NATIC

RALPH COTTON'S
WESTERN CLASSIC
A RANGER'S TRAIL

AUTHOR'S WORK SELECT EDITION

"One of the best Western writers today."
...*Western Horseman*

COTTON-BRANCH PUBLISHING

Ralph Cotton's
Western Classic
A Ranger's Trail

Author's Work Select Edition

Copyright © 2019 Ralph Cotton

All Rights Reserved

No part of this book may be reproduced or transmitted in any form or by any electronic or mechanical means including photocopying, recording, scanning, or by any information storage and retrieval system, except in the case of brief quotations embodied in critical articles or reviews, without written permission from the author.

He may be reached at **www.ralphcotton.com**
or **ralphcotton@yahoo.com**

Front cover photo from 123RF

Author's photo on page 301 by Shay Morton

Cover design and book layout by Laura Ashton
laura@gitflorida.com

ISBN: 978-1686874079

COTTON-BRANCH PUBLISHING

Printed in the United States of America

DEDICATION

To Mary Lynn . . . of course

Dear Readers,

This is the first Arizona Ranger Sam Burrack novel I have written since my recent appointment as an Arizona Ranger (Hon) to this highly esteemed law enforcement organization. Since publication of *A Ranger's Trail* has dovetailed well with my appointment, I felt it only fitting that in addition to dedicating this book to my wife, Mary Lynn—as I do all of my books—I also dedicate this, the 39th novel in the *Big Iron Series*, to all the members of the Verde Valley Company No. 17 (Capt. Gary Jordan, commanding officer), of the ARIZONA RANGERS, based in the Sedona-Cottonwood area of the Grand Canyon State. I do so with special thanks to: MSgt. Nick Cain 17-118 Historian / Training Sergeant. I am much obliged to Sergeant Cain for his steadfast support and encouragement throughout the appointment process.

The few pages you are about to read before hitting the trail with Ranger Sam Burrack and his Appaloosa stallion, Black Pot, is the true story of Ranger Carlos Tafoya. I believe you will recognize the similarities between my Arizona Ranger of fiction, and Carlos Tafoya and all of the brave real life Arizona Rangers who were historically out-numbered, yet with great courage, stood against a wild and lawless frontier.

Private Tafoya's Story

One of the original 13 Arizona Rangers, Private Carlos Tafoya, and his partner, Duane Hamblin, were in hot pursuit (on horseback) of the notorious Bill Smith Gang through the territory's White Mountain wilderness. They were accompanied by Apache County Sheriff's Deputy Bill Maxwell and his brother, noted tracker Arch Maxwell. Bill Smith was known far and wide as a dangerous outlaw and die-hard horse thief.

Tafoya had been a ranger less than a month. Ranger records reflect the last name of Tafolla was also used by him; the exact reason remains unclear, although oftentimes back then, government bureaucracies logged surnames based on incorrect phonetics or the way a name "sounded," and the individual did not bother to correct those "in authority." During the background investigation and interview of next-of-kin for the Peace Officers Memorial in Phoenix, the discrepancy was corrected.

The chase proceeded into the badlands south of Big Lake on the Black River and here is where some of the record-keeping gets a bit murky. The Officer Down Memorial Page and other sources claim Ranger Tafoya was killed in the line of duty on that tragic day, October 7, 1901; however, most reliable sources, including the authoritative *Arizona Rangers,* by Bill O'Neal, the dedication page on M. David DeSoucy's pictorial of the same title, Tafoya family records, and even Ranger Captain Thomas Rynning's own personnel records, state that Tafoya met his unlucky demise late the following day, near midnight on October 8th.

In any event, here is what happened: "...the posse trailed the gang into their camp on Reservation Creek. They crept within 300 yards of the outlaws and at sunset the two rangers and Bill Maxwell advanced into the outlaw camp and ordered them out. Bill Smith emerged dragging his rifle. At 40 feet from the lawmen, he brought the rifle up and opened fire. Deputy Maxwell was shot in the forehead and died instantly. Private Tafoya was shot twice in the torso but continued to fight. Two outlaws were wounded, but the gang escaped."

Before losing consciousness, Carlos pulled a silver dollar from his pocket and gave it to one of the posse members. "Give this dollar to my wife," he gasped. "It and the month's pay coming to me is all she will ever have." He died at midnight. He was 36 years old, and was survived by his wife and three children.

Captain Burt Mossman took the dollar to the governor and asked for a pension for Aceana, Tafoya's wife. The Legislature approved a $25 per month pension for the widow of the first Arizona Ranger killed in the line of duty. (The next two Legislatures cut it to $12.50 per month. The final Territorial Legislature increased it to $20). —Source: Tafoya family records.

Captain Mossman brought fire and brimstone down on the White Mountains, but Outlaw Bill Smith was said to have escaped the Rangers' manhunt and fled to Argentina; he was never apprehended.

According to Texas State Historian and Honorary Arizona Ranger/Author, Bill O'Neal, the Bill Smith Gang, a "band of rustlers, made their headquarters in northern Graham County, where Smith and his younger brothers and sister lived at their mother's home on the Blue River, near Harper's Mill.

"As a young man, Smith had drifted into Oklahoma Territory, where he reportedly served an apprenticeship in rustling and other frontier chicanery with the infamous Dalton brothers. By the turn of the century, he was Arizona's most notorious cattle rustler...."

In 1898 he escaped from the jail in St. Johns and fled to New Mexico for a year. When he returned to Arizona Territory, he was wanted for train robbery; he continued to steal cattle and horses. During the first week of October 1901, the Bill

Smith Gang was spotted heading south near Springerville with a herd of horses stolen from rancher Henry Barrett. Barrett teamed up with Hank Sharp, Pete Peterson and Elijah Holgate to form a posse; they rode to Greer where they met up with Rangers Tafoya and Hamblin, who had already been assigned by Capt. Burt Mossman to track down the gang and bring them to justice, dead or alive.

The posse followed the trail three miles south to Sheep Crossing of the Little Colorado River and on to Lorenzo Crosby's ranch on the Black River. There the posse enlisted Crosby and the Maxwell brothers, Bill and Arch, both regarded as superb scouts and trackers.

The rustlers' trail led south to Big Lake, then Dead Man's crossing on the Black River and on to Pete Slaughter's ranch where, according to the signs, the gang had camped. The posse pitched camp at the same site, then the next day, October 8th, followed the trail six miles down the west bank of the Black River.

There is no more beautiful or forbidding wilderness in America than the Black River Country, according to author and historian Bill O'Neal. "In October, the temperatures are crisp during the day and frigid at night, and the forests are a riot of orange and red leaves, with a thick carpet of pine needles on the ground. Soaring mountains bristle with towering pine and spruce trees, cedars and junipers. It is a difficult country to traverse: the narrow, winding valleys are too thickly forested for easy passage, while the steep mountainsides offer treacherous, boulder-strewn angles littered with fallen timber. Breaks in the timber from high on the mountains reveal breathtaking views of wild beauty, but the almost impenetrable wilderness provided a natural hideout for fugitives. Rustlers regularly found refuge in the area, and the nearby western border of New Mexico offered an additional avenue of escape."

On Tuesday, October 8, the outlaws were in camp at

Reservation Creek, in a gorge 200 yards wide and 100 feet deep near the headwaters of the Black River. The gang had shot a bear and late that cold afternoon were engaged in skinning the beast. Some of the gang members had started supper, while bloodhounds prowled the camp perimeter. One hound nervously barked out an alarm, and Bill Smith scrambled to the top of a rim for a look. He darted back to camp with news that several men were approaching. Al and George Smith began to move the horses out of the clearing.

The posse had heard the trio of rifle shots that brought down the bear, and a ride of half a mile brought them to a bloody trail in the snow. Sign indicated that two men were packing out freshly killed game on a horse, and the posse, sensing their prey, followed the trail in the final hour of daylight.

The nine posse members tied their horses to a cluster of bushes and crept the last 300 yards through the snow on foot. They moved in from the west as the sun set between Mount Ord and Old Baldy. The outlaws thus enjoyed the protection of a shadowed gorge, while sun rays, highlighting the rim to the east, made it difficult to fire into the rustlers' camp. Most of the posse men crawled to prone positions on the rim, but the two rangers and Bill Maxwell boldly advanced into the clearing. In the open, they were starkly silhouetted against the whiteness of the snow.

Barrett shouted from the rim for the lead man to get down. Hamblin flattened onto the ground, but Tafolla (Tafoya) and Maxwell ignored their danger. Maxwell called out an order to surrender.

"All right," replied Bill Smith. "Which way do you want us to come out?"

"Come right out this way!" directed Maxwell.

The outlaw leader walked toward the lawmen, dragging a new Savage .303 rifle behind him. Suddenly, Smith brought up the Savage repeater and opened fire from a distance of forty feet. Tafolla went down, shot through the torso, while Maxwell was hit in the forehead and died on the spot. Smith darted for cover as the other outlaws began firing from behind tree trunks. Tafolla gamely emptied his Winchester, and his companions opened up from the rim. Most of the rifles were loaded with black powder cartridges, and a haze of white smoke began to spread through the gorge as gunshots echoed off the surrounding walls. Barrett's fire was especially effective; the rancher was armed with a Spanish Mauser, captured in Cuba, and the smokeless, steel-jacketed rounds ripped through the little pine trees that shielded the outlaws. Two rustlers were wounded, shot in the foot and leg, and one of their hounds was killed. After a few moments, the gunfire ended as the gang retreated into the timber.

During the shooting, (Ranger) Hamblin had worked his way around to the outlaw mounts. He found nine saddle horses and a pack mule, drove the animals away, and put the rustlers afoot. Desperately, Smith and his men pressed into the wilderness and escaped into the sudden mountain nightfall.

Back in the clearing, Tafolla lay on his back, shot twice through the middle and moaning for water. Bill Maxwell was dead; his big hat had three bullet holes in the crown. As the posse closed in they found the dead hound, along with saddles, bridles, camp gear, and personal belongings that the fleeing outlaws had abandoned. Tree trunks throughout the gorge were scarred with bullet marks. The clearing forty miles south of St. Johns would become known as the Battle Ground.

Bill Maxwell's hat was left on the ground, and cowboys who later had occasion to ride through the Battle Ground superstitiously refused to touch the bullet-riddled sombrero. Maxwell was carried to where the posse had tethered their horses and was laid out on two saddle blankets. Hank Sharp and Arch Maxwell rode east for help to the Mormon community of Nutrioso, where the Maxwell homestead was located. Hamblin, Barrett, Peterson, Holgate and Crosby stayed behind to provide crude care for the agonized Tafolla. Before he lost consciousness, Carlos, realizing that he was dying, pulled a silver dollar from his pants pocket and handed it to Barrett.

"Give this dollar to my wife," gasped Carlos. "It, and the month's wages coming to me, will be all she'll ever have."

He died at midnight, the first Arizona Ranger from the 1901-1909 era killed in the line of duty.

More about the fruitless manhunt that followed the gunfight described above can be found in Bill O'Neal's classic: *The Arizona Rangers,* (Eakin press, Fort Worth, 1987, pages 16-18).

Special thanks to then-Lt. Col. Richard Ellis for his contribution to this original article, and to Arizona Ranger MSgt Nick Cain for providing the photo on page 11 of him pointing to Ranger Carlos Tafoya's name on the Peace Officers Memorial.

*The only thing necessary
for the triumph of evil
is for good men to do nothing.*

Edmund Burke

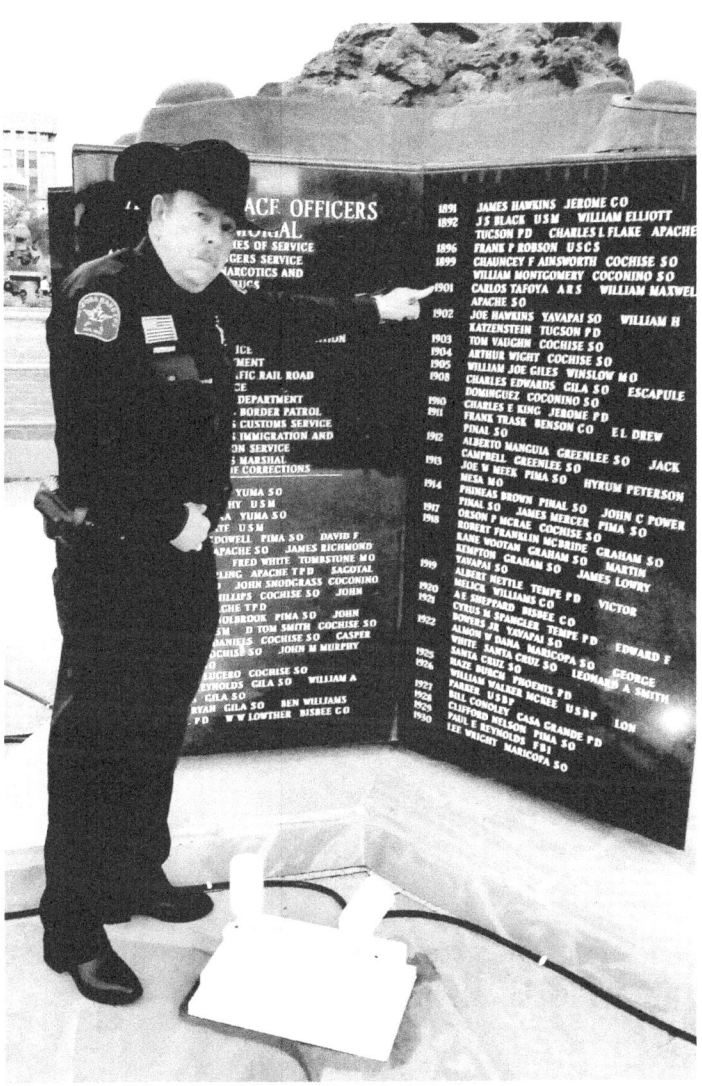

**MSgt Nick Cain at the
Peace Officers Memorial
Identifying Ranger Carlos Tafoya**

PROLOGUE

Arizona Ranger Sam Burrack lay stretched out on his belly atop a narrow dusty butte. Through his battered field telescope, he looked down at the scene unfolding on the meandering desert trail below. Wind and sand whipped and swirled around him. To his right, down there, roughly a mile out on the furnace-hot Grande Chihuahuas floor, a former French battlewagon ambled along behind four big Belgium horses, making its way to Esplanade Ciudad. Being familiar with the wagon, Sam knew it had started from the old French Corporation-owned silver mines some twenty miles away.

The mines had been renegotiated and allowed to remain in operation by the French even after the Mexico-French Revolution, which booted most things French out of existence —but not something as valuable as the Mexican silver mines. Sam knew the wagon would stop for nothing or no one until it reached Esplanade. He knew the wagon delivered monthly payments to the bank in Esplanade, where it was then disbursed to the town. A large payment went to the bank. The bank then made payments to town merchants, to livery barns for hay and livestock feed; to residents and tradesmen, teamsters, bridle and tack makers; to blacksmiths and all others holding a marker for services rendered.

For services rendered, Sam told himself. He'd learned there was even a modest amount distributed among the citizenry, a sort of goodwill and welfare remunerations, to keep the money flowing—*the French wanting to keep everybody happy,* he told himself, watching through his telescope; the

Mexican government wanting to help them do it. That was how things worked here, ordinarily. Only today, he didn't think there would be too many happy citizens once they saw what fate was about to do to them. He reached a wadded-up bandanna out front of his telescope and wiped dust from the lens. What was about to happen in Esplanade was none of his business, though, he'd been told. He remembered Ranger Captain Reginald Jamison's words the last time they'd spoken —*What was that, six, eight weeks ago ...?*

"In fact, avoid contact with the French unless it's absolutely necessary," Captain Jamison had told him. "Some of the French still consider themselves an occupation force." He shook his head slightly at the irony. "Get the man you're after and get out. Things are touchy enough between the Mexicans and the French without us butting in between them. Do we understand each other, Ranger Burrack?" he'd asked.

"We do, Captain ...," Sam had assured him.

None of his business ... okay, he reflected. He shifted his lens away from the French wagon detail, over to his left, to the cloud of dust he'd looked for and spotted this morning when he'd first started scanning the desert floor. These were the riders whose trail he'd been following for four days. They were coming clearly into sight now. The past hour he'd watched them turn from little wavering black dots, like ants rising up out of the sand. Now they'd become the recognizable shapes of men on horseback—these riders he had waited here for, before the battlewagon ambled into the game. He glanced back toward the wagon and let out a breath as it completed passing the butte and made its way on to Esplanade, growing smaller in the swirling dust and sunlight.

Sam lowered his telescope but continued watching the trail, squinting against the blowing dust, his .50 caliber Swiss rifle lying close beside him. He'd spent the day and half of last night, deciding how to best do this. That is, take down the leader of the Wild Bunch, Max Carver, AKA the *Gentleman*

A Ranger's Trail

Bandit, and at the same time try not to get on cross-sides with either the French *soldats* —or the Mexican *federales* .... He let out a breath of contemplation. There was a lot to remember working this side of the border these days. But he had a feeling he was about to start getting it all worked out.

He stayed focused, squinting, watching as the five dusty riders drew closer on the trail below. Four of them rode abreast; the leader, Max Carver, rode only a few feet ahead of the others. One man rode in the rear, a few yards behind, leading six horses on a lead rope through a low swirl of dust. He wore a bandanna pulled up over the bridge on his nose. Sam saw the rider turn his head back to the rising dust behind him, checking the back-trail. But fortunately for Sam, instead of trailing the gang from behind, he had chosen to get up onto the long line of rocky hills and stick high above their flank. High-siding them, Apache style, as it was known among scouts and savvy frontier men.

I'll start with you, Sam said silently to the distant rider, squinting down at him and the string of horses pounding along behind him. Three of the horses carried water skins strapped to their backs. Another horse carried a bag of feed. *There it is ....* The ranger gazed down a moment longer, having decided four days ago that this was their change of horses, led by their horseman, *Cat-eye Eddie Poole,* he speculated.

Recalling Poole's name from a list of Wild Bunch names he carried inside his vest pocket, he scooted back from the butte's edge and stood up in the swirling dust, rifle in hand, sun at his back; he slapped his gray sombrero down the front of his riding duster.

Get to work ..., he told himself. He walked over, off the face of the butte, to a small level spot a few feet down the slope, where he'd left the stallion standing out of the wind-driven sand. He slipped the rifle down into its saddle boot, tied the stiff leather boot cap down over the rifle butt, and gathered his reins. Keeping the rider and horses in sight, he led the stallion downward onto a game path and followed his prey, flanking his dust, knowing that he had the man at striking distance any time he wanted to stop him. Knowing his advantage, Sam let the stallion pick its footing down a thin rocky path toward the pan-flat desert below.

Halfway down the butte, Sam saw the rider and his string of horses slow their pace and veer over off the desert floor, away from the others, into a stretch of tall-standing hoodoos and chimney rock sprawled on an up-leaning hillside. *All right* ... Sam watched the rider and his string disappear around a strewn clutter of downed rock that had once stood hundreds of feet tall.

He looked off again in the direction of Esplanade, only a few miles farther ahead of where man and fresh horses had taken cover. *Good place to wait for your pals, Eddie Poole,* he said silently toward the rider. He stepped up into the saddle and nudged the stallion forward, edging along downward at an angle that would keep him hidden as he made his way along through the large stands of rock.

Cat-eye Eddie Poole, stayed cautious, expectant, the way he always did before a robbery. When he'd led the string of fresh mounts off the desert floor into the shadow of a narrow rock passage, he'd stopped and stood up in his stirrups. *Dead silent* .... He kept his good eye fixed on the desert trail behind him, hearing only the low whir of a desert wind. *Nothing* .... He stayed focused under the hot sun until the tracks he and the horses had made led out to the desert trail and disappeared. He felt some better, yet he continued to look back a moment longer. *Still nothing* ....

When he'd satisfied himself that no one was back there riding up out of the sand to follow him, he nudged his horse forward and led the string up into the rocky hillside.

Rubbing his horse's sweat-dampened withers with a gloved hand, he gave one last look back. *Never hurts to play it safe* ..., he said to himself and the horse beneath him. Unable to see the trail through the tall rocks, he turned forward in his saddle with a breath of relief and led the string farther up the rock pass. Less than fifty yards up the narrow rocky pass he found the familiar sloped clearing he'd scouted out two weeks earlier when they were setting up the raid.

"All right, boys," he said, drawing to a halt, the horses gathering around him, "I'm going to grain you down and water you up—get you ready to romp." One of the horses, a big blue roan, slung his head and chuffed as if he instinctively knew that something would soon be expected of him.

Moments later, when Cat-eye Eddie had finished attending to the fresh horses, and his own, he laid the water skins in the shade of a ground boulder and laid the sack of feed atop a rock nearby. He took his bedroll from behind his saddle and laid it on the ground beneath a stone overhang. He stretched out on the blanket out of the hot sun while he waited for the gang to come roaring in. As was his habit, he loosened his gun belt, unbuttoned his trousers, and gave himself some breathing room. He slid a hand down into his trousers, scratched himself and let his hand lay there.

He dozed a full twenty minutes before the horses awakened him by thrashing and stirring and grumbling, pulling at the rope that kept them strung together.

Poole sprang to his feet. "Damn it, now what—?" he growled. He yanked his hand from his trouser fly and reaching both hands to his loose gun belt, he stepped away from his blanket, out from under the edge of the overhang. He started to curse the horses, but before he could get the swear words out of his mouth, the ranger's rifle butt struck straight down atop his bald head. He dropped quickly, first to his buckled knees, his loosened gun belt and trousers falling down around his boot wells. Then he fell forward onto his face. On the edge of the stone overhang, the ranger stood looking down, rifle in hand, a gathering of small stones laying at his feet. He had pitched several stones one at a time across the clearing, among the horses, causing them to mill and grumble.

Poole stayed knocked out on the ground below as Sam walked down around an edge of the flat stone ceiling and stood over the unconscious outlaw. He reached down and raised a battered Colt from the outlaw's holster, and lifted a hefty Bowie-style knife, leather fringe scabbard and all, from the man's boot well. As Poole begin to regain consciousness he looked around on the ground for his glass eye, searching the dirt with his hand, batting his good eye, keeping the empty socket of his left eye squeezed shut. Sam watched in silence as the outlaw found his glass eye in the dirt and rubbed it clean on his dusty trouser leg and inserted it into his eye socket. The socket, clearly too large for the artificial eye, kept the orb in place by Poole holding his left eyelid in a partial squint, helping keep everything firm where it should be.

Sam spoke down to him as if the two had already been engaged in conversation.

"Who else is riding with you and Max Carver?" he asked as Poole made a final adjustment on his eye. Poole gave him a curious sidelong glance as he rubbed his throbbing head.

"Maybe I missed something here—" He eyed Sam up and down, squinting, looking puzzled. "Who'd you say you are?"

"I didn't say," Sam replied, his rifle at hip-level in a ready position. "But I'm Arizona Ranger Sam Burrack, out of Nogales."

"Arizona Ranger .... That just about figures," Poole said. He wagged his head slowly. "I suppose there's no use in me reminding you we're in *Mejico?* He motioned a dirty hand to take in the land around them. "Old *Mejico,* that is?"

"I'm here by agreement with the Mexican government," Sam said. "Mexico is having a problem with border outlaws. Maybe you heard?"

Poole appeared to search his memory, still rubbing his head, his right hand hanging over his knee near his boot well.

"No," he said after searching his memory, "can't say I've

heard mention of it. I wouldn't though, traveling widely as I do."

"If you try to reach down in your boot, I'll clip your fingers off and leave them laying in it," Sam said in a cool, even tone. "So, if you think you might need your fingers later on ...." He let his words trail away as he cocked his rifle hammer.

Poole raised his hand away from his boot well.

"Take it easy, Ranger!" he said. "You've got my word there's no hidden weaponry in there!"

"I know there's not," said Sam with confidence. "I've already taken your Bowie knife. But I'll shoot your fingers off anyway, just for trying me."

Poole let out a defeated breath.

"I'm obliged you warned me first," he said. "I'd feel plumb-a-fool, losing a handful of fingers over a knife that's no longer there. Fact is—"

"Who's riding with you and Max Carver?" Sam insisted, getting back on subject.

"All right, take it easy!" Poole said. "Let me explain best I can, how I feel about giving out information—"

"He won't tell you nothing, Lawman," Sam heard a voice say behind him. He spun toward the voice, his rifle still cocked, ready, his finger on the trigger. Two men stood facing him, twenty feet away, having stepped out from the rocks. Both held six-shooters leveled at him; one held a wadded-up feed sack. "Gather yourself!" the man continued. "We're bounty hunters, not a part of his bunch."

"I am gathered," Sam said in a strong tone, noting the empty feed sack, already planning the move he would make when it came time to make it. His first shot would take out the man doing the talking—*the leader of the two?* He believed so. Usually, the one doing the speaking was the leader. "There's no bounty here for you. This man is my prisoner. I've tracked him and his bunch a long time," he added as his mind worked fast, preparing for battle.

The other man dropped the empty feed sack to the ground at his feet, and stood staring, stoic, silent.

"So have I," said the talker.

Yep, he's the leader .... Sam noted the man didn't say *Us,* he said *I*. Didn't even mention his partner. "I've kept watch on you—spotted you skirting alongside them yesterday, up there in the rocks. Pretty clever." A thin smile spread beneath his fine-trimmed mustache. "You must be part Injun."

Sam didn't reply.

"I bet we can work out a deal here. Don't you think?" the talker added.

Sam still gave no answer. He cut a glance sidelong at Poole, seeing the wheels turning in his outlaw mind as well. But he knew Poole was no help. If the outlaw saw a hole in this, he would slip through it like a rabbit and be gone. *Alright ... here goes ....*

"Walk away," Sam called out. "Get your horses and ride on out of here."

"Or else?" said the talker. He took a slow sidestep away from the other gunman, still wearing the thin false smile.

Sam stood poised, ready. *Here we go ....*

"Else I'll kill you both where you stand," he said, not mincing words.

"Come on, Ranger, I'm betting we can dicker some—" His words stopped short beneath the hard loud blast of the ranger's big Swiss rifle. The shot bored through his chest, his heart, and slammed him backward. His blood splattered the other gunman's face. The suddenness of the blast caught both the gunmen and outlaw by surprise. Pooled already started rolling sideways, looking to cut away, get around these two and make it to the horses. Sam saw him making his run, but his hands were full with the standing gunman. As soon as he made the rifle shot, Sam swung the rifle away with his left hand, his right hand already bringing his big Colt up from his holster.

A Ranger's Trail

The standing gunman held his big Remington ready, leveled, but his free hand was busy wiping the other man's thick blood from his eyes. He managed two wild shots as Sam stalked forward, taking close aim as he squeezed the trigger.

The ranger's shot hit him squarely in the chest. The gunman fell backward. His gun flew from his hand. Sam looked all around, his smoking Colt still ready, cocked, his finger on the trigger. A few feet from the horses, he saw Eddie Poole sitting sprawled on the ground, leaning back on one hand.

"Don't shoot, Ranger!" Poole grunted. "I'm not cutting out! I've took a bullet in the belly!"

Sam walked on to him and stooped down in front of him, leaning on the butt of the big Swiss rifle. Poole took his bloody hand from covering the wound in his lower right side as if showing proof of his injury. Without a word, Sam reached around behind him and found the wet warm spot where the bullet made its exit.

"It's clean through," he said. "You're going to be all right."

"Oh …? Well, much obliged, *Doctor Ranger!*" Poole said with a sarcastic snap. "What do I owe you for your medical opinion?"

Sam ignored the tone. He looked off along the rock pass leading down to the desert floor. Then he looked back at Poole, seeing how the glass eye had gotten crooked in its socket. He also noted that the eye was not the artificial eye of a human, but rather that of a large mountain cat. *Cat-eyed Eddie Poole,* he reminded himself. "I'm going to bandage you up," he said. "Tell me you can ride." He already reached around the outlaw to help him to his feet.

"Oh? Suppose I can't? What're my other choices, *Doctor?*" asked Poole, still defiant, a painful groan in his voice as he stood and tried to straighten. With help, he looped his forearm across Sam's shoulders.

"Only one," Sam said. "I'll leave you here with a canteen and a gun." They moved to the shade of the stone overhang.

"And a horse, I'm hoping?" Poole asked.

"You won't need one," Sam said. He gave him a flat stare as he helped lower him onto the blanket still laying there.

"A gun, *yes,* but *no* horse?" Poole said. "That's no bargain."

"Yes, it is," Sam said. "I'll leave you one bullet." Again the flat stare. Poole got it this time. The two looked off past the rock passage toward the unseen, far side of the wide desert floor.

"Damn it," said Poole. "How do we know the *'Pache* heard it?"

"This is their desert, you want to take a chance that they *didn't?"* Sam took the Bowie knife from behind his back and cut long strips from the blanket as he spoke.

"Good point," Poole said. "How long before you figure they'll get here?"

"They'll be here before your pals arrive if that's what you're wondering," Sam said.

"It crossed my mind," Poole said, gazing away across the endless sand floor.

"It's likely your bunch heard the gunfire, too," said Sam. "What will they do?"

"Without admitting that I belong to, or ride with, any *bunch,"* Poole said, a legal tone coming to his voice, "I'll just tell you that if my good friend Max Carver, who I *do know,* by the way, thinks I'm in trouble, he'll bring whatever *bunch* he's riding with in here like a whirlwind."

"For the horses," Sam said in a flat tone.

"Well, yeah ... for the horses, too, I expect," said Poole, a little deflated.

Sam watched as the outlaw weighed his options.

"What do you say?" Sam asked. "You want to take my one bullet deal, or can you ride?"

"All things considered, I can ride." Poole's artificial eye had gotten more and more crooked in its socket.

"That's what I figured. Fix your eye," Sam said, the strips of the blanket hanging in his hand. "Let's get you bandaged and get on up out of here."

Poole adjusted his eye and looked off at the horses, then off across the unseen distance.

"Get enough 'Injuns' dogging my trail, I can ride like a wind out of hell," he murmured.

"Good," said Sam, "that's what we'll need."

PART I

CHAPTER 1

Esplanade Ciudad, Mexico

Midmorning sun blazed silver-white in a clear Mexican sky.

Surrounding Esplanade—a town often called *Maximilian City* by its Mexican citizenry—the Grande Chihuahuan Desert lay bleak and forbidding behind a wavering veil of heat.

Out of the boiling sun's glare, a Mexican dressed in dirty white peasant pants staggered along an empty boardwalk beneath a canvas overhang. Carrying two bottles of mescal cradled in an unsteady forearm against a thin striped woolen poncho, the peasant stalled out front of the bank *Banque Nationalle de France Y Mexico,* and continued to stagger in place. The peasant stopped long enough to cling to a support post for a moment, and eyed the surroundings as if seeing the town for the first time. Then, realizing this was the end of the day's useless journey, the peasant staggered across the boardwalk, turned and flopped back against the front of the bank building.

"You, hey *you!* You cannot sleep here, you drunkard!" said the half-Mexican bank manager, Philippe Flippoza, appearing from the doorway. He had stood inside watching the French battlewagon lumber along the stone-paved street.

Damn it to hell ...! Flippoza glanced down angrily at the Mexican peasant. But his anger filled with fear and desperation as he turned his eyes back to the war wagon, now being used as a cargo wagon, drew ever closer toward the bank from the far end of town. The Mexican lay sprawled like a corpse, the straw sombrero down low.

The bank manager's face appeared tense and lacquered with a glassy mask of sweat—he couldn't have this!

"Wake up, you fool, *you drunken imbecile!*" he growled, thinking of how bad this would appear to his bank's French benefactors. He batted the side of his black button-top shoe against the downed Mexican's leg. "You cannot disrupt *business!*"

The peasant's head bobbed once then bowed farther down, the sombrero now hiding the entire slumbering face. The two mescal bottles, one full and one almost empty fell free as the peasant's forearm relaxed, and rolled away on the boardwalk.

The manager gave another nervous glance toward the big iron-plated wagon as it lumbered closer. Atop the tall wagon, a guard manning a Gatlin gun rose into sight on a squeaking platform, cranked upward by two guards inside the wagon. Beside the Gatling gun operator sat an ammunition feeder, a young private who carried long ammunition clips stacked on his lap. On either side of the wagon rode a uniformed guard, a captain, and his sergeant. Their mounts were as equally frothed and salt-streaked from their journey as the four big horses pulling the heavy wagon.

"Fine, you drunken fool," the manager growled down to the knocked out peasant. He whipped a damp handkerchief from inside his black suit coat and mopped his forehead. "Let them drag you away. I hope these Frenchmen horsewhip you until you bleed *mescal!*" He stepped away from the man and stood at the edge of the boardwalk with his white handkerchief in his raised hand.

"Do you wish to *surrender?*" the mounted captain asked as the battlewagon sidled along the boardwalk and stopped ten feet out from its edge. As one, the captain and sergeant, both in French uniforms, loosened at the collar, nudged their tired horses across the ten-foot space and swung down from their saddles at an iron hitch rail. Dust swirled up from the street tiles at their feet.

Surrender? Why no—! The manager looked confused, frightened. Then he caught himself and jerked his white handkerchief down and looked embarrassed.

"You must pardon me, *Messieurs*. I am bank Manager Philippe—"

"Philippe Flippoza," the captain said cutting him off. "We know who you are. Would we bring all this to someone without knowing their name?" he gestured a hand toward the huge imposing wagon.

"Please forgive me, *Capitaine,*" said Flippoza. He turned enough to wag his damp handkerchief at the man propped against his bank building. "I must blame this place and its hellish heat. *Oh, mon Dieu!* The devil himself could not live here!"

The captain took unimpressed note of the bank manager's awkward use of the French language.

"And yet we *devils* live here daily, *Señor* Flippoza," he replied. He looked around Esplanade Ciudad with disdain, responding in neutral English, "We bring *tribute*—payment to reward a people whose nation cannot even pay its lawful debts." He lifted his nose arrogantly at the town in general as he slapped dust from his shoulders. From inside the ironclad wagon, eyes looked out through open horizontal gun ports. The captain walked the side of the wagon facing the boardwalk, a hand propped on the butt of his holstered French revolver. He gave a nod to the sergeant who now stood on the opposite side of the loading ramp, carrying his rifle at port arms.

At the Captain's silent command the young sergeant tapped the butt of his rifle on the wide drop-down ramp. The clank of iron on iron resounded as bolts slid open and latches released inside the ramp. The turning of cranks cried out in the still air; the thick metal-covered ramp moved slowly toward the ground.

"We have company, *Capitaine,*" the French sergeant said quietly between the two of them. He glanced all around the hot dusty street. "Always, money brings them out, *oui?*" he added.

The captain only nodded. "Let them watch, *Sergent,*" he said. "It is too hot to shout at them."

The sergeant nodded. Looking around he watched a young female child of no more than fifteen years old slip from the bowels of an alley beside the bank and stand posed against the corner of a weathered hovel. A ten-week-old yellow kitten circled and mewed and slapped at her ankles. She offered a shy but knowing smile to the sergeant and pushed aside a stand of glistening black hair.

"Mon Dieu!" the sergeant said, partly under his breath, "If only I had an hour to spend with this one."

Hearing the sergeant's lowered words, the captain gave him a sharp look and reminded him in a gruff tone, "If you have an hour to spare I will find something more useful for you to do, *Sergent.*"

Knowing the two Frenchmen were discussing her, the girl gave a short giggle and raised her tattered dress to just below her knee and moved her bare foot back and forth, this young seductress, slowly sifting loose dirt between her toes. The kitten mewed and slinked and rubbed itself on the lower calf of her leg.

"I only jest, *Mon Capitaine,*" the sergeant said, quickly ignoring the girl. He collected himself into a more serious demeanor.

Faces of villagers appeared as if out of nowhere as the wood and steel ramp groaned and lowered. When it bumped and settled, and rested on the ground, more glaring sunlight spilled out of the partially open-top battle rig. A wide length of dusty gray canvas had been rolled back off the low Conestoga style wooden ribs and tied to a cross beam where the gun platform stood raised into place—gun and platform occupying the first four feet of wagon top space.

The dropped ramp revealed four soldiers inside, each having hefted a corner of a battered iron-trimmed military pay chest by its thick carry handles. They stood soaked with sweat, but ready, awaiting an order to proceed down the ramp. Atop the wagon, the gunner and his feeder looked all around warily at the streets, at rooftops, at the wavering desert floor. Yet, for all their attentiveness, neither they nor any of the gathering onlookers saw the dusty black gloved-hand reach out of the edge of the alley just as the girl turned to walk inside. But she stopped with a jolt and stood wide-eyed, startled. She tried to speak, or shriek, but before she could make a sound the glove-hand clasped firm across her face and dragged her out of sight. The yellow kitten looked all around on the ground as if baffled by the girl's sudden disappearance.

In the darkened shade of the alley, two men in long black faded riding dusters stood amid five dust-streaked horses. One held the girl against his chest, his gloved-hand still over her mouth as she clawed and squirmed and tried to wrench herself free.

"Of all the places for you to step into!" the young gunman, Elvin Sloane said close to her ear. The girl grunted and kicked and made a muffled sound into his gloved hand. But she hadn't tried to scream, Sloane noted. He was certain he would have recognized the difference between a scream and the sound she made. *"Shhh!* Hush now!" He whispered in her ear; he shook her, not hard, but hard enough to slow down her struggling with him.

"Damn it, *boyo, get rid of her! Knock her out! It's commencing!"* said an older outlaw, Leonard Dog Fannen, keeping his gruff voice to a whisper, his face hidden behind a ragged bandanna. "Knock her cold!"

Knock her out ...? At the sound of Fannen's words, the girl's eyes widened, terrified above Elvin Sloane's grip. What were these two? Apparitions? Wolves taking on human form?" Her eyes were wide and terrified. "Easy, little darling," Elvin Sloane whispered, relaxing his hold on her a little. "I'm not going to hurt you."

The men looked sinister, darkly dressed, dust-streaked—

demons from the wastelands ...? The alley smelled of them. They carried the wild scent of the desert, and of wood fires, and horses and sweat. She needed to cross herself; she *couldn't!*

"I said, knock her out!" the older gunman demanded.

Sloane whispered to Dog Fannen, careful not to use his name. "I said I ain't going to hurt her. She's just a baby!"

"Baby, my ass—here, I'll knock her out," whispered Dog. He started to reach for the girl; he stopped short as he felt the tip of Sloane's big Remington poke his belly. The yellow kitten had streaked into the alley and put itself in the middle of the melee, slapping and lunging at the girl's thrashing feet.

"Back *off!* I'm turning her loose," said Sloane. Dog Fannen stepped back. Sloane whispered into the girl's ear, "You and your little pussy get on out of here, darling, and don't you go hollering. This bad old man here will shoot you dead in the back. All right?" He gave Dog a hard stare and a flat smile, the Remington still pointed at him.

When the girl nodded that she understood, the young outlaw turned her loose with a little starting shove. She shot down the alley like a scared fawn. Dog gave a side of his boot to her butt as she streaked past the horses, all of them shying sidelong to let her through. A split second, then the yellow kitten streaked away silently in the girl's direction. The suddenness of the darting kitten caused the horses to stir.

"Damn blasted cat!" Dog growled.

"You needn't have kicked that girl," Sloane said to Dog.

"Let's go," said Dog.

From the street, they heard the sergeant's order for the four soldiers to bring the pay chest down the ramp. The four soldiers stepped forward down the ramp as one. The sergeant fell in beside the two in front, everything going as planned. But on the boardwalk, in the blink of an eye, the sprawled drunken Mexican sprang up; a woman screamed as if having witnessed the sudden rising of the dead. The Mexican swept back the sombrero and let it hang behind by its leather string.

A Ranger's Trail

"Yiii-hiiii!!!" Stone sober now, the peasant threw the front of the dusty poncho to one side, revealing a double-barrel shotgun with barrels sawed short, the hickory stock carved down to a pistol grip. The brunt of the first blast shattered the town's scorching hot silence. A barrel load of fiery scrap iron shredded the sergeant's chest and knocked the two front soldiers away from the chest's handles, causing the chest to fall forward; the shift of weight caused the two rear soldiers to lose their hold. The second blast took out one of the fallen front soldiers who tried to scramble to his feet, his face and chest a mass of blood and pulp.

From the alley, Dog Fannen and Elvin Sloane arrived in time to see the gunner swing the Gatlin gun around and grab the firing handle. The gunner was too late. One measured, well aimed shot from Dog Fannen's big Colt Conversion hit the gunner squarely below his right eye. He flipped backward from his seat, off the wagon, and onto the ground in a heavy up-surge of dust. Sloane's quick firing Remington sent the captain, the bank manager and the on-lookers scrambling for cover in every direction.

Atop the wagon, the feeder made a move for the gunner's seat almost before the gunner hit the ground. With quick and practiced precision, he took up the firing crank and pointed the big gun down at the Mexican peasant who had pitched the shotgun aside and drawn a big Colt to replace it. Running wildly along the boardwalk the Mexican peasant pursued the other two blood-drenched soldiers. From the doorway of the bank, the leader of the gang, Max Carver stepped out onto the boardwalk and fired three shots up at the feeder taking over the gun. Each shot hit its target; the feeder-turned-gunner fell away from behind the Gatling gun. The gun barked, gave off a short sudden burst of fire as it swung up wildly and blew holes in the boardwalk overhang. Its new gunner fell headlong onto the wagon bed, dead upon impact.

Hurrying away from the Mexican peasant, one soldier

tried unsnapping his holster flap to draw his revolver on the run; but before his blood-slick hands could get a grip on the gun butt, two shots from the Mexican peasant nailed him in the back and shoved him forward and down. His discarded gun bounced along the boardwalk.

The last soldier, running hard, leaped away from the boardwalk and sped out onto the empty street. Shots from Sloane, Dog Fannen and the Mexican, hit him at once, twisting and turning him on his feet until he sank to the ground, still trying to run. On the boardwalk, Max Carver turned away as if losing interest. A few seconds of dead silence fell upon the town until Carver stepped over to the payroll chest, pushed back his battered sombrero, and aimed his Colt at the iron latch. One shot blew the locked latch from its hasp. Looking around at the empty street, warm gun smoke curling up the back of his hand, he called out to his men, "Gather in, let's finish up here!"

As Carver spoke, he raised the chest lid with his boot and shoved it back until it lay open on its own. Citizens of Esplanade came out of hiding and moved in for a closer look. They stopped short and eased back as Carver reached down and drew a big knife from its sheath down inside his knee-high boot well. He held the knife at his side as he gave the townsfolk a harsh stare. The people stared back with caution; Carver reached down, sliced the leather drawstring from one of six large bags of gold coins—payroll for countless miners in nearby French-held silver mines.

Shoving his knife back down into his boot well, he scraped up a handful of gold coins. *"Para usted,"* he called out to the onlookers, standing tall, holding the coins up for them to see. Then he turned toward the street and drew back to throw the coins.

For us...? Townsfolk looked at each other, puzzled. But only for a moment, then they hurried in closer as Carver sent the coins flying. The coins bounced and jingled on the stone tiles and kicked up little curls of dust as they settled. Townsfolk scurried about, crouched, grabbing, sifting, shouting in laughter. The girl with the yellow kitten, caught up now in the excitement, had managed to circle around the block through the alleyways. She snatched at the coins with the kitten squeezed against her breast. Fannen and Sloane stood watching as the Mexican peasant escorted the French captain and the bank manager, their hands in the air in front of a cocked Colt pistol. Their faces were sweat-streaked, stiff with fear. But as Carver tossed another handful of coins out on the street, the gathering of townsmen surrounding the drunken peasant and the two captives dwindled for a moment.

In the few seconds it took to disperse the people crowding in close, the Mexican peasant looked away as the French captain and the bank manager dropped low and disappeared under the big wagon.

"You see that? They gave our Mexican *peon* the slip!" Fannen said to Sloane, a little critical. "Maybe Teal ain't as tough as everybody—"

"I saw it," said Sloane, cutting him off. "Teal did things just right. You don't like it, next time you be the Mexican peasant."

"I just might," Dog said.

The two looked all around as they spoke, seeing no sign of the escaped captain or the bank manager. Instead, they saw Max Carver summon them over to him with a wave of his hand.

"Get over here!" Carver called out. "Let's take our loot and cut out of here before company comes calling!" He gave a jerk of his head toward a rise of dust in the near distance as he scooped up another fistful of coins and pitched them up toward the now ecstatic crowd.

Seeing the people grab the coins, Dog Fannen's eyes widened. He gave Slone a stunned look. "Come on, *boyo,*" he said, "You heard him, let's get the gold hefted and get out of here."

The two outlaws hurried along the boardwalk, watching Carver shove his knife back into his boot well. "Oh no!" said Fannen, seeing Carver reach down again and bring out yet another handful of shiny gold coins. "Hurry, boyo!" he yelled at Sloane, seeing Carver draw back and throw more of their ill-gotten coins out onto the dusty street. "He's going to break us!" They quickened their pace into a full run.

When the pair slid to a halt, joining Max Carver at the open strongbox of gold coins, their leader stood, gun in hand. They all three gazed at an alleyway that onlookers had directed their attention to.

"They got away from Teal in the crowd!" said Fannen.

"I saw it," Carver said, having caught sight of the French Captain and the bank manager slip from beneath the wagon, dart through the parting crowd and disappear into the long alley. "Let them go. Everything went well. We need to get out of here. It's three miles to fresh horses—more like five miles in this heat." He allowed himself a thin smile and loud enough for anyone understanding English could hear him. "I'm betting the *Capitaine* has had enough of us Wild Bunch riders to last him a lifetime."

In the crowded loft of a hay barn behind the main livery stables, the French captain and the bank manager lay partly emerged in the hot itchy piles of dried wild grass. They stared out through a crack in the barn slats, Captain Jerome Gascoyne with his French revolver in hand. From the same alley reaching out to the stone-tiled street, the captain's horse, a rangy chestnut bay trotted out slowly, searching the air with its nostrils. "Holy God, Capitaine!" said the bank manager. "Your *idiot* horse is giving us away!"

"Shut up!" Captain Gascoyne snapped at him. "My horse is more valuable than you are!" As he spoke he scooted away backward through the loose hay to a short ladder down to the dirt floor.

"Don't leave me here, Capitaine!" the bank manager said in a panicked voice.

"I'm not leaving you," the captain hissed. "I'm letting my horse inside. If they see him, they will kill the three of us!"

"Let me hold your gun!" the manager blurted out.

"No!" Gascoyne whispered harshly. He stepped off onto the rickety ladder and started down, gun in hand. "If you don't keep quiet I will knock you out with it!"

The bank manager made a whimpering sound into his shaking cupped hands.

At the dirt floor, Captain Gascoyne stepped lively over to the front door and cracked it open enough to see out. He saw the outlaws leaving town, coming in and out of sight, passing buildings, adobes and empty lots in turn along the tiled street. From the street where the battlewagon had been left sitting, black billowing smoke rose above the roofline in the hot air. Watching the smoke rise, the Captain hoped they'd at least had the decency to first unhitch the big Belgium horses.

Of course they had ..., he reminded himself, or else the big horses would have bolted away with the big flaming rig. Relieved to see the gang leaving, he opened the door a little more, enough to pick up his bay's dangling reins and coax the nervous animal inside. Then he shut the door and looked out through the front wall planks. Feeling the bay make a determined tug on the reins, he turned loose and let the animal walk over to a bucket of water sitting on the dirt floor.

"Yes, that's it," he said, "Drink your fill. We have a hard ride ahead of us, my friend." As the thirsty bay took water, Gascoyne searched around and found a handful of grain in an otherwise empty feed bin.

From the overhead loft, the bank manager looked down in surprise.

"What is this, Capitaine? In the middle of our peril, you feed your horse?"

"They have left town," Gascoyne said without looking up.

"You can come down now." As he spoke he poured the grain into a small pile in front of the bay. The bay switched from the water bucket to the feed without missing a beat. "When you insult my horse, *Money-changer,* you insult me," he added as the manager stood in a crouch, stepped over onto the ladder, and started down.

"The next time you call him an idiot," he said matter-of-factly, "you will answer to me for it," the captain said with conviction.

The bank manager stopped in his tracks, holding onto the ladder with both hands. "I—I did not mean any harm, Capitaine," he said, shaken by the Captain's threat. "If I have offended you and your horse—"

"Climb down here, *manager,*" the French officer said as if delivering an order. "I have a question to pose to you, and I need your answer this minute!"

"Yes, Capitaine, of course!" The bank manager stopped at the bottom of the ladder and stood as if at attention.

"The Wild Bunch has taken the money and burned the wagon," the captain said. "Is there enough money in your bank to settle all of the accounts due?"

"Why no, Capitaine," said the manager. He paused with a puzzled look and said, "Why do they burn the wagon?"

"When I see them again I will ask," Gascoyne said with a dry sarcastic snap. "For now, listen to what I have to say. I'm going after them. Will you find a firearm and ride with me?"

Flippoza turned pale at the thought. "I—I cannot dare come with you," he said, in a shaky voice. "I cannot ride a horse." He swallowed a dry knot in his throat. "Nor have I ever fired a *pistola.*"

The captain looked at him gravely.

"You have never ridden a horse, or fired a gun?" he asked.

"No, never," said the manager, indignantly. He tried to look unashamed.

"Suit yourself, *mon ami,*" said the captain. He began

A Ranger's Trail

readying his bay as he continued. "You take your chances riding a horse and carrying a gun, or you take your chances here, telling the town you do not have the money to pay them." He gathered his horse's reins. "As for me, I must pursue these low criminals, even if it means they kill me."

"Wait! I can ride a buggy!" the manager said. "I will search this town for a gun and a buggy!" He loosened his necktie as he looked all around as if a buggy might appear and save him.

The captain shook his head and checked the stirrups and tested his saddle with both hands. "Good luck with your search, banker," he said. "I am not waiting for you."

"But—but you must!" the banker said, pleading.

"No. My duty is to follow the Wild Bunch and take back the money stolen from my nation. It was not delivered, so it is still the property of France."

"But what on earth will I do?" the banker said.

"In my country, we have a term," the captain said. "My countrymen would say you have '*Shat* out your luck.'"

"Shat out my—" The banker's words cut short. He watched the captain take the horse's reins and lead the animal to the door. Looking out first, the captain opened the door wide, walked the horse through it and swung up into his saddle.

"I don't even have a hat to protect my head!" the banker said, watching the captain adjust his broad straw hat that he'd managed not to lose throughout the robbery melee.

The captain collected the bay. "I know," he said. "I believe that is what *Shat out your luck* means." He gave a thin, tight smile and touched a finger to his hat brim as touched his boot to the bay's sides.

CHAPTER 2

The ranger held the lead rope to the string of horses, keeping Cat-eye Eddie Poole riding in front of him, the outlaw's hands cuffed, resting on the saddle horn. Walking beside Sam, the blue roan led the rest of the horses, having balked and bullied and shoved his way forward until Sam brought him up front, whereupon the scrappy animal settled and walked along with his head held high, keeping watch on the rocky terrain surrounding them.

Knowing any nearby Apache had heard the gunfire, the ranger, the horses and his prisoner had left the overhang and traveled upward instead of taking a short easily tracked route to the flat desert floor. They had weaved upward among rock stands, hoodoos, and gullies, leaving as little sign of themselves as possible. When they reached a high thin game path hidden out of sight below the skyline, Sam called for Poole to stop. As the horses gathered around Black Pot and the blue roan, Sam watched Poole turn his horse and stop a few safe yards away.

Sam said, "Whatever your pals set fire to is growing worse." He nodded at a rise of black smoke adrift above Esplanade. Both lawman and prisoner had first seen the smoke start to rise moments earlier as they'd climbed the rocky trail from the overhang. On the far side of the desert floor, a roil of rider's dust had risen and grown wider on the low horizon. The dust wavered in a veil of scorching heat.

Poole sat in his saddle with a hand pressed to the blood-stained bandage on his side. He gave a slight chuff and said, "If it's the bank, I hope they took pause to empty it first."

Sam didn't answer. Instead, he surveyed the desert below, gauging how soon the Wild Bunch and the coming desert Apache's trails would intersect down there. As if reading the ranger's thoughts, Poole said, "Like as not you've fed my pals to the heathen Injuns, Ranger." Somewhere on the trail up through the rocks, Poole decided to forego any legal talk or denials. He'd seen the ranger was having none of it anyway.

"Your pals are big boys, Poole," Sam said. "I expect they'll give a good account of themselves." No sooner than he spoke, they both saw a fresh rise of dust in the direction of the rising smoke—*Wild Bunch riders leaving Esplanade...,* they both surmised. The ranger nudged Black Pot forward and gave a soft tug on the lead rope, prompting the blue roan to bring the other horses along. The horses followed the roan's silent command.

"They're the best," Poole offered, watching the fresh rise. "But the *'Pache* are hard fighters in their own stomping grounds. I wish to hell you'd left these fresh horses for my bunch."

Now they had become *my bunch,* the ranger noted.

"It was just as likely the Apache would get there before Carver and your bunch," the ranger said. He wasn't going to mention that the Apache would have sent scouts out ahead of them to make sure they weren't riding into a trap.

"Whatever the case, this is all on your head if Carver and the boys get slaughtered," Poole said.

"I'll be all broken up over it," Sam said in a flat tone. He motioned for Poole to ride on. When Poole hesitated for a second, Sam cocked the big Colt resting on his thigh.

Hearing and seeing the Ranger's move, Poole jerked his horse around to the thin trail. "I was just thinking if I dropped back closer, we wouldn't have to talk so loud to hear each other, is all!" he said, angrily.

The ranger uncocked the Colt quietly and said, "I like it when we don't talk at all."

Grumbling and cursing under his breath, Poole gigged his horse and rode on.

Instead of exposing their position to the open desert floor, Sam directed Poole to turn left onto another thin trail just out of sight below the crest of the hill line. To the right lay the high trail to Codell, where the ranger had started following the Wild Bunch. As they began weaving through more rock and hoodoos in the direction of Esplanade, Poole looked around over his shoulder.

"Say, wait a minute, Ranger," he said. "You never told me we're headed to Esplanade." He tried to slow his horse a little. But the ranger nodded him forward.

"You never asked," Sam said flatly.

"I never thought I'd have to," Poole said. "You said you're after the Wild Bunch. I pictured you'd be jumping hot on their trail, not going back to where they'd already *been!*"

"I figured you wouldn't mind getting your wound looked at," Sam said as Poole started his horse forward again. "It's a thirty-mile ride through these hills to get to Codell," he added. It won't take the Apache that long to figure us out and start to track us." He nudged Black Pot and the horses an extra step forward. "Not to mention if you fever up, or start bleeding again."

"My people are hardy Kentucky stock," Poole bragged. "We never fever up."

"Congratulations," Sam said flatly. "We're still headed to Esplanade."

Poole fell silent and thought about it. Then, as if giving his permission he said, "All right. I guess I can stand some doctoring. What then?"

"The ranger weighed his thoughts for a second, then said, "There's a jail in Esplanade—some *rurales* running it. They'll take you in while you're healing up. Soon as your

Wild Bunch and the Apache are through chewing each other up, I'll start gathering you and the rest of your bunch up and see what Matamoras wants me to do with you." The only man he was after right now was Max Carver, but he wasn't going to tell Poole. As far as he was concerned, once he had Max Carver—a man charged with double murder in Arizona Territory—Poole could ride away.

"Ha! Just like that?" Poole snapped his fingers and chuckled. "Easy as sin, you think?" He hiked himself around in his saddle and stared at Sam with a wide grin, his artificial yellow cat's eye having turned crooked in its roomy socket.

"Easy or hard," Sam said. "It's all the same. My job is to put the Wild Bunch out of business."

"Is that a fact?" Poole chuffed, gave a knowing little grin.

"That's a fact," Sam replied.

"Now does that mean all of us Wild Bunch riders, or just us ones operating below the border?"

"So, you're admitting you are one of the Wild Bunch Gang?" Sam said.

"Just for the sake of our conversation, let's say I am." Poole gave a shrug and an up-tip of his chin. "I expect somebody might have mentioned to you along the way, the Wild Bunch is the biggest gang the west has ever seen? We've got riders I've never even met face to face, and I been with the riders since I was not much more than a pup."

Keep talking..., Sam said to himself.

"I've been thinking, Ranger," Poole said. "Fact is, I can tell you more about the Wild Bunch than you can ever learn on your own."

"I bet you could," Sam said, seeing an offer coming his way. "Why would you do that?"

Poole turned his horse and stopped and chuckled out loud.

"I like you, Ranger," he said. He shook his head as if in bewilderment. "Damned if I know why." He leveled his gaze on Sam, who this time instead of prodding him on, stopped Black Pot and the horse string a few measured feet away and sat with this hand around the butt of the big Colt.

All right. Ready to listen ....

"I like you too, Poole," Sam said in a dry cynical tone.

Poole gave a little laugh.

"Okay, let's drop the *hazazz* and talk straight, Ranger," he said, relaxing a little. His eye went to the big Colt on Sam's thigh, then back to his eyes. "Here it is. When lawmen or bounty hunters come hunting the Wild Bunch, they ain't interested in bringing us in alive."

"You don't say," the ranger replied flatly, careful not to give this wiley outlaw any glimpse into his mind, any clue of what his personal thoughts might be, or what personal weaknesses might tempt him. He'd learned there's more to disarming a prisoner than taking away his weapons. The less his prisoner knew about what he was thinking, the better.

"Yes, I do *say,* Ranger, and we both know it," Poole said with growing confidence. "So, I'm not going to beat around the bush. There was six big fat bags of gold on the French battlewagon. Now it's out of Esplanade and headed this way. All I got to do is show up with these horses and claim my part of it, for providing fresh mounts." He grinned widely, one tooth broken and crooked, two more heavily capped with gold. "You might say I *earn well* for a man born to low and meager prospects. *Eh?"*

Come on, get to it..., Sam told himself.

"It sounds like you might be," Sam said. "What have you got in mind?"

"Ah-ha!" Poole said, perking up a little, hearing a hint of interest in the ranger's tone. "I see you've been thinking about that gold some yourself?"

"It crossed my mind," Sam said, wanting to keep him talking.

Poole chuckled again.

A Ranger's Trail

"If you'll use your head, Ranger, the gold will do more than cross your mind. I'll see that some of it crosses your palm."

"How much gold are we talking about, Poole?" Sam asked.

"If all's gone well today, and I'm betting it did," Poole said, "My cut alone is going to be ten thousand in unstamped gold coins." He grinned widely, his gold-capped teeth shining. "Half that is yours just for looking the other way while I ride off back across the border." His fingers made imaginary little horse's legs riding across the air in front of him. I'm talking five thousand in gold coins—"

The ranger gave a chuff, interrupting him, and looked away.

Poole's grin disappeared, replaced by a look of confusion.

"What's wrong, Ranger?" he said quickly, "What'd I say?"

"Five thousand? We're too far apart to even talk about it," Sam said. He made a gesture to turn and move away.

"Wait, no we're not!" Poole said. "That was what's called just an opening figure. Now that I know you're interested, we'll start getting serious!"

"You want to get *serious?*" Sam said. "Okay, tell me this. How much money do you suppose your pals stole today?"

"We were counting on five bags of coins, fifty thousand a bag. That comes to, let's see—" He hesitated, counting on his fingers. "Uh …."

"Two hundred and fifty thousand dollars," Sam cut in.

"Yep, I believe you're right," Poole agreed.

"And for sitting out here in Apache country, alone, you get only ten thousand dollars?"

"That's not a lot, is it?" Poole said as if having considered it for the first time.

"How do you know there's two hundred and fifty thousand in gold came to Esplanade today? Do you have a person on the inside who tips you boys off, how much gold comes every month?"

"Might be," Poole said, getting crafty all of a sudden. "If there is, I'll never tell who. So don't ask."

"I'm not asking; I don't care," Sam said, realizing Poole had no idea what he was talking about. "But I know if there's enough gold coming from the French mines every month that their troops send out a battlewagon to protect it ..." He let his words trail.

"Not this much every month. Just *this* month," Poole put in. "Sometimes the French just use a big rig to keep anybody from wanting to take a chance."

All right, someone had to have tipped them off, Sam decided. Why else would a gang like the Wild Bunch take a chance, five guns against a battlewagon and a Gatlin gun. This one had to be well worth the risk, and Sam knew enough about Max Carver and the Wild Bunch to know they were no fools. They knew how much gold was coming to town today. *Sure they did ....*

Poole got right back on the subject of bribe money.

"But forget all this *hazzaz,* Ranger. I've got some money that I've been scooting aside, nobody knows about." Again with the shiny cold-capped grin. "I can kick it up to ten thousand—send you away from this hellhole with some real money in your pocket. Nobody ever has to know."

"When do I get this money from you?" Sam said.

"As soon as I get my cut from Max, and get to the place I keep my private money in." He gave Sam a serious one-eyed stare, the artificial cat-eye looking askew and partially hidden in a squint. "Here's the thing. You'll need to trust me for just a few—"

"Forget it, let's go," Sam said flatly, gesturing toward the rocky trail leading down to Esplanade.

"Jesus, Ranger," said Poole, "Won't you even think about it?"

"About trusting you? No," said Sam. "About the money, maybe. But the fact is I don't know of any thieves who manage

A Ranger's Trail

to put aside any money."

"No, it's true, Ranger. I swear it is!" said Poole. "I am your huckleberry when it comes to scheming money for myself. I make something off of every horse job I do for the Wild Bunch."

Sam eyed the horse string, then looked back at Poole.

"Tell me about it. Maybe I'll think it over."

"See," Poole said, getting cagey, lowering his voice and glancing around as if someone might hear him, "Max puts up strong money for these fresh horses every time we make a run. I manage to make some cash for myself by stealing a couple of horses instead of paying top dollar for them."

Sam just looked at him.

"Sometimes I manage to sell these horses two or three times each, then go steal them back when the times come we'll need them." Again the grin.

Sam let out a breath.

"Let's go, I don't want to hear it," he said. "You put your own pals on plug horses you steal from a barnyard?" He shook his head in mock disgust.

"No, No! Nothing like that," said Poole. I only steal the best. I've got two in this string. I bet you can't pick the ones I stole from the ones I bought."

"I don't care," Sam said. Let's go."

"Okay, I'll tell you anyway," said Poole. He pointed out a dark bay, the third one in the sting. "That one and the blue roan … both of them stolen, didn't cost me a dime. Max paid well for two good horses, and two good horses is what he'll get."

Sam gave a glance first at the dark bay, a strong, good-looking horse by anybody's standards. Then he looked at the blue roan, an uncut stallion, far too handsome and intelligent to be on a string headed for what could possibly end in a killing shootout.

"All right, Poole, you do a good job betraying Max Carver. You best hope someday he doesn't find you out and kill you."

"A man's got to make something on the side, Ranger," Poole said. "I don't need nobody judging me—"

"Shut up, Poole," Sam said, his attention honed onto the trail leading up from Esplanade.

Poole tried again. "Now wait a minute—"

"No, shut up," Sam said, speaking in a lowered voice. "Listen to that." He stared at where the trail dipped down out of sight.

"I don't hear nothing," Poole said in the same lowered tone.

"A rider is coming up," Sam said. He gave the cuffed outlaw a shove toward a stand of rock beside the trail. "Come on, whoever it is we'll wait for them out of sight."

Stopping in the rock cover, Poole held his cuffed hands up to the Ranger. "Think we ought to get these things off me, maybe give me a gun, in case we've got a fight coming?"

"Nice try, Poole," said Sam, watching the trail as he spoke. He recognized the quiet tap of iron shoes against trail rock. *A single rider...,* he told himself. Did that explain why he hadn't seen a rise of dust coming out of Esplanade? He didn't think so. Even a single horse would raise a stir of fine Chihuahuan desert dust on even the slightest wind. *But not this rider...,* he reminded himself. *Why...?*

After a silent moment, the two watched as a single rider came into sight, his horse at a walk as he leaned in his saddle searching the narrow rocky path. Through a thick coat of desert dust, the two recognized the uniform of a French cavalry officer. Sam watched intently, wondering if the rider would take note of their eight horses' tracks leading over into the rocks where they stood. He would have to be blind not to see them. Yet, before the rider reached that spot, Sam saw him sit upright in his saddle and gig his horse straight ahead, almost at a gallop.

"He missed us altogether, Ranger," Poole said as the rider moved out of sight. He chuckled. "Dang Frenchman. Why'd you duck him?"

"Never mind," Sam said. This was not a time to be stopping and explaining himself to anyone, let alone a *prisoner*, or a French military officer. Sam wasn't going to tell the officer that he had Cat-eye Eddie Poole, the gang's horse-man, and six fresh horses standing right here beside him. Whatever the officer was doing out here, Sam knew it had something to do with the robbery that had just taken place in Esplanade. He'd been told to avoid the French if at all possible—*All right, Captain Jamison, I just did* …, he told himself in reflection.

"All right then," said Poole, still using a quiet tone. He started to take a step forward out of their rock cover, his horse's reins in his cuffed hands. But the ranger grabbed his hand, and the reins, and yanked him back a step.

"Wait!" Sam said, his voice still lowered. He motioned toward the trail the officer had taken. "Wait 'til he checks his back-trail."

They stood in silence. When a few seconds passed, the click of the horse's hoofs resounded as the rider came back to a point just above the drop in the trail. Like a man craning up enough to peep over a fence, the officer looked back and forth on the trail. Satisfied with his findings, he dropped out of sight, turned his horse and rode on.

"Pretty dag-gone good, Ranger," Poole said quietly. "What made you know he'd do that?"

Sam didn't answer. He didn't *know* the rider would come back to see if anyone was on his trail. But given the circumstances—a roiling cloud of black smoke in the air, gunfire coming from Esplanade, the Wild Bunch and nosy Apache on the loose—odds were good that the officer would want to know who, or what, might be riding in his wake.

When Sam gave no reply, Poole shook his head and said, "He's dumber than I am, if he's chasing down the Wild Bunch and all that gold all by himself—nothing but a big pistol for protection."

I agree ..., Sam said to himself without answering. He gazed back along the trail. The desert floor was partly hidden now behind tall rock lining the other side of the trail. Enough fine dust still swept past on an upper wind to let him know that actions were about to set a-boil. Looking north and down, he saw the obscure roofline of Esplanade and the rough trail leading down to it.

Poole looked off in the direction the French officer had taken, and spit on the ground as if in contempt. "He'll get himself shot by Max and the gang, or scalped by the *'Pache.* Either way, it serves the damn fool right!"

Sam didn't like leaving anyone up here without warning, yet he knew that any man trained by the French military was savvy enough to look down and see what he was riding into. The man's actions made no sense to him. *Careless? Sunstruck...?* He had no idea. He unwrapped the lead rope from Black Pot's saddle horn and gathered the string on his left. Then he swung up in the saddle. Following suit, Poole mounted his horse and took his place a few feet in front.

"Let's see if we can slip out of here before the fighting starts," Sam said.

"But you still going to think about what we were saying, ain't you?" Poole asked as they turned their horses to the trail leading down to Esplanade.

"I'm thinking about it right now," Sam said, nudging Black Pot and the string forward. The blue roan, in the lead beside the ranger's left leg, threw his head over and tried to give Black Pot a sharp nip on his shoulder. The ranger saw it in time and gave the bullying roan a quick slap on his ear. The roan jerked away in surprise and settled down.

"Don't you start too," Sam said to the blue roan as they rode on.

CHAPTER 3

Hearing the sound of the woman Ruby Teal's horse drawing closer out of the dust behind them, Max Carver turned in his saddle, his hand on his holstered Colt, just in case. A bag of the stolen gold coins hung from his saddle horn. Twenty feet behind him, Elvin Sloane and Dog Fannen's gun hands made the same move as they, too, looked back. Fannen also carried a bag of gold. Elvin Sloane carried two bags, one on either of the horse's sides. Recognizing Ruby Teal in spite of the thick dust clinging to her and roiling around her, Carver gave himself a guarded grin.

"Keep up, Teal!" he called back to her. "Back-scouting shouldn't take all day."

"Right, *Boss,*" Ruby Teal shouted right back to him in a sharp sarcastic tone. "I'm-a-coming!" She waved her dusty sombrero back and forth, giving him an all-clear sign.

Carver gave a nod and turned forward in his saddle, still with the slight grin, and a little chuckle under his breath.

Hearing the exchange, Fannen spat in disgust.

"Damn *splits!* An answer like that from *any woman, black, white or half-bred,* deserves a good solid rap in the mouth."

Sloane looked at him in mock surprise. *"What?* You don't think he should shoot her, hang her? Set her on fire, throw her off a cliff? Dog, are you going soft on us?"

Fannen gave him a hard narrow stare.

"You might be too damn young, or plain *simple-minded* to see it, boyo, but this world is changing faster than you can twirl a pistol—and ain't none of the changes worth a damn."

Elvin Sloane let the simple-minded remark go. He shook his head, having long given up on any response to the old gunman's philosophy. He looked back at Ruby Teal as she galloped forward out of their cloud of dust.

"Jesus, Dog," he said. "I've seen Ruby shoot. You might think about keeping that kind of talk to yourself."

"Hummph," said Fannen, also turning in his saddle and seeing Teal with her bandanna pulled up across the bridge of her nose. She had tied another bandanna around her horse's muzzle. Covered with a thick coat of dust, both horse and rider resembled some apparition just up from the lower bowels of the earth. "I'm told to ride with her, so I do," Fannen continued. "But never think I consider her or *any woman* equal to a man—"

"Save it," Sloane said, cutting him off as Ruby Teal sidled up and reined the horse down from its gallop on Sloane's right, opposite of Fannen. Sloane reached over and pulled the bandanna from her horse's muzzle as she settled the dusty animal.

"Obliged," Teal said, taking the bandanna he handed to her. Her horse sneezed and shook its head. Dust billowed. Teal dropped her horse back a step and took off her bandanna and shook it out. She took off her hat, shook it off and slapped it up and down the front of her poncho. When she stepped her horse back beside Sloane, the two of them lifted the bag of gold on his right and looped it over onto her saddle horn. "Obliged again," she said to Sloane. She patted a gloved hand on the bulging bag and said, "Come to *Mama!*"

"Hummph," Fannen grumbled and looked away.

Now that Teal had checked their back-trail, Max Carver, still riding ahead of the others, veered left up into the rocky hill line where he knew Cat-eye Eddie Poole would be waiting with fresh horses. He stopped his horse for a moment and turned facing the others. He gave a short guarded hand signal to Ruby Teal, who gave a sigh and started to once again lift the bag of gold from her saddle horn.

"Oh well, easy come, easy go," she said to Elvin Sloane who reached over again to help her make the lift from her saddle horn to his. Sloane nodded.

"Don't worry. I watch your gold like it's my own," he said.

"I know it," She replied, reining her horse away and touching her boots to its sides.

Following Carver's signal, she rode away in the direction Carver had given her. She knew what he wanted, He wanted her to flank his trail and get up into the rock cover, ahead of him and the others. Carver slowed his horse's steps, giving Teal a few extra seconds to move farther up into the rocks and half-circle the hillside opposite the overhang where they were meeting Poole.

But as the three moved forward at a cautious walk, just before rounding a turn hidden by tall rock, Carver raised a hand and stopped the other two in their tracks.

"What's this, boyo?" Fannen asked under his breath, moving forward and stopping beside the younger gunman. He kept a firm hold on the rifle across his lap.

Without taking his eyes off of Carver, Sloane spoke sidelong to him.

"I don't know … something on the ground," he said quietly, watching Max Carver look down and all around on the rocky trail. "Some tracks, maybe." He turned his gaze to Fannen, eyed him up and down. "Why don't you back away a little—keep one bullet from killing us both."

"Pardon *the hell* out of me," Fannen growled. But knowing the younger gunman was right about them needing to spread out, he gave a rough pull on his reins and backed his horse up a few steps. Ahead of them, Max Carver straightened in his saddle, waved them forward with his raised Colt. He moved, nudged his horse around the large standing rock hiding the clearing, toward the overhang he remembered from when he and Poole had first scouted the site.

Rounding the turn a few yards behind their leader, the other two stopped short when they saw Carver stepping down from his saddle, his Colt already in hand. He walked forward, leading his horse by its reins.

"Jesus ...," Sloane whispered, staring across the clearing at the naked mutilated body sprawled against the rocks edging the overhang. He spoke as he swung down slowly from his saddle. On the ground at the body's feet, a black vulture spread its wings and batted upward, and landed again begrudgingly, a few feet away. As the three stared, the enormous belly of the dead man wiggled and jerked, the rest of the body doing a strange dance like a marionette on unseen strings. In a second, a smaller, younger vulture poked its head out of the man's belly and looked back and forth at the men, a long strand of intestine dangling from its bloody beak. Then it wiggled itself free of its grizzly buffet and hoped down to the ground.

"Holy Moses," said Fannen, also stepping down from his saddle, "is that ole Cat-eye?" He led his horse forward, putting a few feet between himself and Sloane as they followed Carver closer to the overhang.

"Which one?" Sloane replied, nodding toward a second mutilated body lying face down in the rocky dirt. Two more buzzards rose up from atop the body and moved to the side, as if to let the men better assess their gruesome banquet.

"'Pache!" said Fannen, in a low growl.

"Easy does it ...," Carver cautioned the two gunmen in a quiet tone, the three of them crouched, looking up, all around the rocky world surrounding them. "If the Apache did this, our horses are gone." He looked up along the high rock line. "Where the hell is Cat-eye and the horses? Who the hell are these jakes?" As he spoke and eyed the scoured hillside, he caught sight of a young Apache warrior rise up from within the high rocks, a rifle already raised and pointed down at them.

Before either of the three could respond, two rifle shots resounded as one from among the rocks. The warrior froze for a moment as a bullet kicked up a puff in the dust at their feet and simultaneously the warrior's head exploded in a red spray. Carver let out a tight breath. The other two followed suit. They spread out, leading their horses, still looking up, still ready.

"About damn time, Teal," he murmured to himself, seeing the woman outlaw rise up on the steep hillside twenty yards above the warrior. She stood long enough to give Carver an *all-clear* wave, then dropped back down out of sight. Max Carver didn't let his amazement show. He was not so much impressed by her twenty yard marksmanship, but he was greatly amazed at the fact that she had managed to get that close to an Apache scout without getting her throat cut.

After checking the two mutilated bodies, Carver, Sloane and Dog Fannen stood in a triangle not more than five yards apart as Ruby Teal worked her way down from the rugged hillside above them. On a low line of rocks the buzzards stood impatiently craning their bloody heads. Overhead two more winged scavengers circled the clearing. To the west, the cloud of dust had drawn closer ever since they'd left Esplanade.

"I never counted on being here this long," Carver said. "They'll be riding up our shirts in no time."

"Yeah," Fannen growled, "thanks to that glass-eyed bastard letting the *'Pache* run off with our horses."

"Shut up, Dog," Carver snapped. "Cat-eye wouldn't let anybody take our horses, less they killed him first."

"Then where the hell is he?" said Fannen. "And where's the damned horses?"

"Apaches stole them, Dog!" Sloane cut in quickly as Carver narrowed a harsh stare on Dog Fannen.

"Then where the hell is their tracks?" Fannen demanded. As the two bickered, Carver gazed out at the dust, the riders still too far away to be visible but getting closer every second.

"There had to be more scouts than just the one Ruby killed," Carver said. "I figure at least two or three more." He gave a nod toward the hillside behind them. "They took the horses up through the rocks, to make them harder to track."

The three looked around as Teal led her horse down into the clearing and walked over to the gunmen, an open canteen hanging from her free hand.

"What'd you learn from up there?" Carver asked her.

"Whoever took the horses went out of here on a high trail," Teal said. She took a short sip and wiped her hand across her lips. "Don't ask me why though, with their whole party riding this way. I'd think they'd want to join them quick as they could—show off what they stole."

"Damn it," Carver cursed. He gave the two mutilated dead men a puzzled stare. "Who the hell are these two?"

Sloane had looked all around for the dead men's clothes and whatever identification he might have found, but he'd found nothing. Boots, hats and clothing had all vanished, just like the fresh horses.

"If you ask me—" Fannen tried to speak, but Carver cut him short.

"Enough talk," he snapped. "If we don't skin out of here, we're going to be fighting Apache."

Fannen let out a breath and fell silent.

"Our horses are worn to the bone," Elvin Sloane said, the four of them looking out on the desert floor below. "If we have to make a hard run for it, they'll be lucky to carry *us,* let alone all this gold."

"Don't even try to tell me to leave this bag of gold behind," Fannen said, nodding toward his horse standing at arm's length. His horse stood lathered and wet with sweat, the heavy bag of gold, also wet and dark-stained, hanging from the saddle horn.

"I'm not going to tell you, Dog," Carver cut in. "We're going to take the high trail and try to shake these Apache off our backs. Once we top these hills we'll decide if our horses are able to make it away from here. If we need to bury the gold somewhere we will."

"Maybe the rest of you will," Fannen persisted. "I'm not leaving my share behind. That's that," he said with resolve.

"You decide when we get up there," said Carver, Nodding upward onto the rocky steep hillside. "This is not the time to argue about it." He gave a nod toward the two bodies and the vultures waiting for their meal. "Keep these two in mind while you think it over."

"Any ideas who they were?" Teal asked, hanging her canteen over her saddle horn.

"No," said Carver in a short tone. "If you come up with anything, let us know." He turned to his tired horse and rubbed its muzzle. "We're all dying to find out." He paused and took a breath, and said, "Sorry, Teal, I didn't mean to be sharp. It ain't everyday I lose a horse-man and a string of fresh horses."

"I understand," the woman replied solemnly. She took the reins to her horse and led the animal toward the path she had just ridden down.

Carver and the two men looked at each and followed suit. In a moment the vultures watched the four lead their horses up and disappear into the rocks. They turned their beady eyes back and forth at each other, then hopped into the air on batting wings; they soared and hopped back to their places atop the bloating corpses and resumed their feast.

By the time the four led their horses to the trail atop the hill line, afternoon shadows were drawing long under the cooling desert sun. The horses stopped and staggered in place, and stood wide-legged, with their heads lowered as soon as their sweat-darkened reins were wrapped among short standing rocks. Without being told, the woman and Sloane followed Carver's lead. Sloane dropped both of their bags of gold to the ground. But Dog Fannen remained defiant.

"We can discuss it till hell turns to snow, I ain't leaving my share behind."

Carver took note of Fannen's hand resting on the butt

of his holstered Colt. Teal and Sloane also took note. Teal stepped away, leading her horse out of danger, her rifle in hand. Fannen gave her a look over his shoulder, then turned back to Carver as Sloane nudged his tired horse on the rump and moved it a few steps out of the way.

"If you're getting ready to pull iron with me," Dog said to Carver, "let's get right at it."

But Carver raised his gun hand in a show of peace. "Easy, Dog," he said. "It's your gold, and it's your life at stake. Look at these animals, they are plumb spent and you know it. If you ride yours to death, we're not stopping for you."

"I never asked none of you for nothing," Dog said. "and I ain't going to start now."

"Good," said Carver, "so long as we understand each other. If these Apache find the gold on you, they'll likely press harder to catch up to us and see what else we've got."

Fannen chuffed.

"No Apache I ever seen gives a damn about gold," he said. "Sure, there's some who might pick up a little gold if it happen to land on their feet. But most of 'em will kick it out of their way and go on." He shook his head. "Heathens have no use for gold." He spat as if to get a bad taste out of his mouth.

"Used to be, maybe so," Carver said. He jerked his thumb toward the desert floor. "But down there, lots of the warriors who've thrown in with these roaming desert Apache have lived with us *pálidos* much of their lives. They know what gold will buy—more guns, food, battle supplies. They'll take all the gold they can get their hand on." He stepped closer and stopped six feet away. "But if you've made up your mind, I expect there's no more talking to you."

"Now you're starting to get it, Carver," Dog said with a sarcastic grin, "I've always knowed you're a little slow in the head, but damn—!"

He stopped short; behind him, Ruby Teal slammed the butt of her rifle to the back of his skull. He sprawled forward on the dirt, knocked cold, his hand still on his gun butt.

Watching, Sloane shook his head.

"He should have known that was coming from two days away," he said.

"Give *Ruthless* Ruby a hand," Carver said with sly little grin, "get Dog into some shade 'fore he starts frying, and stinking." He motioned toward a stand of rock with shade lying across the ground beneath it. He nudged Dog's gun hand away from his big six-shooter and stooped and lifted it from its holster. He gave a glance at the advancing dust cloud on the desert floor. "We need to hurry it up. Get this gold under some rocks and clear out of here."

Sloane and Ruby Teal looked out at the roiling dust with him.

"Growing up on the reservation I've seen the Apache gather up all my life," Ruby Teal said, "like a swarm of hornets. But I've never seen the likes of this. It looks like the swarm is getting larger as it gets closer."

"Yeah, I've noticed that too," said Carver. He kept the growing concern out of his voice. "If it turns out that Cat-eye ain't dead, I ought to kill him myself—leaving us stuck like this."

"I've never known Poole to short his pals," Sloane said, dropping the bag of gold from Dog's saddle horn.

"Neither have I," said Carver. He turned to Ruby Teal. "Get up ahead of us, Ruby. See what the hell's going on."

Teal nodded and looked all around as if searching for the answer somewhere on the silent hillside.

From the other side of the clearing, at the long trail leading up from Esplanade, a voice called out in a French accent, "Have I arrived at an inopportune moment?"

Carver, Teal, and Sloane spun facing him in surprise, their guns up and leveled at him.

"Never point a gun unless you're ready to use it, Gascoyne." Carver said, recognizing both the dust-streaked

French captain and his uniform.

Noting the three guns held loosely pointed back in his direction, the captain let his own pistol slump.

"Good advice, *Monsieur* Carver," he said. "May I ask what has happened here?" He looked around more. "Where are the fresh horses you were to have waiting? My horse is worn out." He looked toward where the two dead men lay. His horse stood behind him, led by its reins for the last thirty yards. The big French revolver remained leveled in his right hand.

Carver wasn't going to tell the captain that they hadn't brought a fresh horse for him in the first place. "We think Apaches stole them," he said as Gascoyne led his tired horse closer. "But we're not real sure." He gestured down at the closing cloud of dust roiling ever closer across the desert floor. "When they get here we're hoping they'll tell us," he added wryly.

"Yes, well then," Gascoyne said. "While you await their arrival and figure everything out, perhaps you'll be so kind as to give me my share of the gold, and let me get out of here beforehand."

"I'd like to, Captain," said Carver. "But the fact is your horse is in no better shape than ours. We're getting ready to bury our shares up here and make a run for it."

"And my share?" Cascoyne asked.

"You can have it right now," Carver said. "But if you want to stick with us and make a run for it until the Apache are gone, you're going to have to bury it somewhere up here. We're going to travel light. When we come back to get our shares, you'll get yours."

Ride with the Wild Bunch? Hunh-uh ..., he didn't like the idea. But he took a moment, and looked down at the huge roiling dust cloud now hugging the hill line. Then he thought about the two dead bodies he'd seen down the hillside, and looked down at the knocked-out gunman. This was no time

A Ranger's Trail

to argue. And it was certainly no time to be riding alone, especially on a tired horse, with what looked like the largest horde of Apache warriors riding in on them.

He tossed a hand down toward the two bodies, the vultures waiting eagerly …. "Did all of this what happen as a result of these three not liking your plan?" The captain asked in a half serious tone of voice.

"No," Carver said. "We don't know who those two are, but we figure the Apache stole our horses and did all the cutting on them." He pointed to Dog Fannen. "This one is one of us, and *yes,* you might say we had a disagreement about leaving the gold behind." He turned to Sloane and Ruby Teal and said to them, "Tie Dog's hands before he starts waking up. Both of you take your gold somewhere around here and hide it." As they busily followed his orders, Carver turned back to Gascoyne. "Well?" he asked flatly, offering no room for further discussion.

"Yes, I'd like to stick with you," Gascoyne said, watching Sloane and Teal lead their horses away to where Dog lay unconscious.

"Wise decision," Carver said. "Come on, I'll give you your share. You can bury it, like the rest of us, and we can get the hell out of here."

"Which way are we going?" Gascoyne asked.

"Back to Esplanade," Carver said.

"Back to Esplanade?" Gascoyne said as if in disbelief. "Surely you're joking, after what just happened—?"

"We all wore masks. Nobody there saw any of our faces. He glanced up and down Ruby Teal, her white peasant's clothes gone, replaced by her doeskin trail clothes. "We'll hold up at a place we use in the burnt ruins outside of town —nobody goes there. Besides, if anybody does happen to see us, and ask any questions, you tell them you know us." Carver gave a grin. "You won't be lying."

Gascoyne only stared at him.

Carver gave a chuff but stopped grinning, seeing a look of doubt come to the captain's face.

"Tell them we're bounty hunters you hired to track down the Wild Bunch," he said.

Gascoyne still found no humor in Carver's words. Riding back to Esplanade sounded awfully risky, he had to admit, but with the Apache almost upon them, heading away in the other direction toward Codell, on worn-out horses, sounded a whole lot riskier by far. Besides, he reasoned quickly, Carver was right, few people frequented the burnt ruins on the north end of town. The site was believed to be *unlucky*. When the original Esplanade had burned to the ground thirty years earlier, the people left the charred debris lay where it fell, and built the new Esplanade right beside it.

"Yes, of course, *Monsieur,*" Gascoyne agreed with a half-hearted smile. "Why didn't I think of that?"

CHAPTER 4

When the ranger, his prisoner, and the horse string rode onto the main tiled street of Esplanade, the burned up battlewagon had turned into a pile of ash, coals and blackened metal framing. Some brave soul had rescued the Gatlin gun before the fire had grown too intense. The gun lay on the boardwalk, on its tripod's side. Sam had slipped a rope around Cat-eye Eddie Poole's waist and still rode a few feet behind him, leading the string. The blue roan had kept the horses settled, watching them over his shoulder like a demanding drill sergeant. Cat-eye Eddie Poole sat slumped in his saddle, his cuffed hands held close to his throbbing, bloody wound.

Sam moved Black Pot up beside Poole's horse as the townspeople began to gather around, *getting too close ...,* Sam noted. He gathered in the slack of the rope until only a short three feet separated him from Poole.

"Take it easy, Poole," he said quietly between the two of them. "Folks can get really bristled after something like this." Poole stayed slumped, his good eye closed.

"I'm asleep, Ranger," he said sidelong under his breath without straightening in his saddle.

"That's good. Stay that way," Sam replied. He reached over and looped the coiled rope over Poole's saddle horn and took the reins to Poole's tired horse. He opened his duster enough to make sure his badge was clearly seen.

"If you try to make a run for it," he said to Poole in a lowered voice, "I'll turn this big rifle loose on you."

"I hear you," Poole said in lowered voice. "I got nowhere

to run. I'm bleeding like a stuck hog."

"Hold yourself right there, *Señor* lawman!" said a swarthy red-headed Mexican-Irish. He continued eying the ranger's badge as he trotted up a few yards and stopped close in front of them. He wore a leather blacksmith's apron with the top half untied and hanging down his front. The butt of a big pistol bulged on his right side. He managed to get the pistol out and level it in Sam's direction. Sam could see the man's nerves were on raw edge.

"What happened here?" Sam asked, nodding back toward the burnt battlewagon sitting up the street in front of the bank. He already knew about the raid on the bank, but he felt it best to let the man have his say and let off any built up steam.

"We've had a robbery here," the man said, acknowledging the ranger's badge. He looked the horses and Poole over, then lowered his pistol and said, "Our telegraph lines have been cut, but we now have them spliced back together. Soldiers are on their way. You are welcome, but we have all the help—"

"I understand," Sam replied. He gestured toward the dust on the desert floor that was now starting to settle as the Apache slowed their horses to a walk coming onto the hillside. "I came here to keep from fighting Apache, and to get my prisoner patched up." Sam brought the string of horses to a halt at Black Pot's right side, Poole and his horse on his left. "I'll grain and water these horses, and get going soon as I can."

"*Si,* I mean *yes,* of course, Ranger," the man said. "I am Jorge Doyle, the blacksmith. Also I'm Esplanade's *Selectman,* for now anyway. So, water and feed your *caballos*—Your horses that is."

"*Si, comprende,*" Sam said, wanting the man to know that either language was all right by him.

The blacksmith only smiled, and leaned a bit to one side, then the other, checking out both the prisoner and the string of horses.

A Ranger's Trail

A rotund lady with silver-gray hair, wearing a long black dress leaned close to the blacksmith and whispered near his ear. The man straightened and held his head high.

"Por favor, Ranger," he said. "She would have me ask you what this one has done," he said.

Other Esplanade citizenry had gathered in closer, many of them Texans and Arizonians as well as native Mexicans. Sam knew they had been through a lot, yet they appeared calm enough under the circumstances, he thought. He saw more rifles, shotguns and bandoleers of ammunition than usual on a town street like this, but he realized it was partly owing to the gold robbery, and partly because of the large band of Apache riding into the area. The town was stirred up. He knew it. He gestured a nod toward Poole, who was still asleep as far as anyone could tell.

"He is accused of being a horse thief," Sam said. "He denies it, but I'm ordered to take him to Nogales. The Arizona Territory court will deal with him there."

"Too bad," said a broad-shouldered teamster leaning on a hickory pick handle. A coiled rope hung from his shoulder. "We could stretch his neck for him right here in the street."

Other Esplanade citizenry grumbled in agreement with the teamster. Sam stopped it all short with a raised hand.

"Let's have none of that talk," he said firmly. "This man will get his day in a Nogales courtroom. If he's found guilty, the law will handle the matter."

"This ain't the U.S. of A. Ranger, let alone Arizona Territory. We want to hang somebody, what right have you got to stop us?"

The grumbling of the crowd grew a pitch louder. Jorge the blacksmith interceded.

"This lawman is here under an agreement signed between the US Government and our Mexican leaders in Matamoros," he said, speaking above the crowd. "If he has a prisoner in custody, the prisoner is under his protection."

"That's the damndest thing I ever heard of in my life!" said the teamster, getting more and more testy as he spoke. "I moved to old Mex to get away that kind of cock-eyed thinking!"

"It's time you shut up," Jorge Doyle said with firm resolve. He pointed a thick finger at the loudmouthed teamster as it to make his point.

The teamster fell silent, staring red-faced. Jorge stepped closer to the ranger and pointed past the crowd.

"The *cárcel*—I mean the *jail*—is an adobe building just up the street on this side," he said.

"You needn't correct yourself," Sam said, "I speak Mexican."

"*Gracias,* Ranger," said Doyle. "Still, I will speak English."

"Suit yourself," Sam said, dismissing the matter. "Is there a doctor here?" he asked, noting how the crowd had started to settle down some under Jorge Doyle's calm reasoning tone.

"We have a woman healer who births babies and cleans bullet wounds. I will send her to the jail to treat this one," Jorge said. He nodded toward Poole who still appeared to be sound asleep.

Sam touched his hat brim. "Soon as I get this man shackled and treated, I want you to tell me everything about the robbery."

"*Si,* I will tell you what I can," said the blacksmith, although he wondered why an Arizona Ranger would have any interest in the robbery of gold from the French mines. "You will see the bank manager in jail when you get there. He was there through the whole thing."

"Why is he in jail?" Sam asked.

"To keep all these people from beating him to death, Ranger," Jorge said.

"Because his bank won't pay what's owed to us! That's why!" the American teamster shouted within the crowd. "We might still drag him out and beat the living hell out of

A Ranger's Trail

him some more!" He shouted in the direction of the adobe jail, "Hear that, Flippoza? You *mangy cur!* We might just be calling on you again. This time we'll bring our razor straps! If I get my way, you'll hang from—"

The man stopped short as Sam turned in his saddle and gave him a hard glare.

"Next word out of your mouth about hanging, I'll put a bullet in your foot," Sam said calmly. He swung the lead rope around Black Pot's saddle horn and raised his big Colt, cocked and ready.

The man's face turned pale; his eyes widened. He started to speak, but stopped himself under the ranger's stare. Sam waited for a second as a stunned silence set in over the crowd in the wide street. At length, he lowered his Colt.

"That's more like it," he said quietly. The crowd stood still as stone as he took up the lead rope and the reins to Poole's horse and nudged Black Pot forward at a walk, flanked by his wounded prisoner and the horse string on either side. "Anybody wants to know, I'll be at the jail until this man's wound is 'tended to."

A slow click of hooves resounded on the tile street as the ranger nudged Black Pot and his horses and prisoner forward at a walk. Jorge Doyle stepped in close and walked alongside Black Pot, in front of the horse string. Feeling the blue roan balk slightly at the man walking in front of him, Sam gave a firm pull of the lead rope, letting the roan know who was boss. The roan cocked his head against the rope and grumbled and huffed, but he settled down under the ranger's command.

"Speaking to you now as Esplanade's Selectman, Ranger," Jorge Doyle said. He looked around as if to make sure no one else was listening. "I want you to know I am glad you're here. I didn't mean what I said about we have all the help we need."

Here it comes .... Sam only gave a nod and gazed straight ahead.

"Truth is—" Selectman Doyle said, walking along close,

speaking quietly up to Sam atop Black Pot. "—the robbery has left our citizens without resource. And now, with the Apache coming, there is much fear and anger in the air. The robber chief threw some gold coins into the street. But much of the coins are already spent on drink. Drinking only makes the fear and anger worse."

"I understand," said Sam. He thought of his orders to not get involved with the French troops or the Mexican citizenry, even though a good deal of the people living here were US citizens whose trades or businesses had drawn them across the border. "What about the *federales?*"

"I asked them for help, *twice!*" said Doyle. "But there's been no response. Then I found our lines were cut, so I don't know if the *federales* got my messages or not. Now that our lines are repaired, our operator keeps signaling the outpost in Suderey. Still, there's no response." He paused, then said, "I think the solders are afraid of the Desert Apache. Itza-Chu leads this large band. He is known to enjoy torturing and killing our soldiers."

"I know about Itza-Chu," Sam said down to him. "The past year he's gathered allies from all along both sides of the border."

"Si! And his number of warriors has grown larger than even the old ones here can remember," Doyle said. Without pause he said, "Now that I can speak freely, I must ask for your help, Ranger, *por favor,* for these people." He pleaded with a shrug and stood back from the horses as Sam veered Black Pot and the string to an adobe hovel in a row of buildings on his right. The shabby little building had barred windows and the faded crudely hand-painted word *Cárcel* above the open door.

Sam swung down from his saddle and hitched the string, Poole's horse and Black Pot to a post in a row of worn wooden posts standing from the ground along a low boardwalk. Doyle stood waiting, expectant, until Sam turned to him.

A Ranger's Trail

"I don't want problems with the French or the *federales*," he said. "The French will send troops when they hear about the robbery. I expect the *federales* will do the same. Nobody likes losing gold." As he spoke he slipped his rifle from its boot and let it hang from his hand. "Until the Mexican or French troops arrive, I'll stay here and help you keep order. Meanwhile, I need you to go bring the doctor here while I get this prisoner inside. Then I need you to guard him while I go take a look at the burnt wagon."

"The burnt wagon?" said Doyle. "What is looking at the burnt wagon going to tell you?"

"I don't know," said Sam. "That's why I'm looking."

In the *cocina* behind Mama Flora's Restaurant and Open Air Lodging House, two would-be members of the Wild Bunch, Joe *Little Gun* Mercer and Fedder Dockery slipped forward unseen along the side of the big, dilapidated clapboard building and watched the ranger and Selectman Doyle talking at the hitch rail. A third man, a fast gunman named Morgan Manlen, hadn't bothered getting up from the ground right away and going with his two sidekicks for a better look at the wide street. Instead he remained seated on his saddle blanket a moment longer, taking his time, draining his tin coffee cup. He sat the cup down and pushed up to his feet when an old man cooking the meat turned to him and gave him a nod.

"El alimento está listo," the old man said, cordially.

"Gracias," said Manlen. "I'll tell my pards come and get it." He picked up his saddle blanket and shook it, laid it over his saddle on the ground and walked away along the side of the building to where the other two stood watching the street.

At the front edge of the building, Joe Mercer leaned closer to Fedder Dockery.

"See there, Dock?" he said to Dockery. "I told you that was Cat-eye Eddie riding by. I never forget a face."

"You're right as rain, Little Gun." Dockery replied under his breath as he eyed both the wounded outlaw and the ranger up and down. "I've seen ole Cat-eye in better shape." He continued scrutinizing the ranger as Jorge Doyle followed the two through the open door into the adobe jail. "And if I ain't mistaken, that's that aggravating ranger from Nogales taking him to jail." Dockery eyed the string of horses at the hitch rail.

"That's the ranger all right," said Mercer. He paused for a second then said, "So, I did a pretty good thing, spotting Cat-eye riding by like I did. Lucky for us both I saw him when I did. I told my—"

"Yes, you did good, Little Gun!" said Dockery, cutting him off. "Now let it go."

Mercer gave Dockery a hard look, but kept his mouth shut.

At the rail the blue roan bumped sidelong against Black Pot, demanding more space. Black Pot didn't budge. He slung his head, delivering a hard solid butt against the blue roan's neck. The roan pulled back.

"Wherever Max and his bunch are," Dockery continued, "I've got a hunch that's their fresh horses standing right there." He gave a thin, sly smile. "Think Max would be beholding if we busted his horse-man out that rat-hole?"

"Kill the ranger first," Morgan Manlen's deep voice interceded close behind them.

Both men jerked around, startled by the suddenness of Manlen standing only inches away.

"Jesus, Morgan!" said Dockery. "Let a man know you're standing behind him!"

"Hey, Dock," Manlen said with a dark chuckle, "I'm standing here behind you." He gave a sharp grin. "How's that suit you?"

Dockery grumbled his disapproval, but dropped the matter and looked back at the horses at the rail. Beside him, Mercer did the same.

"Anyway," said Manlen, "I come to tell you *hombres,* the

cook says, *'el alimento está listo.'"*

"I hate it when people come down here and think they have to speak Mexican." Dockery spoke to Mercer, but fully intended his words for Manlen.

"It means *your goat* is cooked," Manlen said, the sharp grin still frozen on his face.

"That's not what it means," Little Gun Mercer cut in. "It means *the food's ready.*"

"Damn, hoss," Manlen said to Mercer. "Ain't that pretty much the same thing I said?"

Mercer just stared at him.

Dockery changed the subject back to the ranger.

"Were you serious about killing the ranger first, before breaking Cat-eye out?" he asked Manlen.

"You bet I am," said Manlen. The smile left his face. Down to business now. "I ain't having that ranger dogging me every time I look around. If you two want to ride with Max Carver and his bunch, saving Cat-eye Poole and these horses will get you closer than anything I can think of."

"We were supposed to already be riding with him on this big job down here," said Mercer. "He as much as gave us his word. But when the time come his whole bunch was gone—"

"Hush up," said Manlen. "If you're going to talk about what should have, or shouldn't have happened, I'll go eat the goat and let you two stay here and sort it all out."

Mercer and Dockery looked at each other, then back at Manlen.

"As far as this big job goes, the deed's been done," said Dockery. "I figure Max Carver owes us something for telling us we were in, then backing out on us. I say join him and his Wild Bunch, or take what we figure is coming to us."

Mercer nodded in agreement.

"Whether we come here to hook up with the Wild Bunch, or getting our hands on their loot, far as I'm concerned the way to do it just rode into town." Manlen gave a nod toward the jail, and grinned. "And I'm just the man who can make it all happen for us." He patted his holstered Colt as he spoke.

Mercer nodded his approval.

"He's right, Dock," he said. "I say let him do it."

"Hold on just a damn minute, Little Gun," said Dockery. He looked at Manlen with a narrowed gaze. "How do we know you can take down the ranger?"

"You're getting ready to see me do it, Dockery," Manlen said in a sharp tone. "I know I can beat him, he knows I can beat him. Hell anybody who has ever seen me draw and shoot knows I can beat him."

Dockery looked doubtful; Manlen continued.

"All the ranger ever had going for him is *surprise,*" he said, "always slipping up on a fella with his gun out and cocked. Not this time. I'm the one slipping up on him with *surprise* on my side."

"He's got a point, Dock," said Mercer. "I've heard that's how the ranger works. He'll manage to slip his Colt out and cock it while nobody's paying attention."

"That won't happen with me," Manlen said confidently. "I'll be the one who pulls a surprise."

"That's fine. But I don't want to be left hanging," Dockery replied to Manlen. "If he kills you, he'll be all over me and Little Gun."

"Just be waiting out of sight then," said Manlen. "When the ranger hits the ground dead, just break ole Cat-eye out and grab them horses. You can do that much can't you?"

Dockery gave him a dubious stare. With no reply he turned and walked back toward the aroma of sizzling meat.

"Don't worry about Dock, he'll be all right," Mercer said to Manlen.

"What about you, Little Gun?" Manlen asked. "Have you got any doubts?"

Mercer looked the gunman in the eye and said, "I believe

I'm standing here talking to the man who's about to kill Ranger Sam Burrack."

"You got it right," Manlen said with an up-tilt of his chin.

CHAPTER 5

Cat-eye Eddie Poole sat in a wooden chair outside of the jail cell, where the ranger had placed him. Now that the ranger and the bank manager had left to go see the burnt wagon, Poole leaned deep against the iron bars with a handcuff around his wrist keeping him secured in place. He watched an elderly Mexican woman tend to his side wound, pressing the bullet holes front and back, alternately, with a knotted cloth of chopped herbs from the desert. As her thin weathered leathery hands dipped the herbs into a pan of water and squeezed it, and pressed it against the front of the wound, Poole sized her up and down, while Selectman Doyle stood close by watching, a forge hammer in his rugged blacksmith's hand.

"How long you suppose before Burrack and the bank man gets back?" Poole asked, feeling for any information he might be able to get to help him plan a means of escape.

"Shut up, Cat-eye Eddie Poole," Doyle said, his hammer ready for any situation that might arise. "The ranger said don't talk to you. So just sit there quiet, and let her patch you up."

"Do you speak *American,* old woman?" Poole asked bluntly, ignoring Doyle's order.

The healing woman only flicked a glance at him, then shook her head and turned her eyes back to soaking his wound.

"Oh, you don't, hunh?" said Poole, with a sarcastic snap to his voice, "Then how do you even know what I asked you?"

"Leave her alone, Poole," said Doyle.

"Porque digo un pequeño ingles," the old woman said without looking up from her nursing.

"Keep your mouth shut!" Doyle said with contempt in his voice.

But Poole ignored Doyle again and worked the woman's words over in his head.

"Because you know some English?" he said to the woman, translating as close as he could. He mulled it over.

"Sí, pequeño," she said, still soaking his side wound.

"A little?" he said, even more puzzled as the conversation went on.

"Yes, a little *Ingles,"* she said. She looked up at him with a wary expression on her face.

"Don't worry, old woman," said Poole, "I'm not going to—"

"I told you to shut your mouth!" said Doyle, his grip growing tighter around the hammer handle. "Don't make me tell you again."

"Oh? Or you'll do what?" Poole asked in defiance.

Doyle took a step forward.

"I'll crack your head," Doyle replied, tight-lipped.

Poole chuffed.

"No you won't," he said. "I've seen my fill of men like you. All bark, but no bite." He nodded at a rifle leaning against a battered desk. "You've got a good rifle standing there, but it ain't enough. You've got to hold onto a hammer." He shook his head slowly. "Naw, you ain't got the sand to hit me with a hammer, or shoot me with that rifle." He grinned. "I'm so dangerous even the ranger knows it takes an armed guard and a pair of cuffs just so's I can get my wound looked over. Your knees would go weak if you tried to hit me."

"You've never been more wrong in your life, Poole," Doyle said, raising the hammer as he stepped closer.

Outside, on the wide street, the ranger and bank manager, Philippe Flippoza, looked over the pile of burnt ruble that had once been a French battlewagon. Flippoza kept a cautious eye on the townspeople who passed them on the street, a few still directing looks of anger and scorn at him.

Sam toed his boot against burnt leather-bound ledgers and partly consumed papers lying scattered on the ground a few feet from where the worst of the fire had been.

"There you have it, Ranger," Flippoza said with a shrug of his narrow shoulders. He nodded toward the nearby boardwalk. "If there is anything of value left here, it is the Gatling gun, and the stacks of bullets—if they are not ruined."

A voice among the onlookers called out, "Don't worry, we're keeping an eye on everything, Ranger. Soon as the gun's cooled off enough we're moving it indoors."

"To where," Sam asked.

"Selectman Doyle said take it to the old church," the man replied. He gestured toward an ancient stone building towering above the far end of the street. "It's always kept Esplanade safe from Apache."

"And we're setting up wagon barricades on both ends of town," another voice called out.

Good thinking .... Sam nodded and turned back to Flippoza, realizing how important the big crank gun would be if the Apache grew bold enough to attack Esplanade. He would check the big gun and the ammunition out himself when he finished here. *But for the time-being* .... He looked back down at the burnt debris at his feet.

"As I told you on our way, Ranger," said Flippoza, "there is little to see here."

"You're right," Sam said, "the fire ate everything." He paused, then said, "When there's gold scheduled to come to Esplanade, I'm sure your bank gets advance notice—and some sort of signed documentation?"

"*Sí,* I mean yes, of course we do," said the bank manager, still keeping a close eye on those passing by, some of whom were now gathering and watching curiously. Owing to the threat of a coming Apache raid, firearms were being worn and carried by men and women alike. Older Native Mexicans carried machetes in their waist sashes, and old musket-loading rifles on shoulder straps. "Perhaps you'd like to go inside my office and see the signed delivery notice?" His nerves had began turning edgier as size of the crowd increased.

"Let's do that," Sam said, looking back and forth at the gathering townsfolk. He followed Flippoza past the Gatling gun and the salvaged stacks of ammunition on the boardwalk. Afternoon shadows were drawing long across the streets and rooflines of Esplanade; once inside the closed bank, Flippoza locked the door and drew a breath of relief. Outside they could hear lingering voices as the sound of shoes and boots moved away. Sam only observed, his rifle hanging loosely in his left hand.

Flippoza saw his own hand shaking as he took the signed paper from his desk drawer. His trembling fingers took two attempts to get the paper unfolded.

"What a coward you must think I am, Ranger," he said, smoothing the paper on his desk and turning it toward Sam to read. "If I had it to do over I would have found a buggy and gone with the captain whether he liked it or not." He spoke quietly; Sam listened and read the signed documentation. He recalled seeing the French captain as he rode past Poole and the ranger on the high trail.

"He didn't try to form a posse—get townsmen to ride with him?" Sam asked casually without raising his eyes from reading the document.

"No," said Flippoza, "the French Captain Gascoyne is a very brave man. He said if I wanted to follow him I could, but he could not wait for me. He said the gold is not yet delivered and still belongs to his nation. That his duty is to recapture it quickly as possible. I am a coward for not going with him." He stared down for a moment, but then looked up, taking pride in the French officer's action. "Going after those murderers took *extraordinary dedication!*" he added. "I envy such courage."

"I understand," Sam nodded quietly, having taken in

every word. Keeping his questions on course, he asked, "All of the other wagon guards were killed right here in the street?" He laid the paperwork back on the manager's desk.

"Yes, all of them," Flippoza said. "They died so quickly, so horribly!" He shook his bowed head.

Sam studied him for a moment. Then he pointed a finger down and tapped it on the paper he'd just laid on the banker's desk.

"This says '*seven bags* of un-struck gold coins.' Does that figure sound right to you?"

"Yes," said Flippoza. "I always count the bags myself. Most times there are five, but sometimes, like this time, there were seven—as the paper says." He nodded at the paper on his desk. "We keep the other two bags here in our vault until railroad guards pick come pick them up and take them to Ciudad Mexico."

"I see," Sam said, picturing a lot of un-struck gold coins being shifted through many hands. *Careless hands? Thieving hands ...?* He wondered, yet he reminded himself he was here to bring down the Wild Bunch, nothing else. Although Sam couldn't help but notice how the man seemed at ease talking about the gold shipment until it came to the bag *count.* There he seemed tense, uncertain. The ranger's lawman instincts pushed his curiosity further. He could stop this at any point and never mention any of it again. *But not right now ...,* he told himself.

"And you counted the bags yourself, this time, like always?" he asked, bringing the question back into focus.

"Yes, *always!*" Flippoza's face reddened.

"Because you always count the bags yourself?" Sam probed.

"Yes, I told you!" Flippoza said. "I always count the bags as they come through the door."

Sam only gave him a blank stare; he'd asked enough questions, now he let his silence nudge the man on.

A Ranger's Trail

"It is my most important responsibility," Flippoza continued. "Each bag is an estimated one hundred thousand in gold—the shipment is never off more than a few coins, which is discovered and corrected when the coins are counted for disbursal—"

"You never wait and count the bags after they're inside the bank?" Sam asked, cutting him off.

"No," said Flippoza, "I count the bags as they come through the door. *Across the threshold* I call it—it is my system. I never vary from it."

Seeing the curious look on the ranger's face, he asked, "What? Is something wrong, Ranger?"

"No," Sam said. "I believe you always use your system. But this time things got out of hand. Men were killed. Maybe you wondered if you were going to die yourself."

"You doubt what I'm saying?" said Flippoza. "You think I am lying about counting the bags of gold?"

"No, said Sam, "I don't think you're lying. I think you're mistaken. I'm wondering how you managed to count the bags *across the threshold,* when they never even made it through the door?"

"Oh—!" Flippoza looked stunned, realizing the ranger was right. He stalled, trying to get the robbery scene straight in his mind. His face reddened. "I always, without fail, count the bags as they arrive—"

Sam cut him off.

"As they *arrive,* or as they come through the door?" he asked pointedly, leaving no other option. "Because these bags arrived but never made it into the bank. Isn't that why the French Captain said they were still *his responsibility?"*

Flippoza considered the ranger's words, then looked up as if a light had come on.

"Yes! That's true. Perhaps— Perhaps this time I did not count them so closely," he said in a halting voice. "Yes, there was so much going on, men were dying—"

"Not *so closely?*" Sam said, lowering his voice as the two of them were speaking in secret. "I think in all the confusion you didn't count them at all."

Filppoza started to protest; Sam stopped him.

"I have nothing to do with the Mexican government. Even less to do with the French. I'm here hunting the Wild Bunch, the same men who robbed your bank. Whatever you tell me doesn't go any further than us. Do you understand?"

Flippoza only stared, stunned, afraid to say anything.

Sam continued. "You have a signed document from the French stating they delivered seven bags of gold. Selectman Doyle and several townsmen say there were five bags taken out of the strong box, and never made it inside your bank." He paused, then said, "I wasn't here and what I say wouldn't matter anyway. If that delivery had been completed, you would have had to either sign the paper, saying you accepted seven bags of gold, or you would have had to refuse to sign it."

"I—I haven't signed it, as you can see," Flippoza said quickly.

Sam just looked at him.

"Why did you say *seven?*" he asked.

"Because I saw the paper said seven," Flippoza replied. "I was not going to argue with it! Not after all that happened!" Sweat beaded on his forehead. "If the townsmen and selectman say there were five," he said, "then I must say there were *five.*"

Sam said, "If you believe there were seven you have to say so. If you believe there were only five, you have to say five. Don't lie because you think it's what people want you to say. Tell the truth and stand with it."

He watched the bank manager's eyes well up.

"I don't know now if there were five or seven! I am so confused," he said.

"Listen to me." Sam said, "If you don't know how many bags arrived, say you don't know. Because that is the *truth* as you know it. Anything else is a lie, and you can never see where a lie is taking you until you get there—then it's too late. The truth is all a man has to save himself. If we quit trusting it, we lose everything."

Flippoza let out a relieved breath and confessed, "I have no idea how many bags arrived here, Ranger. This is the truth, and when the *federales,* or the French ask, it is what I *must* say."

Sam nodded his approval and watched him pick up the unsigned paper, put it away in his desk, and take out a handkerchief from inside his coat. When Flippoza finished wiping his eyes and nose and put the handkerchief away, he formed a weak little smile held up a long key. "I have my own cell key" he said. "If you are all finished here, take me back to jail, *por favor*. Where the people I live with and work with will not be permitted to kill me."

On their walk back to the adobe jail, Sam noted the aura of fear and tension that had seemed to consume the bank manager had lessened considerably. In spite of the fact that there were still people here who blamed him for the gold being gone and the bank not having enough funds to pay them, Flippoza had resolved himself to taking the side of truth. *The truth and nothing but the truth ...,* the ranger quoted to himself.

"Tomorrow I will reopen the bank," Flippoza commented as the two moved away from the people gathered outside the bank and neared the front of Mama Flora's Restaurant and Lodging House. "I know there will be insults directed to me, but I am going to hold my head up and go on about my job."

"That's good to hear," Sam said, the two of them, banker and lawman walking along the wide dusty street, the ranger's rifle in his left hand.

"My fear of telling the truth must seem small and trivial to you, Ranger," Flippoza said. He gave a small embarrassed smile, "Now that I have settled it in my mind, it even seems a little foolish to me."

"Getting to the truth is never foolish," Sam said, glancing

along the street, down the alleyway running alongside Mama Flora's he said, "the only thing foolish is trying to ignore it." As he spoke his gaze moved over three horses standing at the hitch rail out front of Mama Flora's. The three horses stood saddled and ready for the trail, a well-loaded pack mule standing beside them.

"Yes, it is so, Ranger," Flippoza said in a calmer voice than the ranger had yet heard. They walked on ....

Selectman Doyle stepped forward from a battered desk, his rifle in hand as Sam and Flippoza walked in off the street. Cat-eye Eddie Poole still sat outside his cell with his wrist cuffed to the barred door. The woman had finished bandaging Poole's wounds and taking a small coin that Doyle held out for her. Sam and Flippoza stopped and watched as she thanked Doyle and shuffled away, leaving through a small back door into a back alleyway.

From the wooden chair, Poole asked in a gruff voice, "How's a man get himself fed in this rat hole?"

"Start by showing some manners," Sam said as he stepped over and opened the back door enough to look out. He caught sight of the woman just as her long black dress faded into the evening gloom. Then he closed the door, walked over and un-cuffed Poole and directed him into the cell and locked the door behind him.

"Mama Flora is sending over a tray for the four of us," Doyle said. He held out his hand to Flippoza and said, "Now that we've got us an honest-to-God prisoner, I'm afraid I'll have to take back your key, *Señor* Flippoza."

"Of course," said Flippoza, taking the long cell key from his pocket and handing it to Doyle. "If I may, I'll stay the night and go to my house tomorrow after the bank closes."

"You're welcome to stay as long as you need to," Doyle said. "But I believe folks here have settled down considerably." He looked to Sam for a second opinion. Sam only nodded.

"Ha!" said Poole, lying on his cell bunk listening. "Any

A Ranger's Trail

man fool enough to stay in jail when he don't have to, oughta stay in one all the time."

Before anyone could reply, a loud voice called out from the empty street.

"Ranger *Burrack!* This is Morgan Manlen—I know you've heard of me! Step on out here, show yourself. I've come to kill you!"

Inside the jail, Poole rose quickly from his bunk at the sound of Manlen's voice. He took a position at the cell door, both hands gripping the bars.

"You stole a pal of mine's horses" Manlen shouted. "I'm here to square things up."

"Manlen …. You straight up fool!" Poole grumbled under his breath.

Out front, Manlen looked around and grinned toward the spot where Joe Mercer and Fedder Dockery had been standing near their horses, their plan being to gather the horse string from the jail's hitch rail and leave Esplanade as soon as Manlen killed the ranger. But Manlen saw no sign of them. He looked up and around, as if they might have taken to the rooftops with rifles. *No need in that, boys…,* he told himself confidently. He looked back at the adobe jail.

"I know you're in there, Burrack! I know you hear me!"

"Jesus! You're not even half right," Poole said under his breath, looking over at Doyle, then at Flippoza.

"Keep your mouth shut, Poole!" Doyle warned, his rifle ready, its hammer cocked.

What the hell …? Manlen waited a moment for a response, but none came. Farther up the street townspeople, seeing and hearing the lone gunman, started drifting in the direction of the jail.

Manlen waited in a tense silence. He stood as still as stone, like some statue in tribute to a *dangerous gunman.* After a full minute he moved three steps closer to the small jail, getting a bit closer now than was his ordinary practice. But that was all right. The ranger was starting to show himself a coward, he thought, just like he figured he might, without the element of surprise on his side.

"Ranger, *Ranger!*" Manlen shook his head, aware of the townspeople starting to reassemble on the street as they were before, at the burnt wagon site. "Folks are showing up out here! Wanting to see me do some hard killing! Let's not disappoint them."

Manlen waited, tense, expectant. A big clock ticked inside his head. What the hell was this?

"If you don't come out, Ranger, I'm coming in. Anybody in there with you will be as dead as you!" *Damn it, this is crazy ...!* He started walking forward slowly. He'd go right in and flush him out if he had to—"

"Manlen, back here," the ranger said, his voice sounding uncomfortably close behind the big outlaw. *Too damn close ...!* he warned himself.

He spun around suddenly toward the sound of the ranger's voice, his hand already going around the butt of his Colt, swinging it up even as he caught a glimpse of the ranger's big Colt, drawn, leveled, cocked, ready. *Oh hell!* He saw a belch of smoke and orange fire split the evening shadows as the shot resounded along the street. Then he realized he was down, a hard stabbing pain punched into his leg. His gun flew from his hand. *"Jesus! No!"* He shouted, seeing the ranger walk toward him like a stalking panther, cocking the Colt for the next shot.

"Don't shoot! Don't shoot!" Manlen shouted, loud enough for everyone on the street to hear, including Mercer and Dockery who had reappeared beside their horses and mule and stood struggling to untie the horses' reins.

Sam gave the two struggling gunmen a sharp glance. Then he looked back down at Manlen.

"Why not?" he asked Manlen quietly. "Wasn't some *hard killing* what you came here to show these folks?"

Manlen raised a flat hand up toward him, seeing smoke

still curling up the barrel of Sam's Colt, the barrel tilted down at his forehead.

"All right now, *listen, Ranger!*" he said. "That was just some tough gunman talk. I expect you've done some yourself, right?"

"No," Sam said flatly, the big smoking Colt cocked, still ready for the next shot.

"Okay, I'm done here," Manlen said, talking fast. "You got me. You win! I don't want *no more.*" He nodded down at the bullet hole in his leg, just above his knee. "Like as not I'll bleed to death here anyway."

He kept jabbering as Sam looked over at Mercer and Dockery still trying to loosen their horses' reins. Seeing the ranger look their way with his flat expression, the two men struggled harder.

"It's in a *damn knot!*" shouted Dockery. Bystanders watched the two in stunned wonderment.

"How *the hell ...?*" Mercer had no time to wonder. He pulled a knife up from his boot well and made a violent slash through both sets of reins. Hurrying into their saddles, Dockery grabbed the mule's knotted lead rope and tried to yank it loose. But the hitch rail wouldn't give it up and the mule would have none of Dockery's rough handling.

"Damn it to hell!" Dockery shouted, "It's knotted too!"

The mule flew into a wild frenzy of braying and high kicking, finally jerking the rope loose from the rail and spinning and kicking in a tight circle. As the two unnerved outlaws turned their short-reined horses and raced away, the mule continued to kick and buck, scattering trail supplies all over the street.

Sam looked back down at Manlen and said, "You're not going to bleed to death."

"And—and you ain't going to kill me?" Manlen sounded unsure, but relieved.

"No," said Sam, letting down the hammer on his Colt. "If

I wanted to kill you, why would I waste a bullet shooting you in the leg?"

"I'm wondering that myself," said Manlen, in a pained voice. He gripped his punctured leg with both bloody hands.

Sam glanced off at the rise of dust Fedder Dockery and Joe Mercer's horses stirred up in the grainy evening light. The click of the horses' iron shoes on the tile street had stopped as the horses ran off of the hard tile, into the sandy desert floor.

"You let them two trail rats go on purpose, didn't ya?" said Manlen.

He watched the ranger turn back to him with a poker face. Without answering, Sam picked up the downed outlaw's dropped gun and shoved it down behind his belt.

"I wished to hell you'd let me go, too," Manlen said. "This wound will likely keep me stove-up for a week or more." He grimaced. "You've hit the bone—my luck, it's broke to hell."

"There's a woman here who'll 'tend to you," Sam said with no sympathy in his voice. "Soon as you're 'tended, you and I are going to talk."

"Talk?" said Manlen. "Talk about what?"

"About Max Carver and his Wild Bunch," Sam said. As he spoke he motioned toward the open window of the jail where Doyle and Flippoza stood watching.

"What makes you think I know anything about that bunch?"

"You just stood out here and said he's your *pal.* Remember?" Sam said.

"I don't recall saying any such a damn thing," Manlen said, taking the ranger's down-reached hand. Doyle and Flippoza hurried out to help lift the wounded outlaw to his feet.

"Then let's just call it a *hunch,*" Sam said. He gazed off in the western direction the two fleeing outlaws took out of Esplanade.

CHAPTER 6

Inside the small jail office, Selectman Doyle looked all around at a bloody pan of water and blood-stained washcloths.

"This jail starting to look like a field hospital, Ranger," he said. This time the healing woman had tended to Morgan Manlen inside the single cell. Philippe Flippoza stood beside the ranger, his sleeves rolled up, having assisted the healing woman all he could. Cat-eye Eddie Poole lay on his bunk leaning back against the stone wall. He watched closely as Doyle turned the big cell key, opened the barred door and let the woman out. She carried the stained cloth and the pan of bloody water.

"When they stop coming at me I'll stop shooting them," Sam reflected. This time he handed the woman a coin and thanked her for her services. Flippoza stepped over and opened the rear door for her.

"Hell," said Poole, as the ranger shut the door, "I never shot at you."

"And I haven't shot you, Cat-eye ... *yet,*" Sam replied.

"I got hit by a bullet," Pooled said, his artificial eye seated crooked in his roomy eye socket. "Now that I've had time to think of it, that coulda been your bullet as easily as the bounty man's."

"Hire a lawyer," Sam said in a quiet voice.

"I just might once we get across the border," Poole threatened, "but not here. Mexicans don't know nothing about the law—except their own, whatever that is." Doyle looked at the ranger, curiously.

Sam shook his head slightly.

"He's just flapping his jaws," Sam said, keeping his voice lowered.

But Poole heard him anyway and said, "You'll think, *flapping my jaws* when I get out of here and catch up with Max—"

"Why don't you shut your *stupid mouth,* you stinking, flea-bit son of a bitch!" Morgan Manlen shouted from the other bunk, in a loud drug-coated voice, cutting Poole off. Manlen's eyes were shiny and wide from the herbs and mescal the woman had given before going deep into his leg to retrieve the bullet. His leg was wrapped in strips of clean white cloth, his foot resting at a raised angle atop an empty lard tin lying on his bunk. He looked all around wildly for anything in his reach to hurl at Poole, but found nothing.

"I ain't said a damn thing I shouldn't say, *Manlen!*" Poole shouted back at the drugged gunman. "Anyhow, if you're such a favored hand in the Wild Bunch, why are you out here having to look for them—?"

"At least I know where to look!" shouted Manlen. His hand slapped his right hip instinctively, for his gun which was no longer there.

"Hear that, Ranger?" said Poole, also grabbing for a phantom gun. "You want to know where to find the Wild Bunch. This man right here is your *huckleberry!*" He cackled in laughter, then stopped short as pain stabbed deep into his lower side.

"I'll straight up kill you, Cat-eye!" Manlen's hand slapped his right hip again, still finding no gun. His glazed eyes swam around the cell, baffled, as if he had already forgotten why he grabbed for his gun in the first place.

Sam looked at Doyle and Flippoza and motioned them toward the front door.

"Will they be all right alone together?" Flippoza asked as they stepped outside and Doyle closed the front door behind them. At the hitch-rail a young Mexican livery attendant worked at cleaning up along the string of horses he just fed and watered at the rail. The blue roan had nudged the string a few feet away from Black Pot, who stood with his saddle and blanket off and thrown onto a wooden chair against the adobe building.

"I think so," Sam said. "They both work for the Wild Bunch, as needed. I think I'll give them some time to mull things over. There's nothing in the cell they can hurt each other with."

"I'm *flying* here!" They heard Morgan Manlen shout out in a thickly drugged voice.

The three men looked at each other for a moment, then nodded.

"Yep, I think they'll be okay," Doyle said.

"Good," said Sam. He paused for a moment then said, "I'm obliged if you'd both look after these two while I take a ride north of here."

"Sure, Ranger," said Doyle. He looked at Flippoza for approval. The bank manager nodded in agreement.

"What about the Apache?" Flippoza asked. "What if some of the warriors swung north once they got across?"

"That's what I want to find out," Sam said.

"But—But it's *dark out!*" said Flippoza.

"Good," Sam said, "maybe they won't see me."

Flippoza felt a little foolish, but went right on. "You can't just ride out there to *find out!*" he said. "What if you *do* find them out there?"

"Then I'll know more than I do now," Sam said quietly. "If there's another way to find out, I'm all for it," he added flatly. He searched each man's eyes. Neither commented.

"We'll watch about your prisoners and horses, Ranger," said Doyle.

"Obliged," Sam said. He turned without another word and walked away, his rifle in hand.

At the hitch-rail the young attendant had untied the lead rope and led the horse string toward the livery barn only twenty yards from the jail, off of the wide, tiled street, yet in clear sight of the jail office. The ranger saddled Black Pot and slid his rifle into its boot. He picked up his canteen the attendant had filled and left for him, and hung it from the saddle horn. Jorge Doyle had told him about a water basin outside an old Spanish fort. Black Pot was well watered to get them both there.

As the attendant led the horse string away, the blue roan reared slightly and jerked his head back toward the hitch-rail as if agitated by humans interfering in matters only understood by horses. Now the only horse at the rail, Black Pot gave the scrappy roan a toss-way glance and stood waiting, ready, a big strong animal who looked well-accustomed to leaving a town in the dark of night.

Watching the ranger adjust his left trail glove and swing into his saddle, the two men nodded, Doyle gesturing a touch of his hat brim as the ranger turned Black Pot away from the rail, noting the ranger's bare right hand rested comfortably on his thigh, near the big holstered Colt 45 Conversion.

"I still feel apprehensive about him riding out there," Flippoza said. They listened to the slow clack of iron shoes on the stone tiles rise a notch in both volume and rhythm as the stallion brought his steps up to a traveling pace.

"So do I," Selectman Doyle admitted, watching faces appear at open doors as the ranger rode past. "But he knows what he's doing."

"Oh?" Flippoza gave him a questioning look. "Do you know this man?"

"No, but I know the kind of lawman he is by the badge he wears," said Doyle. "With Apache coming, I feel a lot better having him here."

"Me too, *certainly!*" Flippoza said. "And I'll feel even better if he makes it back."

A Ranger's Trail

"Don't say *if*," Doyle corrected him, "say *when.*"

"Oh my, *yes!*" said Flippoza. "'When' he makes it back —*When* is what I meant, of course!" The two gazed in silence at horse and rider growing smaller in the night until the surrounding darkness swallowed them up.

Leaving Esplanade, the ranger moved up off of the flatland trail leading directly to the old Spanish fort. With a half-moon offering him little cover on the stretch of sand, he decided to keep Black Pot and himself in whatever shadowed cover the nearby chain of rocky hills and hoodoos provided. He would stay up in the rocks as long as he could. When he had to come down, he intended to have circled wide of the fort and come into its crumbled walls from the low edge of hillsides instead of the open desert floor. He was hunting the Wild Bunch, and now two more gunmen, Joe Mercer and Fedder Dockery, members of the gang who had made a run for it to join Carver and the others.

He stopped Black Pot at the crest of a slim game path and reminded himself what he'd known all along, that hunting down Max Carver and his riders would not be an easy job. Now, as a kicker he had the Apache leader Itza-Chu with a gathered following of nearly every roaming Apache warrior on the Southwestern frontier.

We'll have to watch out for him, too, won't we? he whispered silently down to Black Pot, trying hard to play down his situation. He rubbed a hand along the stallion's damp withers. Black Pot gave the slightest puff of a breath, as if knowing too well the value of silence here on this sharp, cruel and dangerous killing plane. He sat the stallion for a moment longer and listened closely to the dead of night and the veil of soft chilled wind that shrouded it. It came to him that under these circumstances he could have turned back to Nogales and lain low until the desert claimed both Apache and outlaw alike.

Enough of that. It's not the nature of the job, he told

himself as if cutting himself off. With that, he nudged the stallion forward and down onto the game path.

Three hours earlier when he'd left Esplanade, he hadn't gone ten miles before he began hearing infrequent rounds of distant gunfire, the sound muffled in the folds of purple darkness. In the silence between the sporadic shots he caught the smell of a large Apache camp drifting into his face. It was not a smell of people, but rather the smell of the elements and rudiments that made up their life. He recognized a mixed scent of woodsmoke, of animal and sweat, of dog, horse, and of cattle that had been stolen and driven hard from the Mexican Rancheros to the North. Within the content of life's smell came the rank odor of that which followed closely any large body of animal or humanity on the move.

As he'd ridden on, the smell of the large camp had stayed with him on the rise and waning of the wind. But Sam knew that the smell signalled only the Apache in the near distance. His concern had to remain riveted on the small bands of warriors traveling out of the camp at will, into the villages, the farms and cattle *ranchos* in the outlands. As he let Black Pot negotiate the thin game path, he searched the darkness below, the fallen walls of the old Spanish fort now into view, large stones strewn onto the surrounding beds of sand. Within the vast darkness he spotted a dark glimmer of the water basin lying between the black silhouette of the fort's broken stone walls and the lower edge of the hillside. He waited until Black Pot had taken them down closer to the flatlands; then he stopped and stepped down from his saddle, rifle in hand, and lead the big stallion across a stretch of rocky ground to the water's edge.

While the stallion drank, Sam kept close watch on the darkness in each direction. When both he and the stallion heard the metallic click from among the fallen stones and rocks on the other side of the basin, Black Pot raised his dripping muzzle at the same second as Sam's rifle cocked and pointed in the direction of the sound. Without a word Sam placed his left hand on the stallion's nose and effortlessly nudged him back from the water. Black Pot turned and stepped away: Sam moved quickly around the basin. He recognized the sound as that of a gun hammer falling on an empty cylinder.

As he rounded the water basin Sam heard the sound again. Whoever was pulling the trigger had to be stopped before they figured out what was wrong and corrected it. Black Pot had stepped away from the water in among the shadowy fallen wall stones. But seeing that the stallion was still exposed, he hurried.

He heard the sound of a pulled trigger again as he moved, crouched, around a large stone and leveled his rifle at a woman in ragged bloody range clothes who lay sprawled in the dirt, her back leaning against a stack of broken rock.

"Drop the gun!" he said, moving a step closer, his rifle aimed, cocked and ready. Without looking up the woman let the gun slump in her hand. But she gave the hammer one more dry click as she let the silent gun fall to the dirt between her knees. Sam saw her horse standing out of the purple circle of moonlight, watching him with suspicion.

"It's … empty," she said in a broken voice. In the shadowy half-moon light, Sam saw her nod at the ground ten feet away, in the direction she had been aiming and clicking the empty gun. Sam lowered his rifle a little. He looked at a struggling Apache warrior lying in the dirt, both hands digging and clawing at the leather thongs of a bolo drawn tight around his throat. "Shoot him! Kill … him," she said, her voice sounding more resolved as she spoke. "Just kill him, Mister!"

Without answering, Sam stepped over to her, stooped and picked the empty gun up from the dirt. He shoved the gun down behind his belt as he stepped over to the choking warrior whose struggling turned weaker and weaker by the second.

"No! Let him die!" the woman said, seeing the ranger stoop down and draw a big knife from inside his boot.

"Take it easy," Sam said over his shoulder. He reached the knife blade down and sliced through the bolo thongs, leaving a short shallow cut on the warrior's throat as the tight thongs flew apart. "He's not going to hurt you." He rolled the half-conscious Indian over onto his stomach, pulled his hands behind his back and handcuffed him with a set of cuffs he took from a loop behind his gun belt. He loosened the bandanna from around his neck and used it to blindfold the warrior. Then he rolled the young warrior onto his back and stood up and walked to the woman with the severed bolo balls and thongs in his hand.

"I'm not afraid he's going to *hurt me!*" the woman said, her voice coming back with confidence. "I want him dead for dogging my trail—for trying to *kill me!* Him and his pals!" She gestured an exhausted nod toward the dark desert floor. "I've been fighting them all day." She swung a tired glance at her horse. "Look at my horse!"

Sam looked at the heavy-breathing animal standing slick with glistening sweat. Deeper in the rock shadows he saw the young warrior's spotted pony, standing spread-legged, its head hung low. He looked at the empty bandolier crossing the woman's chest. Here was where most of the shooting had come from, he decided—a running gunfight between her and a band of the wild young Apache. He looked at her again and considered the severed bolo lying in his hand. As he watched her, she struggled to place her palms on the ground and try to push herself up. Then he saw the stub of a broken arrow sticking from the back of her thigh.

"Sit still, *Ruby,*" he said quietly.

She gave no response to hearing her name. Instead she tried a little harder to shove herself up. As she tried, she caught a passing glance at the ranger badge on his chest, showing no response to it either.

"Mister, I'm obliged to you for saving me, but I've got to keep moving."

"I didn't save you, Ruby," Sam said, "I just happened along. You saved yourself." He gestured the broken bolo toward the cuffed warrior stretched face down on the ground, no doubt figuring his next move, Sam thought.

Twice now this lawman had used her name. Still she played it off as if not hearing him. *A lawman ...,* she told herself. *Of all the rotten luck!*

"Can I have that back, Mister?" she asked. She reached a hand up toward the bolo. But Sam was having none of it. He shook his head slightly.

"I'll hang onto it for you—keep you from losing it," he said. He hefted the two stone balls in his hand, the leather thongs hanging severed in half.

When the woman offered no reply, as if reading her mind, the ranger said, "Here's some more bad news for you, *Ruby.*" As he spoke he took another pair of handcuffs from behind his back and stepped closer to her.

"Wait, you're mistaken!" she said. But as she spoke a cuff circled her right wrist.

"Front or back?" Sam asked, holding the other cuff firm in his hand.

A flash of terror streaked across her eyes in the purple darkness. Sam saw it disappear in a split-second, replaced by a cold, killing gaze.

"The cuffs," he said, making himself clearer. He nodded toward the young warrior, cuffed from behind and blindfolded. "Can I trust your hands cuffed in front until we get off this desert? That one's got reason to make a run for it. But you don't, unless you want more warriors dogging your trail."

She seemed to settle a little, enough to start figuring her next move, he thought. She held her left hand over to him and watched him put the other cuff on her.

"How many of those do you carry?" she asked.

Trying to keep it light? Why? he wondered. This woman didn't strike him as the kind who might try to play up to a man.

"As many as it takes," he said with no attempt at levity. He raised her to her feet and helped her limp over to a large wall stone. He eased her down on the large stone with her wounded leg outstretched to the ground.

"This hurts something fierce," she said through clenched teeth.

"There's a healing woman in Esplanade," Sam said. "While it's not bleeding a lot, we best let it alone until we get there." He paused and added, "If we can get there."

"Esplanade, hunh?" she said. She looked closer at his badge. "You're an Arizona Ranger."

"I know that, Ruby," Sam said in a flat wry tone.

"But this is *Mexico!*" she said, as if in revelation.

"I know that too," Sam said. "Folks are always telling me." Anticipating her next words, he said, "I serve out of Nogales. We have a signed agreement with Matamoros." He paused, then asked, "How far back are Max Carver and rest of your pals, Ruby?"

Her voice took on a harder edge. "I don't know who or what you're talking about, Ranger," she said. "And I don't know why you're calling me Ruby."

"I'm talking about Max Carver and the Wild Bunch, Ruby—" Sam said.

"Don't know them," she said sharply, cutting him off.

"You go by the name Ruby Teal, *Ruthless* Ruby," Sam pushed on. "You've only been riding with the Wild Bunch a short while. But you've made quite a name for yourself, scouting, hiding out."

"You don't know what you're talking about," she said, avoiding his eyes. She looked over at the young warrior lying in the dirt. "Saying Ruby's my name. *Ha!*"

"Not you're real name," Sam said. "But I know your real name, too." He held the bolo balls and severed thongs out on his hand toward her. She looked away, out across the purple darkness. "You've become rightly known for using this thing."

"You don't know nothing about me," she said with bitter finality on the matter.

"Have it your way, Ruby," Sam said. "But you need to know, I'm here to get rid of Max Carver and his bunch. If you tell me where they're going to hide out around here—"

"Nobody is *getting rid* of the Wild Bunch," Ruby said, cutting him off. "If you know so much about me, you know that I can take anything you throw at me. I'll never tell you anything."

Sam nodded and said, "I understand. But it's my job to ask." He looked closer at the arrow stub sticking from her thigh. "We've got to get your leg fixed. We can talk more on the way."

"There's nothing more to talk about," Ruby said sharply.

"I need you to tell me what you know about this big band of Apache," Sam said. "A lot of lives might depend on it."

He watched her consider it.

"I'll tell you what I learned out there, such as it is," she said. "But I don't know much—"

Before she could say any more the two of them looked towards the blindfolded warrior as he managed to spring to his feet, and let out a blood-curdling war cry and race toward the sound of their voices. His cuffed hands providing no help in keeping his balance, he veered back and forth crazily. Sam grabbed the woman and jerked her out of the way as the young man streaked past them and struck the rock she'd been sitting on at knee level.

Still screaming like a wild banshee the young warrior turned a high flip above the fallen wall stone and came down on it head first, his scream coming to an abrupt stop. His head made a sickening sound hitting the large stone. His limp body rolled off the stone and landed with a hard thud in the dirt. The two stood stunned, staring at him for a moment in silence.

"My God," Ruby said in an awestricken tone, "the fool killed himself!"

"I think he's alive," Sam said quietly. "Wait here." He helped her sit back down and stepped over to where the downed Indian lay knocked cold. He stooped beside him as he looked all around the darkness with his rifle ready. A sour smell of Mescal rose from the knocked out youth. White foamy vomit filled with bits of green cactus skin spread in the dirt beneath his face. "He's feeling no pain," Sam said. "He's packing a bellyful of Mescal and *sorba*. Probably doesn't know where he is." He noted the boy looked even younger than he'd first thought –*fifteen? Sixteen?* Too young to be out raiding and killing, even for a roaming Apache.

"We'll see plenty more just like him on the way to Esplanade," said the woman. She looked all around the darkness. "I shot as many as I could until my ammunition gave out." She waited a second, then said, "Think maybe you should give me my gun and some bullets for our ride?"

Sam didn't bother answering as he walked over to gather both their horses.

"It's my job to ask," she said, repeating what he'd said moments ago.

Sam stopped and swung his rifle toward a sudden sound of iron shoes clacking toward them across a stretch of flat stone.

"Look out, Ranger!" the woman shouted, seeing the form of a bareback horse plunge forward out of the darkness into the pale moonlight.

The ranger started to pull the trigger, but caught himself just in time as the blue roan circled close in front of him and slid to dust-raising halt. "It's all right, I know this one." Sam called out to Ruby who managed to stand up and watch the big roan spin in place and scrape his front hoof on the ground toward her. "He's a showoff, but he's one of us."

"I can see that now," Ruby said, her cuffed hands motioning the roan to her. "I always get along with horses."

Sam watched the roan settle and step closer to her.

A Ranger's Trail

"What's got you so stoked up, Blue Boy?" she said quietly to the big roan, as if the two of them knew each other. The stallion blew and slung his head away from her. But he didn't move away, Sam noted. *Blue Boy, hunh ...?* A fitting name, he told himself.

The woman stood her ground, her cuffed hands still welcoming the spooked animal until he brought his head back to her. While she rubbed his muzzle, the ranger eyed the animal and saw the bloody foot long graze of an arrow across the top right side of his rump. Dried blood stained the roan's rear leg.

"Looks like he came across some Apache, himself," he said, lowering his voice, glancing back and out across the purple desert floor. He stepped in for a closer look; the stallion stood still for him. "You got yourself in trouble following me," he said quietly to the roan.

The woman kept her cuffed hands on the roan's muzzle, settling him more. Sam looked closer at the arrow graze. "He'll have to be all right until we get back to Esplanade," he said. "We can't spend any more time here."

The two looked out across the dark land together. Somewhere here was the Wild Bunch Gang—the gang this woman worked for.

Hunting Max Carver and his Wild Bunch riders was edgy enough business on its own. With Apache in the mix, Sam knew that every step he took had to be measured and certain if he intended to come out of here alive. Carver and his Wild Bunch were seasoned outlaws. This woman *alias Ruby Teal* knew where they were, but she wasn't giving them up, at least not yet. They could be anywhere.

So, watch yourself ..., he cautioned.

CHAPTER 7

The ranger fashioned a halter from the coil of rope hanging at his saddle horn and slipped it over the roan's muzzle. He paused for only a moment when the gunfire they'd heard start and stop earlier erupted again from the same direction. Sam looked at the woman as she turned toward the sound. But in the purple dark her face and eyes gave no indication that the gunfire might be coming from Max Carver and his men, fighting for their lives. *You are a cool one, Alias Ruby Teal ...,* he told himself, studying her dark eyes.

Away from the gunfire, farther out on the desert floor north of them, more shots resounded, these muffled by a greater distance across the sand. The two turned from the first gunshots and gazed out toward the ones in the distance.

"There must be small bands roaming everywhere tonight," the woman said, still looking out across the darkness.

"So it appears," Sam replied.

Finishing with the roan's new harness, Sam kept a ten foot lead of rope in hand and walked the big animal closer to where Black Pot stood, fifteen feet away, saddled and ready to ride. The young Indian had come-to and tried to sit up on his own, mumbling behind the bandanna that his fall had jarred down from his eyes and left laying crooked across his mouth. The woman, standing near the young man, pulled the bandanna down below his chin and spoke to him in Apache. Sam walked up, rifle in hand and listened as the young Indian replied in a slurred voice.

"What did he tell you?" Sam asked, already knowing, but

wanting to test the woman.

"He says he will kill us both," she said. "I told him he wouldn't be the first one to try to kill you, or me, either one." She gazed at the ranger; she had a feeling he spoke Apache as well as she did.

"Ask him how many warriors are out there," Sam said. He watched her, listening close as she talked to the half-conscious youth. The boy swayed as he spoke and almost fell forward. She caught him by his shoulder and helped him straighten up.

"He says they are over a thousand strong," she said to the ranger. "But I think he is lying."

"Why's that?" Sam asked. He didn't believe the young man's slurred words either.

"I lived at San Carlos as a child," she said with authority. "They would never allow that many men of fighting age to be there at one time."

"I see," Sam said, already thinking the same thing. The Indian youth swayed in place, but managed to stay upright, his hands still cuffed behind his back.

The woman fixed a level gaze on the ranger and said, "Have you heard enough to believe me yet? Or, do you want me to question him more?"

Sam didn't reply. Instead he said, "No matter how many warriors there are, the longer we stay here, the worse our chances of getting back to Esplanade alive." He reached down, pulled the youth to his feet, and steadied him. In the darkness gunfire still resounded from two locations, one near, the other farther away. "Anyway, now that you and I know we both speak Apache, what say we agree to talk straight with each other until we get through all this?"

She gazed at him coolly.

"You asked me to talk to him, so I did," she said. "Did you find me honest in what I said?"

"Yes, you were honest," Sam said. "I'm obliged." He gestured toward the young warrior as he asked her, "How far out did this one and his friends pick up your trail?"

"Not far," she said. "I shot a couple of them and they fell back, except for this one. He was drunker than the rest." She gazed with contempt at the young Indian. "He wanted to prove himself a big man to his pals." Gunfire rose and fell from the location nearest to them.

"All right," Sam said, "Let's get moving before they get any closer."

The woman looked off toward the nearest location of gunfire. Sam saw the look of concern in her dark eyes. She had been scouting ahead of Carver and the other. Now she stood here, caught and cuffed. The Apache had managed to get between them in the darkness, Sam figured. It wasn't her fault, but he wondered if she looked at it that way. Getting caught meant leaving Carver and the others with their hands full.

"They're big boys, Ruby," he said quietly. "If they make it, we'll be seeing them in Esplanade, unless they've got a better place out here to hole up." He looked at her for a reply.

"Don't waste your breath, Ranger," the woman said, turning away from him, "I'm not telling you anything."

"I can see you're not," Sam said. "Do you need help walking to your horse?"

"I can walk," she said flatly.

Sam turned from the woman to the drunken young warrior and gave him a nudge toward the horses. When the three stood beside the horses, Sam took the coil of rope from Black Pot's saddle horn. Stepping behind the young warrior, he tied an end of the rope to the middle of his handcuffs. He gave a short jerk, just to let the young man know what to expect if he tried to make a run for it.

He said to him in Apache, "If you give me no trouble, the people of Esplanade will send you back to San Carlos. I will ask them to do it."

"Or else they will hang me, or cut my throat," the young

A Ranger's Trail

man said in slurred but understandable English. Sam realized the young man was right. On the US side of the border, he would be sent back to the reservation. Here in Old Mexico— Sam had to remind himself that here the rules were all different.

"I figured you speak English," he said, showing no great surprise.

"I learned *Inglis* in the reservation school," the young man replied.

Sam stopped and stood close beside the Indian's paint horse.

"Good," said Sam, "then you'll understand this. Give me no trouble and I'll see to it they don't hang you or cut your throat."

The Apache youth only stared at him. Sam raised the bandanna and pulled it up across his mouth, ending the discussion. He started to help him up onto the horse's back. But the young man gave him a look of contempt and turned his back to the horse. With the slightest crouch at his waist, he sprang up, cuffed hands and all and landed sideways atop the paint. He swung his right leg up and over the horse's neck, righted himself in a riding position and stared down at the ranger.

The ranger only nodded. This young man was fast. Even faster than most.

Good to know, he told himself, looking up at the mounted youth. *The more I know what to expect from you, the better ....*

Before stepping up into Black Pot's saddle, the lead rope to the young Indian in hand, Sam looked at the woman as she settled into her saddle in spite of the pain in her wounded thigh. Seeing his eyes on her, she ignored the pain.

"I can lead Blue Boy if you need me too," she said.

Having already considered and rejected the idea, Sam wrapped the Indian's lead rope around Black Pot's saddle horn and made a half-hitch in it.

"I've got it," he said; with his rifle in hand, he motioned

the Indian and the woman ahead of him, keeping the blue roan drawn up close to Black Pot's side. "I want the two of you within reach, and in clear sight." He gave both of them a quick once-over as was his custom when traveling with prisoners. *What's this ...?* Earlier he had counted four small battered tin conchos on the outside lower legs of the woman's trousers. All of a sudden, her left trouser leg only had three. *Duly noted ...,* he told himself. But he wouldn't mention it. Not now anyway.

"You mean in clear shooting sight, don't you?" the woman said, even as she nudged her horse forward at a slow walk. Sam nudged the big stallion forward with twelve feet between him and the two riders.

"Call it what suits you," he replied to her, "But don't test me. The closer we get to Esplanade, the less you're going to want to make a run for it."

The woman stared straight ahead in the darkness, hearing gunfire growing closer behind them. The ranger was right; this was a bad time to be out here alone with a stub of a broken arrow sticking from her thigh. She had left Max Caver a sign that she'd been here. But that was all she could do. She cut a sidelong glance at the young warrior riding six feet from her left side.

Yes, he is young, she reminded herself. But she had seen what this one was capable of doing, and she'd grown up with young warriors just like him in San Carlos. They were young and foolish, but as deadly as rattlesnakes. They learned the white man's language and wore the strange haircuts and prison boots the staff at San Carlos forced upon them. But they were killers; she knew it. How many had she spotted out there tonight? Certainly not over a thousand, like the young Indian had said. But the way they were spread out in separate groups—*Thirty here, fifty more there. There could easily be two hundred ... maybe more ...?* She couldn't tell. But yes, she would ride to Esplanade with this ranger. After that, she couldn't say what she'd do. She hadn't come out here with the Wild Bunch for her health. She needed money ... *needed it bad!*

She gave the slightest touch of her heels to her horse's sides, the ranger riding close behind her. This was the hand dealt to her. Bad as it was, she had to play it out. Not only did she have to play it out, she had to make it work—she had to *win it.* She looked down at her cuffed hands holding her horse's reins. *So you will!* she demanded of herself, riding forward into the night.

When the ranger and his two prisoners rode away, the rugged stones, remnants of the old fort wall, lay in shadowy silence. But the silence was short-lived. No more than a half an hour later Max Carver and his three horsemen sprang forward out of the darkness. They rode into the moonlit outer perimeter of the old fort at a hard fast pace and slid their worn-out horses to a halt at the glistening water's edge. Looking back, weapons drawn and ready, they sat as still as stone for a moment, listening, even though when they'd left the desert floor, the gunfire had fallen away behind them.

"All right, let's water these cayouses," he said to the others, his horse beneath him straining against the reins to get to the shimmering pool only a few feet away. He slid from his saddle and let his horse go, one rein slack in his hands. The horse stood its front hooves in the water and lowered its muzzle to drink. The other three riders and horses followed suit.

"Forget the woman. I figure she's dead as hell," Dog said in a gruff tone. He sipped water from his cupped hands, keeping watch on the shadowy rock lands.

"Shut up, Dog!" said Sloane. "You sound like you're wishing her dead."

"Boyo, I'm not wishing nobody nothing!" Dog said in a gruff tired voice. "I'm just saying what we already know!" His wet hand wrapped around his gun butt. "We're all dead here anyway! Don't make me shoot you before the Apache get to us."

"Both of you shut your mouths, and keep your eyes open!" Carver demanded, watching the surrounding darkness while the other men and their horse drank. He held his rifle ready to fire at the slightest sign of Indians moving up around them.

"Throw me your canteen, Carver. I'll fill it," Captain Gascoyne said quietly, having dropped from his saddle, fallen onto his knees, and plunged his head beneath the water. He slung his wet hair back and extended a hand toward Carver. His horse stood drinking beside him.

Carver took his empty canteen from his saddle horn and pitched it to the Frenchman. "Obliged," he said almost grudgingly. He let the single rein fall from his hand and moved along the water's edge in a crouch while his horse continued to drink with the others.

In the pale moonlight, Carver stopped and lowered onto a knee where fresh wet hooves and boot prints littered the ground. He followed the prints with his eyes until the greater darkness swallowed them. These fresh prints were all made by shod horses, yet he noted that they were implanted over prints of unshod horses, moccasins and bare feet. He knew the under-bed of prints belonged to the Apache. The top prints, he had no idea. *Settlers on the run?*

Sure maybe .... He took note of a set of boot prints smaller than the rest and it piqued his interest. *A woman? Ruby?* But before he could wonder longer, his eyes caught the slightest glint of metal and his fingertips went to it and raised it from the wet sandy soil. *Damn! Okay Ruby!* He recognized the small concho right away. As he picked it up and felt around it and found three inch deep impressions in the sand. He gave a trace of a smile. Ruby, taking it a step farther, had left him her finger tips—three of them, small prints, poked down in the wet ground, forming a triangle, pointing her direction. Instinctively, he looked all around and once again followed the fresh prints with his eyes.

Okay, Ruthless Ruby, you're still alive, still out there, he said to himself. *Good work. But who's this with you?*

Without time to give it any more thought right then, he stood up and slipped the concho down into his trouser pocket. He turned and started back toward the others when the sound of horses came toward the water basin from along a thin rocky trail.

Before anyone could stop Dog Fannen, the spooked old gunman emptied his big revolver toward the sound of horses' hooves.

A voice let out a scream of sharp pain.

"Hold you fire, Dog!" shouted Elvin. "It might be Ruby!"

Another voice cried out in the darkness, "Holy God! *It's us!* Don't shoot us!"

But Dog wasn't about to let up. He jerked his rifle from his saddle boot and levered a round into the chamber.

"I don't know who us is, you Apache sonsabitches!" He fired a shot and levered another round.

"Jesus! Stop shooting, Dog!" Max Carver shouted, recognizing Joe Mercer's shaky voice. "It's Little Gun Mercer!"

Dog held his fire, but stood ready, not trusting the voice from the darkness. Gascoyne and Sloane had crouched behind a downed wall stone.

"Yes, stop!" Mercer bellowed, "You've hit poor Dock in the head."

"Damn it to hell!" Carver cursed. *"Dog,* fire another shot and I'll kill you where you stand!"

"All right, I'm done." Dog replied. He lowered the rifle and fell silent.

"Come on in, Joe!" Carver shouted at the dark trail. Then he said in a growl, "Now that we've let every Indian in the desert know where we are."

The four stood watching as Joe Mercer and Fedder Dockery's horses stepped out of the pitch dark into the pale moonlight. Dockery, wounded, sat with his bare head bowed in his hand, against a waded up bandanna. The bloody bandanna covered a long bullet graze just above his left ear.

"I ought to kill you, Dog Fannen, you *rotten bastard,*" Dockery said angrily as their horses drew closer and stopped.

"Had I known it was you, Dock, I would reloaded and kept shooting," Dog said.

"That's enough, both of you!" Carver said. He helped Dockery down from the saddle and sat him on a rock. "Mercer, tie the bandanna around his head. We've got to get out of here."

"You're damned right we do," Mercer said hurrying down from his saddle. "We've had Apache up our shirt tails every since we left Esplanade."

He looked all around and asked, "Where's Ruthless Ruby, anyway?"

"We're thinking she didn't make it," Carver said, not wanting to mention he'd found the concho and the sign she'd left in the wet dirt.

"Damn it," said Mercer. He shook his head in bewilderment. "I always heard Apache never attack at night."

"Why don't you stick around here and tell them?" said Carver. "It would solve a lot of our problems."

Gascoyne gave a dark quiet chuckle. Joe Mercer started to say something but Dockery cut in, saying to Carver, "Damn lucky thing we found you, Max. "There's a whole lot going on you need to hear about. First of all—"

"Hold it, Dock" Carver said, cutting him off. "Anything you think I need to hear about ... you save it until we're out of here. This is not the time or place to be hearing about anything 'cept how to keep hair on our heads."

"But this is things you need to hear, especially if you're headed for Esplanade."

Dockery took on a sullen look and fell silent.

The group watched while Mercer tied the bandanna around Dockery's bullet-grazed head. Then, as one, they mounted their horses and rode away into the night, each of them looking back over their shoulder and all around the rocky hill land surrounding them.

"Hey, Little Gun," Dog Fannen said to Mercer in a hushed but taunting voice, "Since these *'Paches* don't attack at night, you could make camp and get a peaceful night's sleep, 'til long about daylight." He cackled at his little joke.

Again, Cascoyne gave a dark quiet chuckle.

"Smart son of a bitch!" Joe Mercer growled in reply.

CHAPTER 8

The ranger and his two prisoners moved slowly but surely throughout the night on the rocky hill trails toward Esplanade. The young Apache on the longer lead-rope, tied to Sam's saddle horn, the blue roan on short lead, drawn only inches from Black Pot's side. The woman, riding beside the Indian, had taken on the role of unassigned trail scout—a role she likely fell into from habit, Sam decided, noting her gaze at the dark rocky ground beneath the horse's hooves—too dark to see anything without stopping and stepping down from her saddle. After gazing down for a moment she would raise her face and search both sides of the rocky narrow canyon walls.

Good enough, Ruthless Ruby, Sam thought, watching her. He'd take all the help he could get. Through gaps in the rock walls and hoodoos, the range caught a view of the purple shadowed desert floor lying lit by random campfires strewn out and sparkling in the night. He could not recall a time when the Apache revealed themselves this way. His only explanation for it was that the roaming Apache leader, Itza-Chu, having seen his fighting ranks grow larger over the past months, held no respect for the Mexican Army, or that of their French allies.

A bad mistake, Itza-Chu ..., Sam said silently. Open campfires in the middle of the night? Bands of young warriors, drunk and on a killing spree, lit up on herbs and powerful concoctions of *cocaina* and alcohol? Hunh-uh, Itza-Chu. *Not for long ...,* he told himself. They rode in silence, into a stretch of trail that became narrower as they rounded a high-walled

A Ranger's Trail

turn into a rugged pass.

Suddenly Sam's thoughts were interrupted at the loud squall of a panther up among the rock shelves above his prisoners' heads. Immediately, the Apache's horse spooked and sprang forward. In spite of the rope attached to cuffs behind his back, the youth tried to hold the horse back with his knees. But the scared horse would have none of it. Sam tried to unhitch the rope from his saddle horn, but before he could the horse shot out from under its rider and the boy fell onto the rocky trail.

The woman's horse fell back a few fast steps, but she pulled the horse in check with both cuffed hands drawn hard and sharp on its reins. Sam saw the streak of the panther flash through broken moonlight and pounce atop the downed Indian. Throwing the lead rope aside, as well as the rope on the blue roan, Sam jerked his rifle up to his shoulder. This was no time to worry about a shot being heard. The cat mauled and slashed at its downed prey even as it began its task of dragging that helpless prey, flailing and kicking, into the rocks.

In the second it took for the ranger to seek a clear shot, he heard a deep whistling sound and saw the woman let go of a bolo she'd twirled above her head. Instinctively, he might have pulled the trigger anyway, but as the cat raised a paw for a deadly swipe, the bolo, spinning too fast to be seen in the shadowy light, spun around the cat's throat and its raised claws. Pinning the cat's raised paw to its throat with tightly-drawn leather thongs, the bolo sent the panther backwards, thrashing on the ground, confused and trying to free itself.

Without wasting a second, Sam raced forward on Black Pot, letting his rifle's hammer down on the way. The woman leaped down from her horse as Black Pot streaked past her. The roan stayed back, keeping his distance from the thrashing cat. The Indian's horse stood close beside the roan as if seeking his protection.

Stopping ten feet away, keeping Black Pot out of the

panther's reach, Sam swung down from his saddle and hurried, closing the gap between himself and the raging cat. Raising his rifle with both hands he brought the butt down hard on the cat's skull as the shaken animal tried raising its free paw to clutch at the thongs choking the life out of it. The first blow of the rifle butt stunned the animal; a second, a deliberately less powerful blow left it lying limp in the dirt. The young Indian watched wide-eyed above the bandanna still taught around his mouth.

The woman came up as Sam stooped down over the cat and sliced the bolo thongs with the knife from his boot well. His rifle lay across his bent knee. Even with the tightness gone from around its neck, the cat still lay unconscious from the rifle blows.

"I'm tired of cutting these things off of your targets," He said to the woman, pitching the bolo and the severed thongs to the ground.

"Not more than I am," the woman replied coolly. She stooped down over the bleeding Apache, untied the bandanna from around his mouth and whispered "Be silent," cautioning him in Apache. The Indian spat and blew and collected himself, heeding her subtle warning. Both he and the woman turned their eyes to Sam as they heard the half-conscious cat give a weak mournful growl.

"Cut his head off," the young man said bitterly in English. His voice was more sober now. "Look what he has done to me." Blood spilled freely down his chest.

"It's not a *he,*" Sam said. "It's a *she*—and a momma cat, too, it looks like." He noted the partially swollen teats along the cat's sagging belly. The woman turned back to young man and pressed the bandanna against the flow of blood. It only helped a little. "Likely, she would have dragged you away, chewed you to death and carried chunks of you up her den, to feed her brood," Sam said.

"Give me the knife, I'll cut out her heart!" the young

warrior said.

"Be still," the woman said to him, this time in English. "You're bleeding a lot." She pressed the bandanna more firmly to the deep slash of claws—the wound bleeding worse than the many others.

Sam stood, rifle in one hand and dragged the cat off the thin trail by its hind leg and left it lying at the bottom of a crevice that ran jagged up the steep rocks. As he left the cat he noted it was breathing better.

Walking back to the downed Apache and the woman, Sam looked at the two round rocks the woman had used to produce her replacement bolo.

"I suppose if I throw these rocks away you'll just make another bolo, first chance?" he said. As he spoke, he loosened his own bandanna and tossed it down for her to use on the Indian's wounds.

"There's no shortage of rocks around here," she said. "Do you want my word I won't do it again?" Sam noted a trace of defiance in her tone. Instead of answering her, he stepped over to her horse and looked at its reins. They were shorter now. *Freshly cut ...,* he noted to himself.

"I used my spur," she said, as if she knew he was wondering how she cut the leather reins. She gave a one-shouldered shrug. "They were too long anyway."

Sam knew himself as a man who missed very little, especially something coming from a prisoner. She was lying about the spur. He was certain of it. He hadn't seen her raise a boot from her stirrup, which she would have to do in order to cut the leather reins. She had a knife on her somewhere.

Duly noted ..., he told himself.

Instead of commenting on the matter, he said, "I make it an hour or less we'll be down this hill line, headed into Esplanade." He gave her a telling gaze. "You'll stay in front of me. Keep watch on this one, try and keep him from dying on us." He looked at the young Apache, seeing the severity of his wounds. Reaching into a shirt pocket he took out the key to the handcuffs. "If we don't get you to town, you're dead," he told the young warrior. "Think about that before you try making a run for it."

The young Apache stared at him with much of the anger gone from his eyes.

"I won't run," he said, his voice already growing weaker. "I want the white man's medicine."

"In this case, it's an old Mexican healing woman," Sam said. "But she'll know how to stop the bleeding," he thought about it and added, "If she didn't before, she does now. I've brought her lots of practice."

Sam handed the key to the woman and watched her un-cuff the Indian. He saw the questioning look on her face when she finished and held the key back out to him on her palm. She had to admit to herself, she didn't understand this lawman. She knew he hadn't bought her answer about cutting the reins with her spur. He knew she was lying. *Why don't you say so ...?* She asked silently.

Sam only returned her gaze for a moment as the Apache rubbed his freed wrists. Blood spilled freely from behind both the blood-soaked bandannas.

Gambling with her interpretation of the ranger's thoughts, the woman closed her fist over the key. "Obliged," she said quietly.

Sam gave a nod, without voicing his consent. He watched as she un-cuffed herself and handed him the key and the cuffs. She stood up from beside the Apache, her hands dark with his blood.

"Take the blanket out of my bedroll," Sam said, nodding toward Black Pot. "Fold it and lay it on his chest. Take my rope and wrap it around him good and tight."

She hurried to Black Pot and back while Sam helped the Indian up into a sitting position. Blood poured, from the wounds.

A Ranger's Trail

"Be advised," he said, as she pressed the folded blanket to the Indian's chest, "if you turn your hand toward me in any way, bolo or otherwise, I'll shoot you down like any other prisoner."

"Oh?" she said. She hurriedly wrapped the rope around the young man as Sam held the blanket in place. Without pausing she asked, "Do you realize I could have used this bolo on you?" she nodded at the stone and the severed thongs on the ground. "Or, when the panther struck, I could have rode away into this pass and kept riding?" She made three more wraps around the young warrior's chest.

Sam stared at her, then helped her snug the rope down and tie it off firmly. He wasn't going to let her know what he realized or didn't realize.

She studied his face in the shadowy moonlight—a man with *no* hollow threats and *no* shallow warnings, she decided. *A man who's hard to figure, and likes to keep it that way ....* All right, she could deal with that. *No threats, no warnings ....* She realized she was much that way herself. Life was serious and dangerous. They would both agree on that. The slightest trace of a weary smile came across her face, then left.

The two raised the Indian to his feet and helped him up onto his horse. Sam held onto the paint horse's reins. The young warrior swayed, his eyes nearly closed—*loss of blood ....*

"All right, Ranger," the woman said. "You told me that the closer we got to Esplanade, the less reason I'd have for wanting to get away. You were right. You'll have no problem with me between here and town."

Sam understood, and agreed with everything she'd just said. Still, he stood his position. He had every right and reason to search her for whatever she'd used to cut the reins, especially now that the cuffs were off. This was no place to be traveling un-heeled, he thought. Under the circumstances he wished he could trust her with a gun. *But you can't ...!* he cautioned himself quickly.

He repeated his words clearly, with deliberation, "Be advised, if you turn on me—"

"I know, I know, Ranger," she said. "I'm trying to tell you, you were right. I don't want to get away from you. I want to get away from *this.*" She gestured a bloody hand, taking in the land and the predicament surrounding them.

Sam had listened closely, weighing not only her words, but her tone, the look in her eyes, her whole demeanor.

"I understand," he said, knowing he was accepting some sort of truce from her. Yes, he'd realized it could have been his throat the bolo wrapped itself around, instead of the panther's. She could have twirled the bolo, turned in her saddle and made her move, quick as a snake. Could he have stopped her? *Maybe. Probably.* He didn't know. But the fact she hadn't tried to move on him, showed him something—something he didn't care to admit at the moment. It was time to ask her for more.

"Who is this one?" he asked, indicating the young warrior on the ground.

Sam's words caught her by surprise. She stared at him as if dumbfounded.

"I saw the two of you talking back and forth," he said, bluffing, but playing a strong hunch.

The woman let out a breath.

"So that's why you let us ride close together," she said. "To see what I could learn about him."

Sam didn't answer. Of course that was why, and she should've known it.

"Okay," she said. "He told me he's Itza-Chu's grandson. There, do you believe that?"

"I believe, you," Sam said, not showing his surprise. "Do you believe him?"

"I have never known an Apache to lie about such a thing as who is his father, or grandfather," she said. "Yes, I believe him."

A Ranger's Trail

"What's the story out there?" Sam asked her, helping the Indian right himself atop the horse.

"Their true strength is between a hundred and a hundred and fifty warriors," she said. "Which is about how many we both thought, right?" she asked.

"Sounds right," Sam agreed. "Why are they gathering up down here?"

"Most of them are desert Apache, even the roamers," she said. "Itza-Chu believes they need to make peace with the people below the southern Mexico border. Who knows why?" she shrugged. "Maybe he saw a vision ... had a dream. Maybe a coyote told him."

Sam noted resentment of the Apache in her voice.

"I think I understand," Sam said. "While the main body is moving south for a peaceful visit, the young warriors like this one need to stretch their legs a little." He shook his head, considering it.

"I don't judge my Apache kin, Ranger," she said. "My pa was a U.S. Army officer. I don't judge my white kin either."

The wounded warrior sat slumped forward against the blanket tied to his chest. The bleeding had slowed but not stopped. As Sam listened he'd began reasoning why she'd turned the bolo lose on the panther instead of on him. If this was Itza-Chu's grandson he could prove to be her way out of here. Had she put that bolo around his neck instead of the cat's, she could have delivered Itza-Chu's grandson to him and rode away free and clear. Had the cat killed the young warrior it would have meant the end to any such plan. Saving the young man from the cat, she still had a chance of getting the hand-cuffed warrior to his grandfather someway. But Sam knew now, whatever her plans might have been, or might yet be, they didn't include him.

"Why did he decide to tell you so much?" he asked, the two of them walking over to their horses, Sam leading the young warrior's paint horse by its reins.

"Here's where I might lose you, Ranger," she said with hesitancy. She paused, but for only a second, then said, "His grandfather, Itza-Chu, or *Great Hawk,* as he was called then, has spoken to him about my mother and me, back when I was a little girl and we lived on the San Carlos reservation."

Sam fell silent as they stopped at their horses.

"Surprised?" she asked. Her voice had turned softer, not friendly, but not as *unfriendly* as before.

"Not so much," Sam said. He turned and looked at her, seeing the moonlight shine and play in her dark eyes. "I told you I know who you really are. I know your real name. I know who your father was and what happened to him over in the blood lands." His voice softened. "I'm sorry, Julie."

The woman only offered him a lowered look.

"Please," she said. "I'm *Ruthless* Ruby Teal, remember?" She raised her eyes to his; he saw them glisten wet in the moonlight. "Julie Wilder would never do what I'm doing out here, Ranger, riding with Max Carver and his Wild Bunch. I won't say why, not right now anyway." She paused, then added in an even softer voice, "Soon though ... maybe?"

She raised her eyes to his. Sam saw pain and shame well up and glisten, yet she seemed to let only a drop of it spill down her cheek. Sam instinctively reached his thumb beneath her eye as she searched his face in the pale light.

"All right, *Ruby Teal,"* he said quietly, wiping the single tear away. "I won't ask why you're doing it. It's your life, and your name, whatever you choose it to be. Until you say otherwise, Ruby it is then—"

He watched her eyes soften on his. For a moment she fell silent. Sam believed she was asking herself whether or not she could trust him. He wanted to tell her she could, as far as keeping everything they'd said strictly between them. But he wouldn't mention it. He still wanted to know the Wild Bunch's hideout. *You're still working your job ...,* he reminded himself.

"Thank you, Ranger ... for understanding," she said

almost in a whisper. She started to place a hand on his chest, but she caught herself and stopped. Sam was glad she did. Glad, yet also feeling an urge to tell her it was all right—she could have placed a hand on his chest, right then, right there. He would not have stopped her. Would he—?

From the place where he'd laid the unconscious panther, came a stronger growl that cut his thoughts short. The two turned toward the sound in time to see the panther scramble away, limping a little from where the bolo made a tight grab on its paw. Leaving the moonlight, the cat turned into a streak of yellow as it scurried up the jagged crevice and disappeared into the shadowy darkness.

Sam looked down at the arrow stub sticking out of the woman's leg. The strip of cloth tied around it was soaked black with blood, but not too much of it had escaped the bandaging and ran down her leg. *Good ...,* he thought. They were close to Esplanade. They could make it. The Apache avoided towns when they could. They preferred the desert, the rock lands and plains.

"How are you holding up?" he asked the woman.

"It's mostly gone numb on me," she replied. "I'm better in the saddle than out."

"Then let's get you back in the saddle," Sam said. He raised her arm over his shoulder and assisted her to her horse.

"Careful. Ranger," she said, standing against him, "People will start to talk."

Sam didn't answer. There was nothing suggestive or flirtatious in what she said—just a quick line to lighten their situation, he thought. But to himself he had to admit there was something about her that was getting to him. He knew her story, how tough her life had been. He knew what had happened to her Apache mother, to her father, the U.S. Army Colonel. Now that she had admitted herself to him, he felt some strange need to protect her, to let her know everything was going to be all right, at least while she was with him.

Stop it ..., He cautioned himself, *She's a prisoner.* He collected himself, helped her into her saddle and handed the reins up to her. She looked down away from his eyes, and said quietly, "I didn't mean anything, what I just said."

"I understand," the ranger replied, just as quietly.

"I'm not a loose woman," she said. She paused then added, "You're decent to me ... that's all I should've said."

"I understand," Sam repeated. "As prisoners go, you're not so bad yourself." He reached behind his back and brought the gun he had taken from her. "I loaded it, all six. I know you realize what that sixth bullet is for if it comes down to it."

She took the gun and nodded her thanks. She checked the gun and laid it on her lap. "If they caught me alive, I'd ordinarily say they won't harm me." She glanced at the wounded Indian, who sat slumped, half-conscious in the pale moonlight. "But this young bunch of warriors don't act like any I've ever known."

"I know," Sam said, "that's why I'm arming you. If things go bad, you decide what to do with that sixth bullet." He laid a gloved hand on her horse's neck and tried to sound reassuring. "I think we'll be okay though." He rubbed the horse. "It's just that you never know."

Their eyes met and held for a moment.

"Come on, now," Sam said, "let's get this boy to town — get off this hill line before something else tries to feed on us."

CHAPTER 9

Near dawn, Max Carver and his Wild Bunch reined up at the base of low sand hills covered with mounds of charred frame work and discarded rubble. Among the riders, only Jerome Gascoyne looked surprised at the shabby surroundings.

"Wait right here," Carver said to everyone. The horses were blown and frothing.

Here ...? Gascoyne looked all around in surprise, but he kept silent. Three skinny coyotes raised their heads above a pile of debris. They blinked red eyes at the riders, then vanished from sight. Gascoyne raised in his stirrups for a broader view of the endless abandoned dumping site. Not far from his side, Dog Fannen leaned cross-armed on his saddle horn and observed the Frenchman's reaction to their hideout. He gave a dark chuckle.

"Looks like our *French guest* doesn't cotton much to our trail lodgings, Max," he said to Carver while he stared at Gascoyne.

Gascoyne ignored Fannen and looked at Max Carver.

"You told me we were headed back to Esplanade," he said.

"You heard me right," said Carver. "And here we are. This is the burnt section of Esplanade." He nodded toward a hazy glow of lantern light in the morning gloom. "If you want to go deeper into town, knock on some doors and tell them we're here, go right ahead." He gave a slight grin and pushed up his hat brim. "But keep going the other way when you leave."

Dog Fannen spat and stared narrowly at Gascoyne.

"Yeah, Frenchy," he said, "don't go pointing them our way, I'll give you what I gave ole Dock here. Eh, Dock?" He gave the wounded gunman a cruel little grin. Dockery stared at him with pure hatred, a bloody cloth pressed to his wound.

Gascoyne looked away, back onto the early dawn haze.

"If you don't like it here, don't feel bad about it," Slone said to Gascoyne, hoping to bring tempers down between Dockery and Fannen, "neither do we."

"Yeah," Dog Fannen joked with sarcasm, "usually we do all our hiding out in some plush places, like Zelda's in New Orleans or Fannie's in San Francisco—the finest hotels and brothels money can buy." He gave a jerk of his head toward Carver. "Our *boss*, Max here is just trying to cut our costs. He's always looking out for us. We get into Esplanade this morning, we'll rent the whole place and bring in a mariachi band—"

Having talked to Fedder Dockery and Joe Mercer along the trail, Max Carver cut in, saying, "You never shut up, do you, Dog."

The old gunman gave a guttural growl in reply.

Max went on, saying to everyone, "I've had to change our plans, for now. Everybody's staying right here while I ride into Esplanade and see what's going on there." He gestured toward Joe Mercer and Fedder Dockery. "Dock and Little Gun here tell me there's an Arizona Ranger there holding Cat-eye Eddie Poole and Morgan Manlen in jail—both of them shot to hell."

"Jesus," said Dog, "What's a ranger doing down here in Old Mex?"

"Doing as he damn well pleases, it sounds like," said Carver. "He dragged Cat-eye into town. Then shot Morgan Manlen down in the street when Manlen tried to take our horses back from him."

"So, Cat-eye is still alive?" Dog commented.

"Yes, he is," said Carver. He looked from face to face among the haggard gathering of riders. "The lawman who stole our horses is there with our animals—held up in the livery barn."

"He shot *Madcap* Manlen down in the street?" Dog said as if in disbelief.

"Yes," Max Carver said flatly. He stared at Dog Fannen for a second, then said with a curious tone, "I never heard Manlen called 'Madcap' by anybody." As he spoke he produced a long sulfur match. He struck it on his saddle horn and raised it overhead and moved it back and forth in the early morning gloom.

"Then, maybe you don't know him as well as some of us do," said, Fannen, standing by his words. "Morgan Manlen is one of the wildest, deadliest gun-handlers there ever was."

Sloane put in, "Manlen *is* known for being lightning fast with a gun, Max. I've heard it myself."

"Just feel free to butt right in when I'm talking, boyo," Fannen said to Sloane like some angry father.

"I'm just saying, is all," said Sloane.

"Yeah?" said Fannen. "Well I don't need you backing up any damn thing I've got to say."

"Both of you keep quiet," Carver said, seeing a lantern glow move back and forth up on a ledge near the top of a pile of rubble. "Here's our signal."

Carver waited for a second, then blew out the match in his hand and stepped down from his saddle. Atop the debris littered ledge the lantern light disappeared.

The six men led their horses up a narrow twisting path over and through all manner of junk, broken furniture, dried garbage and refuse. Rats scurried away from their pickings at the slow drop of horse's hooves and the sound of men's boots rustled through the debris on the littered path. As Carver brought them around him atop the narrow ledge, an old Wild Bunch robber gunman named Sid Tully stepped forward from the shadows with the darkened lantern in one his hand and a rifle hanging in his other.

"I'd about given yas up," the old robber said in a guarded tone, "figured your top knots might have ended up on hanging from some warrior's pony." He took the reins to Carver's horse and pulled it away from the path as others walked up one by one and handed him their tired horse's reins as well.

"It's been rough as a cob," Carver said. "We missed changing horses. Ours were too blown to head any other direction. So, we stuck to our plan and came here." He walked alongside Tully as the old man led the horses back under the stone shelf overhang and though a rock opening that took them to other side of the hill.

"We're glad you did," Tully said. "Itza-Chu's bunch has the desert turned upside down right now. But we brought in grub, coffee and whiskey, just like you said to do. We can hold up here." They walked on, the horses gathered beside Tully. The rest of Carver's men walked spread back behind them.

Once they were out of sight from every direction, Sid Tully squatted down and relit the lantern and kept the flame trimmed low and blue. Carver and his five men looked around, seeing the shadowy faces of Sid Tully and two additional men who'd been waiting there in the darkness for them.

Carver spoke up in a calming voice, seeing his men tense up. "All of you except our Frenchman here know Seaway and Dub Porter?" he asked. The men acknowledged with an exchange of nods. Carver gestured toward Gascoyne who stood watching. "This is our French captain," he said. "He might not want his name spread around while he's with us a short time, so just call him 'Cap.' He looked at Gascoyne for approval. Gascoyne's face revealed no opinion on the matter.

The three hideout men nodded and appraised Gascoyne. The gunman, known only as Seaway looked at Dockery who stood with a blood-soaked cloth tied around his head wound. "What happened to you, Dock?"

Before Dockery could answer, Dog Fannen cut in, saying, "I shot him, Seaway." He gave a casual so-what shrug. "Shot him right in his damn fool head." He sounded proud of himself.

Seaway stared at him, confused.

"Why?" he asked.

"'Cause I felt like it," Fannen said with flat cruel grin.

Fedder Dockery sat boiling mad, but he kept his mouth shut.

"It was an accident," Carver said, seeing it would be up to him to keep tempers at a manageable level. "What say we get a long pull on that whiskey you brought?"

"Sure enough," said Tully. He turned to Seaway and Dub Porter and said, "Get the front door closed and covered up. Then attend to these worn-out cayouses."

"What about my head wound?" Dockery asked.

"What about it?" Tully asked

"Can I get a dry cloth for it?" Dockery asked, sounding a little put out. "I'm so bloody I'm drawing flies here."

"Fix him up, Seaway, until he can get himself into town," said Tully. "There's a healing woman there," he said to Dockery. Dismissing the matter he turned back to Max Carver. "C'mon, Max, let's get farther back under this hillside—get that whiskey started around." He nodded toward the sound of distant gunfire. "We can sit here and drink while they chew each other up out there."

Ahead of the ranger and his prisoners the black silhouette of the town stood out against the gray-blue rise of morning. In the final mile before entering Esplanade through the opposite end of town from the burnt district, Sam and the woman came to a halt at the same time. Beside the woman, the young Apache sat unsteadily atop his horse, slumped forward, partly supported by the bloody saddle blanket bound to his abdomen. The desert lay silent to their left; but on the trail in front them two dead Indians lay sprawled in the rocky dirt. On the other side of the dead Indians three young braves sat staring at them, their rifles, bows and lances in hand.

Both Sam and the woman realized that if the warriors

were here to kill them, they would have already been dead. These warriors had come for their wounded companion. Knowing whose grandson their companion was, Sam had already considered what he would do when the Apache came for him. He and the woman watched intently as the older of the three young warriors stepped his horse forward, giving only a glance at the two dead Indians lying in the dirt as he reined his horse around them.

As a warning to the young warrior, Sam's right hand cocked the hammer on his rifle standing propped on his thigh.

"That's close enough," Sam said in a low menacing tone, speaking in Apache. Beside him the blue roan managed to hug up close against Black Pot.

The young warrior stopped and replied, but instead of speaking Apache he spoke in stiff border English.

"This one go with us," the warrior said.

Sam started to answer, but before he could, the wounded young man called out in weak and halting English, "No, Naiche, I go with ... them to town."

The lead warrior, Naiche, looked curiously at the ranger and nodded him forward for an even better look. Beside Sam, the woman gave the wounded young man's horse enough rein to take a step forward. On Sam's other side, the blue roan began to turn surly toward the approaching Indian. He whinnied and jerked his head hard against the lead rope.

"Not now, Blue Boy ...," Sam said silently, giving a hard jerk back on the rope. The roan settled, but not without first grumbling an angry protest.

As the lead warrior stopped a few yards from the wounded brave and appraised him in the grainy blue morning light, the brave struggled and sat upright, straightening himself on his horse's bloody McClellan-style cavalry saddle.

"I go to town ... to stop my ... bleeding," the brave said haltingly, but with determination. "Tell Itza-Chu ... I return soon."

A Ranger's Trail

"We can kill these people and take you to Itza-Chu *now,*" the lead warrior said in whiskey-slurred Apache, with no thought, or perhaps no concern that the ranger or the woman might speak his language.

"No." The wounded Indian shook his bowed head quickly. "I won't ... go with you," he said, returning the talk to English. "I won't last ... that long."

The lead Indian bent forward a little in his saddle as if needing an even closer look. Beside Sam, the roan stamped the rocky dirt and blew through its nostrils. The woman pulled back the reins on the young Indian's horse.

"You heard what he said to you, *Naiche,*" she told the lead Indian in a scolding tone, letting him know she knew his name. "Now go and let us get him into town. "Keeping us here is only going to kill him. Do you want to kill him, *Naiche*"

The lead Indian thought about it for only a second, then backed his horse and waved his two companions to the side of the trail.

"Go to town," he said. He looked the woman up and down. Sam wondered if he was going to demand she stay with them as hostage until the young warrior returned from town. Whiskey and peyote was pressing hard on an already unstable situation.

"Move out with him," Sam said quietly to the woman, not wanting to get her into a hostage situation. Knowing the tension that awaited any strangers riding into Esplanade after such a violent night, he wanted to warn her to wait for him outside of town. But he didn't dare trust these three warriors hearing a word he had to say. It was time to get out of here, period. Hopefully, she would know on her own. He looked back at the lead warrior as the woman put her horse forward at a walk, leading the young Apache beside her. He slumped back down in his saddle.

"Keep moving. I'll catch up," Sam said, staring hard at the lead warrior as he spoke to the woman. Following a nod from their leader, the two young warriors grudgingly backed their horses a short step to let the woman and their wounded comrade pass.

The lead Indian looked Sam up and down with contempt. "You go on, too. Join your people," he insisted in a gruff tone.

"I'm in no hurry," Sam said flatly, keeping a low even tone.

The lead Indian didn't like a white man showing no fear of him.

"If I decide to," he pointed out, "I can tell my warriors to kill the woman and bring me the son of Itza-Chu's son."

"I know," Sam said. "That's why I don't mind waiting here." He spoke calmly, firmly, his finger on the hammer of his cocked rifle. He could smell the strong concoction of cheap sour alcohol on the Indian's breath.

The Indian looked at the rifle and smirked. "You could not stop me from sending these warrior's after him," he said.

Here we go. Just what I was afraid of ..., Sam told himself. He realized they were about to go back over everything they had settled on when the lead Indian sent the woman and the wounded young man on to town.

"I know I can't stop you," Sam said. "But if either one of your warriors heads forward, you'll be dead before you hit the ground." He knew he was trying to talk sense to the man though a heavy fog of whiskey and peyote.

"How do you know I won't have my braves kill you when you do decide to leave?" the leader said, as if nothing had just been agreed to.

"I don't know," said Sam, "any more than you know that I won't kill you before I leave."

The lead Indian sat silent for a moment. Sam saw a dark swirl of peyote madness ebb up across the edges of his mind as he tried mulling things over. After a moment of dark thought, the Indian scowled at Sam, and started to bring his braves forward with only a twitch of a finger. But then he stopped, just as Sam was ready to press back on his rifle's trigger and send the man's forehead flying through the air. But the leader nodded at his warriors with a slowly raised hand.

"I said we will let them take Itza-Chu's grandson to town —so we will."

Sam felt relief flood over him, yet he kept his rifle ready, a fact the Indian looked suddenly sober enough to understand.

Without another word, Sam backed Black Pot a step and turned him and the blue roan upward onto a dark path still blackened by the shadows of lingering night.

"I will see you again, Lawman," the leader called out, showing his two followers something to his credit even though they had witnessed Itza-Chu's grandson being the one responsible for stopping any bloodshed. With no reply, Sam gave him a look over his shoulder and put Black Pot and the blue roan forward at a walk.

Riding up deeper into the dark shadows of rock, the ranger saw the hillside below opening in a silvery mist as morning light pushed its way up the far edge of the earth. By the time he found a less rocky path skirting along the steep hillside, he knew the three warriors would be out of sight on the trail below, as would the woman and the wounded young Indian.

At a place where the trail below disappeared around a turn toward the dim lantern lights of the waking town, Sam took Black Pot and the blue roan down through the rocks until the rugged path intersected with the wider trail on the flatlands. The blue roan grew restless and tugged at the lead rope. Sam righted him, realizing the horse was telling him something. When he stopped the horses and listened for a moment to the silence before turning onto the trail, he heard what had now become the familiar sound of the woman's bolo make a circular whooshing sound off to his right. Instinctively, he ducked low, wrapped the roan's lead rope around Black Pot's saddle horn and rolled off his saddle onto the rocky ground. His rifle came up cocked and ready, but the sound of bolo twirling stopped suddenly.

Sam eased his grip on the rifle, seeing the bolo plop down from overhead like some giant spinning insect. In a slow final spin it landed onto the rocky trail twenty feet away, far enough away that Sam knew she hadn't intended him harm. The roan let out a whinny and tugged against the lead rope.

Recognizing the roan's voice, the woman walked out of the rocks toward him, leading her horse and the wounded Indian's paint. Sam noted the young man was bowed low in his saddle, not moving.

Walking Black Pot and the blue roan forward, Sam met the woman as she stooped down and silently picked up her bolo and shook it out and hung it over her shoulder.

"It also makes a good calling card, times when you're not sure who you're calling on," she said in a lowered tone.

Sam only nodded. Once again she could have used the bolo on him, but she didn't. Instead she had been there lying low, waiting for him.

Good move .... If that was the message she wanted him to get, he'd gotten it right away, he told himself. He'd wondered if she was savvy enough to know not to ride into a town threatened by the desert Apache. And she had—a half-Apache woman leading a wounded Apache warrior. Yes, she was capable, as savvy as anyone he'd ever met on this wild frontier.

"Is he still alive?" Sam asked in a lowered voice, his eyes scanning the growing morning light as he spoke.

"He's alive," she replied. "I don't know for how long though." She looked into his eyes in the grainy morning light. "I wasn't riding in there alone," she added. Sam watched her take the bolo from her shoulder and drape it from her saddle horn. He saw her favor her wounded leg as she started to swing up into her saddle. Cradling her forearm he gave her a boost up.

"Good thinking," he said, as if it had never crossed his

mind. He turned to Black Pot and stepped up into his saddle, taking the blue roan's lead rope in hand. The woman gave herself a guarded smile and touched her horse forward, the wounded Indian badly slumped in his saddle beside her.

PART II

CHAPTER 10

The ranger, the woman, and the wounded Apache waited on the flatlands a hundred yards out on Esplanade's main trail. They sat their horses for a full twenty minutes behind a short pile of rock until morning sunlight spread high across a clear blue sky. Three dead Indian horses lay strewn on the flatlands. Behind the town a spiral of black smoke rose from a pile of burning cinders that had the framework of a nearby barn.

With his telescope raised to his eye, Sam looked closely at three freight wagons lined across the dusty tiled street. He counted a half-dozen rifles lined along the wagon sides, all of them aimed out in the direction of him and his prisoners. Other men and women alike lined the roofs of the town, rifles in hand. Sam looked at the blacksmith, town selectman Jorge Doyle standing up in middle wagon bed gazing out at him through a battered pair of binoculars.

"Come on, blacksmith, I've got a man bleeding out bad here," Sam said under his breath, raising both arms, waving the telescope back and forth slowly.

Inside the wagon, recognizing the ranger through his binoculars, Jorge Doyle let out a breath of relief.

"Hold your fire," he said to the line of armed townsmen on either side of him, "it's the ranger."

"What's he doing riding with Apache?" a townsman asked.

"I don't know," said Doyle. "Stop shooting long enough and we'll ask him!"

But almost before he'd finished saying the words a shot exploded from one of the men lying prone inside the wagon near his feet. The blacksmith jumped, startled by the sudden blast.

"Hold your fire, *damn it!*" Doyle cursed. From the roofline another nervous rifleman let a shot rip out toward the ranger and his prisoners. Doyle jumped again.

"Stop shooting!" Doyle bellowed. His voice resounded along the empty street.

Out behind the pile of rock, the woman gripped her pistol with both hands, ready to return fire, for all the good it would have done her.

"Are you sure these folks know you, Ranger?" she asked in a tense voice.

Instead of answering her, Sam kept his eyes on Doyle standing in the wagon bed, waving his right arm, as if saying he had things under control.

"They're strung tight," Sam commented. "Lucky we didn't go riding in before daylight."

"But everything's good now?" the woman asked, still holding on to the pistol.

"Everything's alright, he sees us now," Sam nodded, watching Doyle continue to wave. "Gather the Indian. The two of you keep close to me all the way in. Don't make any sudden moves. I expect these folks have had a tough night."

As they mounted their horses and rode forward, Sam sidled near the woman and asked in a lowered voice, "Is anybody going to recognize you here?"

"What do you mean?" she asked in turn.

"I mean from the robbery?" Sam said, "You were here, weren't you?"

"If I was here, do you think I would tell you?" she said.

"I think you need to tell me something," Sam said. "Legally, I don't have a thing on you or your pals either one. As soon as this desert settles down, you're free to ride. But I want to know what to expect once we're looking these folks in the face—"

"Nobody saw my face," she said grudgingly, cutting him off. "That is, if I was even here—*which I wasn't.*" She offered a thin little smile and stared straight ahead. Sam let it pass. He looked her up and down and found himself wondering as he had before whether he was looking at a straight up outlaw or woman in great distress. *Maybe both ...?*

He knew what had happened to this young woman back along the Kansas-Missouri border. When her father had been killed she'd thrown in with an old hired gunman named Baines Meredith who taught her to kill like a professional with all manner of weaponry. When her training was complete she left Meredith and hunted down the men who killed her father, one after the other until it was done. Then she had gone back to her father's ranch and dropped out of sight. What had happened to bring her to the outlaw trail—riding scout for Max Carver and the Wild Bunch?

She turned her face to him and said, "Don't worry, Ranger, I'm not going to put you on the spot. I'm not *wanted* anywhere on your side of the border."

Sam nodded as she looked straight ahead. Riflemen had started to gather at the wagon barricades as they rode closer. The wounded young Apache sat unsteadily in his saddle. The blue roan rode along between the woman and the ranger as if in charge. *A curious-looking group ...,* the ranger told himself. He had a lot of questions about this woman, but that would have to wait. He'd met few outlaws who didn't have some reason, either real or imagined, that had led them into their lawless pursuits. He felt grateful that this time, at least, fate had not put him in the position of having to bring this one in tied face down across her saddle, because something about this woman told him that there would have been no other way.

Sam's thoughts were cut short as he and the woman both saw a band of mounted Apache warriors appear on the horizon as if they had come up from the core of the earth.

"Uh-oh," the woman said, "here's our welcoming party!"

As they both booted their horses into a run across the flatlands, the young Apache found just enough waning instincts to lay forward on his paint and hold on while the woman led them alongside her. Ahead in Esplanade, a large church bell rang out, announcing the coming attack in a blaring urgent tone. Quickly, the gathered riflemen were back inside the wagon barricades and spread back along the roof line. Shots began to explode from both directions between the Indians and townspeople.

Riding hard, the ranger and the woman made it into Esplanade just as the Apache gunfire began whistling past them and their horses. Once behind the wagons, Jorge Doyle and several townsmen bounded down from the wagons and crowded around the newcomers, grabbing their horses and helping them down from their saddles.

"Say, what're you doing traveling with this bloody Injun?" one of the townsmen shouted after helping the young Apache down from his horse. He stared at the wet blood on his hands as if it was contaminated.

"Get him over to the jail," Sam said, "to the healing woman, before he bleeds to death."

"So what if he bleeds to death?" another man said. "It'll keep us from hanging him!" two townsmen started to let the young Indian fall to the ground, but Sam stepped in and grabbed him just in time. The woman helped him.

"This way," Sam said to her, motioning toward the small jail where the banker, Philippe Flippoza stood watching with concern, holding a short shotgun at his side.

"Hey! This one is an Injun, too!" one man said. They looked the woman up and down with suspicion and sudden contempt in their eyes. "The hell do you mean bringing them here?"

"Get out of my way," the ranger warned them both. There was no room for disagreement in his tone. The men stepped back.

The Indian's arm and chest slathered with blood as Sam

wrapped it over his shoulder. The woman took the Indian's other arm and the two started walking almost in a trot toward the jail. The two townsmen who had given Sam a hard time looked at each other sheepishly, then hurried forward, picked the Indian's feet up from dragging in the dirt and hurried along carrying him.

"We meant no harm, Ranger!" one man called back over his shoulder above the sound of rifle fire still resounding back and forth between the barricades and attackers. "We'll get him to the healing woman, for sure."

Jorge Doyle trotted along beside Sam, a rifle hanging from his hand.

"We were getting worried about you, Ranger," he said.

"So was I," the ranger replied as they reached the front of the jail and Flippoza threw open the door for them. "Have my prisoners gave you any trouble?"

"Naw, nothing like those savages out there," Doyle said, referring to the attacking Apache warriors. They've been jabbing at us all night like coyotes—run in, hit us and run out. Now that you three are inside they'll slack off. We've taken a few wounded."

"I see," Sam said, noting a wounded townsman seated on the floor leaning against the wall, a bandage around his head. Another man sat beside him, his arm in a blood-stained sling.

At the wagon barricades and along the roofline the rifle fire waned as the mounted warriors circled away and pulled back deep on the flatlands, making themselves more difficult targets. Seeing Doyle look at the women with question, Sam said, "The Apache were chasing her. I found her."

"By the saints! Ma'am, you are lucky this ranger came along," Doyle said, his expression softening some toward the woman.

"I know," the woman said, giving Sam a look. Then she nodded at the wounded Apache. "He was one of them dogging me," she added.

The three of them looked at the warrior as the two men laid him on a table the old woman had set up for herself in the middle of the floor. The healing woman had also brought in a helper overnight, a slightly younger woman dressed in the same black cloth.

"Thank the *Sainted Mother* you both made it," Doyle said, looking at the ranger and the woman with an arrow stub sticking from her thigh.

"I ran out of bullets," the woman said, "or I would have killed him."

She gestured again toward the wounded Indian and gave Doyle a level gaze. Doyle noted her seriousness on the matter.

"I'm sure you would have, *Señora*," he said. "Let's get you looked at."

He waved the healing woman's helper over to them and pointed out the arrow wound. The helper nodded silently and led the woman to the sheriff's desk that had been pushed to one side of the office and cleared, in order to serve as a surgery table for the wounded.

"This one says he's Itza-Chu's grandson," Sam interjected, directing the subject back to the wounded brave.

"You believe him?" Doyle asked.

"I do believe him," Sam said. "Some on his pals showed up drunk, wanting to kill us and set him free. He sent them away." He stared at Doyle to gauge his level of belief.

"Sent them *away?*" said Doyle.

"Told them he wanted us to bring him here for help," Sam said.

Doyle shook his head.

"These younger generation Apache are a whole different breed," he said. As he spoke he glanced over at the woman who lay atop the desk, the healing woman's helper hovering over her wound. "Time was, a young buck would stake himself out and die before he would take help from a white man. Maybe the reservations are doing some good after all."

A Ranger's Trail

Sam didn't answer; he looked around the small jail office that had been quickly converted into a field hospital. Blood stained the floor below the desk. In the cell, Cat-eye Eddie Poole and Morgan Manlen both lay knocked out, sprawled inside the cell, leaning sidelong against each other for support.

"The rifle fire doesn't seem to disturb them," Sam said.

"I hope you don't mind, Ranger," Doyle said. "We've kept them loaded with whiskey and laudanum. It was the only way to shut them up! They wanted us to arm them and let them help. I didn't trust them. They got louder than the Apache. We figured whiskey and laudanum is more humane than knocking them in the head every few minutes."

"I understand," Sam said.

"What about this woman, Ranger?" Doyle asked in a lowered voice. "Is she—that is, I mean …."

"She's *part* Indian," Sam said, making it easier for him. I know a little about her and her father. He was a well-respected cavalry officer—name of Wilder. Her name is Julie Wilder." He gave Doyle a pointed gaze. "Folks of good repute, the Wilders." He let his gaze linger long enough for Doyle to understand that he wouldn't allow her being part Indian to have *anything* to do with *anything*.

"Of course they are, I'm certain," Doyle said. He paused long enough to welcome a change of subject. "What did you find out about this horde of Apache?"

"Not much," Sam said. "There's a lot of them gathered up, but still a lot of them spread out across the desert. It's hard to get a good tally. I'm hoping they're not going to stick around here much longer." He nodded toward the wounded young warrior. "He says his grandfather, Itza-Chu, wants to make peace with the tribes south of here."

"How far south of here?" Doyle asked. "All you've got down through Sonora are what's left of the Chiricahua and White Mountain bands—roamers, desert bands. He's already got peace with them."

"I understood the grandson to say Itza-Chu wants to try to make lasting peace with the Sonora Yaqui tribes."

"Looking to the future, huh?" Doyle said. "Well, I wish him luck with that. If any tribes can hand the Apache their asses, it'll be the Yaqui. Their rebels are kicking the hell out of our *brand-new* Mexican government everywhere. Something the French failed to do."

"Listen how quiet it's got out there," Sam said, the two of them noting the silence that had come upon the tile streets now that the warriors had withdrawn deeper back across the rolling flatlands.

Doyle gave a tired smile.

"If we're smart we'll go get some breakfast and coffee right now while everything is settled down," he said. He motioned toward the door. Seeing Sam look toward the woman he added, "I'll have some food and coffee sent over for Miss Wilder until she can join us."

From across the office, the woman turned quickly upon hearing her real name called. She shot Sam a hard cold stare. But there was nothing he could do or say to explain himself right then. Instead, he gave her a cautioning look as he and Doyle headed out the door, rifle in hand. The woman glanced around and realized no one had paid attention to her name being called. She saw Cat-eye Eddie Poole, the only one there who would know her by sight. He was still knocked out, mouth agape, leaning sidelong against the equally unconscious Monroe Manlen. She deftly touched her fingertips to the fresh bandage on her thigh, her trousers down to her ankles and off of her wounded leg. *Of all times to be wounded ...!* But that's all right, she assured herself. You can ride. It'll hurt something fierce, but pain's nothing new. She clenched her teeth, raised her throbbing leg and shoved her foot down into her trouser leg. The two old women looked her up and down and turned back to their work.

Doyle had caught the quick silent exchange between the

woman and the ranger on the way out of the adobe jail. As the front door closed behind them and they started toward Mama Flora's Restaurant and Open Air Lodging House, Doyle spoke as he stared straight ahead.

"Your prisoner, Eddie Poole, is a horse thief, huh?" he said.

"Right," Sam said. "You saw the horses."

Doyle only nodded and went on, saying, "And this woman is a traveler you just happened onto out there in the desert hills —she was fighting the Apache?"

"Right again," Sam said, preparing for whatever came next. He had not lied about anything. No legal lines had been crossed between the US and Mexico, or France, or any other place that he could think of. He was here to bring back a murderer, Max Carver. He was ordered to do so with as little involvement as necessary. *Easier said than done ...,* he told himself, looking all around at the town under siege by a staggering number of desert Apache.

Doyle fell silent for a moment, still looking ahead.

"One thing I always like about Mexico more than I do the United States," he said, "is that here, people know when to pry into your business and when to shut up."

"I've always admired that myself," Sam said. A slight smile moved across his lips, then left. "The fact is, Eddie Poole is a straight up horse thief. I caught him with stolen horses."

"And I have no doubt the woman *really* is a traveler you found out there fighting off the Apache," said Doyle."

"That's the truth of it," Sam said. Then he added, "The truth as I care to share it, Selectman."

Doyle considered it, then said. "Good enough. You rangers always deal square with everybody I've known of."

"We do the best we can," Sam said humbly.

"If I ask you anything else will I be *prying?"* Doyle queried.

"You could be," Sam said quietly, not wanting to go any deeper into his business for being here.

"All right then, I'm done with it," Doyle said. "If I can help without *prying,* let me know. Otherwise, I'll keep my mouth shut."

"Obliged," Sam said, touching his hat brim. He was expecting questions to turn toward the Wild Bunch robbery. He was glad when Doyle let it go.

In the distance, more gunfire erupted fiercely across the desert floor. Just as the two started to turn into the alleyway running alongside Mama Flora's to the *chimnea* out back, a Mexican *vaquero* ran to them from the wagon barricades waving his rifle over his head.

"Uh-oh," said Doyle, "I knew coffee and breakfast sounded too good to be true." The firing intensified.

"Señor Doyle!" The *vaquero* shouted as he ran. "Come *pronto!* The Apache overrun us! There are too many of them!"

"This way, Ranger!" Doyle said without answering the vaquero. He directed Sam toward the church's bell tower. They quickened their pace; a wide cloud of dust filled with gunfire and war-cries swept in, filling the air. The *vaquero* ran alongside them.

At the bottom of the stairs leading up the side of the church to the bell tower, Sam said, "Hold it!" Stopping at the bottom of the stairs he said to the two stopping with him, "Do you hear what I hear out there?" He paused with his attention piqued toward the distance—a faint sound of a bugle. When it resounded again, this time louder, a faint bit clearer, Doyle and Sam turned to the *vaquero.*

"Who is it, Peto?" Doyle asked the *vaquero.*

"It is the French!" the *vaquero* said. "No other nation on earth allows *musica* that bad!"

"Ah, yes, the French," Doyle said, as if the information had suddenly occurred to him. The three bounded up the stairs as gunfire ripped the air around them. Splinters flew from the wooden window ledges. "Once again the French get here before our *federales*," Doyle said in a voice raised about the fray. "Want to know why, Ranger?" he asked as they hurried up the bell tower stairway up the side of the adobe church. Sam only looked at him.

"Usually, they get here first because our *soldados* are scared to death of the Apache!"

"The French are too hard-headed to fear the Apache," Peto the *vaquero* said.

Doyle laughed, his voice rising above the endless stuttering blasts of the Gatlin gun as they bounded the last few feet up the rickety stairway and onto the stone roof. The church bell stood tucked inside the tower on the next level down. Bullets struck the large bell through the large four-way stone opening that housed it.

"But today they arrive ahead of our army because they have had hundreds of thousands in gold coins stolen from under their noses!" His laughter grew louder. "Our heros! *Hurrah pour la France!*" he shouted amid the sounds of battle.

Sam looked all around on the ground below the church tower just in time to see one of the riflemen stand up in a crotch in the wagon bed and fly backwards when a bullet slammed into his chest. Another of the riflemen lay dead in the dirt beside the wagon. Out beyond the thick stir of dust, a muffled sound of the French army bugle made its way through the heavy gunfire. Ten feet away one of the two men operating the Gatlin gun fell forward with both hands on his chest and dropped over the stone edge of the roof. The other gun operator flattened to the roof as bullets zipped past him.

This was no time to be making jokes, Sam told himself. He grabbed the selectman by his forearm and shook him a little to settle him down.

"Pay attention, Doyle!" he said. "They've figured the location of this big gun. We've got to move it down to the bell housing, before they shoot it to pieces. They can do a lot of damage before the French army get them chased away."

Even as he spoke bullets zipped through the air like angry hornets, some of them thumping against the short adobe walls surrounding them, some hitting the big bell in the space below their feet.

"You're right, Ranger," said Doyle, a bullet whistling dangerously close to his head. "Help Peto and me move it and set it up. We'll handle it until the French get here. Right, Peto?"

"*Sí*, right, we handle it," said the *vaquero*.

CHAPTER 11

With the Gatlin gun moved and reseated inside the four arched stone columns housing the bell, Sam, Doyle, Peto, and the old man who'd been firing the big gun hurriedly lined up a large stack of loaded magazine clips. Sam and Doyle grabbed the gun by its firing frame and shook it, testing the gun for steadiness as the old man and Peto prepared to wreak hell on the streets below. The warriors had managed to move in closer, many of them more visible now through a lesser veil of dust.

Seeing two warriors appear from an alleyway and run along the tiled street toward the narrow street leading to the livery barn, Sam grabbed his rifle and swung it up into play. Beside him, Doyle began firing a big French horse pistol at the two. As both warriors fell dead on the street, Sam saw the woman, *Ruthless* Ruby Teal, now known to be Julie Wilder, come running with a limp from the direction of the jail, a smoking Colt hanging in her hand. Four more Indians appeared out of an alleyway and ran head-on toward the limping woman.

Noting the woman with the Indians running toward her and the look on Sam's face, Doyle stuck fresh rounds in the smoking French revolver and said, "Go get her, Ranger, I've got you covered!"

Wasting no time, Sam hurried out onto the rickety stairs and down to the street. He saw the woman shoot one of the Indians twice in his bare chest as he raced in her direction. As Sam reached the street he raised his rifle butt to his shoulder and sent another Indian veering sidelong through a large glass window. Gunshots sped wildly past him. From the wagon barricades, the riflemen had heard the commotion on the street behind them and turned toward the remaining two Indians. One Indian fell dead in a volley of rifle fire. The other, still breathing, crawled a few feet in the dirt until more rifle fire hammered him to the street.

"Are you alright?" Sam asked, having grabbed the woman around her waist, sweeping her into the shelter of an alley stacked with cargo crates.

He held her at arm's length and looked her up and down. The crates stacked deep in the alley partially muffled the sound of the fighting. In the distance the French bugle resounded. The air reeked of burnt powder.

"Yes," she said, "I'm alright." As she spoke she let herself slide down the clapboard wall she leaned against. Seated, she stretched out her leg and cautiously kneaded the sore flesh around the wound in her thigh. Sam eased down the wall with her.

"What are you doing out here, *running?*" Sam asked. "You can barely walk."

"I was coming to help," she said with a firm tone in her voice. Sam saw a fierceness flicker in her dark eyes. The smoking Colt lay in her right hand in the dirt beside her.

"You were coming to help?" he said. He glanced toward the livery barn, then back to her. His gaze settled in on the fierceness. She looked away for a second. "Look at me, Ma'am," he said, firmly but gently. He tipped her face back to his with his fingertips, his rifle barrel warm across his knee, and studied her eyes closer for whatever truth he might discern in them.

"Okay, that was a lie ...." The woman admitted. She let out a breath and lowered her face for a second. Then she leveled her gaze back at him.

"You were cutting out, weren't you?" Sam said, realizing

he had no legal reason to hold her here.

"Still am," she replied, a little out of breath, but with a look of resolve. She raised her hand from kneading her wounded thigh and placed it on his forearm, bracing herself to stand up.

"I can't let you leave here in the middle of Indian battle," Sam said quickly, even as he eased his hold on her hand. "It would be suicide."

She raised her hand from his arm and cupped it on his cheek, feeling the slightest bit of beard stubble.

"No, Ranger," she said, "Suicide would be me killing myself, or allowing these warriors to kill me instead." She shoved the Colt down behind her belt. "Neither of those two things are going to happen here. I've got too much to do to let dying get in my way." She offered a faint smile, but the ranger wasn't letting up.

"Sorry, Ma'am. I can't let you ride out of here," he said. "Not until this is over." He raised his rifle to his shoulder and took aim on a warrior riding hard along the street. Before Sam could fire, a rifle shot from a rooftop knocked the rider from his horse and sent him rolling and tumbling, dead in the dirt.

The woman studied his eyes closely as Sam turned back to face her.

Her smile turned serious. The fighting around them was letting up as the French bugle grew closer. Apache who had breached lesser guarded spots in the town's perimeter were pulling away.

"Ranger, you said I'd be free to go once we got Itza-Chu's grandson here and I got my wound looked after. We're here. I'm looked after, and now I'm leaving." She glanced toward the sound of the French bugle. "Besides, they might be asking questions I don't feel like answering."

Sam knew she was right. He also knew that once she slipped herself through this horde of Apache she was as capable and savvy of making it out alive as anybody he knew. Still, he was here to hunt down Max Carver. He had to keep that foremost in his mind. He leaned back against the clapboard wall and let out a breath.

"Before you cut out, tell me where to find the Wild Bunch's hideout," he said almost matter-of-factly.

"That was never a part of the deal," the woman said with resolve.

Sam gave a slight smile.

"I thought I ought to try," he said. "I'll never find it if you don't tell me."

"Somehow, I don't believe you mean that, Ranger," she said, giving back a half-smile herself.

"You could tell me anyway ... make my job here easier," he said, sounding only half serious himself. "Call it something I can remember you by?"

Without a reply, she suddenly cupped his face in her hands, firmly but gently, and she kissed him deeply on his lips. He started to resist, but the feel of it, the taste of it, told him how wrong that would be—how he would never forgive himself should he do such a thing. He slipped his arms around her and the two stood in the resounding gunfire and bugle call for a moment, knowing somehow that when that moment was over, it would be gone forever.

She whispered softly against his cheek, "I'm glad I met you, Ranger Sam Burrack." She stepped back and smiled at him, at arm's length, still not turning him loose.

Sam shook his head a little, deeply amazed by this strong, beautiful woman. "You beat all I've ever seen, Miss *Ruthless Ruby.*" He paused as if to catch and correct himself. "I mean, Miss Julie Wilder," he said favorably.

She gave a single nod of approval.

"Yes, I'm *Julie Wilder* again," she said softly. "I'm Julie Wilder, *heading home.*" She started to draw him to her again—just one more long warm kiss. But she caught herself and took a step back. "Get back up there with the big gun, Ranger," she said, even though the big gun was firing less intensely,

A Ranger's Trail

"and you take care of yourself."

"I will," Sam said, "but I've got your back 'til you reach the horses." He picked up his rifle from against the clapboard wall. He watched, rifle cocked and ready as she turned and slipped out of the alleyway and hurried away in the direction of the livery barn.

Sam stood watching the livery barn until he saw the woman open the main door just enough to slide inside, then close it behind herself. Looking in all unobstructed directions, Sam made his way out of the alleyway and headed back to the church bell tower. Dead Indians lay strewn along the tile street. Armed townsmen had come out of their firing positions and began to gather as the French bugle stopped and the sound of the cavalry's horses' hoofs roared onto the street on the other side of the wagon barricades.

Selectman Jorge Doyle and Peto the *vaquero* sat collapsed on sandbags beside the silent Gatlin gun. Jorge looked up at Sam as he poured water from a gourd over his bowed head. As Sam neared, Doyle stood up and pointed out across the distance at the dust line left by a dozen fleeing Apache on horseback. A few more warriors ran along behind the riders on foot. Behind the fleeing Apache, he saw streams of dust rise behind seven French cavalry troops in hot pursuit.

What's this ...? A dozen mounted Apache warriors running from a handful of French cavalry—leaving some of their own warriors behind, stranded on foot ...? *Hunh-uh!* He wasn't buying it.

"There's some easy pickings out there for your big rifle, if you want them, Ranger," Doyle said.

"I'll pass," Sam said. He looked dawn as the rest of the French Cavalry trotted in along the tiled street. "Looks like the French have saved the day." As he spoke he glanced out at the fleeing Apache as they rode down over a rise and disappeared in a roil of dust. Then he looked back at Doyle.

"Yes they have indeed," said Doyle. He dipped the water

gourd into a bucket of water and handed it to the ranger. As Sam took it and raised it to his lips, Doyle nodded down in the direction of a thin trail leading away from the livery barn. On the trail, Julie Wilder rode away on the blue roan, a spare horse trotting close beside her on a lead rope.

"*Uh-oh!* There goes the woman, Ranger," he said, not sounding too excited about it. "Are you going after her?"

"I've got her," Sam said quietly.

"You've *got her* ...?" Doyle said in disbelief. "What does that mean?" He looked to Peto who gave him a shrug. They both looked at the ranger.

"It means, *I've got her,*" Sam said bluntly.

Doyle turned his curiosity back to Peto and said, "Hear that, Peto? He's got her."

"*Sí,*" Peto nodded vigorously, "The ranger, he got her," Peto said.

"Anyway, she's not my prisoner," Sam said. He swallowed a drink of tepid water. He stood watching the woman leave, riding wide away from both the French and the fleeing warriors. *Wise move, getting out of there,* he commented to himself, noting how the blue roan with its slightly odd splay-hoofed gait looked right at home beneath the woman.

"They're riding onto a trap," he said bluntly to Doyle and Peto, looking out as the warriors on foot appeared to slow down their pace before dropping out of sight over the rise.

"Say what?" said Doyle, both he and Peto standing and looking out with him.

Sam nodded toward the Apache on foot.

"They're luring the troops farther away from their main force," he said. "As soon as the troops top the rise and head down the other side, there'll be more warriors waiting down there for them. This is an ambush move to take some soldiers hostages. My hunch is, they'll want to trade some soldiers to get Itza-Chu's grandson turned loose."

"No offense, Ranger," said Doyle, "but what makes you

so sure their ambush will work?"

"It's their game on their *desert,"* Sam said. "They've been playing it and winning it for a long time." As he spoke he pointed out the warriors on foot moving too slow up the rise, letting the French get closer than any retreating foe would ever allow.

"I think you might be right," said Doyle, watching and considering the ranger's words as he stared out through the sun's harsh glare. "They're not trying very hard to get away."

"Not at all," said Sam. "They're just drawing the soldiers along behind them until they get them surrounded, on the other side of the rise."

"Come on," said Doyle. "I think we better warn the French!" As if on cue, heavy firing erupted from the other side of the rise. But Sam noted it began to wane almost as quickly as it started. By the time these two warned the French, Sam figured the ambush would be near completion.

"You and Peto go warn them," Sam said. "I'm going to get out there, see if I can get a jump on this thing before more people die." He gave Doyle a firm look. "I'm taking the young warrior with me," He added. "See if he can stop this thing before they start haggling over prisoners."

"You brought him in," said Doyle. "Far as I'm concerned you can take him with you, if he's able to ride. I have to act for the good of the town."

"He's patched up and rested some," Sam said. "He'll have to be able to ride."

"Si," Peto agreed. "If the French find out he's here they will kill him anyway—for all the Apache to see."

"Get going, Ranger," said Doyle. "If the French see you and him leaving I'll cover for you, as best I can."

Without another word, the three men descended the rickety stairs down the side of the adobe church and split up. Selectman Doyle and Peto headed toward the wagon barricades where a relieved crowd had formed around the arriving French cavalry troops. Walking through the smell of gun smoke and scattered bodies of townsfolk and Indian alike, the ranger hurried to the livery barn. Among the stalls of curious stolen horses he'd confiscated from *Cat-eye* Eddie Poole, he checked Black Pot and the young warrior's horse over good, then saddled them and led them out through the side door, to the rear door of the jail.

The banker, Philippe Flippoza, and another townsman named Ben Knopp stood in the rear door of the jail with rifles in hand. The both took a step back as Sam brought Black Pot and the young Apache's horse to a halt, jumped down from his saddle and hurried to the open door. Flippoza lowered his rifle; the townsman raised his rifle across his chest as if to block the ranger's way.

"Get the Indian up and ready to ride. I'm taking him out of here," Sam said quickly to Flippoza.

"You can't do that, Mister!" said Ben Knopp. He looked at the bank manager. "Can he, *Señor* Flippoza? I heard the town wants to hang this rascal."

"Si!" Flippoza said before Sam could reply for himself. "This is the ranger I told you about. The Indian is his prisoner —he brought him here. He can take him away."

The townsman lowered his rifle and stepped back. Behind him stood the young Apache who had watched the sporadic fighting from a small window. Sam saw the young brave stagger and catch himself against a support post with his cuffed hands.

"Are you able to ride?" Sam asked, stepping in closer, ready to catch the young man if he needed to.

"I rode here," the brave said, sounding weak but belligerent. He looked around behind Sam, blurry-eyed. "Where is the woman?"

"She's gone," Sam said offering no further explanation. He stepped in closer, taking the handcuff key from his short pocket. "Give me your hands," he said to the young brave.

A Ranger's Trail

The young man managed to stand straighter and hold out his cuffed hands. He nodded at the key in Sam's hand and said, "If you did not come back, how would they take these off me?"

"It wouldn't have mattered to you," Sam said. "You heard him say they were going to hang you."

The young brave chuffed with contempt but he couldn't argue the ranger's reasoning. Sam took away the cuffs and watched for a moment as the young man rubbed his wrists.

"What do they call you?" he asked, realizing he had no idea who this young man was, other than the fact he was Itza-Chu's—*Great Hawk's*—grandson.

"I am Taza," the young warrior said.

"Star," the ranger interpreted. "Your name is *Star.*"

Taza almost looked impressed by the ranger knowing what his name meant. But he caught himself and gazed away out the open door.

"Look at me, *Taza,*" the ranger said. His voice carried just enough command to make the young warrior turn and look him in the eyes. "I know there's an ambush going on out there. The Apache will be taking hostages, for *trade*. If I trade you for some French hostages it will keep more of your people and mine from dying. Are you going to help me do this?"

"Instead of *hanging?*" said Taza. He almost gave a tight smile. "Yes, I will help you make the trade. But we must hurry if you want to bring these soldiers back unharmed. There are seasoned warriors out there who will carve out their eyes for killing our young braves." Even as he spoke he gave the banker and the other townsman a sharp stare as he turned unsteadily toward the open door.

"Santa Madre!" Flippoza said under his breath as Sam turned with his free hand on Taza's shoulder, steadying him.

At the horses, Sam offered Taza help getting up into his old wooden-framed McClellan saddle. But the young warrior ignored the offer and struggled upward with a dark look shadowing his brow. Sam knew this young man would not show pain if it killed him. This looked like a good day for that sort of toughness, he thought. Stepping up atop Black Pot he laid his rifle across his lap. He made sure Taza saw him pull a soiled white handkerchief from his hip pocket and start tying it to his rifle barrel.

"Will these warriors recognize a flag of truce?" he asked.

"Not if you are carrying it," Taza said. They will shoot you and drag you and your flag of truce over the rocks." He reached over and snatched the handkerchief from Sam and held it in a fist. "When they see me carry it, they will know it's not some white man's trick."

"Then you carry it," Sam said, getting the response he'd hoped for. "Keep it out of sight until we get out of town."

The two turned their horses to a small back street leading out of town. When they passed small houses and businesses and started onto the flatlands, Doyle and Peto and the French cavalry stared out at them.

"Who *is this?*" asked the mounted French lieutenant who had led his cavalry troops to Esplanade. He fumbled for a pair of small binoculars hanging from his saddle horn.

"That's the Arizona Ranger I was telling you about," said Doyle. "He's with us." He and Peto stood among the troops who were still on horseback, milling around the town square.

"Oh?" said the lieutenant, sounding skeptical, hurriedly wiping dust from his binoculars. "And what is he doing with an Indian at his side?"

"That's his trail scout," Doyle lied hurriedly. "He likely is going out to try to talk to the Apache."

"Talk to them?" said the lieutenant. "All they understand is the taste of gunpowder and cold steel!" He finally raised his binoculars to his eyes and looked back for the ranger and the Indian.

"I agree with you, of course, Lieutenant!" said Doyle. "But this ranger seems to have a knack for keeping down trouble—"

A Ranger's Trail

"What trouble?" the lieutenant asked, cutting him off. He jerked his binoculars down from his face, leaving two half moons of brown dust under his eyes. "It appears to me we have squashed any trouble these heathens have wrought upon us."

Peto had to stifle a laugh and look away from the lieutenant.

"Why is this Mexican laughing?" the lieutenant asked Doyle. "Did I say something amusing?"

"No, Lieutenant," Doyle said, looking down to keep from seeing the lieutenant's half-circled eyes. "I'm afraid *mi amigo* here is, as you French would say, *simple d'esprit*. But he is a good *vaquero*."

"A simple-minded *vaquero* ...." The lieutenant stared at the two, unsure if what Doyle said was the truth.

"Rider coming, Lieutenant," a trooper called out, breaking the tight silence. He stood in his stirrups, looking out at an exhausted horse struggling across the sand flats. The bloody trail scout on the horse's back wobbled in his saddle like a man half-dead.

"One rider?" the lieutenant shouted in English, looking out at the buckskin clad trail scout, a French-Cheyenne of desert ancestry, bloody and dust-covered, riding hatless in the scalding sunlight. "What the hades is this? Where's the rest of the cleanup patrol!"

"Here we go, Peto ...," Doyle whispered under his breath in dark anticipation of the bad news they were about to hear.

"They are prisoners of the Apache, Lieutenant," the trail scout called out as he managed to rein his horse to a halt facing the officer. Still catching his breath, he added, "They only released me to bring you the news. There's an Apache prisoner here. They want him back. They'll trade the soldiers for him."

Doyle and Peto gave each other a knowing look as they listened. Doyle leaned slightly and said to Peto in a lowered tone, "The ranger has a way of staying on top of things, eh?"

"Sí, he does," Peto replied.

When the ranger and Taza topped the crest of the hill and started down to where the French soldiers had ridden into a crushing ambush, warriors began gathering on either side of them, escorting them, but keeping a respectful space from them. Even the riders from far parts of Mexico and the lands south were told it was the grandson of Chief Itza-Chu (Great Hawk) riding in beside a white man, a symbol of truce hanging from his rifle barrel in a warm stir of air.

Sam noted that the young warrior was holding up well for a man who had lost so much blood and had so little time for his body to restore itself. He kept Black Pot sidled close to Taza in case he needed to reach out and steady him in his saddle. Ahead of them the warrior Naiche sat atop his horse with a dozen armed warriors flanking him. Thirty yards to the right a group of captured French cavalrymen sat hatless, bootless and blood-stained in the blazing sun. They watched intently as Sam and the young warrior rode in and stopped a few feet away from Naiche.

"You carry the white man's banner of surrender, for them?" Naiche said in a tone of contempt.

"No," said Taza. "I carry nothing for the white man." He moved his rifle barrel back and forth slowly with the ragged soiled cloth hanging from its tip. "I carry this as a sign of truce, in order to talk about what is needed to stop bloodshed."

Sam watched and listened closely, realizing that Naiche was no longer red-eyed drunk and swaying in his saddle. Holding hostages must have given him a sense of power that Sam had not seen during their last encounter.

"I take hostages in order to trade them for you, Taza," Naiche said.

"I was not a prisoner," said Taza. "You knew I came here to see the healing woman."

"There were no soldiers when you came here," said Naiche. "They would have held you prisoner when they found out who you are."

Taza nodded toward the ranger and said, "This man told no one who I am. When he saw I'm strong enough to ride, he came to me with horses and we left before the French knew who I am ... so I am free."

Naiche fell silent for a moment, considering his position. Then a faint sliver of a smile creased his lips.

"This is good," he said. "You are free. We will kill the soldiers and ride away." He turned a strong look at the warriors gathered around him. They nodded in agreement.

"No!" Taza called out loud enough to get the warriors' attention. They fell silent and turned forward facing him. "I rode with this man to have the soldiers set free." He turned his attention from Naiche to the warriors, looking at each of them in turn as he ordered, "Gather their horses and let them go."

Only a few warriors looked to Naiche for direction. Most of them turned away to go about doing Taza's bidding.

For a moment, Naiche looked stunned by Taza taking over his command of the warriors. But there was little he could say that wouldn't put him in a bad light to Great Hawk and the desert Apache leaders. He softened his tone and tried another approach. He gestured toward Esplanade.

"Taza, we can kill everyone there and burn their bones to ashes before this day is gone. This is the kind of victory we can show the tribes south of here when we go to make alliances with them. They will see we are strong."

"You are wrong, Naiche," said Taza. "The tribes south of the desert will see we are coming to them with both the Mexican army and the French army on our trail. They won't become our friends ... they will see we are bringing war into their midst." He looked around again at the few remaining warriors siding with Naiche. "When we have gathered all of our desert warriors, you will take this matter to my grandfather's lodge and tell him you did not agree with me ... but you did obey me."

The warriors understood. Without another word, they turned their horse and rode off to gather French soldiers' horses. Seeing the flat, exhausted expression come over Taza's face, Sam took the canteen hanging from Black Pot's saddle horn, uncapped it and handed it over to him.

With effort, Taza took a sip and handed the canteen back to him. As Sam capped it, he looked off into the direction where he'd last seen the woman ridding.

Taza said in a flat tone, "I see on your face, you must now follow the woman and claim her for yourself."

Claim her for himself ...?

"No, Taza," he said. "I'll be doing my job, following her." He wasn't about to reveal anything about the woman, who she was, where she was going, or why he was following her.

"Go now," Taza said. Warriors will take the soldiers closer to town and let them go." He looked at the ranger and saw his hand had already taking up the slack in the big stallion's reins, ready to ride away toward the desert floor. "Ranger," he said. "It can take us days to round up all of our people. Until we do, watch all the signs."

"Obliged, Taza. I always do," Sam said. He touched his fingertips to the brim of his sombrero, turned Black Pot and rode away.

CHAPTER 12

Near dawn they had arrived at the hillcrest where they'd hidden their gold. The attack had swept forward like a black cloud up along the line of hills running through the burnt section of Esplanade. The fury came upon them so hard and sudden that Carver and his Wild Bunch had been caught off guard in spite of an armed guard posted at the cavern's hidden entrance. They'd been sitting, drinking good whiskey — passing the tall bottle carefully from hand to hand as if it were filled with liquid gold.

And now look at us ..., Carver thought to himself. He and his gang had spent the night running for their lives. The Apache had stayed back in the night and sprang out at random, like coyotes, the young warriors striking at Carver and his men with arrow and spear, then falling back and vanishing. True, Carver and his men had left a few dead Apache lying along their trail, yet every time they'd pulled the trigger, their shots had served to pinpoint them to the warriors who roamed and searched for them in the night.

Damned heathen Apaches ....

Carver craned upward in his stirrups, looking back through the pale grainy dawn with tired eyes. Around him his men gathered in close, also staring back along the narrow hill trail.

"I ain't heard nothing for a while, Max," said Sloane. "Think they've fallen back?"

"No," Carver said bluntly.

"Why not?" Sloane said, a bloody hand pressed to his side wound. His voice was weak, the voice of man dying but who had not yet admitted it to himself. He gave Carver a questioning look. "We've been running and fighting all the way from the burnt section—"

"I'll think they've pulled back when we get our gold and get a long ways out of here," Carver said, cutting him off. The men heard the impatience in their leader's voice.

"These horses are blown," Dog Fannen put in. "We're all as bloody as a hog slaughter." He glanced around at the others and added, "Except for you and me, that is."

"And me," said Jerome Gascoyne. "I'm still unscathed."

"Unscathed ...?" Fannen chuffed with contempt. "Hell, you ain't even one of us, Frenchy," he said sharply. "You're just a blockhead who threw in with us for one job, and one job only. The sooner you're gone the better—"

"Shut up, Dog," Carver said. "He fought for his share. That makes him *with us,* far as I'm concerned."

"Yeah ...?" said Fannen. "Far as I'm concerned I'm thinking had he been standing guard instead of Old Sid Tully, he would be laying back there with his throat cut and Sid would still be with us. *Alive!"* he emphasized, giving Gascoyne a menacing stare. The French captain stared right back. He'd done his part. He had money coming from setting up this job. Once he had it in hand, he was gone. Until then, he wasn't backing another inch from anybody, including the Apache.

"You're not even making sense, Dog," Carver said. "Old Sid is likely dead because he wasn't paying attention like he should have been." He swung down from his saddle. "But you're right about these horses. Let's walk them, rest them down while we find our hidden gold and hole up here."

Fannen chuffed in disagreement. "To hell with holing up," he grumbled. "Let's gather our gold while we can, and cut out." He gave Carver a guarded look between the two of them. These men were bleeding to death right before their eyes. The longer they waited, the less likely they were to ever see all the gold again. Fannen could not abide the thought of it.

"We'll hole up right here in the rocks for right now," Carver said, loud enough for the others to hear him.

"Stay ready," Dog Fannen cut in. "These heathens like to slip in among their foes and kill them without anybody hearing them. They did it to Tully, they did it to Porter. They'll do it to the rest of us."

Fannen stopped talking when he saw Carver's harsh stare.

"Dog's right," he said, giving Fannen some credence. "Keep watch." He looked from face to bloody face. "Attend to yourselves the best you can 'til one of us can get to you. We'll help you dig up your gold."

Help dig up their gold ...? The men looked at each other wary-eyed. Too tired and haggard to even grumble, the bloody outlaws swung down from their saddles around their leader. Dog Fannen gave them a harsh look that sent them walking their tired horses away along the rocky trail. As the men and horses shuffled far enough away and dissipated in among the rocks, Fannen sidled in close to Carver.

"You know these poor bastards won't make it out of here, Max," he whispered. "One more good hit from the Injuns, they're all dead. Why don't I get each one of them aside and put them out of their misery?"

Max shot him a cold hard stare.

"Wait, Max! I see what you're thinking," said Fannen, "But you're wrong. This ain't about the money, or cheating anybody. We wouldn't know where to look for their buried money anyway." He spoke quickly, fearful the look in Max Carver's eyes. "This is for their own damn good. You know what the Apache will do to them—"

"I'm going to act like I didn't hear any of this, Dog," said Carver shutting him up. "These men are our pals. We ride together and we stay together—die together if we have to." As he spoke his hand fell around the handle of his Colt. "We're all the Wild Bunch. I'll hear no more of this kind of talk."

The Gentleman Bandit ..., Fannen thought to himself.

Then, "All right, Max, take it easy," he said, backing off. "To tell the truth I'm glad to hear you feel this way. I hated thinking about doing it."

"Good," said Carver, "Now get it out of your of mouth and off your mind." He stepped away, over to where Seaway had managed to get down from his bloody saddle, but appeared to be unable to turn loose of his saddle horn and step away. "Take a hold of my hand, Seaway," he said to the wounded outlaw. Let's get you out of sight before Apache come calling."

"*Gentleman Bandit*, my aching ass," Fannen whispered under his breath, watching with displeasure. He watched as Carver and the wounded Seaway walked away into the shadowy dawn among a bed of large rocks.

"I'm not ... hurting anymore, Max," Seaway said as Carver lowered him carefully to the ground. "I believe I've run out my string …."

"Don't talk like that, Seaway," Carver said. "Lay still here awhile, get your strength up. Then we've got to keep moving."

"Don't leave here 'til I'm done for," Seaway said. He tried to clutch Carver's arm, but his strength was spent. His bloody hand fell to his chest. "I've seen what ... these heathens will do to a living man."

"Nobody's leaving you, Seaway," Carver said. "If you knew me better, you'd know that I don't leave a man behind."

"The *Gentleman Bandit ...,*" Seaway rasped. "I've heard that about you," he said in a waning voice. "I wish I had … known you better …."

"Lay still," Carver said. He raised the corner of the bandanna circling the dying man's neck and swabbed his bloody face with it.

"There's things I need to say, Carver, I'm a ... Pinkerton …." said Seaway.

A Pinkerton ... of all damned things.

"Just lay still," Carver replied in a soothing voice. "It doesn't matter now." He watched Seaway's eyes go blank.

From a few yards away, Fannen said in a harsh whisper, "You coming out Max? We've got other wounded men here."

"I'm coming," said Carver. A couple of minutes passed. Fannen started to say something more in his guarded tone, but before he could he saw Carver move into sight out of the rocks and walk toward him, wiping his hands on Seaway's bloody bandanna.

"How's he doing?" Fannen asked. As he spoke he looked all around at the morning light spreading more clearly across the purple-streaked sky and the shadowy desert floor below.

"He's dead," Carver said gravely.

"Bled out, did he?" Fannen asked.

"Yep, the best I can make it," said Carver. "Anyway, he's dead." He took his horse's reins and the reins to Seaway's horse. "I said some words over him," he added. He pulled both horses over beside him.

Fannen stood in silence looking at him curiously.

Said words over him ...? Dog almost chuckled in disbelief. But he caught himself, seeing Carver was stone serious.

"Did you sure enough?" he asked.

Carver only gave him a look. He reached up and rubbed each horse on its muzzle, looking Seaway's horse over good.

"How well did you know Seaway?" he asked Fannen.

"I didn't know him," Fannen said with a shrug. "He showed up a few months ago at Hole-In-the-Wall. Old Sully and Dub Porter both vouched for him. Why? Is something wrong?"

"What's wrong is *he's dead,*" said Carver. He started leading the two horses along the narrow trail where the men had spread out and taken position in the rocks. "The rest is going to be dead, too, if we don't get out of here and get help for them." Walking forward with the horses he spoke in a low tone to the men in the rocks. "It's just Fannen and me, coming in," he said. "Don't be shooting at us. We need to see what shape everybody's in."

"Bad shape," a raspy voice replied among the rocks.

A moment passed as the two led their horses toward the raspy voice.

"At least Seaway's got no gold buried," Fannen said quietly.

"Forget the gold," Carver said in disgust. "I hate losing a man."

"I know you do, Max," said Fannen. "I'm just saying, losing him didn't cost us nothing, is all. I hate thinking of gold lying buried up there and never being seen again."

"We're headed there to get the gold just as soon as the horses are rested and everybody's able to ride," Carver countered.

"We better not wait long,' said Fannen. "These boys are barely hanging on as it is."

"Our job is to keep them alive, at *all costs*, Dog!" said Carver, his voice turning tense.

"Take it easy, Max," said Fannen. "I've got us covered. If they can be saved, we'll save them." They led the horses on toward the sound of the injured voice in the rocks.

Fannen stepped over closer to the voice, recognizing it as Elvin Sloane's.

"It's me, *Dog*, coming in, Sloane," he said. "Don't you go shooting at me, you hear?"

"I'll take care of him, Max," Fannen said, looking at Carver with a grave expression. He lowered his voice. "He was looking bad."

"Do the best you can for him," Carver said. "I'll go to the next one."

"Keep an eye on the desert for Injuns," Dog said.

Carver gave him a cold stare and didn't reply.

Knowing he'd just said the wrong thing to the gang's leader, Fannen walked away quick enough to put off any unfavorable words between himself and Carver. Stepping into the rock shadows, he followed the trail of large, dried, blood drops. At a rock where he saw a bloody handprint he stopped and called out in a lowered tone.

"I know you're hurt bad, boyo," he said. Don't forget it's me here and start shooting."

Sloane's weakened voice replied, "I know ... it's you. Dog. I hope you've brought me ... some water."

Fannen touched his fingertips to the canteen hanging by a strap around his shoulder.

"I've brung you some, boyo," he said. "Ole Dog never forgets a pard."

"Especially one ... with gold buried nearby?" Sloane questioned, letting his suspicion be known.

"You're talking out of your head, boyo," said Fannen, stepping into sight among the rock shadows. "So I'm not going to take offense. I'm going to have you tell me where your gold is buried." He shook the canteen a little and added with a friendly grin, "Then you can drink your fill, and put fresh bandaging on your wounds and go scratch it up like a couple of groundhogs!" He ended his words in a slight chuckle. "What say you, boyo?"

"No way ... in hell, Dog," the younger outlaw said in a broken voice. "Why would I tell you ... when I can show you?"

In one quick step, Fannen sprang forward and clamped his boot down on the blood-smeared pistol lying in the dirt in Sloane's hand.

"I figured you'd be pig-headed about this, boyo," he said. He stooped and took the pistol from Sloane's hand. Straightening enough to move the canteen a little and draw a long knife from its sheath in his belt, he stared back down at Sloane.

"Here's the truth," said Fannen, knife in hand. "You're dying." He shrugged. "I'm taking you to the gold, but not before you tell me where it's at, just in case you don't make it there. I can't be wasting my time."

Sloane reached out a weak hand toward the canteen. But Fannen pulled it back.

"Hunh-uh, boyo," he said. "Not until I hear what I came here to hear."

Sloane dropped his weak hand to the ground beside him.

"Go ... to hell," he said. He kept a stare fixed on Fannen, not seeming to care about the knife in his hand. "Start cutting," he said.

Fannen returned the stare. It was the stare of man bluffing at poker. *But why now? Why here?* Fannen knew the young man would give it up before he finished carving on him. But as the thought ran through his mind, a realization came to the old outlaw like a light coming on in his mind. He grinned and stepped forward again. He uncapped the canteen and set it aside against a rock four feet away. "We both know where the money is, boyo," he said. "It's underneath you. Now roll off of it and get yourself some water, before I change my mind and cut your heart out anyway."

"You're crazy, Dog!" said Sloane. But Fannen saw him try to tighten up in place.

"Have it your way," Fannen said. He laid the sharp edge of the knife along Sloan's hairline. "I'll keep the water for myself."

"Wait!" Sloane jerked his head back away from the knife edge. Fannen only watched as he rolled over toward the canteen, reached his bloody hands out and grasped it. Fannen helped him raise the canteen to his lips with a slight smile. He eyed the freshly turned earth around the bottom edge of the rock Sloane had been leaning against.

"And there we are," Fannen said with a dark chuckle, shoveling out loose dirt with his cupped hand. Beside him Sloane strangled on a gulp of tepid water. "Take it easy, boyo," he said. "The water is all yours. Don't drink too fast."

Sloane looked around at him gratefully, even as Fannen began pulling the dirt-covered bag of gold out from under the rock.

Fannen opened a bag, scooped his hand inside and let

coins fall through his fingers. Sloane, with his thirst sated, looked around above the canteen at Fannen.

"Okay, Dog, I'm finished drinking," he said, his voice sounding a little stronger. "There's the gold. Help me take on … some fresh bandages and let's get up out of here."

A sharp gleam sparkled in the old man's eyes. He held back a gust of dark laughter.

"Boyo," he said, quietly, almost sympathetically. "How big a fool would I be to do all that?"

Captain Jerome Gascoyne spotted the body lying draped across a half-sunken boulder in the hot sun, shirtless, hatless and bootless. A spear stood slantwise from the bare back in a dark pool of blood, swaying on a hot breeze like a banner claiming some grizzly new territory. Max Carver and Fannen had agreed that the Apache would infiltrate their midst and strike them in silence. He hadn't believed it at first. He thought they'd said it to keep the wounded group pulling together, waiting for Carver and Fannen to tell them their next move, but here before him lay proof they were right. A blood flow had dried glistening black down the side of the rock where the body lay.

Carver had been right. So what …? Gascoyne stayed crouched in the rocks and looked all around, slyly, a big Remington pistol in hand. It changed nothing for him, Gascoyne thought. He was the *Frenchy—the outsider*. All right, he would rely on none of them. He was within reaching the spot a hundred yards ahead where he'd buried his gold. It was up to him to get it and go. He owed the Wild Bunch nothing. They would feed him to the Apache if it came down to choosing one of them, or himself. So be it, *mes amis,* he said to himself.

He wasn't going to sit here and wait for either Carver to lead him, or the Apache to kill him, the way these wounded men were doing. This was a time to think and act boldly. He had not served as an officer in one of the greatest armies on earth by being timid. *Rise up, Capitain*, he ordered himself, His chin tightened with pride. While he had stayed low in the rocks, his horse had stood exposed to any spears or arrows waiting on the hillside. *En enfer avec eux...*, he told himself. He gave a sharp defiant smile. *Yes, to hell with them ...*, he repeated to himself in English, as if the Wild Bunch might hear his thoughts and at last see the kind of man he was.

He stood up, lifting the reins to his tired horse. He'd started to lead the animal forward when a long faint moan rose from the body stretched out on the rock twenty feet away. Startled, he swung the Remington toward the body, then caught himself, collected himself and led the horse forward, looking back and forth among the rocks.

When he reached the sunken boulder and stepped up around on the short side where he stood almost face to the face with Fedder Dockery.

"Help me ...," Dockery rasped, his eyes glazed, his lips swollen and cracked. The same dark wide ribbon of blood ran down this upper side of the boulder and gathered in the dirt at Cascoyne's boots. Cascoyne's tired horse stood looking on through caged eyes.

"Yes, water," Gascoyne said almost in a whisper. He started to turn to the horse for the canteen hanging from its saddle horn. But Dockery's weak voice stopped him.

"No ...," he said. "Help me ...." His voice faded from his cracked lips.

Gascoyne looked at him, doubting the man had any idea who he was, or what he might do for him. He saw where he had been scalped, but the scalp was still there, still attached to the back on his head. Some cruel Apache joke, he decided. Then he noted Dockery's bloody eyes were open in a strange unnatural manner, and it came to him the man's upper eyelids had been sliced away.

"Help ...," Dockery managed to rasp again.

This time Gascoyne understood. He dropped the horse's reins and climbed up onto the boulder. He realized that this man had been speared after his shirt and jacket were removed.

A Ranger's Trail

He saw no sign of Dockery struggling to get a hold of the spear, or cover his eyes or scalp. The spear had been stuck there with precision, its wielder know exactly how and where to place the steel tip, not to kill right away, but to leave the man completely paralyzed while the sun cooked him alive.

Gascoyne dared not question himself. He stood over Dockery, shoved the Remington down into his waist and wrapped both hands tight around the spear's shaft. He jerked the spear up fast, hoping to minimize the man's suffering. Yet, surprisingly, there was no response, no cry of pain. The only sound from Dockery was a slight exhale of breath. *The breath of a dying man ....*

Cascoyne raised the bloody spear tip three feet up from the spot where he knew a man's heart lay beating in his chest. Quickly, and with no show of mercy, he stabbed the spearhead down through soft and hard matter alike and felt it strike and scrape against the hard boulder Dockery's body lay on.

All right. Done .... He left the spear standing in Dockery's back. Without looking down at the dead man, he stepped off the side of the boulder onto his horse's back and nudged it away from the grisly scene. If there were Apache eyes watching him, he didn't care. To hell with the Apache and everybody else, the Wild Bunch included. He was digging up his share of the gold and getting out of here. Even as he considered his next moves, he looked all around at the rugged hillside, playing with the question of where the other outlaws might have buried their shares.

He smiled to himself as he reined his horse through low rocks and patches of gravel, hot sand, and barrel cactus. Only a fool would leave here without first searching the ground for what might appear to be a good hiding spot—some recently overturned dirt, or rock, or some careless scraping of a blade or of gloved fingers. He and his tired horse meandered about on the scorching hillside, keeping close watch for any of Carver's men, while the sun bore down as if to deliberately kill him.

CHAPTER 13

The ranger had followed the blue roan's unusual splayed hoofprint through dust and brush, staying back just far enough to not confirm the woman's suspicions if she thought he might be following her. *If that made sense ...,* he reminded himself with a faint and dusty smile. He'd followed her throughout the night in this same manner. Her trail skills were not to be underestimated—nor was anything else about her. Twice in the night he had found signs of her turning around wide and backtracking herself. Luckily he'd stayed just far enough away that it didn't matter. She would lead him to the Wild Bunch, to their leader, Max Carver.

And that's what matters..., he reminded himself. He watered Black Pot at the stone-lined water reservoir outside the ruins of the old Spanish fort where she and the blue roan's tracks led him. And he rode on.

He was relieved to see the blue roan's tracks turn diagonally upward off the desert flats into the hill line above the burnt section of Esplanade. He knew she could handle herself, but the less she was seen the better, until word got around among the Apache that their raiding spree was over. Reining Black Pot up onto the same thin trail she had taken, he was not surprised to see how far she'd first ridden past the burnt section, and he was even less surprised when her tracks turned back. She'd taken a long way around and past the place she was headed—an old trail ploy used to shake any followers off of her backtrail.

He wondered for a moment if Ruthless Ruby Teal, now

reclaiming her real name, *Julie Wilder,* had noticed the telltale sign the blue roan's hoof left in the dirt. Yet, as trail savvy as he knew her to be, Sam reminded himself that there were some details so small that only the most wily and wary tracker would see it—*and lawmen, of course,* men whose lives depended on the slightest revelation waiting around the next turn in the trail. And that included the most dangerous of outlaws used to staying ahead of a hangman's rope or a bounty killer's gun, he allowed, thinking about it.

Wily? Wary...? He didn't think of himself as being either, but if his life depended on a slim unnoticeable eighth of an inch offset in a horse's hoof, so be it.

But he didn't see Julie Wilder as being that kind of person. Going from Ruthless Ruby back to her real name revealed things about her. She was not used to hard life-or-death tracking. Maybe Ruthless Ruby would have been, given time. But not Julie Wilder. *Anyway,* he thought, *if she did know about the roan's hoof, she would not have ridden him.* She would have known Sam was on her trail, even now. He looked up the hill line and all around.

She didn't know, he decided. Her *signs* didn't tell him she knew. *So there* .... He nudged Black Pot on up the rocky trail.

Moments later, atop the thin path where a wider trail reached back into Esplanade's burnt section, Sam spotted a dead Apache lying sprawled along an edge of rock. He stopped Black Pot and stepped down from his saddle with caution, rifle ready in hand. Looking all around, he saw an Indian pony standing a few yards farther up the trail picking at a stand of wild grass.

When he stepped over to the body and looked closely he saw the dark imprints of a bolo strap that had circled the warrior's neck with pressure and tightened itself deep. Sam nodded and dropped Black Pot's reins and dragged the body out of sight. Then he led the stallion to where the hard-boned desert pony stood grazing leisurely.

"Sorry to cut your meal short," he said quietly. "You'll do better down out of these rocks—less wolves," he added.

He picked up the single leather rein and led the pony and Black Pot onto the trail. He stooped and inspected the hoof marks on the dirt, finding the mark of a thin worn-out horseshoe. As he looked, the pony stuck its muzzle down close to his neck and looked all around in the dirt, being nosy.

"Does this belong to you?" Sam asked, nodding at the print in the dirt as if the pony knew what he was saying. He checked the pony, and found three unshod hooves and one front hoof wearing a thin hand-formed shoe. "Yep, it's yours." He rubbed the horse's nose. "By the time this shoe came off you'd be horse stew somewhere." The pony raised its head and looked at Black Pot and blew out a strong breath.

Black Pot returned the strong breath and shook out his mane.

"You two try to get along," Sam said. He drew a big knife from its sheath behind his gun belt and turned back to the pony. "Let's get rid of this loose shoe before it causes you trouble down the trail."

He led both horses into the hidden opening some of the Wild Bunch had created in the hill of junk and refuse. A few yards inside, he spotted a dim flicker of lantern light glowing in the darkness ahead. Before the light from the front opening played out, he stopped and stooped down and studied the ground which lay battered by horses' hooves. Dark dried blood lay in splotches among hooves leading out of the hillside and onto the trail. In the gang's hurry they had left the entrance exposed. In the tracks on the ground Sam saw that less of the horses were shod, meaning the Apache had Max Carver and his men greatly outnumbered.

He stood and ventured farther back deeper into the waning light leading both horses into the darkening hillside.

Moving with caution, he didn't stop again until the flickering glow of the lantern reached him and cast a shadow on his boots. When he did stop he stood at the opening of a large clearing filled with standing rock and an empty rope line along the wall above a scattering of dried horse droppings. Here was the hideout he'd wanted to uncover. In spite of the woman refusing to tell him where to find it, she had mistakenly lead him to it on the back of a headstrong blue roan with an offset hoof. *Good enough ....*

He looked all around the shadowy cave hideout, the lantern flickering on walls splattered with blood, on an overturned table filled with arrows and bullet holes, on overturned chairs. The value and secrecy of this place had dropped to zero when the Apache came calling. In the shadows he looked off in the direction the woman and the blue roan had taken out away from here. He reminded himself that the roan's tracks were atop both the shod and unshod horses leading out along the hill trail. *Good for you, Julie Wilder*, he thought with a strange sense of relief. If she could stay behind the gang and he'd stay behind her, this could all be over soon. He estimated that at best she had no more than an hour—an hour and half lead on him. On Black Pot he could close that lead pretty quick.

He turned to lead the horses back out of the cavern and get on the trail. But he stopped short and looked at the double barrels of the scattergun pointed at him less then fifteen feet away. The ranger didn't make an instant move for his gun owing to a young woman standing at the man's side with both hands clutching her large stomach.

"One wrong move and I'll k-kill you. Mister!" the young man said in a trembling voice.

"Tommy don't want to shoot you!" the young woman said, her labored voice equally trembling in fear. "But he will—!"

"Shut up, Millie, *please!*" the young man shouted at her. "I've got him covered! Let me handle this!"

Sam stood silent and still. *Tommy, huh?* He looked them up and down. Whoever these two were, he was certain they weren't a part of the Wild Bunch. He saw desperation in their eyes, heard it in their voices.

"Easy with that scattergun, Tommy," he said to the nervous young man. He held his rifle out arm's length to his side as he spoke. "Whatever's going on here, I don't think anybody needs to get shot." He motioned his face around the cavern. "There's been plenty of killing here—"

"You shut up too!" the young man snapped at him. "Now drop the rifle right now!"

"I'm going to lay it down real slow, Tommy," Sam responded in a calm voice. He stooped slowly, laid the rifle at his feet and straightened, the horses' reins still in hand. "I'm a lawman from Arizona, here on business, Tommy."

"A *lawman?* Oh, Jesus, that's just my luck!" the young man sounded on the verge of tears.

"Tell me what's wrong, Tommy. Maybe I can help." As Sam spoke he nodded toward the young woman. "Looks like she's about to give birth any minute. Am I right?"

The young man let out a tight breath and started to give Sam a civil answer. But he caught himself. His grip stiffened on the shotgun and he shouted angrily, "It's none your damn business what she is or ain't about to do, Lawman!"

"Tommy," the girl said in a pained voice, "he's only trying to help us!" Her hands held firm around her huge round belly. Sam noted her breath was labored and sharp.

"We don't need his help, Millie!" the young man said, giving Sam a harsh stare. "All we need is them horses—and we're taking them." He jiggled the shotgun nervously at Sam and demanded, "Drop those reins, Lawman and step back out of our way! I won't ask you again!"

"I can't do that, Tommy," Sam replied in calm voice. "She's in no shape to be on horseback. Even if she was, leaving here right now will put you both right in the hands of any Apache still wandering around out there." He narrowed his gaze. "Do you have any idea what they will do to this woman, or to you, too, for that matter?"

A Ranger's Trail

"Tommy! Tommy—!" the woman said in a tone of panic.

"Shut up, Millie!" the rattled young man shouted. "Can't you see he's only trying to scare us?" His jaw tightened toward Sam. "Lawman, this scattergun will cut you in half—"

"No, Tommy, *listen to me!*" the young woman shrieked.

"I'm through listening," the young man said.

"Tommy! I've peed all over my feet!" the woman said in desperation.

Tommy glanced at her bare feet, glistening wet, planted in a wide puddle of water, its source still streaming down her legs.

"My God Millie," Tommy said. "Couldn't you wait—?"

"She hasn't peed herself," Sam interjected, keeping calm. "Her water has broken."

"Hunh?" Tommy said in a dumb voice. The shotgun slumped in his hands.

"It's what happens right before a baby is born, Tommy," the ranger said. He looked at Millie. "Your baby is on its way, Miss."

"He's lying, Millie!" the frightened young man said.

"No, he's not, Tommie," the terrified girl remarked. "I heard about it. It's true!"

"Here's something else that's true," Sam put in, "you need to get off your feet and get ready." He looked from her tired pained face to the young man's. "And you best get ready to deliver this baby."

The young man turned stark white. "I—I can't do that," he said. "I've never done nothing like that—"

The shotgun slumped more. "Then get out of the way," Sam said, seeing the woman was on the verge of having the baby standing up. He stepped forward and pushed the shotgun to the side and walked past Tommy to the woman. He cradled her thin forearm and turned her toward a ragged blanket lying on the dusty floor. "Go get the lantern and bring it over here," he ordered Tommy as he led the young woman over to the blanket and helped her lie down, "and turn the wick up. We're going to need more light."

"Is this—Is this going to hurt awfully bad?" the woman asked Sam in a pained and shaky voice.

"I expect it is, Millie," Sam replied in calm voice, "But remember, you're not the first woman to ever go through it, and you won't be the last. Tommy and I will both be right here with you the whole time."

"What if you hadn't ..." she paused, letting her words trail, then swallowed hard and started again. "What if ... you hadn't come by when you did?" she said with slight gasp of pain. "I don't know what we'd have done."

Sam stooped down beside her and helped her lean back against an upthrust of rock. He began rolling up his shirt sleeves.

"Don't think about *what if,*" he said kindly. "Just think about how real soon you'll be holding your new baby on your lap." He looked around as the young man and the lantern light drew closer. Tommy stopped and kneeled down beside him and raised the wick; light grew and expanded about the small cave.

"Why ain't she had it already?" he asked Sam with concern in his eyes and voice.

Sam just looked at him. Lantern light flickered on the blood-stained walls and rock surrounding the three of them.

"We've got a little ways to go, Tommy," he said. "Take her hand. Let her squeeze your hand as hard as she has to."

The young man watched, appearing horrified as the ranger unbuttoned the wet dress and spread it open in order to pull it up past her waist.

In anticipation of what was about to happen, Tommy said, "I hope I don't throw up."

"You won't," Sam said flatly.

"How do you know I won't?" Tommy said.

"Because I'm telling you not to, Tommy," Sam replied in

A Ranger's Trail

a resolved tone of voice.

An hour later, after assisting the woman and her nervous young husband in birth of a baby girl, Sam attended to the child's birth cord and made sure both woman and child were doing well. Then, with the release of a deep breath he stood up and poured water over his hands from his canteen and took a longer than usual drink and capped the canteen and laid it beside the woman as she dozed, nestling the baby in its ragged makeshift blanket. Picking up his sombrero, Sam put it on and stood up. He picked up Tommy's shotgun from where it lay on the ground, clamped it under his arm and walked over to Black Pot and the Indian pony.

"Where you going?" Tommy blurted out, eying his shotgun under the ranger's arm, the ranger still carrying his rifle in hand.

"Watch about your family," Sam replied over his shoulder.

Family—? It took Tommy a second to understand. He glanced all around, lost-like, until his eyes rested on the tiny bundle in the crook of Millie's arm.

"Oh, I get it," Tommy said. He sounded a little relieved, but still eyed his shotgun in the ranger's hand as the ranger took his battered telescope from Black Pot's saddlebag.

"I'm going out front and look around," Sam offered as he walked away toward the front of the cavern.

"I—I didn't get sick, Ranger," Tommy called out from the flicker of lantern light.

"Good." Sam nodded and walked away down the stone corridor toward the slant of sunlight at the entrance.

When he arrived at the entrance, he stood to one side and let his eyes adjust to the sun glare before stepping out with caution. Once out, he immediately took cover in the shadow of a nearby long abandoned mule cart lying overturned in the rocks and debris. Squinting, he pushed his sombrero back and looked up at the sun just long enough to gauge its position.

Seemed like all day ..., he told himself, realizing the

whole birthing hadn't taken over an hour—an hour and a half at most. Still, it had put more distance between himself and the woman. He would have to push hard just to get her back in sight, let alone catch up to her. He adjusted his sombrero atop his head, raised his telescope and looked all around the hills ahead of him and the desert floor below. Time had moved over onto her side, he told himself, scouring with little hope for any sign of her. But he'd catch up ... somehow.

Before lowering his telescope he did a double take as he caught sight of a Mexican army column snaking into sight on a trail running toward him no more than a hundred yards away. He thought of Selectman Doyle's words, *you'll know the Apache are gone when the Mexican Army ventures out.* As he considered Doyle's words, Sam broke open Tommy McCoy's shotgun, looked it over, then snapped it shut. Doyle had been right, Sam told himself. But at least the Mexican army showed up in time to help two travelers like Tommy and Millie McCoy. Sam let out a breath and leaned Tommy's shotgun against a rock and rolled down his shirt sleeves.

"Don't shoot, Ranger," Tommy called out from just inside the cavern entrance. "It's just me, Tommy."

"Come on out, Tommy," Sam said, his hand closed around his rifle in case the young man had any more treachery in mind.

Tommy stepped into sight, his battered hat in hand.

"I just come to say, Millie wants me to thank you for your help—and I do too," he added, looking embarrassed. "I feel plumb awful, what I did and all. I mean what I was going to do—take your horses, and so forth. I'll never do nothing like that again."

Sam didn't reply. Instead, he picked up Tommy's shotgun and pitched it to him. Catching it in surprise, Tommy gave him a puzzled look, as if in disbelief.

"It's not loaded, Ranger," he confessed. As he spoke he broke open the shotgun as proof. "See ...?"

"I would not have given you a loaded scattergun, Tommy," Sam said with a level gaze. "You still need a horse though, to get Millie and the baby somewhere safe."

"But I wasn't going to try to take yours," Tommy said, "Not after all you've done—"

"How'd you know about this place?" Sam asked, cutting him off.

"What place?" Tommy looked all around.

Sam took a patient breath.

"This place." He nodded at the cavern entrance. "How'd you know it was here?"

"We didn't," Tommy said. "We just come running by here on foot after our mule fell dead under us. Apache kilt our other mule and took our wagon down on the flats. They were behind us."

Sam listened closely for any attempt at deception. He heard none.

"We hid in the rocks when we heard riders coming up the trail. They was white men running for their lives, Apache right behind them. The warriors followed the white men right into the hillside—it was plumb spooky, seeing men and horses disappear into the hillside!" He paused then said, "We laid low until they all come riding and shooting back out of there—white men still in front, Apache still chasing them." He shook his head. "We was desperate, Ranger."

"Desperate enough to kill me for my horses," Sam commented flatly.

"I would not have shot you, Ranger, as you know." He nodded at the unloaded shotgun and added, "Even if it had been loaded."

"I believe you, Tommy," Sam said. The sound of the Mexican army column's horses resounded along the rocky trail, drawing closer.

"You do?" Tommy looked surprised.

Instead of replying, Sam said, "They will likely escort

you and Millie and the baby to safety."

"Or, we could ride with you?" Tommy put in.

"I can't take you, Tommy," Sam said. "But I've got some shotgun loads for you, and I'm giving you the little desert barb." He leaned toward the cave opening and let a sharp whistle, summoning Black Pot. In a moment the big stallion clopped into sight, the spotted barb a step behind him.

"I'm forever obliged, Ranger." Tommy hung his head in shamed for having tried to take the horses by force. "If ever I can—"

"Listen to me," Sam said, hearing the army drawing closer. "I'm telling these soldiers what happened here." He saw fear come into the young man's eyes. But Sam handed him the reins to the barb. As Tommy took the reins, Sam continued, "I found you and your wife hiding from the Apache here in this cave. You and I argued over the horses. Before anything was settled your wife started having the baby. We helped her through it." He paused, studying Tommy's eyes. "That's how I'm calling it. Anything you want to add?"

Tommy looked stunned for a second, considering it. It was all true, but the ranger had stripped it of any darker details. "No, I expect there's nothing more I can say—" He started to say more but Sam cut him off as the front two riders of the Mexican column appeared up around a rocky turn.

"They'll likely take you to Esplanade," Sam said, staring straight ahead at the soldiers as they wound into sight. "Bringing in travelers will make them look good—here, give me your hand," he added. As he spoke sidelong to Tommy he reached over and pressed three Mexican gold coins onto his outreached hand. "When you get there, ask for Selectman Doyle. Tell him I asked him to put you folks up for a few days. There's an old healing woman there. Get her to look at Millie and your baby."

Before Tommy could say anything, Sam stepped forward toward the arriving soldiers, his badge in full view, his rifle and Black Pot's reins hanging in his hand.

"*Hola,*" he called out to the arrived soldiers as the rest of the column came up two at a time into sight. They young soldiers looked surprised. One of them called out to the rest of the column riding up.

"*Hola, a ti, Señor. Quédate donde estás,*" a dusty young corporal demanded. He switched partly to English and said, "*Mi capitán* will wish to speak with you."

"*Sí,*" Sam agreed. Yes, he would stay right here. He wished to speak to the *capitán,* as well. He'd caught sight of a dust-covered Apache body lying across the back of a rugged little desert barb, painted up for battle, being led by the soldier riding nearest to the corporal. Sam's attention had riveted onto the two leather strips hanging from the dead Indian's neck. Two well-rounded rocks the size of a small fist hung from the dangling ends of the leather strips.

PART III

PART III

CHAPTER 14

Sam explained his and the couple's situation to a young Mexican Captain by the name of Rodrico Nunez. As Sam spoke, the captain eyed the debris-strewn surroundings with suspicion. His column had followed a random trail of dead Apache and lone horses since leaving the flatlands. He knew, as did most of the Mexican Army, that these rocky trails and cavernous hillsides were often found to be crawling with outlaws and renegades from both sides of the border. He listened closely while Sam finished telling him about the couple and how staying here with them had cost him precious time tracking down the very outlaws who had taken sanctuary here.

"I see," Captain Nunez said in good English. Finding no problem with the ranger's story, he let out a weary breath and looked Tommy up and down. He had motioned three of his men to dismount and look inside the cave for the woman. In a moment they came out with the woman, baby in her arms, seated on a folding field gurney they had carried in with them. The two carrying the gurney sat it down gently in the shade of the overturned mule cart.

"I hope you have learned a lesson about traveling here with Apache running rampant?" the captain said. Tommy started to speak, but not risking the young man possibly saying the wrong thing, Sam cut in, saying, "He will remember this from now on, *Capitan.*" He gave the officer a nod of respect and added, "I am much obliged for you escorting them out of here."

Again in good English, the captain said, "Our Mexican government is forever diligent in protecting all who are within our boundaries."

Sam knew better, but he let it pass. Gesturing his rifle toward the body lying over the desert barb, he asked, "What about this one?"

"This one ...?" the captain shrugged, with a slight grin. "He is dead as you can see. We take him with us to show the people in Esplanade that we know how to handle Apache marauders."

"Killed by a bolo?" Sam ventured, already certain of what had happened.

"Yes, by a bolo," the captain replied, not trying to take credit for the kill, "the most crude of all peasant weapons!" He leaned a little in his saddle down toward Sam and gave a bemused smile. "Killed by a squaw! A *woman!*" he said with further bemusement. "Is it not hard to believe?"

Sam gave a noncommittal nod. "Where's the woman now?" he asked.

Nunez gave a half shrug. "My forward scouts saw her kill this one from a higher trail. They rode down and surrounded her—pinned her down for over two hours." He let out a breath and grew more serious. "But these squaws, they are like snakes." He snaked his hand through the air. "She got away through a hail of bullets." He shook his head. "I don't blame my scouts. They are the best. This squaw was very wily. She had good fortune on her side."

Two hours ...

Sam only nodded in agreement and asked, "How long ago was this?"

The captain glanced up at the sun's position in the wavering hot sky.

"An hour, perhaps?" he said. He gestured toward the next hillside standing high beside them in the wavering hot sky. "What is your interest in this man-killing squaw, Ranger?"

Nunez asked, seeing Sam gather his stallion closer by a slight pull on his reins. "Is she with the outlaws you pursue?"

"I think this woman is following them too, *Capitan,*" Sam said, revealing no more than he had to. "With your permission, I'll take my leave now, and get on her trail."

Do so with my blessings, Ranger," the captain said, taking on the authority afforded to his rank. "If you come upon the squaw, I suggest you shoot to kill."

"Much obliged for your advice, *Capitan,*" Sam said, being courteous. He took a step back and turned to Black Pot who stood waiting. Stepping up into his saddle, he gazed over at Tommy and Millie McCoy and the bundle of ragged cloth gathered around their newly born baby. *You have ammunition and a good horse,* he said to himself. *And you're all three alive ...,* he added. Glancing around the harsh desolate rock hills and the wavering desert floor beneath them, he adjusted his rifle across his lap. *What more do you need ...?* He touched his heels to Black Pot's sides, putting the big stallion forward on the narrow trail. Behind him, he knew the soldiers and the McCoys stood watching, Tommy holding the barb's reins in his hand.

The ranger rode away, letting Black Pot loosen up until they reached a better length of trail along the high hillside. Then, with the slightest touch of his boot heels, he gave the big stallion full rein.

I'm asking a lot, big fella, he said to the stallion, in that silent voice held secret only between two warm-blooded mammals of joined purpose. *Give it all you've got ....* He felt Black Pot stretch out beneath him, fast and smooth in a rising swell of dust roiling sidelong on a hot upper wind.

This is how he would do it—how he would make up his lost time, he told himself. He and the stallion would work the trail at every turn, the way they had done numerous times past. When the rough terrain contracted and filled itself with broken boulder and loose gravel, he would slow to a stop, get down and hand lead the stallion if need be. Let the animal cool-out while he checked the ground, making certain he was still following the blue roan's hoofprints. When the trail opened and cleared before him again, he would take seat leaning low in the saddle and let Black Pot race flat out, belly down, and shoot the trail like polished lightning.

An hour later he spotted the first drops of blood on the rocky trail among the blue roan's tracks. So she or the roan, one, *was* wounded, he reasoned. From what the captain had told him, he was betting it was her. He couldn't see the roan making it this far through this rugged terrain with a bullet wound. The roan was a tough animal, though. He wouldn't exclude it.

And you are a tough woman, Julie Wilder, he said to himself, knowing how difficult it had to be if she took a wound and refused to allow the pain to show to any watching eyes. He considered it.

Let's get in close, he said to the big, sweaty stallion. He gathered the reins and checked the trail ahead of them. It wasn't the best, but it appeared to get worse as the trail continued upward.

Pour it on for us, Black Pot, he said silently to himself, as if the big stallion understood him. Through the ranger's hands and heels the stallion knew what was being asked, and he took on the trail as if with a vengeance.

They rode hard.

By late afternoon as shadows darkened in deep pockets along the hillsides he paused on an outer turn of a narrow trail and took a long scanning look through his telescope. "And there she is, Black Pot," he said with a breath of relief, watching the woman lean forward on the blue roan, the big roan digging with his hooves, taking in a rough upward trail. "How hard was that?" he said, patting a gloved hand on his stallion's sweat-streaked withers. He collapsed the telescope, shoved it into a pocket on his rifle boot, and rode on at an easier pace.

When the woman had felt the bullet hit her low in the back on her left side, she knew by the impact that it was bad. But she couldn't stop, wouldn't stop, nor was she about to let them see her falter in her saddle. If they knew she was wounded they would have pursued her like scavengers—she had no time to shake these soldiers off her trail. She was close to the hilltop where they had hid the gold. Too close to let the likes of the Mexican army stop her from getting there. Lying flat atop a wide stone ridge, she gazed almost straight down at the four Apache warriors on a cliff less than a hundred feet below as they passed a clay jug of whiskey back and forth.

Come on! Come on...! She coaxed in impatient silence, her left hand pressing a blood-soaked cloth against the front exit wound in her side.

She had been watching the drinking warriors below her for a half hour, knowing that from their position they had clear view of the trails leading to where she needed to go. The best route was a narrow game trail right across a ravine not far ahead of the warriors. But to take that trail meant she would be sky-lighted and in perfect view for a full half mile. Sky-lighting herself to these four seasoned-looking warriors, drunk or sober, would be suicidal. There was nothing she could do but wait and hope that they—

She stopped in midthought and jerked her head around toward the blue roan when she heard him let out a deep grumble and stomp a hoof on the stone shelf. She'd stood him fifteen feet away in the slim shade of a cut-wall, his reins tied to an overhanging juniper. She gripped her rifle tighter when she saw four Apache who'd appeared out of the rocks and made their way to the flat cliff. They stood encircling the roan, looking at her, bleary-eyed and unsteady on their feet. The roan lunged and bellowed and yanked at its tied reins, and reared as a warrior reached for its bridle.

Without wasting a second, she swung her rifle around at the Indians. But seeing her move, the warriors closed in around the roan, as if to use the animal for cover. It wouldn't work. She saw that the Apache were armed only with knives and steel hatchets—one carried a short lance. They saw her cock the rifle hammer, aimed, ready to fire. Her finger started to press back on the trigger. As much as she needed the roan, and as much as she'd come to like the animal—

Before she could pull the trigger, the big roan reared up again as the warrior tried to grab his bridle. This time the stallion, standing high on its rear hoofs, savagely pawing the air, let a long loud whinny and slung its head so hard, it yanked the overhanging scrub juniper from it rocky perch and slung it wildly back and forth, spewing dirt and gravel from its roots. The Apache backed away from the short spiky tree whistling back and forth at them. The roan half-circled steadily, advancing on them, forcing them back, kicking bucking, using the juniper like some thick deadly broom meant to sweep them off the ledge.

Oh yes, they're drunk! Julie noted, on her feet now and crouched, aiming the rifle, looking for a clear shot as the roan kept up its relentless attack on them. No Apache she'd ever known would have taken this treatment from a horse, even one swinging a tree in its reins. One of the Apache turned away from the wild unstoppable roan and ran toward Julie, hoping to somehow get past the rifle in her hands and take it from her before she took her shot. His plan fell short.

The rifle bucked in the woman's hands. She levered up a fresh round as the Indian slid backwards on the stone shelves, dead. She knew the shot would alert every Apache still prowling these desert hills, but it couldn't be helped. She took another close aim, but her shot was foiled as the roan's sharp, jagged juniper whistled in a wide circle, slapped the warrior hard across his face and sent him backwards dangerously close to the edge of the cliff. He sprang up and ran away through the rocks.

The remaining two drunken warriors tried to get back and away from the roan's wild if unwitting attack on them.

One managed to get out of the flying juniper's deadly range. The other Apache dropped and rolled in beneath the swinging tree, closer to the roan. As the roan slung its head one way, the Indian leaped up, clamped himself around the roan's head and neck and held on. The roan stopped suddenly and stood blowing and snorting. The juniper fell from his reins and rolled away. Seeing his fellow warrior get the stallion settled down, the other Indian faced Julie as she took aim on his chest. He walked toward her, knife in hand, determined, ready to die. She knew she had to kill him with one shot. Wounded, he would still be upon her and take her down even as he bled to death.

She held her ground; her finger pressed the trigger. Yet again the blue roan injected himself back into the melee. The big stallion found his second wind and blew up in rage, like an ignited powder charge. He slung the warrior viscously from his neck and lunged forward toward the other Indian just as Julie made her shot. She saw the man and his knife stalking toward her; and she saw the roan peripherally as it made a high leap upwards, half-turning on its front hoofs, balled and ready as it touched down and made a hard full-bodied kick with both rear hooves.

Julie's shot may have met its mark, she didn't know. The roan's hooves shot out, straight yet coming up high, catching the man full force on the side of his head as Julie's shot exploded. Julie saw the Indian sweep sideways from in front of her, his neck twisted at an odd angle the split-second the roan's hooves raised him and launched him out over the cliff's edge. The man flew out and down, soundless, his arms spread like the wings of an eagle. Seeing this, and hearing a hard slapping sound rise from the ledge below, the last warrior rose in a crouch and took leave, vanishing back into the rocky hillside.

Levering another round just in case, Julie stepped to the cliff's edge. She lowered herself flat into her belly and looked straight down. The warriors she'd seen earlier where still there, looking up in bewilderment from a circle around the body that had just fallen into their midst. The warrior had splattered on the stone facing like an overripe tomato.

My God ...! Even from this height, had she not been able to clearly see all of the blood, she could see the Indians and their horse were badly splattered. One squatted and scooped up dust to wipe his hands and face with. Another took off a battered slouch hat and stood slapping it against his leg. The horses shook out their manes.

All right, time to go .... She pushed back from the edge on hands and knees. They knew someone was up here. They would have to come up and investigate. This stretch of the desert hills were still crawling with roaming warriors, both drunk and sober. She believed the raid was over and they were on their way out, but what did it matter? As long as they were still here, she still had to avoid them—especially now that she had just been seen killing two of them.

She glanced around for the fourth Apache but saw no sign of him. He would tell the others. Of course he would. She slapped dust from the front of her and walked over to the roan. The big stallion stood at ease watching her as if he'd been standing here all day and nothing of any importance had taken place.

Yes, time to go ...! And go quick! she reasoned. She reached around and felt the wet cloth she had rolled tight—the thickness of her thumb and stuffed into the bullet hole in her lower side. *Still there ....* She placed a hand flat on the larger cloth lying behind her belt on her lower stomach, holding firm to the bullet's exit wound. Soreness was sharp and relentless front and back, but she could stand it, she told herself. She felt the pain as she gathered the blue roan's reins and pulled herself up into the saddle. Shoving the rifle into the saddle boot, she drew her Colt from her belt and kept it in hand as she turned the roan toward the trail.

"We're in trouble, Blue, let's get out of here," she said in a guarded tone. The stallion perked its ears at the sound of her voice, but he settled again quickly as he felt her hand close on his reins. A slight touch of her heels put him forward at a quick pace. But as he started around the high rock turn in the trail, Apache warriors appeared out of the rocks on foot, and swooped down on them. The blue roan slid to a halt and reared against the attackers.

The woman, pistol in hand only managed to get off two shots before the sheer number of attackers overpowered the roan and brought it nickering loudly to the ground. Julie rolled away, trying to get back on her feet. But the attackers would have none of it. As she tried to aim her Colt a pair of strong hands forced it down then twisted it away from her. She looked at the face of the man now holding her gun pointed in her face and recognized him.

"Naiche!" she said in a breathless tone. She tried pushing herself up to her feet. There were too many hands holding her down.

"Yes, it's me, Naiche," the warrior said in a strong voice. He shoved her backwards to the hard stony ground, and gestured the others to step away. "Did you think I would forget you?" He formed the thinnest sliver of a mirthless smile. "No, I don't forget! I gave Taza his say, as it is right that I should have. But now he's gone, and you belong to me!"

Julie looked all around at the many hard weathered faces, some lit with anger, some lit with alcohol and strong *cocaina* and cactus buttons.

"I belong to no one here," she asserted sharply. "I come from the same place as the rest of you. Many of you know my mother—" Her words cut short as she heard the roan, being held down onto his side, let out a loud long whinny as she saw a warrior flash a long knife in the air above the stallion's exposed throat.

"No!" Julie screamed. "No! Turn him loose!"

Standing over her, Naiche gave her side wound a sharp kick with the toe of his moccasin. The pain was too intense to allow her to do anything but roll into a tight ball on the ground and gasp for air.

"Cook as much horse meat as we need," Julie heard the big warrior say through her darkening veil of pain.

"No! No...!" she gasped still hearing the blue roan rage in terror. She knew her consciousness was fading fast. All she could think of was the blue roan, how gallant he had been trying to protect her. She thought of the knife she carried in the well of her calf-high range moccasins. Could she grab it? She thought of it as the world spun around her. *Grab it and do what with it ...?*

Another sharp kick from Naiche's moccasin caused a wave of tight blinding pain to close fast around her like a fisted iron glove. In spite her pain, she struggled, trying desperately to cling to the small sliver of consciousness she still processed. But it was of no use.

Blue ..., she murmured, the warriors surrounding her drawing even closer, four of them still holding the big stallion down, ready to butcher.

Standing above her, Naiche looked over at the downed roan. The warrior with the raised knife looked at him with question, awaiting word from their leader to cut the stallion's throat. Naiche started to give the warrior a nod to go ahead. But he stopped for a second, looking down at the woman laid out beneath him like a warm breathing sacrifice to some powerful war god.

"No!" he called out to the waiting butcher. "Let the horse up!"

"Let him up?" The warrior lowered his knife as he looked around with bewilderment at the others.

"Yes! Let him up!" Naiche said in a harsher tone. "Give me the knife, I will kill him myself when it's time. Hobble him for now!"

All of the Indians looked at each other.

"All of you, *go now!*" Naiche ordered. "I will make work of the woman and her stallion. I will meet you on the trail with horse meat for all of us."

Surprise left the warriors' eyes; now they looked at each other with wily understanding. This was the woman who had helped Taza. It was Taza's order that she not be harmed. But Naiche knew that Taza couldn't ply wrath upon him for something he did not know about. And if the woman tried to kill him while he butchered the stallion even Taza or even Great Eagle himself could not blame him for killing her. It would be his word. No one else's.

CHAPTER 15

She regained consciousness only moments later with dull jolting pain in her side and her lower back. Looking around she realized how much those few minutes had altered this violent world surrounding her. The warriors were gone, except for Naiche who stood at her feet, a knife in his hand, still looking down at her. In the deepening twilight shadows, she saw the blue roan standing relaxed in a circling glow of firelight. Naiche's horse stood a few feet away, equally relaxed, its head lowered against the creeping darkness.

"Yes, the blue stallion is still alive," Naiche said. "But only for now." He stepped around so that she could see him up close, and see the knife he held. He gestured the glistening blade toward the blue roan. "How long I let him live, is up to you."

Julie saw where the conversation was headed. She made no reply. Her eyes went to the iron hobbles one of the warriors had pin-locked on the blue roan's front shins. She tried to concentrate on the knife she always carried in the well of her high moccasins. *Is it still there?* she asked herself. *Had they overlooked it?* She dared not reach for it with him standing over her, watching every move, her in a weakened condition.

"Did you hear me, *woman?*" he demanded of her. She saw him start to draw back his foot for another kick. She raised a shielding hand toward him, palm first.

"I—I heard you," she stammered needing to regain all of her consciousness as quickly as she could. She glanced around as she spoke. "I'll do anything you tell me to do," she said. "But turn the stallion loose first. Take the hobble off of him—"

"Shut up!" Naiche snapped at her, the knife gripped his fist looking threatening. "I tell you what to do. You do not tell me!"

She stared straight at him, the way no squaw should ever do in defiance of a man's higher position, especially a man regarding her as his enemy and holding her life or death in his closed fist.

Naiche stared down at her with murderous contempt. He could kill her at any time, even after slaughtering the stallion before her eyes. She couldn't fight him off. He had only to beat her senseless and do to her what suited him. Yet, something about beating her senseless wouldn't do. He stared at her exposed leg, her partly torn open shirt. She looked more white than Apache. He was curious about her. He wanted to take her there in the dirt; but he wanted her awake and aware. He wanted to hear what sounds a white woman like this might make as he bored himself inside her, especially while he still wore the warm blood of her dead stallion on his hands.

He looked over at the blue roan, then back down at her.

"I will free him," he said. But as he spoke Julie sensed deception in his voice, saw it in his eyes.

He shoved the knife in his belt and turned away from her. She took a deep breath as he started walking toward the firelight where the roan stood watching him through the growing darkness. Julie summoned up all her strength while his eyes were not on her. She bent her knee enough to get her hand down into her calf-high moccasin. To her relief she found the bone handle of her big knife resting against her leg. She slipped the knife from the high moccasin and held it hidden against her side. Testing her waned strength she forced herself to raise up enough to look over at Naiche as he stopped and loosened the pins on the hobble and held it up by its chain for her to see. Now, to get to her feet and get to him, she ordered herself to wrap herself around his back and stab him to death.

"He is free," Naiche called out. He held the roan's reins in one hand and jiggled the hobble chain in his other, above his head. The roan was fidgeting, trying to draw away from the man. But Naiche held firm, even gave a hard jerk on the reins, causing the bridle bit to clamp hard onto the stallion's bare gums behind his front teeth. The roan froze in place.

Oh no! Julie told herself, sensing danger before it showed its face. She saw Naiche drop the hobble and pull the knife from his belt. He held it up.

"You will learn to never tell Naiche what he must do!" he shouted. *Oh no ...!* He planned on keeping her, she decided as he turned his back to her and adjusted his stance for a deep thrust of the blade into the roan's lower throat. The roan pulled away, but the warrior reined him back roughly. As the blue roan settled, unwittingly standing still to meet his own death, Julie saw that this was her only chance—a slim one at that.

She rose to her feet in a hard run, still weakened, but giving it everything she had. Ahead of her she saw Naiche draw the knife back. She was too late. She wouldn't make it in time. She let out a long bellowing scream.

"No, *you son of a—*" But her words cut short as a sound like that of a sharp ax sinking into wood resounded in the clearing. At the same time she saw the knife fall from Naiche's hand as his head broke open like a shattered gourd and blew forward in a wide bloody streak across the roan's back. With its reins free, the roan kicked sidelong away from Naiche's falling body. It took Julie only a split second to recognize that a gunshot had slipped in out of the falling darkness and taken the situation over. No sooner than she realized what had broken open Naiche's head, the sound of the shot caught up with the bullet, rumbling in like a sharp delayed clap of thunder.

She had no idea who had made the shot or if they would be making another one. But she saw the roan still exposed within

A Ranger's Trail

the circle of firelight. Having gone berserk by the spray of warm blood slathering his back, the stallion whinnied loudly, rearing and stomping the dead Indian into the hard dirt. It took only short reasoning to further realize that whoever had just killed Naiche had used the firelight to make the shot.

"Blue, let's go! *Get out of there!"* she bellowed, running hard in spite of her weakened condition. She slid to a halt at the edge of the firelight. The roan saw her and circled away from Naiche's body and made a fast run past her, slowing just enough to allow her to leap forward, grab his fluttering mane with both hands and swing up onto his wet bloody back.

Guiding the roan with her knees, and her hands on his withers, Julie rode him back through the firelight at a run.

When she and Blue raced past Naiche's horse, she reached down and grabbed its dangling reins and swept the nervous animal alongside them.

As they rode away on the thin path, opposite the side of the clearing the Apache had used, she reached over and lifted Naiche's rifle from the saddle ring holding it onto an old McClellan style wooden-framed saddle. Behind the wooden saddle cantle she saw one of her quickly made rock bolos hanging down the horse's sides. *Good ...!* She might need it. She wasn't sure how long she had been unconscious, but she had little doubt Naiche's warriors had heard the shot. *Let them come ...!* she told herself as she levered a round up into the chamber of the battered Winchester. She was ready for them. She had a rifle, a knife, her bolo, a good stallion beneath her and another horse to spare. Naiche's horse seemed more than willing, maybe even grateful to go wherever she was taking him.

From the next hill over, eighty feet higher than the clearing where Naiche had held the woman and the stallion captive, the ranger stood with the big Swiss rifle still smoking in hand. He had looked all around the settling darkness as soon as he'd taken the shot. It was risky taking a shot so far off with the only light being the flicker of the campfire. He'd thought about that as he watched Julie and the blue roan cross his field of vision. Fortunately the shot did its job without a hitch. Had the Apache heard it? *Of course they had ....* He looked at the far off flickering firelight once more, knowing the Apache would soon be returning to this spot to investigate the gunshot, then on to the next hillside.

"And that's that," he said quietly to himself.

Naiche lay dead with most of the top of his head missing. Sam took a deep breath and turned and walked to where he'd left Black Pot and a spare horse standing by a tall cutbank in the rocky hillside. The spare horse was another abandoned desert barb who had taken up with him and Black Pot along the way. He must have a knack for taking in strays, he thought. This one's rump was splattered with dried blood from its former rider. Sam ran a hand down each horse's neck in passing and climbed up a thin jagged path leading up the bank to level ground overlooking the desert floor. In the thinnest veil of remaining daylight, little more than shadowy silhouettes of Naiche's warriors split up on the sandy trail and rode away.

The fact that only four of them were heading back toward the hillside where they had left Naiche, confirmed what he thought—this Apache raid was over. The ones riding away across the desert were moving slowly, heading home, he decided. The four riding back this way were doing so at a good trotting pace, but certainly riding with no urgency. They were curious about the rifle shot. They would ride back to where they would find their leader, Naiche, lying dead by the fire. Would they follow the blue roan's tracks out of there?

We'll see, he told himself, turning back to the short steep path leading down to Black Pot. The woman was moving fast, but he would have no problem tracking the roan. The woman was trail savvy enough that he knew she would keep a careful watch of her back trail—maybe even double back to make sure she wasn't being followed. But on that matter he knew the roan was his ace in the hole. With the stallion's splayed hoof, Sam could follow from as far back as suited him. The woman would not want to double back too far.

She would be in a hurry, but Sam knew she was savvy enough not to risk the roan or the other horse on these dark rocky hill trails. After all, he reasoned, at the end of this ride she would have gold coming to her. The thought of it would keep her moving—but not without caution, he reminded himself, half stepping, half sliding down the path in the cutbank.

"Easy, boys," he said in a low soothing tone, noting how finicky both animals had become. He drew the barb's reins and brought it up next to Black Pot and rubbed its muzzle. The horse settled some. Upon seeing Sam return, and hearing his soothing tone of voice, Black Pot settled right away. But Sam noticed the big barb's attention was concentrated on a short rock pile across the clearing. Looking close though the darkness, Sam saw two pair of red eyes staring back from over the edge of a rock. To the left of the rocks another pair of eyes staring. To his right, a fourth pair shined fiery red.

"All right, I see them," he said low and calmly to the dead Indian's jittery horse. As he spoke he reached out with his big Swiss rifle and shoved it down into the double rifle boot behind Black Pot's saddle. He wasn't going to use the rifle again tonight if he could keep from it. He didn't want the Apache to hear the same sound they had heard only moments ago. Anyway, he reasoned, these were desert wolves, used to roaming long and hunting in large packs.

If this were a lone hunter like a Mexican panther, a rifle would be his best defense. With a pack of hungry wolves, this close, he wanted as many rapid shots as he could carry in hand —and these wolves *would be hungry,* he told himself. With the Apache roaming their domain, they'd been forced to lay low. Now they were coming out to catch up on their feeding.

He drew his big Colt and stepped up into Black Pot's saddle. Keeping the spare horse reined close beside him.

"Let's go, nice and easy," he said almost in a whisper to the two animals. *They scented your fear,* he said silently to them. *Now the fear is gone, they're wondering why* ... He nudged Black Pot forward, leading the spare horse beside him, hugged against his leg. These wolves would soon catch the scent of fresh death lying on the next hillside, and hear the call of others in their pack drawing them in toward tonight's meal.

Adios, Naiche, he said to himself. At some point on the next hillside, the Apache warriors would soon meet up with the wolves. There they would have to deal with the feeding wolf pack, and decide what to do with Naiche's ravaged remains. At least Naiche would have kept both desert groups off of his back, for the time being. He was closer to the woman than he had thought he would be. With continued good trail and fortune he would be caught up with her before daylight.

He gave the slightest touch of his heels to Black Pot, and they rode on, the spare horse close beside, appearing grateful for their company on this harsh, wolf-infested desert night.

The woman knew it was risky riding up on a dark water hole in the dead of night with shifting wind now at her back, announcing her arrival to any nostrils keen enough to catch scent of her and the two horses. But she had learned from her days from the Apache on the San Carlos reservation, the only way to know the strength of your luck was to test it. So she would, she told herself—but she would not do so blindly. All the creatures inhabiting the desert floor would be out tonight, searching for food, for water. She would move in as silently as the rest of them, ready for whatever the night held in store for her.

Yes, she was testing her luck, but so far her luck had held itself strong and worthy against both unpredictable fate and most dire circumstance. *Testing her fate* had worked in her favor and brought her this far. Like any other warm-blooded species prowling the night, she was going for the water that both she and the horses needed—water the two animals had smelled and leaned toward a half hour earlier when the wind was still in their faces. Since then the wind had reversed its direction.

Not good ..., she cautioned herself. Still, she rode slowly upward on a short, steep path, her rifle ready, a pistol in her waist and her bolo she'd recovered from Naiche's horse draped over her left shoulder for quick access.

As she started around a large boulder standing like a sentinel at a turn in the narrow path, the nearby guttural sounds of snarling, growling, feeding wolves stopped her cold in her tracks. Blue and the other horse heard the wolves, too, and froze in place, ready to turn and bolt away. Julie held the reins firm and inched Blue forward until she could see the shadowy silhouettes of a half dozen wolves bowed over a dead horse near the water's edge, less than twenty yards away.

As soon as she saw the animals attending to their feast she began inching the blue roan backward, the spare horse coming unfrozen and moving right along with them. But suddenly the wolves raised their head almost as one. Their fiery red eyes snapped toward her and the horses. Without a second of hesitation, she raised the rifle and fired into the wolves as the pack formed closely knit between her and their dinner.

Her shot brought a sharp yelp followed by loud splashing as the wolves gave up their bloody meat and darted away in every direction including across the shallow water hole. But she knew they wouldn't retreat very far, not with this much fresh red meat at stake. She instantly levered a fresh round into the rifle chamber as she turned the blue roan around with her knees and let him spring forward back down the steep rocky path.

Fifty yards later after a hard, dangerous run, the horses half running, half sliding, the woman reined the roan down, the other horse following suit, and turned facing up the path leading down from the water hole. In the dim glow of a half-moon she searched the hillside. Nothing moved—no flash of dark silhouettes bounding silently over rock and sparse brush in pursuit. She breathed in relief and rubbed the roan's damp withers. The spare horse sidled up tight against her leg as if to claim his share of praise. She rubbed his neck and started back down the trail, her attention still partly focused back in the direction of the feeding wolves.

"No water tonight," she said quietly to the horses. "Okay?" She gazed all around and up at the trail to her right where a tall bent cactus stood sky-lighted in the pale purple glow of the moon. She looked down at the flatlands and back up at the trail, again at the tall cactus. Recognition set in. "Anyway ...." She let her words trail as she studied the dark rugged terrain. Atop the next hill the gold lay waiting. There was no doubt that this next hill was where she and others had buried their shares. *"We're here,"* she murmured, forcing herself to settle down and take control of a soaring feeling in her chest.

Her next words she said in silence. *We'll rest a few minutes up there.* She nodded at the upward trail ahead. As she spoke to herself, her hand tightened instinctively around the rifle chamber. She looked back once again at the trail in the direction of the water hole. "Then we'll all go home," she whispered to the horses.

Three miles back along the grainy moonlit trail, the ranger had shortened the gap between himself and the woman. When he'd heard the distant echo of the rifle shot in the rocky hills higher up to his right, he kept Black Pot and the other horse at the same steady pace. He had little doubt the shot had involved the woman, yet he knew of no way his pushing closer just yet would either help or change anything. He rode on and upward and stopped where he saw the fresh tracks on the dusty ground leading up toward the big boulder standing atop the trail.

He rode steadily upward until at length he saw where the roan's and the dead warrior, Naiche's horse's tracks led up on to the steep path, but overlapped themselves coming back down. He paused and looked all around

Something didn't suit you up there, Julie Wilder, he said to himself, taking in the purple moonlight, the blackened overhangs dotting the hillsides. He had a hunch the rifle shot he'd heard earlier had come from up there. *Here's where we make up some time,* he said silently to himself, to the horses. He stopped the horses and sat for a moment. He wasn't going up the trail just to turn around and come back. He had no idea how far the woman had ridden up before turning back. It didn't matter. He had a sense of things winding down.

This was the break he'd been hoping for. Riding up this steep little path would cost her. He looked up at the boulder, a mile up and a mile back, he judged. How long was she up there? He had no idea. He turned Black Pot with a touch and turn of his knees and rode down, following the tracks of the blue roan's telltale hoofprints.

CHAPTER 16

Dog Fannen led the recently deceased Elvin Sloane's horse beside him on his way to the cave where Max Carver awaited his return. Four bags of gold hung down the horse's side. Fannen knew he could take the horse and the gold and cut out here and now, but to do so would have him watching over his shoulder for Carver the rest of his life. He'd already decided he would have none of that. He would kill Max Carver straight up—take his share too.

What the hell .... He gave a slight shrug. He'd spent the day killing his fellow outlaws, and although he hadn't been ordered by him to do it, Carver knew damn well he was going to kill them when he sent him to check on them. Without saying so Carver had sent him to clean up what was left after the Apache had chewed the gang to a bloody pulp.

Okay, job well done, he thought, complementing himself. Right before dark, he came upon the mutilated body of Fedder Dockery lying dead on a rock, his lidless eyes cooked and swollen from their sockets. *Tough break, Dock* .... Truth be told he'd been looking forward to killing Fedder Dockery himself. *Damned heathen Injuns.* He blew a small pebble from his mouth that he'd been carrying in his jaw to stave off his thirst.

When he reached the narrow crevice in the hillside he rode right in, both horses' hooves clacking and echoing along the stone corridor ahead of him.

"It's *Dog,* I'm back, Boss. Don't shoot," he called out without stopping.

He watched a flickering firelight grow clearer as he neared the far end of the stone corridor. When he stopped and slipped down from his saddle at a widening open to the large underground cavern, he led both horses inside and saw Carver standing fireside with his rifle in his hands. Forty feet overhead above the fire, gray smoke hovered and dissipated up into the mass of interlocked stone mantling the wide cave.

"Nobody else made it?" Carver asked, looking only mildly surprised.

"No," Dog said flatly. "I don't think we expected anybody would, did we?"

"No, I suppose not," said Carver. With a sad breath he said, "Too bad. They were damn good men." He avoided Dog's dark gaze as he uncocked his rifle and leaned it against a tangled pile of dried brush and kindling lying near the fire. Dog took note of the leaning rifle, and of Carver's gun belt wrapped around his holstered Colt and placed atop the pile of kindling.

"Yeah, too damned bad," Dog said. He motioned toward the bags of gold hanging from Elvin Sloane's horse. In doing so he took a short casual step closer to Carver's rifle and gun belt. "All being said and done," he added in a cool tone, "that's a wicked load of gold we've got there." He almost offered a slight grin, but he stopped himself. "I can't say I'm sorry it all belongs to the two of us now. Can you?"

Carver didn't answer.

"I know we talked about it some earlier—" Dog stepped over close to Carver's rifle as he spoke and idly leaned his own rifle beside it. "—but you started getting all bent sideways over it. So, I let it go." He managed to stay standing within arm's reach of Carver's gun belt, the butt of the big Colt close to his right hand. He shrugged a little. "As it turns out, I expect we'll just split it all between us?"

Carver seemed not to notice how well Dog had positioned himself to the guns.

"We'll each take our share and maybe a little extra for all our trouble," Carver said. He stood with a firm expression on his dusty, sun-hardened face. "Most of it we're taking back to *Hole-In-The-Wall*. I think that's what these men would want us to do."

"Yeah, you can bet your sister's *ass they would!*" Dog couldn't keep from laughing out loud. But his laughter stopped when he saw that Max Carver—the *so-called* Gentleman Bandit—was dead serious.

Dog, now settled, said in a somber voice, "Boss, don't try to tell me you're stupid enough to believe something like that."

Carver only stared at him without a word.

Dog took a deep breath and let it out in a chuff, his hand ready to grab Carver's holstered Colt.

"Let me put it another way, Boss," he said. "Don't try to tell me you think *I'm* stupid enough to believe something like that!" He snatched Carver's Colt from its holster, cocked it and aimed it at Caver's chest twelve feet away.

"I don't know, Dog," Carver replied in a low even tone. "Looks like you're *stupid enough* to believe I'd stick a loaded gun right at your fingertips when there's a wagonload of gold at stake."

"Oh ...?" Dog's expression changed a little, not much. He only gave a quick glance down at the Colt in his hand. "Now I've got the drop on you, you're going to try to bluff me down? Tell me this shooter of yours ain't *loaded?*"

"I forgot if it's loaded or not, Dog," Carver said in a calm even voice. "But squeeze the trigger back, you lousy son of a bitch. We'll find out together."

The big Colt tensed in Dog's grip for a second. But instead of firing it, he eased his grip and turned it over in his hand, checking it as he gave a thin smile of satisfaction. He could see the back edges of brass cartridges in the cylinder without opening the loading gate. *Five rounds,* he noted. *So, it was a bluff,* just like he thought. The gun *was* loaded. He cocked the Colt and leveled it at Carver's chest. He squeezed the trigger.

"Adios, Max," he said. "I can't say I hate doing this ... fact is, I've always wanted to!" The hammer fell, but the gun made no sound above the metal on metal click as the hammer struck a spent brass shell.

"Son of a bitch!" Dog shouted, realizing he'd been had after all. He hurled the useless gun at Carver and reached for his own. But Carver's hand had already gone behind his back and came streaking forward with a hideout .36 Colt Pocket gun. A shot blazed in his hand. The bullet sliced through Dog's right shoulder, only staggering him a step. He still got off a shot, but it missed Carver and ricocheted off the stone wall. Dog tried to raise his lowered gun for another shot. But he couldn't. He gripped his wounded right chest with his left hand. Blood ran between his fingers.

"Wait, Max, wait!" he shouted. He tried again to raise his gun. Still no good.

Wait ...? Carver gave a dark chuckle, stepping forward. Switching his Pocket Colt to his left hand, he reached down and pulled a long vicious-looking knife from his boot well. "I've waited all day to cut your beating heart out. Now that the gold's here, I'm not going to wait!" Another dark chuckle.

Dog saw a crazed, wild look in Carver's eyes as he stalked closer. He tried to turn and run, But Carver was near enough to reach his boot out and trip him. Then he stood over Dog and stared down at him with a dark ugly grin.

Dog tried scooting backwards, talking fast, "You can't kill one of your own men this way, Max—You're *The Gentleman Bandit!* It ain't in you! You only kill when the *job* calls for it."

"You've never been more wrong, Dog!" Carver said. Shoving the pocket gun into his waist, he grabbed Dog by a boot and pulled him back. "I'll do more than kill you. I'll cut you in ways and places these Apache ain't even *dreamed* of!" He stood over Dog, his knife raised, and bent down to grab him by his shirt.

As he bent farther down over Dog and stabbed him in the chest, the wounded old gunman yanked Carver's pocket gun from his waist with his left hand and shot him in his belly just above his belt buckle. Carver turned him loose, leaving the knife sticking high in his chest and backed away, bowed at the waist. He gripped his wounded belly. When Dog pulled the trigger again, Carver grabbed the gun barrel and pulled away as it fired. Dog drew his holstered Colt; Carver knocked it from his hand. The two rolled bloody and fighting on the sandy dirt floor.

In the dark hours of early morning, she had unwillingly fell asleep. Unable to keep her eyes open or her mind from wandering she'd bowed forward in her saddle and drifted aimlessly on a warm, quiet cloud. For the moment the pain that had grown to a rage burning deep in her wounded side had left her. Yet, as she slumped deeper onto the wound the pain seemed to seek her out. She tried adjusting herself against it, but it was no use. The pain gnawed steadily and mercilessly at her until at length she awakened just in time to catch herself falling from her saddle.

Feeling her weight sinking dangerously low on his side, the roan swayed slightly, scooping himself up under her enough to save her from a bad fall. He stopped short in midstep, the dead Indian's barb stopping close beside him. The woman instinctively caught and balanced herself.

"Buen chico ...!" she murmured, the soft sound of her voice helping to awaken her. She straightened quickly in her saddle and looked all around the moonlit darkness. The blue roan stood perfectly still beneath her as if allowing her the time she needed to collect her senses.

"Good boy," she whispered, this time more conscious, and in English. Then she'd moved slowly and gathered the reins that had fallen down the roan's sides. "Both of you," she added, gathering the barb's reins which had also fallen from her sleeping hand. Before stepping the roan forward she smelled and saw the small pool of runoff water lying only ten feet ahead of them. Had she the energy to smile she would have. Instead she turned in her saddle and let herself down as gently as she could while the pain pulsed hard in her side. Then she led the horses to the water's edge and dropped down onto her belly between them and drank deeply, refusing to give into the raw aching wound.

Her shirt felt only damp around the wound, front or back, a sign that very little fresh bleeding was going on. That was good, she knew. She would do nothing to the wound right now. She had no time for it, neither to clean it, nor to be slowed down by it, she told herself.

Pushing through the pain up onto her knees she looked all around again, seeing a thin sliver of light mantle the distant horizon. She wasn't sure how long she had dozed off—not long she hoped. They were still on the same rising trail they'd been on, the moon and stars were still where they had been earlier, the moon a little paler now as morning stirred off the far edge of the earth, otherwise all the same. She gripped the watering roan's front leg with both hands and pulled herself to her feet.

It was then that she'd heard the first shot. No sooner than she stood up, the shot rang out in an echo not far up the hillside. The woman ducked instinctively, then caught herself and gazed up the trail in the direction of the echoing gunfire. Both horses raised their dripping muzzles and searched the darkness up the rocky trail. Julie waited intently for a moment until another shot rang out from the same spot on the dark hillside. *Pistol shots ...,* she told herself. Then she whispered to both horses, "We're here, boys!"

Ignoring the pain in her side, she gathered the spare horse's reins and pulled the two animals close together. Another pistol shot echoed down the hillsides as she turned and pushed herself up atop the blue roan, and turned him in the direction of the gunshots, knowing that her gold lay nearby. She had no idea what the gunshots meant, but whatever was going on there would have to wait. Before she rode in to find Max and whoever was left of the gang, she would uncover her hidden gold and keep it close at hand.

With a slight touch of her heels the roan moved forward in the grainy dawn. As the ground leveled beneath them and the lay of the land became more familiar, Julie guided the horses through prickly carpet cactus, rock and dried brush to the exact spot where she'd buried her gold. Without hesitation she eased herself down and lifted the edge of a flat rock and scraped sand from under it, uncovering the bulky canvas bag she'd buried there.

With a breath of relief she hefted the bag up and cradled it in her arms. On the shadowy ground she saw hoofprints and upturned rock and dirt where Max and the others had already unearthed their shares. Struggling against the pain in her side, she swung the canvas bag up atop the roan and climbed up and put the horses forward toward the rise where she'd heard the earlier gunshots. She had her share and she was ready to go. But she would check on Max and the others first. She owed them that much.

A half a mile up the hillside trail where Carver's Wild Bunch had each buried their share of the stolen money, Captain Jerome Gascoyne had also heard the earlier gunshots and looked across the morning darkness in their direction even before the echo had fallen away. He had been lying low among the rocks since late afternoon, having searched the hillside longer than he had intended in the blazing heat. He knew the heat had taken a toll on him being able to think clearly. Fortunately, in his muddled state of mind, his hillside wanderings had led him correctly to the spot where he'd hidden his share of the gold. He'd recovered the dusty bag from under a large rock and hung it over his saddle horn.

Yet, instead of taking his share of the gold and leaving,

as he had first intended, he'd gone right back to searching the hillside in the blazing afternoon heat until at length his thirsty, worn-out horse had collapsed down on it haunches like a dog and refused to move. Only with much coaxing and cursing did he get the horse to stand and stagger along behind him until he'd found this well-hidden spot. From here he'd been able to watch for any comings or goings of Carver's men without them seeing him.

All he had seen so far, though, was an hour earlier when he'd watched the old gunman, *Dog* Fannen, ride his horse into a wide crevice in the rocky hillside. Four of the bags of gold hung behind Fannen's saddle, draped over his horse's rump and tied down with rawhide strips.

But then these gunshots ..., he told himself. He lay waiting, watching for another half hour as dawn crept up the far edge of the earth.

All right! Stop waiting! It was time for him to act boldly, go inside the crevice and take the gold, all of it. *And do so quickly!* If there was one thing he'd learned in the wretched, horrible land it was that gunshots of any kind drew the Apache and any other armed, miscreant lunatics like sugar drew flies. He started to stand up into a crouch, but the sound of hooves scraping on stone caused him to duck down and watch from around the edge of a rock as a lone rider leading a spare horse rode slowly into sight and kept moving toward the crevice he'd watched Dog Fannen ride into.

Not so fast, Capitain, he told himself, seeing the bag of gold hanging down the first horse's side. *What have we here ...?* He settled back onto the ground and watched as the rider drew close to the crevice and stopped and studied the place for a long moment before stepping down and stalking forward silently, rifle in hand.

Ah! It's the woman ... Ruthless Ruby! He straightened and studied the figure closer as the recognition came to him through the pale gray dawn. He watched her slip down from the roan's back, holding the heavy bag of gold against her chest. *Perfect ...!* One rifle shot from right here, right now, and he would double his share of the robbery. He smiled to himself. But he would wait. How long? Not long, he thought. Lying here had taught him that *good things did indeed come to he who waits.*

He'd watched Dog Fannen ride into the crevice opening carrying bulky canvas bags hanging on his horse's side. Now here was the woman, *Ruthless Ruby,* carrying yet another one! *Oh yes, Capitain,* he told himself, *this will prove to be worth the wait!*

CHAPTER 17

Julie Wilder had only ridden a few yards into the open crevice leading into the cave. When she realized how loud the horses' hooves resounded along the rocky stone corridor, she stepped down from the saddle and led both animals off into wider space just off the dark walk path. Wrapping their reins around a rock spur, she took down the gold bag and set it out of sight behind a loose pile of dust and rock. With her rifle in hand and the bolo draped over her shoulder, she walked toward a thin light glowing in the distance where she could see the crevice widen and open into a dimly lit cavern.

She stood for a moment just outside the opening, listening to the voices of Fannen and Max Carver. They both sounded testy and quarrelsome with each other. She waited until a lull came into the conversation before calling out to them, "Hello, the campfire. It's me, Ruby." Her rifle was ready just in case. "I'm coming in?" It was a half-question, half-statement.

A silent second passed while Fannen and Carver gave each other a surprised look. Then Carver made a nervous grin toward the dark corridor.

"Jesus. Ruby, *yes!*" Carver said. "Get yourself on in here!"

She stepped into sight staying close to a stone edge, her eyes making a quick sweep of the wide cavern. The stone walls were smudged with smoke from countless ancient fires. Hand drawn stick figures, like the scribbling of children, lined the smoother wall surfaces, carrying spears and shields. Three horses stood at a place along the right wall that looked more like a converted sleep area than a hitch line for animals.

"Where the hell have you been, woman?" Dog asked her roughly. "We all gave you up for dead!"

"All …?" she questioned with a raised brow. Her eyes darted to the bags of gold lying near the fire. "Where is everybody?"

"We're everybody," Carver cut in. "The Apache have slaughtered the rest of us." He gestured toward the gold near the fire. "We've rounded up everybody's shares, except yours and the Frenchman's." He looked her up and down, noting the rifle in her hands, the Colt in her waist, and her quickly constructed bolo hanging from her shoulder. "Now you're back, we'll help you find yours."

"I just dug mine up and reburied it," she said, not about to tell them her share was in the dark corridor, waiting with her horses.

"Nearby, I hope," Dog said, sounding friendlier than she could ever remember.

Instead of answering Dog, she turned her face from him and looked Max Carver up and down, the blood spot on his shirt above his belt buckle. Her eyes went back to Dog who had dropped his hands to his sides, revealing the knife handle standing in his chest. A thin trickle of blood ran down his dirty shirt. Then, looking back at Carver she said in a low voice, "What's going on here, Max?" The rifle tensed in her hands. "I heard shots coming up the trail."

"Nothing, woman," Dog cut in. "We just was talking about divvying this gold up and skinning out of here before the Apache come calling—"

"Shut up, Dog," said Carver, cutting him off. "The shots was us trying to kill each other over this gold, Ruby," he confessed, looking ashamed. "We had just quit tangling when you showed up."

She nodded at the pocket gun in Max's hand.

"So, you'll be putting it away now, I expect?" she queried.

"Of course," Max said. He put the gun behind his back

and down into his waist. He stared at Dog.

Julie looked at Dog's Colt lying in the dirt a few feet away. Dog took a step toward the Colt, the big knife looking out of place buried in his chest.

"I ought to put mine away too, I reckon," he said. But he stopped cold in his tracks when he heard Julie cock her rifle behind him.

"Hunh-uh, Dog," she said quietly. "Maybe you best leave it lay there for now."

"That's all right too," he shrugged. "I'm easy to deal with." He stood four feet closer to the gun than when he'd started.

"Move back over here," Julie said.

"I don't like complaining," Dog said, stepping back over to where he'd stood before. "But moving around hurts worse than a bad tooth, this thing sticking in my craw." He gestured toward the knife handle.

"It means a lot, you coming back to take up with us, Ruby," Carver said, trying to sound deeply moved by the woman's actions. "I was telling Dog that if only you—"

"Save it, Max," said Julie, not letting him finish. "I came back for my share—figured all of you were either dead or had lit out by now."

Dog's demeanor changed quickly back to his belligerent self.

"If you come for your share, go get it and get the hell out of here. You heard the gunshots. You know there'll be Apache here most any minute."

"The Apache have started pulling out," Julie said. She looked at the bags of gold. "How'd Elvin Sloane get it?" she asked.

"Injuns, that's how he got it," said Dog. "Like everybody else. What do you care how they kilt him? He's dead, that's all."

"Why are you asking?" Carver cut in.

"We became pals," said Julie. "He's got a young woman in Colorado with his baby in her. Asked me if anything happened to him, would I take his money to her."

"That's truly touching," Dog said with sarcasm. "But the fact is, I don't believe a word of it." He looked at Carver for support. But Carver shook his head.

"Hold on, Dog," Carver said. "Elvin told me he had a woman carrying his baby in Colorado. So, I believe Ruby." He offered Julie a thin smile.

"I don't," said Dog. "So, if you want to give her some money, or anybody else you can think of that might need some, go right ahead. But it comes out of your cut."

"Jesus, Dog!" said Carver. "It's not coming out of *anybody's* cut. It's Elvin's share. He earned it!"

"Earned it? *Ha!*" said Dog. "Are you forgetting? The sumbitch stole it, just like all the rest of us did." The louder he spoke, the closer he tried to move toward Julie.

"Don't blackguard the dead," she warned him in a level but firm voice."

"Like hell I won't," Dog said. "If you don't like hearing him cussed at, maybe you're in the wrong game, little woman!"

As Julie's eyes stayed on Dog moving closer, Max Carver's hand slipped around to his back and closed around the butt of the Pocket Colt.

"Leave her alone, Dog!" he said. "She's getting an extra share. What she does with it is her business."

Dog stopped in his tracks and said without taking his dark eyes off of Julie's, "Is that a fact?"

"That it is," Carver said calmly.

Dog's voice softened, a half smile came to his face.

"So, you've got her, Boss?" he said, his tone almost pleasant.

"I've got her, Dog," said Carver. Go pick up your gun. Let's get busy here."

Julie turned her eyes back to Carver, puzzled, only to see

the Pocket Colt cocked and aimed at her while her rifle was still turned toward Dog.

The two of them had gotten her good. She kept the rifle clenched in her hands. If he meant to kill her he would have already done so without saying a word.

Dog side-stepped to his gun lying on the dusty stone floor. It took all of his effort to stoop and pick it up, his wounded chest pounding with each beat of his heart. When he did straighten up with the gun in hand, he said in a weakened shallow voice as he cocked it toward Julie, "Let's kill this *puta* and be done with her."

"That's a good idea, Dog," Carver replied. "Except, I'm wondering if you're able to load these bags on the horses." He nodded at the bags lying on the stone floor. "Because *I'm not,* and we need help to get done and get out of here."

"And you think I'll load the gold and watch the two of you ride away with it?" Julie asked, the rifle slumping in her hands. "I'm wounded myself," she threw in.

Dog started to take closer aim on her, but realized Carver was right. Neither of them were able to load up and cut out.

"Listen to me, both of you," Carver said. "There's a way out of this for all of us." He looked at Julie. "Put the rifle down, ease that Colt from your belt and lay it down."

"Then what?" She asked with caution.

"Then, help us load the gold bags and we'll let you leave here alive. My word on it," said Carver.

"What about the extra share?" She asked, already knowing there was no way she was going to trust these two again. She knew she wouldn't be leaving here alive, no matter whose word she had on it.

"Damn it!" Dog cursed. "I'd sooner kill her right now!" He raised the Colt and took a clearer aim.

From the dark cave entrance, a voice called out, "Drop the gun, Fannen, or I'll kill you where you stand!"

All three outlaws swung their eyes to the dark entrance,

just as the ranger stepped into sight of the flickering firelight, his rifle chest high, ready and aimed, appearing to take in all three of them at once. Dog stood firm for a second until he saw Carver lower the Pocket Colt. Then he shook his head in disgust and let his Colt slump in his hand.

"Damn it *to hell!*" he growled. "I don't know why we even carry guns out here! You can't fire a shot without bringing in every damned lawman, Injun, or some other kind of no-good sumbitch—"

"Shut the hell up, Dog!" Carver barked at him. "This ain't over!" His eyes fixed on the ranger. "Is it, Lawman?"

"It is for you, Carver, if you don't drop that gun right now," Sam said in a tone that left no room for further discussion. Carver let the Pocket Colt fall from his hand.

"Easy, Ranger," he said. "There's plenty of gold here to go around. Right, Dog?"

"What …?" Dog's eyes snapped up in surprise from his Colt he'd dropped onto the stone floor. He caught himself and said with sarcasm, *"Oh …. Why hell yes,* there's plenty to go around." He shrugged and added in the same sour tone, "Anytime I rob a place, I can't wait to spread it out to every mullet-headed sumbitch that wants part of it." His raspy voice fell silent, cut short by the deep pain in his badly wounded chest.

Sam looked closer at Julie Wilder, still holding her slumped rifle.

"You too, Julie," he said, gesturing for her to give up the rifle.

"Oh? *Julie* is it?" Carver said. How long have you and Ruthless Ruby been rubbing flanks?"

Neither Julie or the ranger answered Carver. Instead, Julie leaned her rifle against an ancient set of stones formed centuries past into a crude table.

"How did you track me, Ranger?" she asked. Knowing she had taken all reasonable precautions to avoid being followed.

"It wasn't easy," Sam replied, not about to give up anything on the matter.

"So it was you who blew Naiche's head off?" she said, fishing.

Sam only stared at her for a second, then at the other two.

"Before anybody gets jumpy and does something stupid, I'm going to tell you why I'm here." He paused for a second, then said to Carver, "I came here looking for you, Max Carver. You're wanted, *dead or alive,* for murder in Arizona Territory."

The woman and Dog Fannen both looked on in stunned surprise.

"Murder ...?" Fannen said with a wide, mean grin. "Well, well," he said gazing at Carver, "He told me he's a killer. I didn't believe him."

Carver ignored him and said to the ranger, "You came all this way to take me to Arizona ... to *hang?"*

"If they find you guilty, yes," Sam said, "hanging's one possibility."

"I bet you're hoping I won't go back though," Carver said. "Am I right?"

Sam stood facing the three with his back to the entrance eighteen feet behind him. Before he could answer Carver, he saw a look come over Julie Wilder's face. *Something or someone behind him --?* He didn't know which, but when the bolo came off of her shoulder in full twirl and she shouted at him, *"Duck!"* he did so instantly. Above him he heard a low whistling sound as the bolo shot spinning through the air only inches above his head.

Turning quickly, crouched, he saw the French officer, Jerome Gascoyne, stagger forward, choking, one hand digging at the leather thongs wrapped tight around his neck, his other hand holding a gun out at arm's length, firing wildly at the ranger.

One shot from Sam's big Swiss rifle silenced Gascoyne's

gunfire and slammed him flat on his back, dead. His eyes and mouth lay stretched open wide, aimed up at the smudged cave ceiling, above walls, shelves and sub-ceilings littered with warring stick figures perpetually charging each other with their crude weapons and shields.

"See ...?" said Dog Fannen, making a point. "Another *crazy bastard* drawn here and killed by the *curiousness* of gunfire!" As he spoke he gave a dark chuckle and reached down for his Colt, his chest throbbing in pain. Seeing him make a move, Carver started to reach down for his Pocket Colt.

But as soon as Sam saw Gascoyne going down, he spun around toward Dog Fannen, anticipating the old gunman making a move. The big Swiss rifle's chamber was empty, but Sam's black-handled Colt replaced it in his hand, cocked and pointed.

The ranger's shot hit Fannen three inches to the right of the knife handle, placing the bullet squarely in the gunman's heart. Fannen staggered backwards and down, his Colt going off, knocking chips of stone down from the ceiling.

Sam spun toward Carver, ready to fire, but Carver hadn't made it down to the Pocket Colt. He froze halfway and slowly stood up, giving Julie an embarrassed look. He kept his hands spread chest-high.

"Well, *Ruthless Ruby,*" he said. "At least it won't be *my shot* that draws any unwanted company."

Julie started to reach for her rifle, but she stopped and said quietly to Sam, "I didn't lead you here, Ranger, but you have the man you came for. Any reason I can't leave now?"

"What about your side?" Sam nodded at a small fresh spot of blood on her shirt.

"I'll be all right," she said, "soon as I get this place behind me." She gestured at Carver who stood looking away from them. "Think he'll go along with you without any trouble?"

"We'll have to wait and see," said Sam. "Nobody likes

attending their own hanging." He paused a second then said, "I met a Mexican cavalry patrol on the way here. You might want to get moving."

"I wish …." She stalled for a moment then started again. "I wish we had some time, Ranger. I wish I knew you better."

"Me, too," Sam said, "Knew you better, that is." He offered a thin smile, then put it away. "I'm walking this one back a ways into this cave. When I get back, I hope you'll be gone. It'll be easier explaining when the time comes." He felt like warning her to hide the bulk of the gold somewhere on this vast desert lands and return for it some other time. But he decided she already knew all that. If anybody knew how to handle this much gold in a place like this, this woman did. He gave a slight nod and let out a short breath, watching her pick up her rifle and her Colt.

She adjusted the Colt down behind her beaded rawhide Apache-style belt. "You take care of yourself, Ranger Sam." She said softly.

"Thank you, Miss Julie, I will," Sam replied in the same tone. "You do the same."

They stood close, facing each other. Both of them wanting to say something, but neither of them finding the right words. Finally, Julie touched his arm and said quietly, "Someday then?"

Sam nodded. "Someday then …."

He watched her walk away, out the entrance toward where she'd left her own bag of gold and her two horses. Then he turned to Max Carver who stood a few feet away, looking in another direction toward a narrow corridor across the cavern from them.

"Over there?" Sam asked.

"That will do," Carver said. He started walking across the cave toward the narrow corridor.

"Lead the way," Sam said, and he followed close behind him, shoving Carver's pocket gun down into his belt.

Moments later the two stopped farther back inside the narrow corridor where daylight seeped down slantwise, casting a thin golden veil of light on the stone work and the dusty floor. When the corridor opened wider, the ranger walked around one side and Carver the other until they stood facing each other from twenty feet. On the dusty floor a large rattlesnake gave an angry warning and crawled out of sight among a pile of downed wall stone. More stick figures lay broken on their backs and upside down in stone piles, as if stricken down by their gods. Sam raised the Pocket Colt from his belt and pitched it across the space between them. It landed in a puff of dust at Carver's feet. The outlaw leader picked it up and checked it as he spoke.

"Ranger, everything turned bad for us when you—*a US lawman*—*stole* our getaway horses," he said.

"I know," Sam said calmly, not wanting to comment on the irony Carver was implying. He wasn't going to discuss anything of any *philosophical* nature that had happened to Carver and his gang. *Irony ...?* Anyone who felt so inclined could look back and study the case themselves and make their own conclusions, *philosophical* or otherwise. He reminded himself he'd come here for Carver, no one else. *To kill him ...?* he asked himself. But he offered himself no answer.

"I should kill you for that alone," Carver said, starting to get his bark on. "What about Poole?" he asked when Sam didn't comment.

"I left word to let him go," Sam said. "If the Apache didn't overrun Esplanade, I expect he'll head back to Hole-In-the-Wall."

Carver nodded and said, "We could split the gold, you and I." He stared at Sam for an answer, the Pocket Gun ready in his hand.

"No we can't," Sam said, his big Colt hanging in his hand. "They charged you with a double murder. But how many others have you killed?"

A Ranger's Trail

Carver gave a dark chuff and said, "These are violent times we live in, Ranger. A man who can't kill quick without hard-cause won't likely—"

His words stopped short as he jerked the Pocket Colt to fire. But the ranger's big Colt came up faster, and one shot nailed the outlaw hard in the center of his chest. He jerked back a step then sank to his knees. The ranger's smoking Colt stayed leveled, ready to fire again. But Sam lowered it as dark blood seeped from Carver's lips and he fell forward face first on the dusty floor.

Walking over, Sam checked to make sure Carver was dead. As he looked down at his body, his blank staring eyes, he heard the sound of gunfire echo out on the hillside. With his rifle and the big smoking Colt in his hands, he turned and walked back to the main cavern. There he raised both guns over his head when he saw a stout Mexican sergeant and three other soldiers he recognized from their patrol the day before. The soldiers had been looking all around and were startled by Sam's sudden appearance. Sam noted the woman was gone; so was the gold, except for one bag still sitting in the dust.

"Hold your fire," the sergeant barked at his men. "It is the Ranger from Arizona!"

The soldiers lowered their rifles. The sergeant walked toward Sam sweeping his hand about the cave. Dog Fannen and Jerome Gascoyne's bodies lay dead on the stone floor.

"I see you have been busy! Did you get your outlaw, Ranger?" the sergeant asked.

"I did," Sam said. "He's back there, dead." He gave a nod in the direction of the narrow corridor where Carver lay in the ray of sunlight.

The sergeant quickly told his men, "Go get this outlaw and bring him out here." He looked at Sam and said, "I will shoot him too. I must make certain he is dead, eh?"

"Be my guest," Sam said. "I'm headed back to Nogales."

"Ah, that is good," The sergeant said with a thin smile.

Sam nodded. He understood what was going on. By the time this story made its rounds, the sergeant would be the one who killed the outlaw leader of the infamous Wild Bunch. Sam didn't care. He'd done what he came here to do. "I heard shots out there," he said.

"Yes, we found three Apache hiding in the rocks," said the sergeant. "They might have been waiting to attack you! Lucky for you we discovered them. You might now owe your life to me and my men—the Mexican Army," he added proudly.

"Most gracious, Sergeant," Sam said, doubting if any *live* Apache would have still been hiding out there in the rocks. He gestured toward the bag of gold on the stone floor. "That's gold coin from the Esplanade robbery," he said. "You'll find a horse out on the hillside carrying another bag of it." He nodded at Gascoyne's body. "That'll be his horse." He offered no opinion on what Gascoyne might have been doing out here, or what his intentions might have been. That hadn't been part of his job here, he thought.

"You are mistaken, Ranger," the sergeant said, shaking his head. "We found a horse, but sadly, there was no bag of gold on it."

"That's too bad," Sam said. "It was just a hunch I had." As he spoke he dropped the spent cartridge from his big Colt and replaced it, and slipped the gun down into its holster. Maybe the Frenchman hadn't dug up his share. Maybe it was still hidden on the hillside—maybe the woman took it on her way out. He didn't know, and he likely never would. He was done here. He swung the big Swiss rifle up over his shoulder and walked away, out to where he'd left Black Pot and the dead Apache's horse. He thought about the woman as he dropped the reins from the Apache's horse and gave it a slap on its rump with his hat. *Watch out for wolves ...,* he said silently as the freed desert barb lopped away through dirt and rock. He stepped atop Black Pot and gathered his reins. He looked in the barb's direction, but saw only a stir of dust it left in its wake. He looked off in the direction the woman, Julie Wilder, would have taken. By now, her dust had settled, leaving not a trace of her in sight. *Someday, then?* she had said to him.

Someday then ..., he thought to himself. He gave the big stallion the slightest touch of his heels and put forward onto the narrow trail, his rifle across his lap, looking Northwest in the direction of the border line.

Black Pot ... Let's go home ....

THE END

For more about Arizona Ranger Sam Burrack, be sure to read the following preview of *Montana Red*. For more about the character Julie Wilder, read the preview of *Blood Lands* following *Montana Red* on page 270.

Hope you enjoyed the 39th book in the *Big Iron Series*. Following are the first few chapters of *Montana Red*, the 1st book in this long-running, popular series.

THE SEARCH FOR

MONTANA RED

**The Ranger Lives for the Hunt.
The Outlaw Lives for the Killing.
Now They Are About to Come Face to Face at Last.**

Arizona Ranger Sam Burrack is a man of courage with a lightning-quick draw. His goal is swift justice, and his aim is as sure as death. With a .58 caliber rifle behind his saddle and a list of outlaws next to his heart, he tracks his prey relentlessly, alone, and to the bitter end.

No one under the badlands sun would put the Ranger's skills to the test like Montana Red Hollis, a man more brutal than any beast and more cunning than any desperado the Ranger has ever hunted. No one is safe from the wrath of Montana Red and, until the Ranger took up the search, no one was brave enough to stop him. Now, on the high badlands where the fastest gun rules and only the strongest survive, a bloodthirsty killer is about to meet his match.

From master storyteller Ralph Cotton comes an extraordinary story about lawmen and the lawless—and of gun justice in the rugged American West.

PROLOGUE

MONTANA RED

*Here are preview chapters from Ralph Cotton's **Montana Red**, the first book in the **Big Iron Series**. **Montana Red** is available in both softcover and ebook versions.*

Buenos dias, Ran-jur, the little girl had said, smiling, her face slightly shying to one side as she padded barefoot past him along the dirt street. A strand of black hair swept forward and glistened across her face. She pushed it aside with the tip of a finger and walked on, an empty brown water gourd swinging on its leather loop in her hand. The rain season had come and gone with no rain falling and none to speak of the season past. About her the land and sky stood stark and unyielding, as dry as the heart of a broken stone.

The frayed edge of her thin serape dragged along in the dirt behind her, stirring a low rise in the burning dust. When the ranger did not answer but only looked up from his thoughts and tipped the brim of his tall gray sombrero, she slowed but did not stop, and turning quarter-wise she looked back at him as she moved on toward the well.

A gaunt red chicken cocked up from its pickings in the dirt and scolded her, and fled from her path in a flurry of dust and batting wings. A single dry feather stood in the heat, then lighted back and forth to the ground. She walked on, with the chicken watching from beneath a spent and tilted wagon where so long it had sat broken that a single clump of pale dry grass had weaved upward through its bleached spokes.

Like all things abandoned in that bare fiery basin, dust had lapped in and crept up the wagon's brittle spokes until the wagon seemed to have grown unnurtured from the barren earth itself. The rib caging of some small creature lay glistening white near the wagon, half sunken where some predator of the night had left it.

On her way back, with the gourd full of water resting heavy down her side, she smiled again, cupping her free hand near her cheek to hide the gap left there by a missing front tooth.

"Hola," he said, this time as she passed. With a gloved finger he pushed up the brim of his sombrero. And this time he returned her smile and added as she shied her face, "Aw, don't you fret about that tooth. It'll grow back twice as pretty." Friendly now, yet his eyes and his voice seemed lost and distant in a way she'd never seen before, and she cupped her hand closer and did not look back again until she stood before the open door to the adobe. Then she stole a guarded glance back to where he sat in the wooden chair beneath the shade of the ragged canvas overhang. A hot breeze licked at the canvas.

He sat looking back down at the ground now, his sombrero tilted forward. Bowed in prayer, she thought, or—if her young mind could fashion such a thought—perhaps succumbed to something dark inside himself.

Midmorning heat wavered atop the billowing canvas and up the sides of the crumbling adobe walls behind him. His horse stood in the shade near him and lifted its nose west toward things unseen. The shade about them stood out in its darkness against the white hot glare of sun, the two of them appearing to be drawn into a black hole and swallowed up on the hard flat belly of the land. Beyond the crumbling adobe stood the well some twenty yards off. Beyond the well stood no artifice of humankind's manifestation but for a small frail corral patched and strung with scraps of board, dried mesquite, and knotted wire with strands of mane and fur entwined in it. Beyond that, nothing, except a low drawing breath of wind over sand and a narrow trail snaking off across the desert floor. Dry stands of pale wild grass and mesquite brush stretched outward to the far end of vision.

He looked small and brittle and ancient to her against the long backdrop of earth and sun, him with his tall sombrero pulled low across his brow and his broad duster collar raised against his cheeks. Her mother had told her that he had many things on his mind today ... and *yes* it was so, she thought.

She squinted in the sun's glare, concerned for this man who always before would bring her rock candy when he brought flour and tins of beans and corn to her and her mother. She had been asleep when he came to the door last night and had only heard his voice and her mother's voice from some far away place. In a second the door had creaked shut again and the voices ceased, yet she knew that had she been up, he would have swept off his dusty sombrero in a grand gesture and bent down to her to say something in his broken Spanish just to make her laugh. She knew he liked hearing her laughter.

She was allowed to take candy from *this* man, and from *this* man only, because her mother had said that in *this* man there was no meanness, no harm to come—no *evil* to be read or felt. Not in *this* man. Yet today there was a darkness about him she'd never seen before. Seeing it frightened her. She was not frightened *of* him, but rather *for* him; and for reasons she did not understand, she crossed herself and whispered the name of the Virgin Mother under her breath as she swung open the sun bleached door to the adobe and stepped through it out of the heat. Today she saw no laughter in him.

Beneath the dusty canvas overhang he stirred restless in the rickety wooden chair until at length he stood up from it, propped a dusty boot up on it, and adjusted his belt and holster and the brim of his pearl gray sombrero. He stared off, out to where the burnt land turned into a long narrow haze and bled blue-silver upward into the sky. Beside him, the big dun horse jerked its sweat darkened head and blew and grumbled and looked down, scraping a hoof on the hard dirt.

Horses knew man better than man knew horses, he always thought. He whispered something to it under his breath and watched its sharp eyes bore back into his. A wisp of damp mane raised on the wind, and the horse nickered low and breathed deep, and held his gaze until he turned and looked away.

His Christian name was Sam Burrack, but to be honest about it, he'd almost forgotten it over the years. If paperwork was forced on him he simply initialed it in a loose scrawl, "SB.RNGR." He had short tolerance for paperwork and had managed to reduce his to a single list he carried in his breast pocket at all times. His records were easy to keep and simple to understand. Should a man's name appear on his list it meant that man was *wrong.* Should a man's name become crossed off his list, it meant that man was *dead.* After a time he'd even dropped the SB, and for years had only scrawled "RNGR." As far back as he could now remember everybody called him *the ranger*, and nothing more. Even other rangers called him *the ranger,* as if unlike themselves who had taken on the title along with their oath, their badge, and all the more formidable trappings of the job, he had somehow been born with the title instead of a name—the job having taken the man as surely as the man had taken the job.

And the job had swallowed him.

The job ....

He straightened and raised his boot from the chair, and stood in the dirt beside it, still staring off, yet no longer seeing the land or the sky, seeing instead the picture of the young woman's cold dead face where she'd lain in the dirt in the black puddle of blood, and where the dust had blown in across her naked body and her hollow open eyes as if dust and dust alone had come at the sound of her dying plea.

Though it had been over a month, the picture remained, as clear in memory as it had been in flesh. Beside the dead woman he saw as clearly the body of the Indian boy, half of his head gone and flies swarming there. What he'd seen he could not abide, and at the dark picture of it he winced and looked away and still could not shed himself of it.

The picture clung deep in the center of his being and all other thoughts that came and went were only thin clouds passing across some terrible mountain. Behind the passing of the clouds the terrible mountain remained. Nothing moved it. A tendon stiffened in his neck and he swallowed against it and ran a gloved hand along the dun's damp mane.

When he spotted the lone rider come up out of the distant haze, he picked up the reins to the dun horse; yet it seemed a full hour would pass before the rider swung the big bay off the dirt street and beneath the overhang. The bay stood wet and frothed and slung its head, the heat of it filling the space around them. "What did he say, Captain?" The ranger asked as the captain's boot touched the dirt.

The young captain turned to him sweeping off his hat and slapping dust from his trousers.

"You sure don't waste no time, do you?" he said.

"Got none to waste," the ranger replied. "Was it Red Hollis or not?"

The captain stalled for a second, wiped a hand across his sweat streaked jaw, then let out a breath and said, "Yes, it was Montana Red Hollis, just like you said. Him and three friends of his. But they're long gone north. Judge said forget them for now. We can't spare a man. And he said tell you if you expect to get any expense reimbursement from now on, you best start holding receipts."

"What's the others' names?" The ranger stepped in and

ran his gloved hand down along the bay's neck. The horse bobbed its wet head up and down and sniffed against him.

The captain cocked his head to one side. "You're not listening to me, are you?"

"Sure I am," the ranger spoke without turning to him. "Judge said I better keep receipts. So I will." He rubbed the horse under its chin, and asked, "Now. You gonna tell me their names?"

"Well ...." The captain pushed his hair to the side and sat his hat back on his head. "It's a couple of drifters named Hurley Yates, and Donald Kurtz. Real bad eggs. But it doesn't matter to you. Judge said we got more trash pouring up out of Kansas than we can shove back with both hands. He said tell you."

"You said there's *three* of them." The ranger cut him off, turning to him, his eyes fixed on him.

"What? Oh ... there is. Third one's a young cowboy named Bennie Burdett. Judge figures he's just a cowhand got into bad company and got pulled into it."

"Just pulled into it, huh?" The ranger nodded and glanced down. A hot wind swung through, lapping the canvas overhang up and down in its frame. Dust swirled.

"Now listen to me *good,*" the young captain said. He raised a dusty gloved finger for emphasis. "The judge is just as torn up about this as you are. We all are! But this isn't the time. We've got too many miles and too few men to cover them." He stopped. Seeing how the ranger stared at his pointing finger, he lowered it and rubbed his hand on his trouser leg. "And the thing is, we've got jurisdiction problems. The United States federal government's saying we can't go crossing lines unless we've got permission to do so, in writing."

"In writing?" The ranger pitched an arm up and let it drop. "Well, *there* we are. Now if Red Hollis and his boys'll put it *in writing* every time they get ready to go on a killing spree, we'll have ourselves a *dandy* thing here."

"I knew you'd act this way," the captain said. "But you can't go and that's that."

"Can't go?"

"You know what I mean." The captain settled and gazed off toward the adobe where the little girl had come forth at the sound of their voices and stood watching from the open door. A silence passed beneath a hot gust of wind until the captain said in a lowered voice nodding toward the child. "That little girl— Isn't she ...?"

"Yep, she is."

"My, my." The captain rubbed his chin. "Does she know who you are?"

"No. Not altogether." He'd stepped back along the side of his dun horse, flipped open his saddlebags, and took out a dusty bottle of rye. "I come through here when I can. Try to help out some." He uncorked the bottle and handed it to the captain.

The captain took it without taking his eyes from the little girl. He threw back a shot, let out a whiskey hiss and handed the bottle back. "Is this why you wanted me to meet you here? Thinking this would move me some way?"

"No. But here's where we are." The ranger corked the bottle and bounced it gently in his palm. "Your daddy was a good man. I know what he'd be telling me about Red Hollis right about now."

The captain only nodded slightly. "It's different now. There's just so many *crazies* out there ... more every day it seems. I think the world's lost its mind or something. You ever wonder what it's all worth?" He still watched the little girl until her mother appeared at her side, looked over at them and drew the child back.

"Nope. I just cross them off my list and go on to the next. It's better that way."

The captain rubbed his eyes and turned them away from the closed door. "Think her mother will ever tell her?"

The ranger dropped the bottle back in his saddlebags and closed the flap. "What good would come of it? She never knew her father, or what he was. At least you got to know yours. That's worth something to you, ain't it?"

The captain pushed his hat brim up an inch. "So, you're just some kindly old gentleman who comes by now and then?"

"They've still got to eat. I killed him straight up for what *he* done. They weren't no part of it."

"Was he worse than Montana Red Hollis?" The captain turned his eyes to him.

The ranger shrugged. "He was just one more killer. They're all about the same in the end. His luck was *up* the day he killed your daddy. It was *down* the day I caught up to him."

"But still ... Montana Red Hollis?" He glanced down at the big pistol on the ranger's hip, then back up to his eyes. "I don't like you going after him alone."

"Don't make him bigger than he is," the ranger said. "It's just a manhunt, no more no less."

"It's never *just* a manhunt when you go out there." The captain nodded out into the wavering distance. "This is not a one-man job."

"It'll come down to one man though. It always does." He smiled a little.

But the captain didn't smile. "Montana Red Hollis is one of those fast gun-handlers you hear about lately. He draws and fires from atop his holster. How quick are you on the draw?"

"I don't know. I always draw before I get there. It's just one less thing to do." He smiled again. "But I'll work on it, if it makes you feel better."

The captain ignored his smile again. "Don't go in shooting first and asking questions later, all right? It would look good on you if you brought somebody in *alive* for a change."

"I always give them a choice," the ranger said.

"But not when you get to Montana Red," the captain said. "You won't give him any, will you?"

The picture of the dead woman and the Indian boy streaked across the ranger's mind. "What do you think?"

"You better not."

Another silence passed as the young captain glanced away, back at the closed door of the adobe. Then he shook his head and looked back to the ranger. "I don't understand you sometimes."

"Neither do I, sometimes." The ranger let go a breath, stepped over and raised a boot into the stirrups.

"Well ... I'll cover for you best I can with the judge," the captain said as the ranger turned his horse and stepped it out of the shade.

"I know it." The ranger raised a gloved hand and adjusted his sombrero down on his head.

"We didn't meet here today," the captain said. "Never met, never talked. I haven't seen you since *February*. But you start keeping some receipts, you hear me?"

"I hear you."

The captain murmured something under his breath and watched the ranger's horse right itself toward the distant swirl of heat and dust, and where above it a buzzard swung low and circled as if in waiting. He smiled a thin smile to himself and shook his head as he saw the ranger stop the horse in the dirt street outside the adobe and raise a small bag toward it in his gloved hand. "You beat all," the captain whispered under his breath.

"Did you think I forget you, little princess?" the ranger said, speaking down to the child in his broken Spanish when she ran out to him and reached up and took the bag.

She replied in Spanish that no, of course she had not thought that. Her mother told her that she had seen him like this before and that he had much on his mind regarding his job.

His job .... He smiled and leaned from his saddle and placed a gloved hand on her cheek.

"When I come back through, I expect I'll see a brand-new tooth more shiny and pretty than any I ever saw."

"Si," she said; and stepping back a step she went on to say how her mother had told her that these teeth she shed as a child would all come back like before, only stronger and better, and the new ones would last her a lifetime. *"Gracias,"* she then added, holding the bag of rock candy. In her dark eyes he saw his reflection, small and distant, and he watched his hand draw away from her cheek.

She blinked and visored her eyes with her hand, and his reflection disappeared, gone and away into the breadth and depth of all shadow and light that wrapped itself around him. Behind him at a glance he saw the young captain step up into the stirrups and move his horse out of the black slice of shade and onto the dirt street toward the well. The girl had stepped back farther and made room for the ranger to heel his horse forward.

The ranger raised his faded bandanna up across the bridge of his nose and adjusted it with a gloved hand. At the door of the adobe he saw the child's mother stare at him through caged eyes. He stared back at her across the bandanna until beneath him the dun horse rose high-hoofed and restless, grumbling, stepping side-wise and swishing its damp tail. Then the woman raised her hand slightly and nodded; and he gave the horse reins and moved off.

Red Hollis, he said to himself, catching a flash of the two bodies in the dirt and the flies and the dried black blood; and in his mind, along with the scene came the stench of it, as real as the wind and the heat around him. *Montana Red Hollis* .... His inner voice spoke the name, yet even in silence the sound of it seemed to echo out across the badlands and beckon back to him, taunting him like the cry of some crazed beast ... calling him to come and give chase to it, to hunt it down in its lair and there destroy it.

CHAPTER 1
MONTANA RED

He was a good gambler if nothing else, he thought. He knew when a streak had run its course and was about to change, one way or the other. For the past six weeks his luck had held, running good and strong at the tables and even better with the ladies. But now ....

Through the open window he kept an eye on the lone rider coming in down there on the far end of the wide rutted street, the big sweat-streaked dun horse jutting its head high to one side in spite of the white froth swinging from its muzzle and its wet mane clinging down its neck. He'd watched the rider appear up out of the desert at a great distance, and he'd sipped on the bottle of whiskey and watched, watched through the shimmer of heat and dust, and through the dirty lace curtains as they licked back and forth in the hot wind.

He'd sipped rye whiskey until the rider drew in deeper from the edge of town, then he'd taken one last long swig, corked the bottle, pitched it on the bed and began stuffing his belongings into a faded purple carpetbag. His name was Joseph Sharpe, but the players and whores called him Gentleman Joe. He could outbluff the devil betting hell against Cincinnati if he had to—but not today. Today it was time to fold and fade.

Gentleman Joe had become a master at the art of leaving a town. He could quit a place at the drop of a hat and disappear like smoke, leaving neither a trace nor a whisper.

He'd killed a whore up in Creed four years back. Her name was Peg-Leg Molly, a name he'd never forget. How could he? She was the only person he'd ever killed, the only person he'd ever *shot* for that matter. He was drunk at the time, and she'd robbed him in his sleep. She'd taken his watch, his stickpin and ring, and was about to cut his throat for good measure. But that's when his luck kicked in.

A fly had lit on his nose, waking him just in time to catch a glimpse of a straight razor near his cheek. Rolling away off the lilac-scented bed and onto the hard wooden floor, he'd gotten both feet beneath him when Peg-Leg Molly came screaming at him like a wildcat. His hand found the little derringer inside his vest and he jerked it out and shot her down—put just one tiny hole right above the yellow plume trim on her bustline.

Damn .... He'd thought about it ever since, time to time, especially when he saw the glint of a badge.

He always saw the way she'd just backed across the room, sighed and sat down in a chair. *You ... shot me*— The razor fell from her hand and in a minute she was dead. No struggle. Just a small hole like that and she'd sat down and died. Hardly any blood at all, only a thin red trickle down her bright yellow dress.

Of course he didn't stick around to explain. No sir! No sooner had her eyes glazed over, than he'd left without stopping long enough to even pick all his money up off the floor. He'd managed to snatch up his watch and stickpin and go. And he'd been running ever since.

You'd think that four years of running and hiding would be enough, that maybe it was all forgotten, that no lawman would even remember it anymore, and maybe they didn't. Maybe most of them didn't. But that one down there now—riding in on a sweat-streaked dun with the tied-down forty-five Colt stretching nearly to his knee—that one would remember. That one never forgot anything.

Damn! When he latched the single leather strap on the carpetbag, he ran a hand across his wet forehead and stepped back to the window. It was boiling hot in the room facing the street. The cooler rooms were all along the back of the building, out of the sun. But he'd asked for this one just to keep an eye on the town's comings and goings. Now he was glad he did.

He jerked the watch from his vest pocket, checked the time and put it away. In twenty minutes the stage would roll in from Wakely, then head over to Grafton; but he wasn't about to wait that long.

He held one curtain still and looked down through it, shadowed by the darkness of the room against the sun's glare. Now the rider turned his horse to the hitch rail across the street and just sat there for a second. Peculiar-looking from this angle up here—a riding duster hanging from beneath a wide round sombrero, one side of the duster pulled back and hooked behind his long holster. A glint of sunlight shone of the butt of the big pistol. Two gloved hands stuck out from beneath the sombrero brim, holding the reins.

He saw the gray sombrero turn, taking in the street; and although the sombrero made no attempt to tilt up toward him, he stepped back from the window just the same. Still watching, he saw the rider swing down from the saddle and stand for a moment, watching the boys from the Flying Cross shove each other back and forth in the street out front of the saloon. They were drunk now and going at it. Playing rough, getting rougher.

So that's him .... The thought crossed Gentleman Joe's mind, that if he was a braver man, a gunman, he could get one good clear shot off from up here and end it. He could do that. Sure he could. It had only taken one tiny bullet hole to kill Peg-Leg Molly.

He slipped the nickel-plated thirty-eight from his pocket and eased it past the curtain into the sunlight. A sudden flash of sunlight streaked off the shiny pistol barrel. It startled him. He jerked the gun back inside the window and saw his hand tremble. Who was he kidding? He couldn't do it. He didn't have it in him.

He was no gunman. He was a gambler, nothing more. What if he missed? What if he only wounded him? *No* .... He shook his head. *Bad odds.* He dare not think it. Not about this man. Better to run, get out now through the back, grab a horse and go. Yet he only stood there watching like a man charmed by a snake.

On the street, the ranger stretched, pressing a hand to the small of his back. He watched the Flying Cross boys from twenty yards away; and when he'd spun his reins around the hitch rail, he stood beside the big dun, watching them even closer as he took off his gloves and stuck them in his duster pocket. The Flying Cross boys were busy, cussing, spitting, threatening anybody foolish enough to walk their side of the street. They hadn't noticed the lone rider come in, didn't see him untie the leather straps and let down the rolled-up canvas atop his saddlebags.

One of them threw a whiskey bottle high in the air, let out a long squall and exploded it with a blast from his pistol. "Damn'er Hurley, let's shoot sumpin! I ain't shot nothing all day!" He let out another whoop and fired two rounds straight up. Townsfolk scurried. The ranger caught a glimpse of two women hike up their dresses and slip into a doorway. A parasol dropped to the boardwalk and rolled off into the dirt. Faces peeked through windows, then dropped down. Signs on doors turned from open to closed with the flick of a nervous wrist.

"The hell ya'll looking at? Hunh?" From amid the Flying Cross boys, the tall gunman, Donald Kurtz, stepped into the middle of the street waving his pistol. He spread his feet, pulled off a shot, and blew a hole through the barbershop window. Then he hooted and laughed and looked all around, spinning his pistol back into his holster, his big teeth shining beneath a mustache streaked with beer foam.

But then his laughter fell away and his grin faded as he caught sight of the tall gray sombrero and the riding duster stooping down in the middle of the street. He saw the man was doing something there, setting something up? Some kind of equipment? What?

"Look at this, boys," he said in a low tone, spreading a curious smile. The stranger in the duster did not look up from whatever he was doing. He kneeled there—*a Mexican, maybe? Now wouldn't that be some fun*—his face hidden beneath the gray sombrero, out there busy, on one knee, clicking something together, snapping something in place. What was all this?

The cowboys stood silent for a moment, just watching. Then Kurtz called out, *"Como estes—" Aw hell with it.* "Hey, you there, greaser! The hell ya think you're doing? Hunh?" He took a step closer when he got no response. "You're in a bad spot there, in case you don't know it." He glanced at the others, grinned, then added, "You're squatting right where I'm getting ready to empty this pistol. *Comprende?*" He patted his hand on his pistol butt and had started to lift it from the holster when the duster stood straight up and stepped to the side. *Huh-uh. No Mexican standing there ....*

Kurtz's hand tensed but stopped; his head cocked to one side. In the middle of the dusty street stood a tripod, four feet high. "The hell's that?" Kurtz took a step back, opening and closing his hand, his palm rubbing the butt edge of his pistol. One of the others laughed behind him.

"I know. He's a photo-grafter," said one.

"Gonna take a likeness of us for pos-terity," said another.

Kurtz grinned again, wiped a hand across his mustache, and said in a mock tone, "Naw, that's too short for a bunch of long-legged ole boys like us. Maybe he wants a likeness of our boots. Is that it? You taking a likeness of our boots?"

"Maybe he takes tin plates of little-bitsy fellers," one said with a laugh.

Then Kurtz called out to the stranger in the duster, "Is that it? You looking for some little-bitsy fellers? Gonna take their ...." His voice trailed down, and he stood staring, seeing the tip of a long holster tied down right about knee level. A ranger's badge shone on the stranger's chest. A breeze raised the brim of the sombrero an inch and held it there.

The ranger had just pulled off his duster. He hung it on the tripod, took a good solid breath and started walking toward them, calm and steady, drawing the long pistol and letting it hang in his right hand. "No," he said; and he kept walking closer as he slipped his left hand inside his shirt and took out a wrinkled piece of paper.

"I'm here to take in four men." He held the paper up, tapped it against the breeze, and without glancing at it, he said, "Hurley Yates, Donald Kurtz, Bennie Burdett and Red Hollis ... dead or alive." Just like that, *dead or alive*, the *alive* part sounding more like an afterthought, something he'd shrugged off more or less and hadn't really planned on. "Any of you cowboys are free to leave. But you better do it now before we commence."

He waved the paper slightly, still coming closer, a determined bearing about him. He was no taller than average, but swinging a lot of iron in that right hand, that right shoulder stooped a bit low. "Are you Donald Kurtz?" the ranger called out.

"Who's asking?" Kurtz felt a nerve twitch in his jaw. Now he *knew* who was walking toward him. The ranger kept coming. "Whooa now! Stop right there!" Kurtz's hand tightened on his pistol butt; his eyes locked on the big pistol swinging back and forth in the ranger's hand, the tip of the barrel brushing past his knee, coming closer.

The ranger didn't so much as slow down. He kept coming, steady, unwavering. "I mean it!" Kurtz shouted, loud. But he took a step back. Behind him, four of the Flying Cross boys spread out. One man slipped around the corner of the saloon and ran, his boots pounding through the alley toward the livery barn.

"Are you Donald Kurtz?" Now the ranger's eyes bored into his as he came closer, ten yards, then nine, eight, seven.

Montana Red

"That's right, I am." He took another step back, and stopped. Nobody in their right mind came this close to a man. It had Kurtz shaken. "And now I *know* who you are, Ranger! But you ain't taking me *no damn place,* not alive—"

"Fair enough." The next thing Kurtz saw clearly was the big pistol explode on the upswing from ten feet away, then he caught a glimpse of his left boot spinning through the air above him as he hit the ground. The very *last* thing he saw was the sky tilting out of shape, churning red, and the ranger walking past him, sweeping his free hand down, picking up Kurtz's pistol as he went. And Kurtz's world went black and silent there in the dirt, even as the sound of gunfire exploded above him.

Like four solid steady beats of a large drum, the big pistol bucked in the ranger's hand, from one man to the next, as he walked forward in the dirt street. He felt a bullet burn through the sleeve of his shirt across his forearm, but he didn't flinch. By the time the last man started to fall, he'd walked so close to him, he reached out, shoved the man's gun to the side and grabbed it from his hand just as it went off. Fire streaked past his side, then he pitched the smoking gun away.

The last man dropped straight down beneath a drifting gray haze, rocking back and forth on his knees, holding his stomach. "Oh Lord," he gasped. He looked up at the big pistol pointing down at him. "You're him, ain't ya? Kurtz is right. You're that ranger, ain't ya?"

"Kurtz is dead. Where's Bennie Burdett, Hurley Yates, and Red Hollis?" He cocked the big pistol and held it close to the wounded man's face. "You just as well tell me before ya die. Might make it better for you once you get where you're going."

"Yates lit out. Bennie's ... at the ... Flying Cross. Don't know ... where Montana Red's at." He rocked forward, then caught himself. "I hope you find him though." He struggled for another breath. "So's ... he can kill ya. Same as you kilt us."

"We'll see." The ranger pulled bullets from his belt and replaced the five he'd spent. He stepped back, looking around at his handiwork in the dirt street, a master craftsman inspecting a finished project. He swallowed the dryness in his throat. Turning his head slightly, he slid a gaze up through the hovering drift of powder smoke, to the window where one curtain had been hanging straight and still as he rode into town, the window from which the flash of metal had come— the flash he'd seen dance across the toe of his boot as he'd stood there beside his horse.

One curtain had hung still and straight while the other fluttered in the breeze. How blind would you have to be to miss that? Now both curtains licked back and forth. Whoever'd been there was gone.

He shoved the big pistol down in his holster and looked out past the edge of town at the wake of dust left by Hurley Yates. And that *was* Hurley Yates, the one who'd ducked out around the corner before the shooting started. *No sign of Red Hollis though. He might have to thin out half the outlaws in the territory before he got to that one ....*

He turned and walked back to his horse, slid the big fifty-eight caliber Swedish rifle from its boot and walked back to the middle of the street, running a hand along the barrel. Townsfolk ventured out now, walking carefully, cautiously there among the dead. One of the two woman slipped from the doorway and hurried out to the parasol in the dirt. She snatched it up, shook it, and hurried away with it under her arm. The wounded man still rocked back and forth in the street, but now his words were slurred when he spoke. "Sheep-licking bunch of trash," he said. A red string of saliva swung from his lips.

When the ranger had put his duster back on, he snapped the rifle in place on the short tripod, kneeled down behind it, adjusted the sights, and stared off at the stream of dust in the distance. This was not the way he wanted it, not a back-shot. But he'd figured coming in—throwing down on this many at once—somebody was bound to make a run for it. So he'd prepared himself for it.

He took a short porcupine quill from his duster, took off his sombrero, pinned up the front of the brim and put it back on. He relaxed for a second and glanced up at the window with the billowing lace curtains. *Who in the world would stick a shiny gun out in the sunlight that way? Nobody he could think of. Nobody who knew what they were doing. Not Red Hollis ....*

Then he glanced around the street at the anxious faces watching him, and at the dying man, the man not rocking now, but down on his side, scrapping his boots back and forth in the dirt, struggling for purchase on the earth, finding none. Dark blood puddled about him. His boots were soaked with urine. He babbled now, low and mindless, cursing the dark shadows moving about him in the street. His hand scratched in the dirt toward the pistol three feet away.

"When ya gonna shoot him?" said a voice beside the ranger.

The ranger turned and looked into the wide-eyed face of an old townsman, leaning near him, squatting with his palms on his knees.

"When I'm good and ready," the ranger said.

The townsman nodded toward the rise of dust far away, then back to the ranger. "Well, it's for sure he ain't getting no closer. That's a hard shot, even for a big rifle like that—the dust and all."

The ranger glared at him and the man backed off a step, then leaned back down on his palms. "Reckon you'd just be wasting all them big bullets, hunh? No sense in that."

The ranger sat studying the stream of dust until a dark spec rose up out of the narrow tip of it, ascending up above the thick brown cloud, climbing the rising land toward the foothills at the end of vision.

Then he leaned forward into the butt of the rifle, aimed it, locked it on the tiny dark spec, followed it as it climbed higher, then eased his finger back against the trigger until the slam of the butt stock jarred him to his bones. The sound of the shot cracked along the front of the buildings, jarring them as well, and echoed off through the swirling heat.

For a second even the wind seemed to stop and watch, holding its breath as the tiny dark spec climbed higher. Another second passed, then the townsman clucked his tongue in his cheek. "Too bad ...." But in another second, he squinted and turned his head to one side, not believing his eyes as the tiny spec seemed to split in half, and the top half sailed off to the side and fell as the bottom half climbed higher into the foothills. "Well, help, my time ...."

The ranger leaned forward, pulled down the sights on the rifle, and stood up dusting his knees. He stared off at the distance as he untied his faded bandanna from around his neck and pressed it against the graze across his forearm. "I'll pay you a dollar to take out a wagon and haul him back here," he said without looking at the old man beside him.

"What if he ain't dead?"

The ranger just stared at him.

"All right. I'll do it then." He nodded toward the bodies in the street. The last man lay dead now, face down in the dirt, dust settling on his back, his fingers only inches away from the butt of the pistol. "How much to haul them out of here and tidy the street up some?"

The ranger unsnapped the rifle, picked up the tripod, and kicked it shut. "It ain't my street," he said, and he walked away to the hotel with his rifle and tripod over his shoulder.

When he stopped at the desk, the clerk came running in behind him from the street and swung around the counter, smoothing back his hair. "Whooie! Now that was something, I'm telling ya. I never seen such carrying on in my life."

The ranger swung the rifle and tripod down onto the counter, reached down and turned the register around. He ran a finger down the list of names. "What's the number of the room up there on the right end, facing the street?"

"Now see here!" The clerk tried to turn the register back around but the ranger grabbed his hand, picked it up, moved it aside and laid it down on the counter.

"The number. If you please."

"It's number seven," the clerk said; and although his hand had not been squeezed hard, he looked down at it and rubbed it as the ranger ran his finger down the register page.

Mister J. Jones, huh? Figures. He turned and walked to the stairs, leaving the big rifle on the counter. "Watch that for me," he said. And he walked up the creaking stairs without bothering to quieten his steps. He knew the room would be empty, knew it had been since about the time the shooting started. Whoever Mister J. Jones was, he was at that very moment putting distance between himself and this place.

Inside the room he looked at the bottle of whiskey on the bed, saw where Mister J. Jones in his haste had taken one last drink and pitched it there, leaving a wet stain where whiskey had ran down the side of the bottle. He picked it up, pulled the cork, and sniffed the bottle as he sloshed it around. He threw back a drink. When he'd corked it and pitched it back on the bed, he looked around the room, taking his time.

All that remained of J. Jones were two aces and a king on an oak dresser; and he picked them up and saw where the corner of each card bore the slightest thumbnail scar. *Gambler ... that figures too. The shiny gun.*

He walked over and looked out the window toward the west, the way he'd rode in, the way J. Jones had watched from this very spot through the lace curtains. From here, Jones could have picked him off too easy with a rifle—not much harder with a pistol, if he was any shot at all and had no qualms about it.

Whoever Jones was, he was no killer, that was plain enough. That being the case, he wondered what reason the man could've had for running. Everybody in the territory knew that he had no truck with gamblers, even those who marked their cards.

He took the wrinkled paper and a pencil stub from inside his shirt, unfolded the paper and ran his eyes down the list of names. At the top of the list was the name Montana Red Hollis, beneath it Hurley Yates, then Donald Kurtz, then Bennie Burdett. Beside each of the top four names he'd written the words "Killers, rapists." Now he circled Red Hollis and Bennie Burdett's name, and marked the other two off the list.

The list ran long with other names, some marked out, others now faded and barely legible—the ones down there near the bottom. On the very bottom of the list, he could no longer make out anything at all. Some of those names he knew by memory, others he just considered pardoned. Once the bottom of the paper turned worn and ragged and crumbled apart in his hand, unless that person was a hardened killer, he figured they'd served their time ... hiding out in the badlands.

* * *

It was dark when the gambler settled down and stopped looking back over his shoulder. The horse was winded and blowing froth as he led it up into the shelter of rock. He himself was breathing hard; and he dropped down on a flat rock with the reins hanging from his hand. Something dark and shiny slipped from under the rock and away into the darkness.

His hands trembled. He wiped dust from his face on his coat sleeve and thought of the bottle of whiskey he'd left back in the hotel room—needing it now. He thought of the breakfast he'd had that morning, eggs, pork, hot coffee, rich and strong and poured full of fresh cream. *Damn.* He hadn't eaten since. Nothing else had touched his empty stomach all day but the bite and burn of rye whiskey. Now he missed it, the food, the whiskey, even the bed, which wasn't the best he'd ever slept in, smelling as it did of old urine and strong lye soap.

Maybe he should've stayed, laid low and taken his

chances. There was no reason to think the ranger was looking for him, not after what he'd seen going on in the street. Then again, his name was somewhere on the ranger's list. Who could say; maybe he'd come to clear that list of old business. If that was the case, what chance would he have had against such a man. He saw part of what happened to the Flying Cross boys before he hightailed it out of there. He could've been next.

Montana Red Hollis. Wasn't that one of the names he'd heard, lurking up there behind the curtains, afraid to drop the hammer on the man. *Hollis, Hurley, Kurtz, Burdett.* If only they'd killed the ranger, that would've solved his problem. But now Kurtz and Hurley were dead. He'd seen Kurtz fall without getting off a shot, and he'd watched from a mile away and seen Hurley Yates spill from his horse like a bag of bones. Was there any way in the world to get away from this ranger?

And where in God's name did he find a rifle that could make a shot like that? It almost didn't seem fair, riding off, thinking you'd made a getaway, then all of a sudden your heart's blown out of your chest. Didn't seem right somehow.

He'd taken a chance and rode over to Hurley's body laying there in the sand, lifted his shooting gear, a canteen of water, and a long boot knife. Never in his life had he seen such a hole in a human being. He tried not to look at it, but he couldn't help himself. Right there where the man's heart should've been was a hole you could've looked straight through and saw the ground, had it not been for the blood and gore ...

He shivered, stood up and pulled Hurley's pistol from the holster draped across his saddlehorn. He turned the forty-four in his hand, a stripped-down Colt with a shaved front sight. At least he now had something better than the short barreled thirty-eight, if he needed it. At least, if it came down to it now, he could put up a fight if the ranger got him cornered.

Who was he kidding? If it ever came down to it—him and the ranger faced off in a life or death battle—he just as well pitch this pistol in the dirt for all the good it would do him.

How do you stop a man like him? It was as if he wasn't even human, walking in like that, that close! Killing Kurtz before he even got a shot off. But it would been different if the ranger ever caught up to Montana Red Hollis. Hollis was not from the same cut as Kurtz and Hurley. It would've gone different if Hollis had been there today. You bet. In spite of what he'd seen today, if it came down to the ranger and Montana Red, as a gambler he'd have to go with Red. That's what the smart money would do.

He might not be a gunman but he sure knew how to figure odds, and Red Hollis ... well, nobody would take the ranger against Red Hollis, no matter how long the odds.

He spun the dead man's pistol on his finger, almost dropped it, but caught it, and looked at it again. There, alone in the darkness, he felt embarrassed for a second, as if someone might have seen him fumble the big forty-four.

He glanced around and slipped the pistol back into the holster. Who the hell was he to even speak the names of men such as these. He'd been spooked by the flash of sunlight off the barrel of his pistol. What would he have done had he pulled the trigger? He pictured the pistol going off in his hand, missing the ranger by a mile and kicking up dust in the street, the ranger turning, looking up at him with hollow eyes, the big pistol raising. *Damn* ...

He shivered and shook his head, clearing it; and he sat on the flat rock and folded his arms against the chill of the desert night until he fell into a restless sleep, missing the hot room on Front Street and the smell of the musty bed.

CHAPTER 2
MONTANA RED

The bar was not lined with drinkers as it should've been on a night such as this. All the tables stood empty save for two, the one where a young whore called "Little Honey" dealt herself hand after hand of poker, then played against the five blind cards she laid out across from her; and the table back in the shadows against the far wall, where the ranger stared into a half-empty bottle of rye.

The bartender chewed his warm cigar and swatted flies with a bar rag. You'd think after all that had happened today in the street the place would be packed, alive and kicking, and buzzing with voices. But few ventured in because of *him—that blasted old ranger*—being there. Those who did stop in were quiet and subdued. They only drank one or two, and they only mentioned the weather as they shot a cautious glance toward the rear table. Then they moved on.

Damn ranger. The bartender slung the rag over his shoulder and crossed his arms on the empty bar. By now the word had gotten out to the Flying Cross. Any second the whole crew might step through the door. If they did, he'd already made up his mind to crawl along the floor behind the bar and skin out through the back window.

When Little Honey raised her face and rubbed the back of her neck, she saw the ranger staring at her and gave him her best seductive smile. She could not read the expression in his eyes when he nodded, beckoning her over to him, but she knew that behind every nod there was another dollar to be made, for any woman who knew her business. She knew hers.

She stood up just slow enough to let the slit in her dress fall away from her bare leg, then she walked over slowly—no hurry here—letting him get a good look at her wares, wanting to look just a little bored, a professional look. She watched his eyes for any sign of what he was looking for, any clue as to how she should play it. Yet his eyes said nothing to her.

He raised a boot beneath the table and pushed out a chair for her. "Oh ... a gentleman." She touched a hand to her breast, raised her brows slightly, and sat down. This might not turn out to be the easiest dollar she ever squeezed off, but on a slow night what could she do ....

"Buy you a drink?" He leveled his gaze into her eyes, and before she could answer, slide the empty glass across the table with his fingertips, filled it, and kept his hand around the bottle when he sat it down.

She shrugged and said, "Sure," and touched the tip of her tongue to her lips. "Will you be joining me?" She raised the glass slightly.

He raised the bottle, tapped it against her glass and waited until she took a sip. Then he threw back a drink and watched her eyes for a second. "I'm looking for a man," he said. His expression was the same, indiscernible, almost grim.

This one could take awhile, she thought. She relaxed, shifted sideways, crossed her legs and draped an arm over the chair back. "Well, then, aren't we *all* ...." She waited a second, then a quiet laugh spilled from her lips. But he didn't so much as raise a brow.

"He's a gambler. Left town today, but he's been playing here. Drinks single-cut rye. Been winning pretty good, I figure." He watched her eyes to see if she'd lie—if so, how much. "He was staying over at the hotel. Corner room facing the street. Goes by the name *Jones*. Know him?"

She studied his eyes, deep-set and gun-metal gray, piercing, too sharp and deep to look into for long, she thought. Eyes that could cut flesh and chill bone. "I know him," she said, and she glanced away, then back to him, only this time not directly. This man was at work, nothing more. There was no room for play here. "Of course, if I had a dollar for every *Jones*, or *Smith* I've known in the past year, I wouldn't be charging a dollar for *telling* somebody about them." There it was; she was working here too. Let him know it right off.

She threw back the drink and slid the empty glass to the middle of the table. She stared at him, until this time he glanced away, long enough to slip a dollar from his vest pocket and lay it beside the empty glass. "Yeah, him," she said, all business now, sliding the dollar to her as she poured herself another drink. "The young guy, twenty four, twenty five—stud player. I know him. Why? What's he done?"

"For a dollar, you tell me."

Again, the cutting eyes. She felt them on her even as she glanced down at her drink. She ran a finger around the edge of the glass. "Nothing that *I* know of." She shrugged. "Not a bad guy, really. Plays straight, far as I can tell. I think he had some trouble in Colorado. He mentioned it one night, drunk. He might've done something there." She ventured a gaze into those eyes. "Is that why you're looking for him?" She couldn't hold the gaze, but focused instead on the scar that curled across his cheek toward the corner of his mouth. That one had hurt, had gone to the bone. An old scar, she figured.

"Maybe," he said, thinking back, running his mind down the list of names inside his shirt, somewhere down low, where the writing was faded from sweat, heat and time. Somewhere there ... a name.

"But, you're a ranger ... that was in Colorado. You wouldn't be looking for *him* would you?"

"Where's he from back there?" He nodded east toward the bar, but she knew what he meant.

"He mentioned Ohio. But who knows? Whatever he did in Colorado, I don't think he'll be doing it again ... if that means anything to you."

He shook his head back and forth slowly. "What kind of horse does he ride? What kind of gun does he carry?"

She shook her head. "No horse. He came in by stage. Probably left the same way. Carries a shiny little pistol. I can't see him using it though." She smiled, rolled her eyes slightly. "He's kind of a dandy."

"Yeah?"

"Not a lot ... but kinda. I don't think he likes it out here much."

Kind of a dandy .... He thought about it a second, placing faces to traits. Nothing came. "How is he with women?"

She fixed a gaze on him now, cutting eyes or no. *"Details* cost another dollar."

He almost smiled. Almost, but not quite. "That ain't what I mean. I mean how does he treat them? Smack them around? Squeeze them for money ... what?"

"No. He's on the square—was with me anyway. I might even miss him, some." She looped a ringlet of hair around her finger, smiled and let it go. "He spent it when he had it ... and he usually had it. Yep, I'll miss him."

Big spender ... kind of a dandy ... Ohio. He stared at her, not seeing her, but shuffling faces, names, places in his mind.

Colorado. *Creed?* The bank robbery? No, not this guy, not *J. Jones.* What about shooting the whore, Molly Frome? He could see that, maybe. Peg-Leg Molly Frome. Not Peg-Leg because she was missing a limb, but Peg-Leg owing to the way she kept one leg flat and straight down the bed, not giving it all up, not to most of them anyway. Who was it that shot her? Joe something. Joe Sharpe? He'd go with that for the time being ....

"Do me a favor?" He reached over and filled her glass.

She folded her arms. "Watch your language." But then she unfolded them when he reached in his vest and brought up another dollar.

"If he shows up here again, tell him not to try something

stupid on me, or I'll have to kill him. Tell him I'm not looking for him for what happened with Peg-Leg Molly, if that's what he's worried about." He laid the dollar on the table, watched her slide it away, and wondered what she would think if he asked her for a *receipt*. "What do they call you?" He leaned back a little and she thought she saw his eyes soften ... not much, but some.

"Little Honey." There was the slightest suggestion in her eyes now. Not all business, he thought. But then, how could you tell with a good whore.

"Little Honey, huh? Figures," he said. He reached beneath the table, slipped the big holster off his lap and back down along his leg, whipped the rawhide string around his leg and tied the holster down.

She cocked her head. "What do you mean, it *figures*. What's that supposed to mean?"

"I mean, your voice," he said, standing, adjusting his hat. "Little Honey suits you. You've got a real pretty voice, smooth like honey."

"Oh ... well, thanks." She looked surprised; he'd almost smiled again, there for a second. "You're leaving, so soon? Aren't you concerned that the Flying Cross boys could be out there waiting for you?"

"They ain't coming," he said. Then he turned and walked across the floor, out through the bat wing doors, leaving a good six or seven shots in the bottle of rye.

"Whooie!" She smiled and fanned herself with her hand on the way back to her table, carrying the bottle of rye. "I felt like I was outstaring a rattlesnake. Is he as bad as they all say he is?"

The bartender grunted, then took the cigar from his mouth and said, "He's worse! If you've got any sense you'll stay wide and away from that crazy old ranger."

"Oh ... I don't know. I like 'em crazy now and then, just to break the monotony."

"Ha. You like 'em any way you get 'em, long as they ain't polecat ripe and molded over—"

"Shut up, Earl. The hell do you know about anything?" She cut him off, giggled, sat down and crossed her legs toward him, letting the slit in her dress fall open above her knee, giving him a look, feeling warm and wiggly up there under the dress. Warm from the whiskey, restless and wiggly from the slow turn of the night. "So, Earl, tell the truth, do you *miss* it a lot ... now that Tessy's gone back to Omaha?" She giggled again, ran a finger along her bare leg. "I know *I* sure do."

In minutes they began straggling in, one, two, and three at a time, until soon the place was blanketed by a heavy drift of smoke and the rise and roar of idle chatter. "I never seen anything like it!" a voice said. "What all did he have to say, Earl?"

The bartender had thrown the rag on the floor behind the bar and kicked it away. He grinned to himself in the mirror. It was the ranger being there that had kept them away. Now it was the ranger's *having* been there that would pack them in. The bartender hiked up his shirtsleeves above his garters. "Boys, he's something all right. But wait till them Flying Cross cowhands get a hold of him." *Damned old ranger ....*

* * *

He made his camp a mile out in the darkness and picketed his horse to graze in a sparse stretch of wild grass. He'd built his low fire a foot deep in the ground and worked a mound of sand up around it. From a distance his camp would go unnoticed; up close, he had the hearing of a predator, tuned to every rustle of dry brush or bat of wing in the night, there on the desert floor. Above him stars spilled like diamonds and silver dust in a wide trail curved to the dome of the universe. A night creature swung down, then away across the black velvet sky.

He sipped a steaming cup of Duttwieler's Tea, listening to the faint sound of hooves that had stopped just now, no more than ten yards out. A silence lingered before giving way to the soft drop of footsteps on the cooling sand. But no concern showed in his eyes as he kept attending to the big pistol broken apart on the blanket before him. Inside the loose button on his shirt lay a short-barreled forty-four.

"Hello the camp," said a voice just beyond the grainy circle of firelight. Still he did not look up from holding the freed cylinder between both hands, rolling it up and down, looking through it into the low flames. Firelight spiraled back on polished hand turned steel.

"Tea's hot," he said; and he laid the cylinder down, raised his left knee and rested his forearm across it. He picked up a stick with his right hand and stirred the embers, his hand close to the front of his shirt. "Come get you some, Tackett."

"How'd you know it was me, and not the Flying Cross boys?" The voice asked from the darkness, and when the ranger didn't answer, the voice added, "You left a hell of a mess back there, you know." Now the voice came from beneath a wide hat brim as the man stepped closer, leading a sorrel gelding. He stopped across the fire.

"Evening, Sheriff," the ranger said, barely glancing up from cleaning the pistol.

The man grunted, touching a finger to his hat brim. "Evening hell. What was you trying to do to me? Make me look bad?" He squatted down, touched his fingertips to the tin pot, then drew them back and rubbed them together. "Your tea don't smell no worse than it ever did." He stood and raised the flap on his saddlebags, took out a tin cup and wiped his finger around in it. "You had no call to make a move in my town without me."

"Shoulda been there," the ranger said, just flatly, no implication on his part. "I looked around for you first. Didn't see you nowheres. How's the Widow Morris?"

Sheriff Tackett squatted again and reached for the pot, then hesitated and raised his eyes to the ranger. "How'd you hear about me and the widow woman?"

The ranger laid the stick down and picked up the barrel of the big pistol. He looked through it, blew through it and laid it back down on the blanket. Tackett's eyes followed his hand. "Heard it on the wind I reckon," the ranger said. "Ain't none of my business, Sheriff. Just keeping up on the gossip."

"Well, what of it?" Tackett poured tea and pushed up his hat brim. "She's a lonely widow woman. I never took much to playing with whores. She does my shirts for me, you know. I've got four now." He raised four fingers, then smiled. "Everyone of em's crisp as a new dollar. Hell, I might marry her, if she'll have me. You oughta get a woman yourself, let her ease your mind some, instead of you coming in all stoked up and killing off the day drinkers." He cocked his head, squinting. "What'd them boys do anyhow?"

"They were running with the wrong crowd. Kurtz, Yates, Burdett and Red Hollis."

"So that's who you was after. I oughta known Montana Red's name would come up."

"Yep. It's come up a lot lately. The four of 'em raped and killed a white girl and an Indian kid down in my territory. The Indian kid was the son of a chief."

"Hold it. You're saying …?"

"That's right, the chief's *son*. The white girl was a school teacher come down from Chicago, teaching the Indian kid to read." He stopped and shook his head. "Red Hollis will do anything, you know that. I figure the others were just afraid to stop him. So they went along with it."

"My God." Tackett let out a breath. A silence passed. "Yates and Kurtz ain't no good either though. Red never made them do nothing they didn't *want* to do."

"Well … they won't do it again," the ranger said.

"Still, you coulda come to me before you killed 'em. It woulda looked better. You got no jurisdiction around here."

"You was busy getting your shirts done." The ranger smiled a little, sipped off his tea and sat the cup down.

Montana Red

"I thought I'd catch up to Red Hollis here if I got in quick enough. He don't stick anywhere very long. I shoulda killed him a long time ago."

"Montana Red *was* here, gambling and drinking with the cowhands. But he left five days back. He lays down higher up, up around them ridge towns. Thought you'd know that?"

"I do, but there's no telling where he's at up there. Figured I'd catch him down here. Hoped it anyway."

"Dang it. What do you suppose got into them Flying Cross boys? It ain't like them, backing the likes of that bunch. Donahue's gonna throw a fit. You killed off a third of his line crew."

"They were whiskey drunk. Just feeling rowdy, I reckon. They might not'a known what Hollis and his friends did. They was just sticking up for 'em because they was drinking together. You know how cowboys are—men who drink together, die together, I reckon, the way they saw it. A man like Hollis has a way of making everybody around as bad as he is. Burdett's holed up out at the Flying Cross. I'll get him come morning."

"You can't go out there. Not as riled up as Donahue's gonna be. I'm surprised he and his boys ain't rode in already. You just don't know him like I do."

"Yeah? Well—" The ranger blew a fleck of dust off the pistol butt. "Your Mister Donahue'll just have to blow wind, far as I care. I tried to let his boys go, but they all chose to throw down on me."

"He ain't *my* Mister Donahue," Tackett said. "I'm my own man here."

The ranger lifted his eyes from the pistol for a second. "Oh? Wanta ride out there with me? Maybe you can explain it all to him ... keep me from having to kill him."

"Naw sir, hell no. You can't explain nothing to Donahue, and I ain't having him down my back for the next year over this."

"Your own man, huh?" The ranger looked back at the pistol and turned it in his hand.

"I *am* my own man, but Donahue's powerful enough to make or break a lawman in these parts. I ain't a danged fool."

"Since when is one man more powerful than the law?" The ranger narrowed his gaze.

Tackett wiped a hand back and forth across his forehead. "Well, Donahue's been good to me, far as that goes. Now I'd of helped ya today, if I knew what Kurtz and them done. But you can't expect me to go out there tomorrow and take a chance on ruining what I got going here, can ya?"

"I suppose not." The ranger shrugged. "It don't matter. Red Hollis has been let go too long. If I'd killed him sooner, none of this other would've happened. I'll just drop by the Flying Cross, take down Bennie Burdett, and ride on. If I don't keep after Red Hollis, he'll soon kill again. He's acquired a strong thirst for it."

"I don't begrudge you hunting Red Hollis. You oughta get yourself up a posse first. Nobody'd blame ya."

"Hear what happened to that five-man posse tracked him over on Wind River?"

"I heard. But you still orta get one up. Things ain't like they once was. You need somebody to cover ya—"

"You offering?"

"No sir. Not me. I got no stomach for manhunting anymore." He shook his head. "Time was when I would've ... but I *can't* do it."

"Know anybody who *can?*"

Tackett felt his face redden. He rubbed it, "No, but surely—"

"So there's your posse," said the ranger. Another silence passed as he reached out, picked up the bandanna from the blanket, and started wiping the barrel of the big pistol. He snapped it in place and picked up the cylinder. "Hollis still wears them crossed pistols on his belly, I reckon?"

"Yeah. Best I know, he does—slicker than lightning with 'em too." Tackett sucked a tooth and nodded. "You know, you ain't the only lawman in the world. Somebody'll take him down sooner or later, if you don't."

"Meanwhile, he keeps on killing. I saw the bodies. Looked more like an animal had a hold of them." His throat tightened; he swallowed. "I haven't been able to see much else since. Won't till I set it right. I believe he might tasted their blood."

"Aw-now," Tackett said. "How you know that?"

When the ranger only stared at him, Tackett added, "Still and all, it don't have to be you that stops him. There's others, *younger* ones than you. Let them go after him. You orta had enough of this kinda killing by now." The sheriff looked down and rubbed his palms on his knees. After a second he said, "Dang it. I'm *asking* you to stay away from the Flying Cross."

The ranger ignored him and said, "She washes your shirts, huh?"

He nodded, still gazing down. "Yep. And I ain't a damn bit ashamed of it. It's took some getting used to though."

"I bet it has. She cook for you?" He connected the cylinder and spun it.

"Some. I'm still partial to my own cooking. Always said a man orta stay shy of a *widow's* cooking ... depending on what killed her husband, of course."

"That's wise thinking." The ranger nodded, held the pistol close to his ear and clicked it, hearing the smoothness of it, hearing the soft perfect turn and drop with each touch of his thumb.

"You owe ole Greely a dollar for toting Hurley Yates's body in. I said I'd get it for him, if you will. Figured you didn't want him prowling around out here looking for ya in the dark, stepping on a rattlesnake or something."

"Sure, thanks." He reached in his vest and pulled one up, flipped it across the low glow of fire. "I'm supposed to ask for a receipt."

"Really? Umm-um. What'll they come up with next?" He squinted, put the coin away and shook his head. "Oh. Greely said for me to tell ya, *'Good shooting.'* Said you stopped his clock with one shot. Somebody already took Hurley's shooting gear and made off with it before Greely got there. Can you believe that? Damned *comadreja* probably. Can't leave nothing laying loose on account of 'em anymore." Tackett sipped off his tea and slung his cup toward the ground. "I'm gone a day, come back, got a string of dead cowboys, a horse theft ...." He shook his head and wiped his finger around in his cup. "It's worse out here every year."

"Don't see how you manage." The ranger looked up, almost smiling again, dim firelight highlighting the scar across his cheek. *Hurley's shooting gear ... a horse stolen ... J. Jones?* He picked up the bullets one at a time, and loaded the big pistol.

Tackett chuckled, then said, "What the heck, don't I deserve a good job after Clinton County, Hayes ... Rileyville? Dang right I do, and you know it. I put my time in. You seen what all I done back then. I ain't fair-haired."

"I know it."

"I know you know it. So what if I ride a little shy of a man like Donahue? Can you blame me?"

"No, I don't blame you. Do what feels right to you, I reckon."

Tackett sucked a tooth. "I still wish you wouldn't ride over there."

"I'm going," the ranger said, "And that's all to be said about it."

"All right then, be hardheaded. I ain't about to mention it again." A silence passed, then he chuckled again. "Remember that night you and Edsen and me threw down on them cattle hawkers outside of—"

"What do you know about Little Honey?" The ranger cut him off. So that's how it is now. Tackett stared at him. *No good ole days here. Not with him. It was always a day's work.*

Still was. "She's a good girl, for a whore," Tackett said. "Why, what'd she do?"

"You tell me?" He reached and poured the last of the tea into his cup.

Tackett grinned. *Fishing, huh? Squeezing information, as if he wouldn't see it. As if he'd been so long out of touch, he wouldn't know when another lawman was grilling him down. Some nerve ....* "I just told ya. She's all right as whores go. Been here a year, ain't cut nobody, ain't clapped nobody out, or cheated 'em much as far as I know. Deals no dirt. Why?"

"Can ya believe what she tells ya?"

"Probably—if the money's right. I told ya I don't play around with whores much. You—of all people—know what they'll do to your head, if ya let 'em."

"I reckon." He sipped the tea. "Ever heard of a gambler named Joe Sharpe? Goes by *Gentleman* Joe. The one they say kilt Peg-Leg Molly over in Creed?"

"Sounds familiar, can't say though. Why?" Tackett cocked his head slightly.

"Had him on my list a year or more. Never caught him."

"Well, I don't figure you *tried* very hard."

"Maybe. I heard it mighta been a clean shooting. She was bad about razoring a man. I tried telling her it'd get her killed someday."

"Lot of folks tried telling her. Sooner or later, it was gonna happen. Blackhearted, throat-cutting whore ...."

"Yep. But you say this Little Honey keeps her nose clean, huh?"

Tackett cocked his head again, "What are you wanting to hear? I told you—" He stopped, then a smile crept across his lips. "Aw, I get it. I see now. You got yourself a little interest there?"

"No, I don't. I just want to know, is all." The ranger glanced away, then back. "What kinda horse got stolen today?"

"Huh?"

"You said while you was gone a horse got stolen—"

"Aw-yeah. Just a stable plug, belonged to the undertaker. A spindly legged paint horse. Won't get far I don't reckon. You sure ask a lot of questions for one cup of Duttwieler's."

"Been awhile since I seen you. Thought we'd catch up some."

"Yeah, sure you did." He stood up, grinned, and picked at the seat of his pants. "What's it all got to do with Montana Red Hollis? Or, are you just cleaning up your list?"

"She's got a nice voice, Little Honey."

"She won't wash your shirts." Tackett nodded toward the big iron. "But I reckon it'd be warmer than sleeping with that cold steel pistol."

"What're you getting at?" The ranger looked up at him, almost smiled again.

Tackett shook his head. "Nothing. Don't mind me." He stepped around and put his cup in his saddlebags, tugged his vest, and stepped up in his stirrups. "I just rode out to pay my respects. Wish you'd stay the hell away from Donahue. There's over a dozen armed men out there." He cocked a half smile. "Not that it matters to me. But it's good seeing you anyway."

He looked down at the low fire, over at the ranger's drawn face hidden partly by the slope of the battered gray sombrero. *A fire, a horse and a clean gun ... all this man had. All he'd ever had. But not him—not anymore. To hell with 'em all, the rapist, the killers, the buggers, muggers and thieves ... whores and razors, lunatics with six-shooters, tasting people's blood. If a man wanted to ride out and face a dozen gunmen ... well, let him.*

He smoothed a hand along his clean shirt collar. "Do you really believe there's a man alive can take down Montana Red?"

The ranger let out a breath and said, "No. None except me. I'll let ya know more once I've killed him."

"Still smug and cocky as ever, huh?" He chuckled and

shook his head. "Reckon there's no point in me mentioning again that you're out of your jurisdiction."

"Nope. I'll stay in my jurisdiction once these hardcases start staying in theirs ... not before."

"I swear. To be a lawman, you sure never paid much attention to the law."

"When you're sheriffing in town, you play by the rules. Out there it'll only get ya killed. Where I go, the only law is what ya make right between yourself and God. The rest ain't worth a spit in a river."

A silence passed. "Then you take care with Montana Red now, ya hear. Keep him upwind." His voice turned low, serious. "If he shoots you, try to die quick. Know what I'm saying?"

"Good to see you too, Tackett," said the ranger.

"Maybe I've helped, some?" He hesitated a second, waiting, but saw nothing obliging in the ranger's eyes. Then he tugged his hat down, grumbled, and turned the gelding. "All right then, dang it. I'll be back here come early morning ... show you the way out there."

"You don't have to go," the ranger said.

"I know it. But if get yourself lost and starve to death, I'll feel guilty for a month."

The ranger smiled, nodded slightly. "I knew you'd go."

"Yeah? Well, I ain't wanting to."

"Neither am I." A second passed as Tackett's horse stepped away. "Bring a shotgun," the ranger called out in a quiet tone.

"Ha— That goes without saying." Tackett raised a hand without looking back.

The ranger watched him until he faded out of the thin circle of grainy light. He thought for a second of the gambler, *J. Jones,* almost certain now that it was Gentleman Joe Sharpe; and he pictured him atop a spindly-legged paint horse—an undertaker's horse—kicking up sand with Hurley Yates's shooting gear hung around his waist, sucking hot air through parched lips ... scared, looking back. He hoped he wasn't riding the same trail as Red Hollis—hoped to God he wouldn't run into him out there. The ranger rubbed his face and touched his fingertips lightly to the scar on his cheek. He didn't want to kill that gambler.

The next preview is from ***Blood Lands,*** Julie Wilder's story.

She moved her sights over to the parson, then to Evans, then to Muller. They fit the description Reese had given her before he died. These were the ones; if by some fluke they weren't her attackers, her father's killers, too bad, she thought. If that was the case, they had simply picked the wrong day to come calling.

Her sights homed onto Muller, the one farthest away, the one most likely to get atop his horse and make a run for it. She rested the sights there and waited, breathing slowly, calmly.

Strange, she thought, how not long ago she had looked for the slightest reason not to kill these men, these men who had violated her, who had taken her father's life, and in that sense destroyed hers. But that had changed. Now, if they fit the description, or matched the names, or came close to doing either, she wanted them dead.

The killing had begun. The quicker they were dead, the sooner she could live in a home of her own—something she'd never had. And more than that, she could hold her head up and live there in peace, like regular, everyday folks—something she'd never known. A tear glistened in her eye, but there was no time to wipe it away. She wouldn't let it affect her aim.

Chapter 1

BLOOD LANDS

*Here are preview chapters from Ralph Cotton's **Blood Lands**, available in both softcover and ebook versions.*

Bloody Kansas: March 1865

At daybreak, in a cold drizzle, Julie Wilder, her father, Colonel Bertrim Wilder, and the colonel's former orderly Shepherd Watson rode up into sight above the low-rise north of Umberton. Upon seeing the three riders and behind them the string of finely attended horses each was leading, Davis Beldon, the livery owner, stepped out of the corral beside his barn and stood in the middle of the muddy street, waving them in with his calloused hand.

"Here comes the colonel, bringing his horses in, just like he said he would, soon as the weather broke," Beldon said over his shoulder to his helper, Virgil Tolan, who stood at the barn door, a pitchfork full of clean straw in his hands.

"Yep, he's doing it," Tolan replied, staring out through the grainy morning light, "but it's not going to sit well with Ruddell Plantz and his militia riders."

Behind the livery barn a rooster crowed into the gray stillness of the morning. "I expect *Captain Plantz* and his *so-*

called Kansas Border Militia will be making themselves scarce now that this confounded war is ending," said Beldon. "Good riddance to them too." A slight smile of satisfaction came to his face as he spit and watched the three riders bring the horses forward along the north trail. "I have no doubt Colonel Wilder would have dealt soundly with those scoundrels, had they tried to stop him from bringing those horses to town."

"All this time he's never once paid Plantz and his militia any protection money like the rest of the 'steaders did," said Tolan. He pitched the clean straw and stepped out beside Beldon, both hands resting atop the long pitchfork handle. "I expect even Plantz and the rest of them knew who to mess with and who not. Some men have guts; others don't, I reckon." He gave his employer a guarded look.

"Well, thank God the extortion is ending." Beldon's smile faded as he squinted for a better view of the three riders, realizing that like most businessmen in the area during the war, he too had paid the Kansas Border Militia more than just a few times to keep his property and himself safe. Beldon decided it best to change the subject. "I recognize old Shep," he said, "but who's the wrangler on Wilder's right?"

"I have no idea," said Tolan, also squinting a bit as he stared out with his employer. "I reckon it's some cowpoke drifter the colonel let winter with him for beans and a roof. There's plenty of them these days."

"Yeah," said Beldon, "and it's going to get worse before it gets any better, war or no war."

No one in Umberton had ever seen or even heard of the colonel's daughter, and for good reason. Julie had not been born to the colonel and his late wife, Laura Nell Wilder. The girl's real mother had been a camp follower known only as Sudie, who'd given birth to the colonel's child during his tenure as a young captain along the wilderness frontier. Sudie had revealed Colonel Wilder's name to her daughter shortly before her death ten years earlier. Over the next decade Julie had written to her father many times, but only recently had she traveled down from the north country to meet him face-to-face.

"I sure hope Colonel Wilder knows what he's doing, taking in every saddle-tramp that blows in off the prairie," said Tolan.

"I expect the colonel doesn't need you or me telling him how to conduct himself," Beldon said a bit sharply. His eyes stayed on the three riders and their strings of horses, most particularly on Julie Wilder, whose identity and gender lay hidden beneath a broad-brimmed Montana crown Stetson and a faded gray riding duster.

Once atop the rise, Colonel Wilder slowed his mount long enough for Julie and Shep to sidle their horses up to him; riding abreast, the three led their strings at an easy pace all the way to the livery corral where Tolan unlatched the gate and swung it wide open.

When the riders and their horses had all passed into the corral, Beldon stepped across the mud-rutted ground toward the colonel, grinning, with his hands shoved down into his back pockets. Tolan closed the gate and walked forward quickly until he'd passed Beldon and stood close enough to take the three lead ropes from the riders. He pulled the horses to the side and began looking them over as they milled around him.

"Morning, Colonel," said Beldon, deliberately showing little interest in the well-cared-for horses. "I expect you realize the price of horses can drop most any day with the war nearly over."

Without stepping down from his saddle, the colonel touched his hat brim courteously toward the two livery men and crossed his wrists on his saddle horn. "One thing for certain about war," said the colonel, "is that it takes *horses* to carry men and equipment there, and it takes *horses* to carry them home again."

Beldon scratched his jaw and said, "Well, I can't argue that. But the thing is, I don't ordinarily keep this many horses on hand. I have to consider my cost in feed and upkeep until the army purchaser comes through Umberton again." He shrugged. "It could be a week; it could be a month."

Julie and Shep backed their mounts a few feet to the side and sat quietly.

"Or you could take them on over to Rulo," said the colonel, leveling a fixed stare at the livery owner, "the way *I would have done* had you not asked me to first bring them to you for an offer." The colonel paused a second, then said, "If need be, I still know the way to Rulo."

"Now hold on, Colonel," Beldon said with a nervous smile, squirming a bit in place. "I'm not about to let you take these animals all the way to Rulo! I'm just looking for the best price. You can't fault a fellow for that."

"No, I suppose not." Colonel Wilder allowed himself a thin smile beneath his wide white mustache. Water dripped from the brim of his hat. "If you need to dicker a bit before you meet my price, let's do it over a cup of coffee, out of the rain."

"Where are my manners!" Beldon said, chastising himself with a mock slap on the side of his wet head. "Of course, let's get inside and get some hot coffee, while I try getting you to listen to reason."

Before swinging down from his saddle, Colonel Wilder raised an arm toward Shep and Julie. "Speaking of manners . . . you both know Shepherd Watson."

"Howdy, Shep." The two livery men acknowledged the old cowhand, who touched his frayed hat brim and returned the courtesy.

"Now for a surprise," said the colonel. "I'd like both of you to meet my daughter, Julie Wilder."

"Your *daughter?*" said Beldon. Both he and Tolan looked doubly stunned, first by hearing that the person beneath the sweat-stained Montana crown was a woman, second, that Bertrim and the late Laura Nell Wilder had a *child* neither of them had ever mentioned. "My goodness . . . ," Beldon added in a hushed tone.

Colonel Wilder gestured his daughter forward with a gloved hand. "Julie, come on over here beside me," he said cordially. "Let me introduce you to some of your new neighbors." As Julie stepped her horse forward, the colonel added, "Even though we will be leaving this part of the country before long."

Recovering from their surprise, Beldon slicked his wet hair to one side. Tolan took off his wet flop hat and held it against his chest.

"Ma'am, it is our pleasure to make your acquaintance," Beldon said, speaking for both himself and his helper. "If there is anything we can do to make your stay here in Umberton more comfortable, please allow us to do so."

"Obliged," Julie said, keeping her reply short and her tone of voice lowered as if its natural huskiness made her feel awkward. She pushed her hat brim up out of courtesy, at the same time revealing her face.

Looking her over without being too obvious, Beldon asked, "You've been back east, I take it, in boarding school, no doubt?" Yet, even as he asked, Beldon silently answered his own question. The young woman sitting atop the big buckskin bay had not been back east, not in any boarding school anyway.

Julie Wilder sat atop the buckskin loosely and comfortably, yet in a confident command, like a vaquero, Beldon told himself, not like some boarding school equestrian. He gave a cutaway glance at old Shep, then back to Julie as she said, still quietly in the same husky yet warm rich voice, "No, sir, I have never been back east. I've been—"

"Not until now, that is," the colonel cut in. "This will be our first daughter and father trip back east. We're both looking forward to it." He swung down from his saddle and held his reins out to Tolan, who stepped forward and took them obediently. "Daughter, why don't you and Shep go over to Molly Lanahan's and order us all three a nice hot breakfast? I'll be right along as soon as Mr. Beldon and I thrash out a price we can both live with."

Beldon looked back at Julie Wilder, expecting her to complete the response she had started, but she didn't. Instead she smiled modestly, saying, "Yes, Colonel," and backed her horse a step as if in dismissal. As she did so, Beldon noted a short jagged scar on her left cheek as she turned her dark eyes away from him.

The young woman had a rawboned toughness to her that presented itself clearly at first glance. Her eyes bore the same haunted look the livery man had seen on countless young drifters, eyes that were sharp and alert, but in sore need of rest, or perhaps reprieve.

Beldon and Tolan turned sidelong and gave Julie and Shep a nod as the two stepped their horses past them, out the gate and up the narrow mud street.

Turning back to Colonel Wilder, Beldon started to speak, but as if anticipating further questions about his daughter, the colonel said tactfully, "I hope you'll both understand that Julie and I have missed many years together. You might say that we're only now getting to know one another. Julie isn't comfortable talking about her past . . . not that it's anything to be ashamed of." He finished speaking with a firm, level gaze.

"Of course not," said Beldon. "Whatever caused you two to be apart all those years is you and your daughter's business. Let's all just be happy that you're together now." The colonel's gaze softened. He smiled. "Obliged, gentlemen. Now, let's go do some dickering."

Watching from the upstairs window of a weathered clapboard rooming house across the street, a young gunman named Nez Peerly saw Julie Wilder take off her hat and shake out her long dark hair. "Whooiee!" he said over his shoulder to his trail pardner, Clarence Conlon. "Charlie, come take a look-see! This ain't no *ordinary* wrangler the old colonel has riding with him!"

Clarence, chewing on a cold fried chicken leg left over from last night's dinner, stepped slowly over to the window, running the back of his hand across his glistening lips and black mustache. Looking down into the street, he caught only a glimpse of Julie's long hair as she placed the hat back atop her head. "What's the deal?" he grunted, still chewing. "I don't see nothing."

Looking disgusted, Peerly said, "Well, maybe you would have if you'd gotten here when I told you."

He looked the big man up and down, eying the chicken leg in his hand and the grease shining in Clarence's full black beard. "That's a woman down there, Clarence." He pointed.

"Down where?" Clarence asked thickly, craning his big head forward a bit.

"Down *there*, gawddamn it!" Peerly said angrily. "The one on the right, riding that black-legged buckskin! She just stuck that big hat down over her head, else you'd seen what I mean!"

"So what?" Conlon shrugged, exposing a slash of dirty white lining in one of the ripped shoulder seams of his ill-fitting uniform. "Long hair don't always mean *woman* where I come from." He sucked grease from a large dirty thumb. "I could stand a little barbering myself."

Peerly stared harshly at him. "Didn't you see the house rules downstairs, 'No food allowed in rooms'?"

"That's not *my* house rules," Conlon said flatly. He switched the chicken leg to his other hand and wiped his fingers on his already badly soiled tunic.

"Do you know *why* that's a house rule?" Peerly asked, getting more and more put out with him.

"I couldn't care less," said the big burly Conlon, turning

his gaze back down to the street as Julie and Shep rode slowly on toward the restaurant.

"Because it draws rats up here," Peerly informed him.

"Rats don't bother me none."

"I can see why," said Peerly, "but as long as we have to share a bed, I don't want rats crawling over me just to lick your whiskers."

"Then sleep on the gawddamned floor," Conlon said gruffly, staring down at the two riders. He watched Julie swing down from her saddle out front of the restaurant. "A woman, huh?" he asked, noting something different about the figure in the wet riding duster. "I don't even remember how long it's been since I laid my hands on a woman's warm furry belly."

Hearing Conlon's voice take on a slight tremble, Peerly stared at him bemusedly and said, "*Quite* a damn while from the sound of it." He stepped closer to Conlon, who stood staring down at the street as if mesmerized. Shaking his head in disgust, Peerly plucked the gnawed chicken bone from between Conlon's large thumb and fingers and pitched it away. "Pull your tongue in and let's get going," he said.

"*Going?* We just *got here* yesterday!" said the big bearded man.

"We're spying here, remember?" said Peerly. "Don't you think Ruddell Plantz is going to want his due *payment* when he hears the colonel slipped all them horses into town? Hell, he might even want to confiscate these horses for our own men."

"So, chances are we'll be coming right back?" Conlon asked, staring down toward the restaurant as if in contemplation.

"Once we tell Plantz about all these big good-looking horses?" Peerly grinned. "Oh yes, I'm pretty sure you can count on us coming back here."

"Then let's go," said Conlon, sucking a piece of chicken from between his teeth. He looked out through the window.

"The rain's stopped anyway."

"Yeah," Peerly said with sarcasm, shaking his head, "I wouldn't want you to ride in the rain." He paused for a moment and looked the big man up and down. "Let me ask you something, Conlon. Would you be riding with us, Plantz, me and the others, if this war wasn't going on?"

Conlon shrugged his broad shoulders inside his too-tight uniform jacket. "Hell, I reckon. Why not? A man's got to do something."

"You don't mind all the killing, robbing, burning, purging?" Peerly asked as if pursuing a point.

"Naw, not me," said Conlon. He offered a wide crooked grin. "Every day, somebody has to die. If it ain't us that kills them, something will."

"Now, there is what I call a real deeply considered opinion," Peerly said, returning the grin.

"Why'd you ask?" Conlon cocked his head a bit in curiosity.

"Just making conversation, Charlie," said Peerly, turning and walking away.

CHAPTER 2

Ruddell Plantz sat at the kitchen table with his tall muddy cavalry boots propped up on the edge, right beside a cold plate of half-eaten beans and hoecake. On the floor near his chair lay the body of Harvey Shawler. In front of the smoldering hearth lay his wife, Mattie Shawler. On Plantz's lap lay a big Colt horse pistol and the feed sack with eyelets that had covered his face as he rode in. He'd taken his Union saber and scabbard from around his waist and laid it alongside his forearm on the tabletop.

At the open door to the Shawler farmhouse, Carl Muller stood holding two young boys by their shirt collars. The youngsters squirmed and kicked, but to no avail. "What about these Shawler tadpoles?" Muller asked.

Plantz hardly gave the boys a glance. "I didn't know they were still alive," he said. He picked up the cup of coffee one of his men had poured him from the steaming pot hanging above the hearth coals, swirled it, then said before taking a long sip, "Kill them both, Carl. Missouri tadpoles today become full-grown Missouri frogs tomorrow."

Muller shot a dark grin to Rance Sawyer standing beside him on the short wooden porch. "See? Ain't that what I told you he'd say?"

"It never hurts to check first," Sawyer said sullenly. He jerked one of the farm boys from Muller's hand and helped drag the two away, down off the porch and farther away from the house. "If you ask me, the war will be over before these two ever make Johnnie Reb's roster."

"But see, the thing is," said Muller, giving a nasty grin, "nobody did *ask* you." He paused, then said as he raised a boot and kicked Davey Shawler forward, "If you want some good advice"—his big Remington pistol came up from its holster and fired a round into Davey Shawler's back—"you'd do well to keep your opinions to yourself, especially when it comes to showing mercy for this Missouri border trash."

"Davey!" young Martin Shawler screamed. He lunged forward against Sawyer's grip, trying to go to his fallen brother.

"Let him go," Muller said quietly. When Sawyer turned the boy loose, Muller let him get to his dead brother, then raised his Remington again and fired.

Sawyer winced at the sight of the two brothers lying dead in their own side yard.

"You see," Muller continued as if nothing had happened while gray smoke curled from his pistol barrel, "the shorter this war gets, the more folks will start to wondering what kind of trouble they might get into over stuff just like this." He gestured his pistol toward the two dead Shawler brothers. "Not everybody realizes that our cause is just."

Hearing the two gunshots from inside the farmhouse, Plantz turned a tired look toward a small bedroom separated from the kitchen by a wool blanket hung over a length of twine. "Parson, are you going to sleep all damned day?" he called out.

After a grunt followed by a short silence, a voice replied from behind the blanket, "How in God's name can a man sleep . . . all this shooting and screaming going on all night."

Plantz gave a dark chuckle. "Now, it wasn't all that bad. Only a couple of young women and these two last night. Muller just shot a couple of boys out in the yard. Come on out and have some coffee with me. Tell me some things."

"Damn it, Ruddell," the voice grunted. In a second a large hand wearing fingerless leather gloves drew the wool blanket to the side. "As long as we've been riding together, you'd think I've already told you all you'd ever want to know."

"Now, I can never get enough learning," said Plantz. He turned and watched Preston Oates, "the parson," step into the room, shoving his gray-black hair back out of his eyes. "I followed your advice too. The blind man is still alive. Hurley and Kenny Bright have him tied to a post out in the barn."

"Thank you," said the parson, "I appreciate it." He cleared his throat and spit into the smoldering coals on his way around the table. Picking up a half cup of cold coffee, he slung the contents out onto the dirt floor and filled the cup from the steaming pot. "I felt very strongly about that."

Plantz offered a thin smile. "I could tell you did. You come near throwing down on Kiley when he started to cut the man's throat."

"Killing a blind man on a moonless night?" said the parson, shaking his head as if in fear. "That's the kind of bad luck we neither one want to bring down on us . . . not when things are going so well."

"Especially a *one-legged* blind man," Plantz added with a feigned sense of caution. "Ain't that what you told all of us last night? Or was that whiskey talking?"

"That was no whiskey talk," said the parson. "That was just me reading all the signs and looking out for all of us." Easing down into a chair across the table from Plantz, he gave the man a look and said, "I know you don't put as much stock in these things as I do. But it's widely known in my inner circle that Napoleon had a blind man put to death the night before his battle at Waterloo." He paused for effect, then added flatly, "It was a moonless night." His beady dark eyes stared gravely at Plantz.

"But was he one-legged?" Plantz asked, showing a trace of a teasing smile.

"Whether he was or not, it's not a matter to treat so lightly," said the parson.

Plantz shrugged a bit, sipped his coffee and said quietly, "Sorry, Parson, I'm just not superstitious the way you are."

"This has nothing to do with superstition, Ruddell," said Oates. "This is a matter of carefully accumulated scientific fact." As he spoke he made the sign of the cross, only instead of making it on his chest, he made a smaller version on his forearm.

Noting the gesture, Plantz said, "Well, fact or not. It's daylight now. I expect we can go ahead and kill this Reb sonsabitch and get on about our business."

"Did we do ourselves any good here last night?" the parson asked. Then, to keep from appearing greedy he added quickly, "Enough to support our *just cause*, that is?"

"Naw, hell, these people have been picked to death the last few years," said Plantz. "We're doing them a favor, killing them." He sipped his coffee. "We're leaving here with a little grain for our horses, a sow hog and some skinny chickens."

"Chicken thieves, then, is what we've become," said the parson, looking down stoically into his coffee cup.

Plantz stared at him in silence for a moment. "You know, I've been giving it some serious thought. Soon as this war simmers on down, I'm thinking about making my own *private* little war. Think you can go along with that?"

"You mean . . . ?" The parson gave a sly grin and let his words trail.

"Yep," said Plantz, knowing he didn't really need to explain himself any further, but doing so anyway. "I mean doing for ourselves what we've been doing for the cause all this time. Instead of throwing the proceeds to the Free Kansas Militia, we keep it all for ourselves."

The parson raised his partially gloved hands as if in dismay. "But there's nothing left now. This is what we should have started doing a couple of years back when there was still something worth stealing around here."

"As soon as this war stops, it'll just be a matter of time

before there's more money circulating than we've ever dreamed of. It'll be real Union dollars too. Not these worthless gray dollars." He gestured a hand toward the Confederate bills strewn on the dirt floor, some of them stained with blood.

The parson sat in silence for a moment as if having to give it some thought. Finally he said, "Hell yes, I'm with you. Only, why wait for the war to end? We could head out tonight, rob and kill all the way to San Francisco, far as I'm concerned."

"We've got a total of eleven men . . . nine of them right out there, Parson," said Plantz, jerking a short nod toward the barn and the surrounding yard. "How many do you think we could count on to ride with us if we broke away from the Free Kansas Militia right now?"

"I'd like to say all of them," the parson replied after pondering it for a moment. "But to be honest and practical, I'm going to say six or seven."

"Yeah, that's about the same number I came up with," said Plantz. Raising another finger each time he mentioned a name he said, "I figure, Carl Muller, Kid Kiley, Goff Aimes, Clement Macky and Buell Evans." He held up five fingers, then added, "Clarence Conlon, and Nez Peerly too, once they catch up with us."

"What about Delbert Reese, or Rance Sawyer, the ones who won't go along with your idea?" the parson asked, lowering his voice lest anyone outside hear him.

Lowering his voice as well, Plantz said, "Well, if there's one thing we've all learned from this war, it's that 'He who is not with us is surely against us.'"

"In other words . . ." Staring intently at Plantz, the parson raised a finger and ran it symbolically across his throat.

Plantz gave him a thin guarded smile. "If it comes to that," he said, "but maybe we tell them we're disbanding, and shake loose of them without having to . . ." He made the same sign across his throat.

"Right, of course," said the parson, catching himself

before he appeared too bloodthirsty. "I meant only as a last resort. God forbid it come to that."

"Yeah, I agree," said Plantz, without much commitment in his voice. "God forbid it come to that." He hesitated for a second, then said, "I've got Peerly doing some checking around, seeing who we can count on when the time comes."

"You say *when*, not *if*," said the parson.

"Yeah," said Plantz with a level gaze, "I suppose I did."

The two fell silent and turned toward the sound of a young gunman named Kid Kiley whose high-welled cavalry boots pounded up onto the wooden porch. "Ruddell! I mean, Captain Plantz, sir!" he said in an excited tone, sticking his head inside the open door. "We're bringing this blind basta . . . that is, we're bringing the *prisoner* from the barn, sir!" He gave a quick, awkward salute.

"At ease, Kiley," Plantz chuckled, rising from his chair. "Get out of the doorway and go calm yourself down. You're panting like a hound on a deer trail." Turning to the parson, he said as Kiley ducked away and pounded back off the porch, "Come on, Parson, let's see how these boys handle this. We'll see who fits in our plans and who doesn't." The two stood with their coffee cups in hand and stepped onto the porch.

Propped up between Kenny Bright and Joe Hurley, Avrial Shawler hobbled toward the house. He turned his blind eyes back and forth aimlessly, searching his endless darkness for any sign of his kin. "Davey?" he called out. His ears piqued for a response. When no response came he called out, "Martin . . . Marty boy, can you hear me? Jed? Speak up, one of you! Where's Sister Loretta? Sister Rose?"

"You don't want to see Sister Rose and Loretta," Muller chuckled. "They're a mess."

"*Jed . . . ?*" Bright said curiously, almost to himself. He looked all around the yard.

Kid Kiley, who had hurried to join Hurley and Bright in accompanying the blind man across the yard, snickered and answered in a mocking, teasing voice, "Here I am, big brother. I'm down over here with a bloody hole in my back, deader than hell!"

Avrial Shawler stopped abruptly and stiffened in place, causing his two guards to stop also. "What have you devils done to my kid brothers?" he cried out. "Where's my ma and pa?" He swung his head back and forth wildly, shouting, "Pa! Ma! Where are you? Somebody answer me, for God sakes!"

"I did answer you, you stupid bastard!" Kiley called out in the same cruel taunting voice. "We're all dead! Every gawddamned rebel-loving one of us! Except you!" He ran in close in a short circle, spit in Avrial's hapless face and kept circling, preparing to do the same again.

Some of the men hooted and laughed; other men only looked on in shame. "All right, Kiley, that's enough!" said Bright, jerking the blind man to the side, away from the circling Kiley.

"See?" the parson said quietly to Plantz, the two observing from the porch. "Kenny Bright is a good man, but his heart just isn't in it, not the way Kiley's is. Wouldn't you agree?"

"Yep, I see what you mean," said Plantz, staring straight ahead. He sipped his coffee, his big Colt in his right hand, hanging down at his side. "All right, both of yas, stand down!" he called out to Bright and Kiley, seeing their tempers begin to flare.

"He started it," Kiley replied. "I'm only doing my job! My job is to *hairy-ass* the enemy any chance I get!"

"This man is no longer the enemy," Bright said. "He's been sent home, out of the war! He's harmless!"

"As long as he's alive, he's still my enemy!" Kiley shouted.

"You've got a knack for harassing the blind and the infirm, Kiley," Bright said flatly. "I can't wait to see you someday have to face up to—" His words stopped short beneath the roar of Plantz's big pistol. Kiley ducked away as if he'd been shot.

"Damn it," said Plantz. "Didn't you two woodenheads hear me tell you to stand down?" He stepped off the porch and sauntered forward, eying both men sharply. Hurley turned loose of Avrial Shawler's arm and stepped away.

"Sorry, Captain," said Bright, one hand on the blind man's thin upper arm, helping to steady him. "I see no need in all this killing . . . and certainly no need in torturing a man this way."

"Torture?" said Plantz, turning his harsh stare to Bright alone. He gave Kiley a gesture with his pistol barrel, sending him away. "This isn't torture. You haven't *seen* torture." He reached out with a muddy boot and kicked Avrial Shawler's wobbly leg out from under him, dropping the blind man to the wet ground. Bright could only turn loose of the downed man's arm.

"If you want to know about killing and torture, ask me about Lawrence, Kansas, the night Cantrell and his men rode through!" He kicked the helpless blind man in the side, causing him to roll into a ball, gasping. "Ask me about Centralia . . . about Whitfield, or Logansport."

"Captain, I—" Bright tried to reply, but his words cut short again as Plantz took him by his forearm and pulled him away from the man on the ground.

Hearing the big pistol cock in Plantz's hand, the blind man said with tears streaming down his face, "Go on, kill me then, you murdering sonsabitch! I ain't going to beg! I ain't going to crawl!"

"Is this daylight enough for you?" Plantz called out to the parson. "Does this fit your *accumulated scientific* tastes?"

The parson only nodded, watching with a firm grin of satisfaction.

On the ground, Avrial Shawler had heard enough to know that his life would end any second. "Ma! Pa! Little Brothers! I'm gone. Can you hear me? I love all of you!" He sobbed and shook his bowed head, his blind eyes seeming to search the wet ground beneath him. "Ma!" he said. "*Please* say something. Let me hear your voice!"

"She can't talk," said Plantz, reaching his pistol out at arm's length. He gave a trace of a cruel grin. "We cut her tongue out." He paused for only a second to let it sink in; then he added, "So she can't tell what we're all going to do to her."

"*Noooo!*" Avrial Shawler shrieked and swung his hands wildly back and forth, trying in his desperation to grab on to his tormentor.

Plantz squeezed the trigger on his big saddle Colt and watched the impact nail the screaming man's head to the ground in a spray of mud, blood and brain matter.

In the sudden silent wake of the explosion, Plantz turned to Bright and said, "You heard him mention another brother, didn't you?"

Bright stared at Plantz for a moment before finally saying, "I heard him call out the name *Jed.* I don't know what he meant by it."

"If you were to guess though," said Plantz, "would you think there might be another brother around here somewhere, maybe somebody who saw everything that just happened? Maybe somebody who will spill everything he saw to the regulars, first chance he gets?"

"I suppose that could be," said Bright.

"Yeah, I suppose that could happen too," said Plantz, staring Bright harshly in the eye. "Why didn't you say something right then, when you heard him mention it?"

"Hell, I don't know," said Bright. "Everybody else heard it; why didn't they mention it?"

Plantz didn't answer. Instead he gave the parson a knowing look. Then he turned to the men gathered in the yard and called out, "Goff Aimes! Get mounted and get up here!"

A tall man with a black powder burn tattoo on his right cheek stepped quickly into his saddle and gigged his horse forward, sliding to a halt in front of Plantz. "Yes, Captain?"

Plantz grinned and said to Bright, "See, that's the attitude a man needs to have around here." To Aimes he said, "Circle this yard a good ways out. If you come upon any fresh tracks, hoof or foot, follow them till you know who made them."

"Then kill them," Aimes stated, as if issuing himself an order. Without having to hear another word from Plantz, Aimes turned his big roan and kicked it up into a trot out across the yard toward the hill line.

"See? Gawddamn it, Bright," said Plantz as Aimes cut his horse back and forth, his head lowered, searching for prints in the dirt. "That's what I need more of."

"I follow orders, Captain," Bright said in protest. "If you are unhappy with how I—"

"Kenny," said Plantz, cutting him off, "I think you'd do well to join another band of riders. This war is nothing *but* killing and torture."

CHAPTER 3

Jed Shawler did not hear his brother Aerial call out his name before Plantz's bullet resounded out across the woods and hollows. But even if he had heard Aerial, he would have been powerless to help him. Earlier, when the militia riders swooped down onto the Shawler farm, their gunfire shattering the predawn stillness, Jed had been tucked away in the cover of a downed cedar, keeping vigil on a large squirrel's nest high up in the bare branches of a sycamore tree.

Upon hearing the gunfire, he had run back to the edge of the woods and looked down into the clearing where the Shawler farmhouse sat beneath its rise of morning wood smoke. Seeing the riders circle the house, some of them splitting off to the barn and dragging his brothers out into the dirt, his first instinct had been to raise his squirrel rifle to his shoulder and draw a bead on the leader of the hooded riders.

"Damn you, Plantz, I'll kill you!" he'd said aloud to himself, recognizing Ruddell Plantz's big dun horse and the man himself, in spite of the grainy light and the white floursack mask over his face. The shot would be difficult at this distance, but he'd made harder shots in the course of his short years, bringing down both deer and elk for the Shawlers' dinner table.

As he took aim, he instructed himself to calm down, breathe deep and make the shot count. He knew how many shots he carried in the leather shooting pouch draped over his shoulder. He'd brought seven loads, enough to bring home seven squirrels for the noon meal. But would seven shots be

Blood Lands

enough to draw the militia away from his family? Enough to save his family from Plantz and his killers?

He didn't know, Jed told himself, centering his rifle sights on Plantz's chest as the man came to a halt out front of the farmhouse. He only hoped that seeing their leader fall might scatter the rest of the men, or draw them hurrying up toward him, giving his family a chance to arm themselves. He felt his right index finger begin its slow, steady squeeze on the hammer. *Now,* he said to himself, knowing from experience at what point the hammer would fall and the stream of fire would belch forth from the barrel.

Yet, before that thin deadly second arrived, his hands began to shake violently; his steady breathing suddenly became tight jerking gasps. He watched Plantz wobble back and forth in his sights until he finally lowered the rifle barrel an inch, batted his eyes and tried to settle himself. *It's a whole different thing killing a man*, he recalled Avrial saying when he'd returned from the war. The image of his brother and his blank lifeless eyes came to his mind. He clenched his teeth with determination and raised the rifle back into position.

"Please, God," he said aloud. But his shaking hands and his trembling knees would not allow him to make the shot. *You've got to do it!* he demanded of himself, trying desperately to calm his shaking hands. Yet, even as he'd struggled for self-control, he watched Plantz swing down from his saddle and step out of sight into the farmhouse.

Jed swung the rifle to a new target, but he realized the moment had slipped away. His hands shook uncontrollably. His breathing remained shallow and tight. The world had begun to swirl around him. He heard his mother scream; then he heard her scream cut short by gunshots from inside the farmhouse. "*Noooo!*" he shrieked in a muted, almost dreamlike voice, feeling what little was left of his nerve and his self-control slip completely away from him. In his hysterical condition, he suddenly hurled the squirrel rifle away, turned and ran wildly, mindlessly deeper and deeper into the woods. . . .

In the front yard of the farmhouse, Delbert Reese heard a sound on the trail and turned quickly, his pistol already raised and cocked. "Captain," he shouted to Plantz, "we've got riders coming!"

Plantz and the others turned their attention toward the sight of two horses coming across an open stretch of land between the Shawler farm and the Umberton Trail. "At ease, everybody," said Plantz. "Hold your fire. It's just Peerly and Conlon."

"Yeah. I wonder what the hell brings them here?" asked the parson, staring intently at the two approaching riders as they galloped into the yard.

"Looks like we missed all the fun!" Peerly called out, looking all around at the bodies, the pillaged barn and house.

"You didn't miss a thing," Plantz said in a grim tone, stepping over closer to the horses as the two stopped. "I thought I told you two to stay put, keep an eye on Umberton for us?"

"Oh, you did. But you're going to be damn glad to see us today, Plantz!" said Peerly.

"I doubt it," Plantz said sharply. "And it's *Captain* Plantz to you." As he spoke he grabbed Peerly's horse by its bridle and held it firmly. "Do you understand me, Peerly? Or am I going to have to give you something to hold on to as a reminder from now on?"

"No, sir, Captain Plantz." Peerly's attitude changed instantly; his demeanor turned serious. "My apologies, Captain." He nodded at Clarence Conlon. "We saw the colonel bring three strings of horses into Umberton. We knew you'd want to know about it right away. So we came running!"

"What about Tolan?" Plantz asked. "When was I going to hear from that hay-pitching son of a bitch?"

"We saw him." Peerly shrugged. "I reckon he would've told you about it first chance he got." Peerly smiled proudly.

"But I knew you'd want to know right off. So I wasted no time. Was I right to do that?"

Plantz nodded his approval, turning loose of Peerly's saddle. "Yeah, you two did right bringing that information to me."

"It was all my idea," Peerly quickly pointed out, not wanting to share any recognition with Conlon.

But Plantz, having gone into rapt contemplation, appeared not to hear him. The parson spoke to Peerly and Conlon, saying, "You two go water your horses."

"Wait," said Plantz, seeming to snap out of his deep thoughts. A sly smile came to his face. "That old colonel is just testing me, that son of a bitch." He turned his eyes back to Peerly and Conlon. "Who did the colonel have riding with him?"

Conlon sat slumped and uninterested in his saddle. Peerly responded quickly, "Two wranglers! One was—"

"Shepherd Watson," the parson said flatly, cutting in and finishing his words for him.

Looking taken aback, Peerly gave the parson a curious look. "How did you—?"

"Because old Shep is always with the colonel," said Plantz, sounding unsurprised. "Who else?"

"You ain't believing this, Rudde— I mean *Captain Plantz!*" he said, correcting himself. "He had a young woman riding with him!" He blurted it out quickly about the woman on the outside chance that once again the parson would finish his reply. When the parson said nothing, Peerly gave him a passing glance, then said, "She was dressed like a man and sat her horse like a man. But she was a woman, no mistaking that. Was there, Conlon?" he said, turning to the big hulk of a man for support.

"She was the prettiest thing I ever saw," Conlon grunted, rising to the question.

"I wouldn't go so far as to say that," Peerly said, taking

over. "Fact is, she was a might on the plain and manly side, for my taste."

"A woman wrangling for the colonel," said Plantz. He turned his amazed expression to the parson. "What do you make of it?"

The parson looked flatly at Peerly and asked as if he already knew the answer, "How old do you say, early to mid-twenties? Dark eyes, dark hair?"

"Yes, that's her," said Peerly, impressed and unable to conceal it. "How'd you know that?"

"It's the colonel's daughter," he said confidently to Plantz, ignoring Peerly.

"Begging your pardon, Parson," said Peerly, thinking he had caught the parson in a mistake, "but it's a known fact that the colonel's wife was barren of child."

"Peerly's got you there," Plantz said to the parson, as if standing neutral between the two in some kind of mental sporting contest. "It is widely known about the colonel's wife."

"The colonel's wife had nothing to do with it," the parson retorted, his confidence unwavering. "This daughter of his came from a whore named Sudie . . . one of the camp followers from back during the Indian campaigns. She took up exclusive with the colonel for a whole winter and got her belly blown up. By the time the baby was born, the colonel was gone on back to Texas. Instead of hat-pinning herself, or knocking the baby in the head when it was born, Sudie decided to keep the girl child." He grinned. "You never know what's in a whore's heart."

The men stared in silent fascination at the parson.

The parson grinned, liking the attention. "She named the child Julie, but being from Wildwood, Virginia, Sudie liked to call the girl her *Wildwood Flower*."

"Damn, Parson," said Plantz. He shook his head slightly in wonderment. "I just don't see how you come up with so much."

"It's a gift," said the parson, shrugging it off. "Sudie's little

Wildwood Flower has been the colonel's deep and best-kept secret."

"Except for you knowing about it," said Plantz.

"Of course," said the parson, a bit smugly, "except for me knowing about it." Pausing as if to reward himself, he pulled a twist of tobacco from inside his uniform coat, bit off a plug and rolled it over into place inside his left jaw.

"A *gift?* Jesus!" said Plantz, with total and unquestioning belief. "I don't know what to think of you sometimes."

"Nor do I, sometimes," said the parson. He grinned, spit and ran the back of his hand across his mouth. Looking back and forth at the other men as if they had become his audience, he went on. "Sudie died young of consumption as many of her occupation do, still working the flesh circuit—railroad camps mostly. But early on she'd told her little bastard daughter all about the colonel. Of course he'd only been a captain when she knew him." He looked off as if in deep contemplation for a moment, then said, "She built him up to be a hero. Must've wanted her child to grow up and try to better herself, I suppose, knowin' she'd come from such good stock."

Looking at the men and seeing their undivided attention to the parson's words, Plantz suddenly grew restless and said, "All right, Parson, before you go passing a collection plate, let's get everything gathered up here and get going."

The parson gave him a look. "Don't you want to hear more about our Wildwood Flower? What she's done all her life? What's she apt to do?"

"Later maybe," said Plantz, seeming to have snapped out of the parson's spell. "Right now, it's time to go."

"But it's always best to hear these things while the information is fresh and pouring through me," said the parson. "There are things about this woman," he cautioned, raising a half-gloved finger.

"I said, *put it away for now*, Parson," Plantz said, a bit sharply. "It'll make for good entertainment around the campfire. Right now I've got other things to do.

Put it away . . . ? The parson stared flatly at him, not allowing Plantz to see how offended he'd become. "As you say, Captain," the parson replied submissively.

"Captain?" asked Conlon. "Are we riding back into Umberton? Make the colonel pay tribute?" He'd straightened upright in his saddle at the prospect of riding right back to town and finding the young woman.

"Hush up, fool," Peerly growled at him in a lowered voice. "It ain't your place to ask such a thing."

Ignoring Peerly, Plantz said to Conlon, "I think not. We'll let the colonel complete his horse sale." He grinned. "We know the way to his house. He's not getting away with anything."

Other Books by Ralph Cotton

The Gun Culture Series

1. Friend of a Friend	*2015*
2. Season of the Wind	*2017*
...More to Come...	

Western Classics
The Life and Times of Jeston Nash

1. While Angels Dance*	*1994*
2. Powder River	*1995*
3. Price of a Horse	*1996*
4. Cost of a Killing	*1996*
5. Killers of Man	*1997*
6. Trick of the Trade	*1997*

* ***While Angels Dance*** *was a candidate for the **Pulitzer Prize** in fiction in 1994. This entire **Western Classic** series has been released and is available from Amazon.com and other retailers, as well as Kindle and other ebook formats.*

Dead or Alive Trilogy

1. Hangman's Choice	*2000*
2. Devil's Due	*2001*
3. Blood Money	*2002*

*The **Dead or Alive Trilogy** is available from Amazon.com and other retailers, as well as Kindle and other ebook formats, as part of **Ralph Cotton's Western Classics.***

Other Books by Ralph Cotton

Danny Duggin (Written for the Estate of Ralph Compton)

1. The Shadow of a Noose	*2000*
2. Riders of Judgement	*2001*
3. Death Along the Cimarron	*2003*

Gunman's Reputation (Lawrence Shaw)

1. Gunman's Song	*2004*
2. Between Hell and Texas	*2004*
3. The Law in Somos Santos	*2005*
4. Bad Day at Willow Creek	*2006*
5. Fast Guns Out of Texas	*2007*
6. Gunmen of the Desert Sands	*2008*
7. Ride to Hell's Gate	*2008*
8. Crossing Fire River	*2009*
9. Escape From Fire River	*2009*
10. Gun Country	*2010*
11. City of Bad Men	*2011*

Spin-Off Novels

1. Webb's Posse	*2003*
2. Fighting Men (Sherman Dahl)	*2010*
3. Gun Law (Sherman Dahl)	*2011*
4. Summer's Horses (Will Summers)	*2011*
5. Incident at Gunn Point (Will Summers)	*2012*
6. Midnight Rider (Will Summers)	*2012*

Other Books by Ralph Cotton

Ranger Sam Burrack (Big Iron Series)

1. Montana Red	*1998*
2. The Badlands	*1998*
3. Justice	*1999*
4. Border Dogs	*1999*
5. Blue Star Tattoo	*2000*
6. Blood Rock	*2001*
7. Jurisdiction	*2002*
8. Vengence	*2003*
9. Sabre's Edge	*2003*
10. Hell's Riders	*2004*
11. Showdown at Rio Sagrado	*2004*
12. Dead Man's Canyon	*2004*
13. Killing Plain	*2005*
14. Black Mesa	*2005*
15. Trouble Creek	*2006*
16. Gunfight at Cold Devil	*2006*
17. Sabio's Redemption	*2007*
18. Killing Texas Bob	*2007*
19. Nightfall at Little Aces	*2008*
20. Ambush at Shadow Valley	*2008*
21. Showdown at Hole-In-The-Wall	*2009*
22. Riders from Long Pines	*2009*
23. A Hanging in Wild Wind	*2010*
24. Black Valley Riders	*2010*
25. Lawman from Nogales	*2011*
26. Wildfire	*2012*
27. Lookout Hill	*2012*

Other Books by Ralph Cotton

Ranger Sam Burrack (Big Iron Series), *cont.*

28. *Valley of the Gun*	*2012*
29. *High Wild Desert*	*2013*
30. *Red Moon*	*2013*
31. *Lawless Trail*	*2013*
32. *Twisted Hills*	*2014*
33. *Shadow River*	*2014*
34. *Golden Riders*	*2014*
35. *Mesa Grande*	*2015*
36. *Scalpers*	*2015*
37. *Showdown at Gun Hill*	*2015*
38. *Payback at Big Silver*	*2015*
39. *A Ranger's Trail*	*2019*

Stand Alone Novels

1. *Jackpot Ridge*	*2003*
2. *Wolf Valley*	*2004*
3. *Blood Lands*	*2006*
4. *Midnight Rider*	*2012*

Author Ralph Cotton

Ralph Cotton is a *Best Selling Author* with over *Seventy* books to his credit and millions of books in print. Ralph's books are top sellers in the Western and Civil War/Western genres, and in 2015 he debuted his **Gun Culture** series with **Friend of a Friend,** followed by **Season of the Wind**. Known for fast-paced narrative and wry dark humor, Ralph's introduction to the Florida crime fiction genre has been well received.

A Ranger's Trail is the 39th novel in the **Big Iron series**, written and released in 2019 in Ralph's Western Classics group of books, as well as an ebook.

Ralph lives on the Florida coast with his wife Mary Lynn. He writes prodigiously, but also enjoys painting, photography, sailing and playing guitar.

Made in the USA
Coppell, TX
13 November 2024